By Chance or Choice

BY CHANCE OR CHOICE

a novel by TONI STATON HARRIS

Epiphany Publishing House LLC

Published by Epiphany Publishing House LLC
One Gateway Center, A-193
Newark, NJ 07102

Editor: Chandra Sparks Taylor
Cover illustration: Rod Bowen
Cover and book design: Stacy Luecker, Essex Graphix

Library of Congress Catalog Card No.: 2001089826
ISBN: 0-9710695-0-6

Printed in the United States of America

First edition

For the man who believed it when no one else could conceive it.
He is the love and lover of my life, my partner, my best friend
and most importantly, my covering.
My Injeel.

In loving memory of Cleon James Burton,
who promised he would always look out for me
and was always the best of all of us.
I love and miss you.

ACKNOWLEDGMENTS

First and foremost, in the precious and most powerful name of Jesus Christ, Your Son and My Savior, Father God, I praise and thank You. For with You, all things are possible and I choose You!

When my editor, Chandra Sparks Taylor, first told me I had to submit acknowledgments with my manuscript, I felt a gush of emotion. I felt triumphant, sadness, confusion and gladness; I felt triumphant that I was actually seeing a dream and a declaration come to fruition. I experienced some sadness that the many arduous nights would now move on to a new declaration. I felt some confusion as to what to say, hoping to omit no one. And finally gladness for my journey for which I would take nothing. Then I started to thank everyone under the sun, praying that no one would be left out. And my wise and fearless little sister Kimmie Q said, "You really have to go no further. After you thank God and your husband, those who love and know you know that you love them and putting their names in your acknowledgement pages won't change that."

So with that advice in mind I would like to thank the following for being instrumental in *By Chance or Choice*: my daddy and mommy (thanks, Mommy, for reading the first pages. Thanks to you both for supporting and unselfishly encouraging me. My heart swells with joy when I think of your unconditional love and support). Kimmie Q (wind beneath my wings, now you have to read it!); Jackie Moore, my big sister, I've told of the many lessons you've taught me. Levolia, thank you for your love.

To my personal angels (ancestors), I can now call by name, and the inspiration for many of my character names as a tribute: Queenesther (I wear the crown proudly), Alphonso (thanks for eating all my candy), Anney Lewis, Uncle Banks (thanks for making them let me ride in the limo), Calvin (the trips to the corner store and always in every kid's corner), Jerry (Just Sweet), Hawk, Gloria (Girlie, Girlie), D-Hawk (You a Harris! Gimme that key), Dwight (Sha Sha Shalazay, Class and Elegance to your life) and Uncle Mac (so many wonderful memories).

Vonda (Wunda), thanks for reading the book as many times as I've written it with patience and love. Thanks for being a wonderful part of the process. Wincey, thank you for being you! Rodney Wright, Jackie, Jon, Tony and (I know by face, not name) the Newark Gateway Hudson Repro Crew, thanks for tirelessly reproducing the manuscript, I can't name the many times. (Told you, Rodney, I wouldn't leave you out.) My first readers: Mommy, Candy (Cherrina), Ametra, Darren B. (Uncle Dawin, my brother and for real, not for play-play cousin) and Mike Jones (What had happened was…). Thanks for your honest feedback. Tony (Bobby), my attorney extraordinaire and Deborah, one of my sisters-in-love who retyped every edit and word with love and at the speed of lightning. To the Statons, Joneses and Harrises (and everyone connected to those families) for your support in everything I do. Mom Nita, the greatest mother-in -love a woman could have. Gayle, thanks for always being in my corner and for your excitement from day one! Many thanks to Mr. James Pringle and the World Famous Harlem Theatre Company, make sure you check out the next book. Susan (J.T.) Hale, thanks for your love and support!

Many thanks to: the Rush's (Chel and Dwayne), the Hoard's (Dawn and Dwayne), the Hale's (Susan and Duane and the girls)—hey, what's with all the Dwaynes? All of you have been phenomenal friends, showing monumental support in so many ways. Dane Chung, you are the man! Thank you so much with all of my heart. You came through with the winning jumpshot at the buzzer.

To my editor, I thank you from the bottom up. You are magnificent and brought magic to my words with extreme talent, kindness and grace. You are one talented and awesome lady. To Gwen Gabriel, may God's blessings shine so abundantly upon your face. Unselfishly you shared invaluable information freely and I can't thank you enough. Many thanks to you, Stacy Luecker. You have been a solid rock throughout the process, above and beyond the call of the duty. I thank you for being a wonderful part of the process! To Eric Luecker, Stacy's husband, I extend my thanks for your support as well. To Becky Pate and the staff at Central Plains, thank you.

Finally, to those I've met only briefly in person or on the Internet, I thank you for the wonderful work you've put out to inspire many. I am in awe of your work…. Mary B. Morrison (this book is evidence of your fabulous advice to show us how to do it), E. Lynn Harris (tools to help turn my perspective to love) and Nina Foxx (The Jules Verne was all that!), Marcus Major (thanks for your liquid poetry and your kind words at OurStory). Also thanks to all African-American authors (legends and living legends) who have paved the way and continue to blaze trails. Thanks to Sandra Gash for your early guidance.

And last but not least, once again my Injeel (Hey, Pumpkin! How ya doin', sweet potato!).

These pages could never hold everyone who has touched my life and who has helped me to be the sum of what I am today. If I have not named you, please blame it on my head and not my heart. I'll catch you on the next go round 'cause this ain't the last.

God bless you all! Enjoy!
From the bottom up,

Toni

Prologue

Talise did everything in her power to disrupt the ocean of tears mounting behind her brow. She squirmed as she sat uncomfortably in a chaise almost adjacent to her boss, K.J's desk, then he ordered her to the executive sofa.

She hated everything about that sofa, including the worn brown leather cracks and the cushions that caved sideways in the very center. She knew that this very seat promoted K.J.'s way with every other female exec in the office and then some. The rumor of him and the underaged mail clerk being caught by the night maids was still hot. Talise tried her best not to be one of his flock but of late his advances had become so overpowering that she feared it might be the only option to retain a small piece of sanity in her life.

No, you wrong, I wanna see you do well but I'm tellin' you he don't want your ass for your brains, he wants the ass. I'm not dumb, I've seen *the way he operates. If you're not careful...*Talise couldn't get the words out of her head as she advanced toward the oversized seat of bereavement.

K.J.'s fat, pink and hairy hands patted the worn-down cushion, beckoning her to sit. His steel-like, rich blue eyes burned through her caramel skin as if she were a door void of kryptonite and he was Superman.

She paused, then eased herself into the chair like a child waiting to be spanked.

"Well, you've got a month."

"A month for what?" Her sheepish glare begged him to cease from allowing his hand to brush her firm and shapely thigh.

"To lower everyone's commissions," he said casually.

"What? What are you talking about?" Talise babbled with anxiety.

"We are moving into the first level of cuts for the year. This round we're cutting commissions by two and a half points. Next level will be three points and finally two more. If we do it in stages, it won't hurt as bad. You have to go to each agent in person, follow up with letters and make sure the data is entered into the system."

Talise's eyes widened as he spoke. Her lips quivered before she mustered the nerve to speak. "And I have to do this in a month? K.J., that's impossible. We have 120 agents and each agent commands at least fifteen commission lines apiece. The task is not feasible. I don't have help and I haven't learned to work the system that well, this quickly—" she babbled again.

He cut her off. "I don't care how you do it, just make sure it's done. That's why I pay my prized marketing rep $40,000 a year." He smiled like a cheshire cat.

No, you pay me $37,000 a year. And that ain't much for everything you expect me to do, she thought. Talise bit her tongue to contain her anguish. "I need more time. It's impossible for me to complete this as well as the projects I'm working on right now in a month with no help. You want me to increase productivity among our agents by twenty percent year-end and while I beg for more business, you want me to cut their livelihood. This isn't realistic," she pleaded between clinched teeth.

K.J. crossed his legs and eyed the silhouette of her round buttocks. He took a deep breath and sighed with an air of accomplishment. "You don't have more time. This is a directive from the home office. There are big plans in store, and well...this is what needs to be done, and you're going to do it. That's it." He chuckled as his hand found its way to the nape of her neck. "You know things could be a little easier..."

Capriciously Talise stood and shook her head. "Then I better get going." She used her petite fingers to massage her temple.

"I guess you better. Oh, and I want first drafts of the outlined plan to execute this and drafts of the follow-up letters on my desk in the morning." K.J., now annoyed, arose and proceeded to his desk. Talise turned as she approached the door and blankly looked in his direction. "I know it sounds like a lot, but you can do it. By the way, lose the red shoes,Talise. They make you look like a whore, and we certainly don't want that. You know I hate red shoes."

"But I don't have on red shoes," she answered.

"Now you don't but you did in Marshelli's office on Wednesday. *Tsk, tsk, tsk.* You also had on pants. One day, you'll get it together. If you don't then you'll be fast approaching new employment." K.J. turned in his chair. She was dismissed.

She carefully pulled the mammoth cherry-oak door behind her and released the crafty brass handle. She sighed. Briskly she walked past the secretary from hell who seemed to snicker at her demise.

"Talise, when you get a chance, you've made some errors on a few files. You'll need to peruse each one. You have an audit coming up soon, and I only pulled a sample. I'll come to your office…." The secretary's voice trailed off.

Talise turned the corners of the office, bypassed several coworkers and headed straight for the ladies' room. It was crowded, but she couldn't hold back the tears any longer. She ran into the stall and lifted her mid-thigh black Kasper skirt and plopped down on the toilet seat. *Dammit, somebody forgot to wipe,* she thought as her face contorted beyond the tears.

By now she was silently crying so hard that her chest heaved in spasmatic spurts. *I can't take this. What am I supposed to do? There is no way in hell I can make all those appointments and enter the information in a month. I need my job—it's practically all I have left. Steff, what would you do? How can I get out of this? Oh, I forgot, he's not talking to me either. My life is like crap. All I have to my name is an ex-job unless I fuck K.J.; an ex-lover; an ex-husband who hunts me down for ten dollars and refuses to give me a divorce; family and friends I've betrayed and let down. How in the hell did I get into this mess anyway? Why does this keep happening to me? I don't deserve this, I've done nothing to deserve all this crap that's being thrown my way. How did I get there? Better yet, how do I get out?*

Talise left the stall and headed to the mirrored basin. She turned on the cold water and splashed her face in effort to clear her now blood-red eyes. *Why do you let them see you cry? Never let them see you cry.* Even after months of turmoil she couldn't get Steffon's words out of her head. And truthfully if he held his arms open wide the way he had done so any months before, Talise would have fallen back into them all over again. And while she regretted what she did, she couldn't say that she would have changed a thing.

Talise splashed the last bit of water on her face, straightened her clothes and blew her nose. Carefully she cracked the large metal door on her way to her office and stood motionless before her once only true friend who inhabited the walls of The Great Raritan Insurance Company. They both blurted "excuse me," before either realized whom they were speaking with. For two of the longest seconds in Talise's life, they stood eye to eye and nose to nose.

Talise noticed her former friend first, so the woman pushed her nose up in disdain, turned sideways and brushed passed Talise as if she were a distant memory.

Talise screamed "I'm sorry," but it was only heard in her mind. Unfortunately, the mess that Talise found herself in had alienated everyone, including her former friend. Finally she entered her moderate-sized cubicle people called an office. It had the same cherry-wood trim and a glass door that gave access to her entire life. K.J.'s watchdog aka his secretary never had to actually go in to find out what was happening in Talise's world.

His secretary grabbed a play-by-play analysis every time she seemed to casually walk by. Her rounds were like clockwork, three times a day, noticing Talise's tardiness, extended lunches or internal visitors and reporting each and every moment to the kingpin, loud and in stereo.

Talise sat at the desk with her head in her arms pondering the day's and week's events. The phone gave her a reprieve for the moment. "This is Talise."

"What took you so long? I was about to hang up." Her gym partner and all-around good girlfriend Chynna always managed to cheer her up.

Talise ran her fingers through her hair while resting her elbow on one of the elevated stacks of files. " I had to get passed these damn files to get to the phone."

"You haven't finished that maniac's project yet?" Chynna asked with concern.

"No. And the asshole had the nerve to give me another impossible project to complete in less than a month." Talise sighed.

"You know, I don't know this guy but from everything you've told me, it sounds like they ruined a perfectly good asshole when they placed teeth in his head."

That gave Talise a hearty laugh.

"I don't get it, girl. Why are you still there? There are a million and one insurance companies…oh no, Talise, stop crying, girl, it's not worth it. Just leave," Chynna pleaded. "I could hook you up with a few headhunters. Please stop crying."

"That won't really help?" Talise said, snatching a tissue from the box sitting on the far left corner of her desk. It was almost empty. "If I try to go to another company, he'll track me down and give me a bad rep. A manager left the company and K.J. bad-mouthed him so badly that the company fired the guy. His power is amazing," Talise reasoned. "Anyway, you going to the gym tonight?"

"Yeah. You?"

"Yes," Talise answered.

"Well is there anybody else there that can possibly help you? Another manager or coworker perhaps?" Chynna asked.

"Not with the mess I'm in. People are avoiding me like I'm the plague. And to make it worse, his secretary is my strongest enemy. She's wielding power to make or break me, and girl, she's breaking me. I think because she's bitter and wants my job, but my boss couldn't give it to her."

"Why?" Chynna asked.

"Cause she has the breath of a dragon. She couldn't meet clients with that breath, we'd lose them all. Once in a while I feel like telling her to beautify America and floss," Talise said as they both howled in laughter.

Talise was laughing so hard that she hadn't noticed her visitor. "Uh, um of course, Mr. Perez, that's perfect. One o'clock on Wednesday. I'll see you then, good-bye."

K.J.'s watchdog had already let herself in. "I'm glad to see you've acquired an appointment so soon," she said with obvious disdain.

If Talise's recent island vacation hadn't tanned her perfectly, her complexion would have been red. *I don't care what you've done, don't let them get to you and don't admit anything, ever…* Steffon's words creeped in again.

"Well, I just came by to warn you. The figures you entered caused an error in the system. I guess your session with K.J. was so fulfilling that you were lost in another world. Anyway, you did something wrong, and I'll be giving K.J. a report in the morning," the secretary said smugly.

"What did I do wrong now?" Talise asked, already anxious.

"I don't know, dear, I'm not familiar with the system you're using now."

No, you only helped design it, Talise thought.

"So like I said, I just came by to warn you. I must get back to my desk and pack up. I'll be leaving in five minutes. I'm sure you'll be here oh, practically for the rest of the night. Oh yes, and how is your divorce going? Did it come through yet?" the secretary asked and bolted out of the door before Talise could formulate her answer.

Bitch, Talise thought. She plowed through one of the files the secretary had so conveniently left for her to peruse. But when thirty minutes were up, Talise, with more of a priority to make Ramon's aerobic class, planned her getaway. She decided against turning the lights off, made a mess of the files, grabbed her bag and sneaked out of the back door. *Oh, well, I couldn't be in a worse position,* she thought.

In record time she found herself at the gym. After an unprecedented two-mile run, Talise joined the rest of the regulars where Ramon, her favorite instructor, was pumping it up on the aerobic floor. He forced her to push every negative out of her body. After aerobics she made her way to the punching bag. Every kick and punch had a name. *This one's for K.J., his secretary, Calvin, Steffon, Stephanie, Gem, Maurice, Vanee and everyone in between.*

"Wow, take it easy. Boy, am I glad that I'm not on the other side of that bag!" On any other day this would have been the voice of a god. He was least 220 pounds of pure muscle, six-one, midnight-black, six-pack abs and a butt of steel. His deep and sensual voice complimented his perfectly chiseled countenance.

Talise threw her gloves onto the ground, looked at the voice speaking to her, rolled her eyes and walked away. Chynna looked on from afar in shock.

Talise purchased a bottle of water from the concession stand and trotted to change her clothes without looking back. Once inside the locker room she stripped off her soggy sports bra and bike shorts. She placed the clothes in her gym bag and reached for a towel to dry off. Fully naked to the world she reached for her purple sweats and proudly put them on when she noticed her audience. The woman showed no inhibition as she took in the full view of Talise's curvaceous, five-six frame before her. For the second time that day, Talise's beauty proved to be a curse rather than a blessing.

Briskly walking out of the locker room, Talise ran into Chynna. "I'm out, Chynna," she said, disturbing Chynna's rap with a body builder.

"Hold up, I thought we were going to go get a bite to eat at Bennigans," Chynna remarked running behind a fast-moving torpedo.

"Even though tomorrow's Saturday, I have to go in."

Talise walked past the reception desk of the gym. Her head was down, so she failed to catch a last-minute glimpse from the personal trainer she and Chynna had fawned over so many times before.

"Wait a minute, Tal. Hold up. What is going on with you? Guys trying to talk to you and you blowing them off. You didn't even flirt with cutie at the desk. Girl, if the job has got you that down, then you need to look elsewhere."

"Girl, guys are not on my mind right now, no matter how cute." In a failed effort to mask her pain, Talise said, "I've had enough. I've tried but nothing has come of it. I used a phone dating service over the last few weeks. What a joke. The only thing I had in common with the three guys the service set me up with was our taste in music. Other than that, well, the first one flipped his wrist and sucked his teeth harder than I did. The second one insisted on ordering for me at the restaurant in an effort to help me maintain my figure. And the last one, oh the last one's imprint on the third finger of his left hand was way too fresh. So I'll be okay. I just need some time. I'll give you a call on Monday, okay?"

"Okay," Chynna said. "But do me a favor, what's um… your friend Gem's number."

"Why?" Talise asked.

"Well it's a surprise." Chynna answered too abruptly for Talise.

"It's not my birthday yet but… anyway it's 555-3742. Hey, I hope you're not thinking of mentioning what's going on with me," Talise said emphatically.

"I wasn't. But I'm apt to try anything to get you whipped out of this funk."

"Well don't. Trust me, my friends have more than enough on their minds. Toodles," Talise said. She walked away and noticed that Chynna headed straight to the nearest pay phone.

Talise drove off like a bat out of hell. Once again she managed to contain her tears until their song played on the radio. She heard the words that asked for a kiss good night. Bittersweet memories of Steffon flooded her mind so deeply that she had to pull to the side of the road just to get herself together.

She recalled his words of wisdom that until now she had ignored.

Talise, you can write this account if you do it right. Cover your ass! Put the account through, subject to inspection and good credit report. This way the guy stays with you until the new business report comes out and you look like a hero. If the account goes bust on the back end, you've done your part and no one knows you're the wiser. You come out smelling like a rose, baby girl.

Stop crying! Why are you crying? You let people see your weaknesses and they use them against you. You would be okay if you organized your desk. I'll help you move at least fifty files. That should catch you up.... Drop that nigga! He's a punk ass and he's playin' you. You just don't want to see it.

Steffon was the most direct guy she had ever encountered. And even though he was rough around the edges, she could always count on him for his honest love. She often encouraged him to go back to school and get his degree. *Naw, baby girl, the streets are really my game,* he would always say. As much as she fell in love with Calvin, he couldn't even match the fervor that Steffon brought to her life.

Finally the light rain startled Talise out of her thoughts. The song ended and she started to drive. She wanted to call someone, anyone, but no one seemed to be available. They either were full of their own lives or had no more room for her. So she decided to leave well enough alone.

As much of a solution as Steffon could be, Talise remembered he could also be a nuisance. And he was only the second raft to the beach. At this point, her first raft, Calvin, had lost all of his air as well. Both floated by when Talise was hanging on to a piece of wood named Maurice by the very skin of her teeth. As each floated by she grabbed on until she landed on what she thought was the land of peaceful sun and sand. It proved to be nothing more than a deserted island.

Chapter 1

The scorching August sun had finally set as Talise Esther Grimes anxiously sped down Route 22 to catch her childhood friend who awaited her at Baystreet Café, located in a quiet New Jersey suburb.

Calvin Miles Jones waited patiently as the waitress set another Amstel Light in front of him. "Um, Hugo Boss," the waitress affirmed as she revealed her lavish bosom while bending over. "And those eyebrows. Now who did you steal those ebony babies from, your mama or daddy?" Pleasantly he smiled with ignorance. His gaze was on the door. "Here's the white wine as well," the waitress stated, "either you are very thirsty or you are waiting for someone." She was working overtime to capture his attention. But he still gazed at the door.

Nervously Talise looked around as she entered the dimly lit restaurant. Calvin's unmistakable aura immediately caught her attention as it had so many other women. It was as if he summoned her without a sound.

"I hope one of these is for me." She sat down in the booth next to him leaning against his broad shoulders. His mesmerizing scent had left a trail. His glass wasn't half-empty before the obviously smitten waitress returned to refill it.

"No, thank you," he said, showing his bright pearly whites. "Of course one is for you, Talise. If it's too warm, I'll get you another one," he said, motioning to the waitress.

"No, this is quite nice. What is it?" Talise asked, taking a sip.

"Firestone. Chardonnay that is," he answered, pleased that he had picked the perfect wine.

"Umm," she said, sighing. "This is really good."

"So are you."

"What? What are you talking about?" she questioned.

"You look fantastic. You were worth the wait," Calvin said seductively.

"Worth the wait? I'm sorry that it took me so long. I had to secure things at home before I came," she answered, smoothing her short sage linen skirt. She noticed him checking her out and she savored every moment. It had been years since she had the full attention of any man—even if it was just Calvin. She had meticulously picked this outfit to show off her shapely thighs and calves. Her three-inch matching pumps made no apology for her thin waist, long legs and smooth hairless cocoa-brown skin. "What are you chuckling about?" she questioned.

"I remember a time in our lives when we could talk about anything. And now we're sitting here, and you haven't stopped looking over your shoulder. Relax. I just wanted to spend some time with you before I leave to go back home tomorrow."

"Oh, that's right.. My parents were happy to see you," she said, changing the subject.

"I'm happy to see you. It's been a long time, Talise."

She blushed as the waitress abruptly interrupted them. By the time they ordered, Talise had settled back into a nice groove. Her third glass of Chardonnay didn't hurt, and even as children Calvin always had a way of making her feel safe and secure. "Yeah, remember how we talked about everything as kids?"

"Yeah. You were every little boy's wet dream back then, but I was proud of you. My girl held back," he said, rubbing her hands.

"You certainly didn't hold out. First it was Shanita. Then it was Jackie, oh, and we can never forget Deirdre. Oh, and whatever happened to Sandy?"

"I don't know. We were kids. A little boy has his needs. Besides, being the star of the football team had its perks. Shoot, I remember coming to a few of your school's B-ball games and you doing a little showing off your damn self. Remember that time you hit that jump split in the middle of the gym floor. Everybody cringed that day." They laughed. "Who were you trying to impress?"

The waitress returned and set the plate of grilled smoked oysters wrapped in bacon in front of Calvin. She placed a plate of scallops prepared in a similar fashion in front of Talise. "I wasn't trying to impress anyone. Just like I'm not trying to impress anyone now," Talise said solemnly as she rearranged the food on her plate.

Calvin slowly sipped his third beer. "So I guess what your parents say is true. You're leaving that Joe—"

"His name is Maurice."

"Just like any old Joe to me. I must say, your parents seem happy about this decision," he said.

"Well so am I," she said emphatically.

"Why?"

"Why am I happy or why am I leaving?"

"Both."

"'Cause he can't eat pussy," she casually said, sipping her drink.

"Huh?" Calvin almost choked on his drink.

"You heard me. He can't eat pussy. And that's because he's too busy sniffing everybody else's. What? The cat's got your tongue. Never heard such language before, huh. Oh, I'm sorry to offend your virgin ears," she said, stabbing a scallop.

"I'm just surprised to hear that type of language from you. You know...I could have saved you a lot of heartache, had you not married him. Hell, I would have stood up, you know that part where the minister says, 'If there is anyone who disagrees with this union'...But what can I say. Grey and I weren't invited to your wedding."

The waitress returned once more, directing her attention only to Calvin. "Are you okay? Is there anything else I can do for you?" she asked as she bent over again to reveal her Lisa Nicole Carson cleavage.

"Sure, I'd love another glass of wine, please," Talise said and snapped her head between them. The waitress turned up her nose and retreated. *Yes, sister, I can give attitude just like you.*

"So enough about me. What's up with you?" Talise asked.

"You know me. Just trying to grow my business and stay single. No wife and no babies. I'm just enjoying life."

"I can tell," she answered, tapping him on his Movado watch and marveling at his diamond tastefully worn on his ring finger. "So my mom told me that you moved again," she said still stabbing at her food.

"Girl, take it easy. You really seem uptight. So when are you heading out?" he asked.

"I have a place, and I'm set to move out the beginning of next month. So for right now I'm just playing it cool and biding my time. You know the phone calls from other women and sudden visits have stopped, but I don't want to be in a relationship where I have to take drastic measures for things to change, because they never will."

The waitress placed the wine before Talise, winked at Calvin and handed him another drink. "This one is on the house," she flirted. Then she slid a small piece of paper to him before walking away.

"See that's the crap I was tired of putting up with. Brothers just don't know when to take a stand. That was Maurice's problem," Talise said, glancing over her shoulder. "Anyway, so tell me about the new house."

Calvin ignored the fact that Talise had again changed the subject. "It's just a little sumpin, sumpin. You know five bedrooms, four baths, living room, dining room, large kitchen, large yard, patio and the works. The master bath has a nice Jacuzzi and I have an outdoor Jacuzzi near the ten-foot in-ground pool."

"I'm impressed. What did you do, sell the other two homes?" she asked, putting her fork down and pushing her plate away.

"No. I'm considering several options, but right now I'm renting them. That's bringing in some extra income and offsetting the mortgage for the new house."

"So, dessert?" the waitress seductively interrupted again.

I have had about enough of this buzzard's intrusive behavior. Goodness, she can have him but can't she at least wait until I leave. She doesn't know if we are here as a couple or not. Bitches... Talise's thoughts led to Maurice and how he never stood up for her. In the four years they had been married, she had dealt with phone calls, visits at her front door and rumors. The last rumor to seal their fate rested in that of a Barbie doll type. The other woman's frame at first sight easily struck that of a brick house as only the Commodores could describe it—36-24-36. Her long fake hair would make Trigger jealous.

She remembered the message on Maurice's pager. MAURICE, MEET ME AT OUR SPECIAL PLACE, TONIGHT AT 11:30. I'M GETTING OFF FOR THE

EARLY SHIFT. He hadn't even come home to offer an excuse. To this day, Talise hadn't figured out how the woman got the message to her husband, considering Talise had swiped his beeper the night before. Finally, after an evening of frustration and lack of an opportunity to confront him, she did what any normal red-blooded, hot-headed and sexually deprived wife would do: She headed straight for her car and combed the neighborhood for two hours until she found their "special place."

It was the local striptease bar, and they walked out hand and hand. Talise still cringed as she thought of how Maurice had caressed the woman's large breasts, then swept a luscious kiss from her cleavage to her apple-red lipstick. Talise gunned the car's engine and headed straight for them. They gasped, then ran. She missed. She promised herself never to miss her target again.

"Hello, earth to Talise…damn, girl, What you thinking about? It's not often a woman has my undivided attention and doesn't appreciate it." Calvin laughed. She tapped him on the arm. The waitress now returned with a portion of the restaurant's homemade hot apple cobbler topped with vanilla ice cream, caramel and whipped cream. "Have some," Calvin said, handing Talise the extra spoon. "Oh, by the way, thanks, but no thanks. I won't be needing this," he advised, returning the piece of paper with the waitress' phone number.

"Humph," the waitress murmured and briskly walked off.

"I'm impressed again. I tell you, I wish more people would respect other people's space…." Talise said twirling the ice cream around on her spoon.

"You know what you need?"

"Oh, here we go. Now you are about to tell me what I need. My parents are at home."

"You need a vacation—you need some time to get away. Besides you haven't seen the new house. As a matter of fact, you haven't seen any of my houses. Maybe you can give me some pointers."

"Thanks, but I just came from vacation with my girls. We went to the Cayman Islands last month, and I actually used up my last week of vacation. I won't get anymore time until January. I don't want to jeopardize my new position at the job. Besides my money is light from that trip."

"First of all, you'd be coming to Charlotte, not the Caymans, so the money wouldn't be the same. Second, you'd be coming to see me, and money is definitely not the issue. Now the time, okay, all you have to do is make it a weekend, instead of a week. I promise you, I'll make it worth your while." He flashed his killer smile.

"So where were you tonight?" Maurice suspiciously questioned.

"Oh, nowhere special. I had to meet a client. Besides why do you care?" she asked sarcastically. She proceeded to strip off her skirt outfit as he gazed sensuously at her figure. Maurice so adored it now that he was confident it was about to be gone. He walked toward her as she bent over and kicked her matching lace panties to the side. He gripped the sides of her toned and curvaceous thighs.

She immediately turned around and cut him off. "Uh-huh…" She shook her head. "None of that tonight or any other night for that matter. Shoulda thought of that when you stepped out of the Dollhouse some months ago." Her eyes grew wild. She was serious and his once tempestuous charm had totally worn off.

"Tal, I deserve another chance. Part of this was your fault too…" He said as she continued stripping and laid between the cool sheets. No matter how hot she may have been, she knew she couldn't give in. It was over, and she had to stand her ground. There was no more room for reason. She closed her eyes, squeezed her thighs, let out a sigh and drifted off.

"This is Talise…"

"Why do you always answer the phone with haste in your voice?" Her mom's bubbly personality even shone through on the phone.

"Ma, I don't mean to cut you off, but I'm busy. What's up?" Talise said, anxiously searching for a file among the pile on her desk.

"What's up? What's up? I don't know whom you think you are talking to, young lady, but…"

"Ma, I'm sorry, I'm just in a rush and—okay, would you just let him know I'm on my way." She took a deep breath. "Ma, I'm sorry but I can't talk to you right now—"

"Well I just called to let you know that you have a package here. Oh, by the way, how was your date with Calvin a week ago? I haven't heard from either of you. Would you like me to open it?" She rattled on.

"It wasn't a date, just a little catching up, and it was fine. No I don't want you to open it and I have to go," Talise repeated with urgency.

"Well the envelope says it's time sensitive and it's from Charlotte. I mean you can pick it up later…"

"Ma, I'll pick it up later but I gotta go…okay, okay, I have it right here and I'm on my way. Ma, I know I'm not getting off 'til late so I'll see you and Daddy later. Love you…" She hung up the phone, grabbed the file and rushed off to the big office around the corner.

The secretary was quick to let her know the boss had been waiting for seven minutes and that he was not happy. Talise chalked it up, squared her shoulders and surmised that this was going to be a long, long day.

"What do you mean you're going to North Carolina? I'm going with you," Maurice shouted.

"Maurice, my grandfather sent one ticket. You can't go. Besides I really need to get away and, you know, sort my head. Maybe I'll come back with a new perspective. I don't know. It's just a weekend, and you can even take me to the airport. How about that?"

"I'm tired of you just picking up and leaving me, Talise. You went to the Caymans with your girlfriends and now you're talking about going to North Carolina without me. I can't take this…."

Yeah well, you should've thought about this the night you chose to meet Christy, you know, Barbie's best friend, at your favorite hangout, The Dollhouse. "I know what you're saying but regardless, I'm going. You're not doing anything! I mean, no new job prospects have come through, have they?" Silence. "My plane leaves Friday at four but I have to be there at three…." Her tone softened. She felt bad that Maurice had been recently laid off and didn't want to rub it in his face. However, it would not be a deterrent to her leaving.

The last Friday of the month at 3:00 P.M. came with no Maurice in sight. Talise wasn't surprised. He hadn't been much on stability lately.

"So you know I don't like this not one bit." Her father's resonant voice almost made her ask him to turn the car around. "What am I going to say when your husband calls the house looking for the number to your grandfather's house?"

Terror swiftly swept her brow. "Well, Daddy, I'm banking on the fact that Mommy is away on vacation and you probably won't be home. You know when the cat's away the mouse will play...huh, huh…" She chuckled. "I'm just going to see Calvin for a short rest before moving out. I don't really want to be in that house anyway. Don't worry, Daddy, everything will be okay," she said, trying to be convincing. She pulled her luggage from the car and flagged down the skycap to aid her.

She hugged and kissed her father on the cheek. "Call me as soon as you get there. I want to make sure you are okay," her dad said. She nodded and headed for her journey.

Talise checked her watch and noticed she still had fifty minutes before boarding. One section of the bar was deemed for first-class passengers only. No one was at the frosted glass doors checking passes so she walked in and decided to pretend.

She felt sharp in her navy-blue flare-legged pantsuit and gold mules as she sat at the long black lacquer bar. She breathed a sigh of relief as she ordered a glass of Firestone Chardonnay. She noticed a very distinguished sandy-haired and impeccably dressed man at a nearby table. She threw a glance and crossed her legs when the bartender interrupted her flirt. "Fifteen please."

Jolted out of her stare she questioned, "Dollars?"

"Bucks, dollars, whatever you want to call it, but that's what I need unless you are planning to run a tab."

She bit her bottom lip and placed her hand in her purse. The bartender rolled his eyes and tipped his head forward. "Madam, you know this bar is deemed for first-class passengers only. May I see your ticket please…"

"Don't worry about it. Place her order on my tab," the deep voice in the Moni suit advised.

"Thanks but I have it," Talise said.

"You certainly do. I wouldn't mind getting it either," he said with the voice of Barry White. "Please join me." He pulled an empty chair to his table. "Please…"

Talise turned up her nose at the bartender, grabbed her glass and her purse and sauntered her sexiness to the chair.

It was three glasses later when she heard the final boarding call for flight number 705 to Charlotte, North Carolina. She thanked her latest suitor, placed his business card in her purse and strolled toward the makeshift passageway to the beginning of her journey. Often warned not to, she looked back. A jade-green Tahari suit was questioning her Barry White about his most recent business meeting, just moments ago. Talise chuckled with the delight of her wine and kept going. His card made it all the way to Charlotte before being discarded in the nearest airport trashcan.

"Oh, man, she is fine. Trust me, you won't be disappointed. Play your cards right and I might give you a good recommendation. Yeah man, ass for days, tiny waist, long hair, brown skin, the works…because I've fallen in the friendship zone that Chris Rock talks about. She's like my little sister…yeah, well I plan for us to hit all the spots tonight. She's only here for the weekend…yeah, yeah okay…peace." Calvin turned off his cell and placed it back in his Coach carryall for men. He eyed the board for Talise's arrival and patiently waited. When he noticed the status change from on time to arrived he briskly walked toward the baggage claim area with delight.

The wine had worn off, and Talise was due for a refill. Her harried gait carried her to the baggage claim area where she was greeted with another deep, sensuous voice. "Need some help with that?"

"Heyyy…" she sang as she turned and held Calvin tightly. "Thanks for the ticket, I really needed this."

"You're welcome." He beamed, escorting her to the car.

"I didn't see this in Jersey. Very nice."

"I didn't drive to Jersey, remember? I flew and had a rental. But this here, this is my baby," he said, tapping the dash of the silver seven series BMW that he affectionately called the Gray Ghost.

They coasted toward the main highway around the mountains where a gold mist seemed to hover. It wasn't twenty minutes before his phone rang.

"Not too much. Just chillin'. Yeah, yeah, uh-huh. Sure will. Ditto. Peace," he said then hung up abruptly. "Anything special you want to listen to?"

"Anything but rap. Not too big on it, you know," she answered.

"Yeah, I know. No problem. We don't have too many stations that play it anyway. You look nice but that outfit doesn't compliment your assets as much as the outfit I last saw you in."

"Thanks, I think. Why do you care?"

"'Cause we are going to hit a few spots tonight and tomorrow, and I want you looking your best. You know, I got some prospects lined up."

"Yeah, well should they warrant it, I'll change. They might not be able to handle it, if you know what I mean."

"Ooh, little Talise has grown up," he teased.

"Yes, I have and don't you forget it." She laughed as he sped up the highway.

Calvin led her to a quaint restaurant. The huge leather-covered doors opened to red-brick walls held together by a wooden floor of a deep burgundy hue. The dim lights hung softly from stiff wrought-iron fixtures over huge wooden tables. No two antique chairs were alike and the place was filled with splashes of azure, aqua and magenta. The fire blazed brightly in the fireplace and gave the place a warm, homey feel.

"So what can I do to make your weekend worthwhile?" Calvin asked, seductively sipping his Amstel Light.

"Well you can start by ordering me a Brandy Alexander, a chocolate hunk of a man with a big dick and perhaps some seafood to tide me over until a real meal comes." She laughed.

"Bold, aren't we?"

"Only way to be," she answered, feeling tingly all over. Dinner ended with Calvin having full knowledge of Talise's reasons for leaving Maurice. He didn't blame her. For four years his friend had been stuck with an adulterer who couldn't satisfy her and turned her life into a soap opera. And it was Calvin's job to make all of that disappear this weekend.

The first stop was a club that stood next to a car dealership. They walked in and all eyes immediately turned to them. Talise had to admit they were a great-looking couple. But she was quick to assert herself to the other cuties in the place and let them know that she and Calvin were just friends. Her eyes landed on a midnight blue-black man with a prominent nose. Just her type with one major flaw: He was in deep conversation with exactly his opposite. Blue eyes, long blond hair and a pouch for a stomach. They headed right toward the brother.

"Banks, what's up, man?" Calvin greeted him. "Hey, Laura, how you doing tonight?"

"I could be much better, Cal. Much better," she said flirtatiously.

Oh, no she didn't. I know she ain't trying to get hurt up in here. She already got one of our brothers, and now she's going to go for another one right in his face, and the brother's not going to step to that. See that's the problem. These brothers let them bitches get away with too much....

"Banks, this is my friend Talise. Talise, this is best car salesman you'll ever meet. In fact he gave me a great deal on the Gray Ghost." Calvin introduced them, jolting her out of her thought.

"Pleased to meet you, Banks, right?" Talise said as her stare prompted the white girl to exit.

"You can't be as pleased as I am," Banks exclaimed, giving her the once-over.

No wonder he allows her to blatantly disrespect him, he's doing the exact same thing. She noticed that Calvin had sauntered off. Banks couldn't have been happier than a fag in Boys Town as her dad often said.

But by the end of the night the three of them had hit two other spots and were having a great time. "Tal—you don't mind if I call you Tal do you?"

"No, many of my friends do."

"Oh, so I'm a friend now," Banks teased.

"I guess. We'll see. That's if Ms. Laura or whatever her name is doesn't mind. Since we're friends, I have to be bold to ask, why do you put up with that?"

"With what?"

"Her blatant disrespect of you. I mean if she could have swallowed Cal and eaten him, she would have right in your face. Not that any woman wouldn't, but dag, she does know that the two of you are friends, doesn't she. Or are you into that freaky stuff?"

"Ohh," he said, nodding in understanding. "That was what the look was about."

"What look? Sure refill me with a rum and Coke, please. Don't worry, the tab is on him," Talise said to the bartender with a smile. Calvin had been missing in action all night, but Talise didn't much mind. She was in good hands with Banks.

"You know the look you gave me when you and Cal first walked in." She gave him a puzzled gaze. "Before we get started clearing that whole nonsense up, I have to ask, are you and Cal sure you guys are just friends? I mean, I know him and I see you. I don't want to tread on my boy's territory."

"First of all I'm not anyone's territory. I date and mingle with whom I choose. Don't bring it up again. Cal and I are just friends, nothing more or less. So if I'm interested in you pursuing me, believe me, it won't be Cal stopping you, it would be me."

"Bold, aren't we?" Talise acknowledged his question with only a smile. "Now that we have that cleared up, let's clarify some other business at hand. I don't date white women, just not interested. I don't knock a brother who does, but I don't. So no, I'm not seeing Laura, she is a coworker. So you can let out your sigh of relief."

"What makes you think I'm relieved?"

"You despise brothers who date white women, don't you?" Banks questioned confidently.

"Who said I dislike interracial relationships?" she asked defensively.

"Your eyes said it the minute you walked into the room and eyed me. Your face said it when you found out it wasn't true," he answered.

Ooh, perceptive isn't he. He gets a big, fat cookie. "Well I don't want to seem racist but I don't so much dislike interracial relationships, I just hate to see productive, good-looking brothers hanging on white girls' tits. It's just a waste," she ended, gulping her rum and Coke.

"A waste of what?" Banks questioned. He rested on his elbow and moved in very close. Too close.

"A waste of time, energy and one of the most precious resources nature has to offer—black men, that is. I happen to love black men and the blacker the better. Besides there are way too many sisters out here who are deserving of good brothers, and it burns my heart to see so many going to the other side. And you know what happens as soon as a brother gets a little bit of money..." Banks had opened a can of worms for Talise. It wasn't until Calvin finally returned that she had regained her composure.

"What in the world has you so riled up?" Calvin asked, approaching cautiously.

"I asked the age-old question that we all know is taboo, why black men should or shouldn't date white women. Obviously Talise is incensed by it. Tell me, Talise, do you feel the same about black women dating white men? Y'all have a whole lot to say about men but what about the women?"

"My question is why. I honestly don't see the attraction in white guys. There is not a white man on this earth to present day that I would consider dating. I'm just not attracted to them," Talise said. "Anyway, black men's standards always seem to change when they date white women. The women they date will be fat with stringy hair and only able to take them home after they have become some famous basketball star and everything is supposed to be okay in Snow White's land. I'll tell you. I'm parched, I think I'll order another one...."

"No, it's getting late, Tal. I'm taking you home. We have a busy day tomorrow." Calvin grabbed her suit jacket and placed it on her shoulders. "It's getting a little cool out."

Talise followed closely as Calvin led her toward the door. Just as she was about to walk through, Banks ran up behind her and whispered something in her ear.

The hour drive to Calvin's place was peaceful. So much so that Talise awoke to find herself in the mix of what must have been an upscale neighborhood with oak trees in every yard. The trees loomed as large as the sky. She wiped the sleep from her partying eyes to see a family of wild bunny rabbits in front of Cal's majestic French doors.

He murmured something about the paying the lawn guy as they entered. He immediately stripped himself of his vanilla trousers. His strong legs stood firm beneath the sexy silk boxers. She couldn't help but notice. He then tore out of his charcoal-gray chest-hugging sweater. It hid abs of steel.

"Just no inhibitions, huh?" she asked not ashamed to notice. "I see you're still taking care of that athletic body of yours."

"Nothin's changed. Got to stay in shape." He led her to one of the guest bedrooms. She immediately began to fill unused drawers and the closet with her things. "I see you're wasting no time making yourself at home." He smiled.

"And you know it. Oh, by the way I don't know what you have planned for us tomorrow but Banks invited me to brunch on Sunday before my flight. He said he'll pick me up by ten so..."

"So...I don't know that you'll be making that date."

"Cal, I'm not little Talise anymore. I'm a grown woman. You offered me this trip to get my head together and have fun. That's all I'm doing...."

"Yeah, well we'll see about that. Good night," he said. "Hey, I'm really glad you came down. I really miss our friendship."

"Me too." She blushed. She changed into her attire for the night. It consisted of her favorite white cotton nightie and a dookie-brown satin headrag. She crawled under the bed only to notice that her only covering was a thin comforter and a sheet. The central air had made her extremely uncomfortable. She got up and scoured to find an additional blanket in the walk-in closet, but she struck out. She then stumbled to the outer linen closet, still to no avail. She was startled by the dark shadow that come behind her and flicked on the light.

"What are you doing?"

"Looking for a blanket. It's freezing in this house."

"Well I don't have another blanket. And I haven't finished decorating the other rooms yet so it looks like you're out of luck," he said as she followed him downstairs.

"No, it looks like you're out of luck. Because you see one of these blankets on this bed fit for a king? I'm taking it." She reached to strip the bed and was hit square in the butt with a pillow. "Oh, it's on now…."

She dropped the blanket, grabbed two pillows and chased him around the room. He used his receiving skills, dodged her throw, picked up another pillow and clocked her on the head. Out of breath she hadn't gotten one good hit on him yet. He ran and then jumped on the bed. She tried to make him fall by shifting the blanket but he was cracking up while steadily pounding her on the head. Finally she retreated and strategized on how she should clobber him despite his brute strength. She did what any desperate person would do: She rushed him. He was so shocked that he fell and they both ended up out of breath.

"That was a great move, Grimes."

"Not so bad yourself, Jones," she answered.

"Man, I haven't heard that in years," she said still trying to catch her breath.

"What, your maiden name?" he questioned and she nodded. "Well I'm sure you'll be hearing more of that soon. When is your divorce coming through?"

Suddenly she became sad. She sat Indian-style on the bed and pondered. She was determined not to allow another tear to fall. He sensed her anxiety and wanted so badly to ease her pain, but this was not the time. Not just yet. He patiently listened for the remainder of the night. Finally they drifted off to sleep, never moving from their original spots.

The next morning Talise was startled awake by the sound of a ringing phone and the unfamiliar smell of burnt bacon. It took her several seconds to realize where she was and what had happened. The slob stain on Calvin's pillow was a quick reminder. She reached across the room for the robe hanging on the door. It was a nice silk, black-and-white polka-dot number that felt smooth against her skin. She was still in the bathroom brushing her teeth and getting her hair together when she heard him yelling for her.

"It's too early in the morning for all that yelling," she said, walking into a kitchen filled with smoke. She noticed the house had a different look in the day. It had modern glass doors, ceilings and windows all over the place. There was so much natural sunlight that there was no need to turn on anything artificial. She walked around the living room and noticed the white leather couch and gold setee. *Wow, this is beautiful,* she thought. She stumbled across an old mahagony desk and noticed a picture of an attractive golden-colored woman with shoulder-length, highlighted hair. She had big pretty eyes that could draw anyone in.

"Who is this?"

He turned around, stunned that he had not put the picture away.

"Candace," he answered casually.

"Oh, who is she?"

"A friend."

"A friend-friend? Or a friend?"

"I don't know the difference."

"Oh, there is a definitely a difference. You see I'm a friend. You know someone you've known all of your life, who you can have pillow fights with, sleep in the same bed with and nothing happens. But a friend-friend is someone who everything happens with. Now is she a friend or a friend-friend?"

He continued to burn his bacon. "What does it matter to a friend?"

"Okay she is a friend-friend. Does she know that I'm here? And would it hurt her feelings to know that we slept in the same space last night. Not that anything happened."

"You are asking too many questions that are not that important. Breakfast is served," he said, taking the photo from her. He placed it back in the living room inside a mahogany drawer.

"I know you don't expect me to eat this. No hard feelings but...perhaps we should have gone out to eat."

"You can't do any better," he challenged, popping her on her butt with his towel.

"Watch me." She placed the apron around her robe, dug in the refrigerator and got to work.

"Thanks, Cal, for a wonderful weekend. I really had a good time. I probably broke my budget shopping with you today, but I had a good time."

"I hope I didn't bore you too much with the parties we had to make a stop at this evening, but I had to go."

"I didn't mind at all. You know I can hold my own."

"Speaking of holding your own, Banks is supposed to come to get you at what time tomorrow?" he asked as he folded back his comforter.

"I think he said around ten, but I'm beat, I don't know that I really want to go. I mean he seems cool and all but I can tell he's slick. I'm not up for that drama right now. I just got rid of one slickster," she said, plopping on the bed. She smoothed out her invariably different attire for the evening. Tonight she donned a cinnamon silk nightie that complimented her skin. She did away with the headrag and conveniently forgot to take off her fiery red matte lipstick. She scooted the covers under her butt.

"What are you doing?" he asked.

"I'm getting ready to go to sleep. What does it look like? Cal, it's not like we haven't slept together before. Remember that time in college when I came to visit you, and you only had one bed?"

"Yeah, that was then, but now I have five beds and you are welcome to choose any one of them except this one. You sleep too wild, Tal, and you dribble." She hit him with a pillow and he laughed. "Don't start. You don't want none of this.... Not only that, I turned the central air down, so you should have no problems."

"Yeah but I'm enjoying your company. Besides my sleeping here has nothing to do with you being shy or Nikki—I mean Candace."

"That wasn't funny, Tal," he said, dropping to the floor to give himself thirty. She watched his masculine physique slide up and down, as he defied gravity. His strong and cut arms were those of a man. A man who would protect what was his. His pants as he ended his sets made her experience things she was not used to feeling when it came to Calvin. *I mean this is Calvin, not, not...* At that moment she couldn't think of anyone to replace the thought.

"Speaking of Nikki, have you heard from her?"

"Haven't heard *from* her, but the last I heard of her was that she was married, divorced and now a single parent." He grabbed a towel from the bathroom, wiped his face and sat down on the bed beside her. "And trust me, Candace is far from Nikki."

"You still love her, don't you. I mean Candace is the spittin' image of her."

"Will always love what we had. Not in love with her anymore. Besides she was more in love with being married, than marrying me. I accepted that, and I moved on. Now it's late and I'm tired. You can stay in here if you want to just stay on your side of the bed. Trust me, with that getup you had on last night, you didn't have to worry about me coming near you, and if you don't play your cards right, nobody else for that matter. Just a hint and word for the wise." He left her sitting up with her mouth open.

He hadn't noticed her attire for the evening. Even so, she seductively slid herself between the sheets and the pillow-top mattress that so enveloped her soul the night before. The satin on her skin and the satin of the sheets provided a sexy rhythm as she situated herself against Calvin's warm, strong muscles. *Ahh, a perfect fit,* she thought. She nestled closer, ignoring the fact that this was Calvin—one of her oldest friends. He rustled. She became unexplainably excited. He then turned over while her sensuality perked, looked lovingly into her eyes and said, "Alright, move over to your side of the bed and don't pull all of the cover. Oh, and don't forget your date with Banks in the morning." Shortly thereafter she heard a snore that could wake the dead. This hit her ego like a ton of bricks.

Chapter 2

As usual Gemmia Barnes rushed around her new two-bedroom starter home nestled in the soft community of South Orange, New Jersey. She was late for what she hoped would be the last night of a dream gig turned nightmare. She was using a flashlight under her dark bed of abyss when the phone annoyed her out of her frantic search.

"Hello…Can't talk long, but speak…" was her usual zippy tone.

"Hey, woman? Busy?"

"Yeah. Right now I'm looking for my brown shoe before I go to New York. I'm late."

"As usual," her friend Stephanie Alphonso chimed in.

"Yeah, yeah," she rebounded sarcastically. "What's up? Oh, there it is."

"Well…" Stephanie let out a long sigh. "I just called to talk a bit, but since you don't have time…"

"No, I don't. But I do have time for you. You got two minutes while I take a pee-pee. Then really I gotta go. I'm already too late to drive, I know I'll hit mad traffic, so I have to train it tonight."

Stephanie thought about it then decided against her soliloquy. "You're on your way out, so I'll save it. But…"

"Is it about that mystery man you have been hiding from us? Problems in paradise or something? I'm probably the wrong person to ask for advice right now," Gem said, zipping her pants. She cradled the phone on her shoulder to wash her hands.

"Gem, honey. You are just as qualified as anyone to give love advice. In fact, when you get some time it wouldn't hurt for you to help me out a little."

"Yeah right. I can tell you everything not to do."

"Would you stop beating yourself up about what you revealed. I mean it's a shocker, yes but we're not judging you. We were just surprised that's all. I might add, a little hurt because you didn't allow me to be there for you."

Gem finished her remaining touches and bit her bottom lip. This wasn't something she had time to get into right now and she wasn't in the mood for Stephanie's psychology moments.

"You have to start healing. Allow yourself some freedom to…"

Oh, oh. Unsolicited advice. I did not ask for unsolicited advice. "Thanks, girl, but I gotta go. Can we talk tomorrow perhaps?" Gem was curt.

"Oh, yeah, um sure. It's not that important anyway. But what is important is that you remember we have to help Talise on Saturday. So keep your calendar clear."

"Oh, shoot. I forgot. Saturday is the beginning of Labor Day weekend. I can't help her then. I have a gig. Why couldn't she move last week when I was sitting around twiddling my thumbs?" Gem said with exasperation.

"Because she wasn't here. She was in North Carolina." Stephanie knew she was baiting.

Gem bit. *We just left the Cayman Islands. For somebody who is always complaining about money she sure is finding it to travel.* "Okay you got me. What or who is in North Carolina?" Suspicious sarcasm had entered her voice.

"You remember Calvin Jones from high school?"

"Calvin? Calvin Jones? Ohhh, not the football player, my boyfriend is a quarterback? Only she didn't know what a quarterback was and he acted more like her big brother than her boyfriend Calvin Jones?" Gem recalled, mimicking what Talise used to say.

"That's the one," Stephanie affirmed.

"How in the world did she hook up with him?" Gem questioned, now really contemplating whether this juicy piece of gossip was worth her being later than she expected or if she should really go.

"Well…"

"Never mind. You know that girl jumps from one lily pad to the next. Why would she get involved with him so suddenly? I mean…" Gem caught her breath and regained her composure. Sometimes Talise had a way of getting her blood boiling. "You know what, I have to go. I'll talk to you later, but tell Talise that I'm sorry but I'm not available."

Gem abruptly scurried out of the door. It was now 11:30. Her train would be at the station at 11:38 for what was normally a ten-minute ride. She also hadn't purchased a ticket, and now that the station ticket clerks had been replaced by machines, she would have to pay the penalty of purchasing the ticket on the New Jersey Transit train.

Normally she was careful not to bring to much attention to herself by speeding through the lamppost-lit streets. She came to a screeching stop at the light and barely missed the white Dodge Neon in front of her.

"Oh no." She noticed the light mist that began to fall. She knew rain in New Jersey almost always meant a delay. *People in Jersey know they can't drive in the rain,* she thought, as time seemed to come to a stop. She waited for the light to turn green, remembering another painful time she had to rush to another gig in her not-so-distant past.

"Violently he wrapped my hands with two belts around each bedpost. I didn't know what was going to happen but I knew it was fierce because I saw a look in his eye I had never seen before."

"Wait a minute. How did he get you to the bed?" Talise asked, while Gem was putting the last touches of sunblock on her extremely long torso.

"I did degrade him now that I think about it," she continued in a daze, not hearing the question. "I mean when I met him he was into every hustle you could think of to make money. Cars, small-time drugs, anything to make a buck. I admit, I enjoyed the material benefits from it too. But when it got too hot, I asked him to stop and that was when the pressure mounted," Gem continued while sipping her favorite toasted-almond drink. "I mean I would snap at him, him at me. Tell him he couldn't do what he needed to do to be a man. All kinds of stuff. It had to hurt."

"There is always room for gentle encouragement," Stephanie chimed in. "But why didn't you tell us, me. I mean there are problems in every marriage. I could have helped, you know."

"I know but I was too embarrassed."

"Let her finish. I want to hear the rest of this," Talise said, crossing her legs and breaking the moment. Stephanie shot her a look.

"Anyway, it all came to head on the last night Terry and I were together. I hopped out of bed. I was going on the road to sing background for the group Jade. Terry was sad I was leaving and so was I. But we were both glad that I was getting away from that maniac. At this point he had totally spun out of control. Anyway I was leaving, and Terry planted a long kiss on my lips. It almost made me turn around and get back in bed—to heck with the tour. Anyway the phone rang and I ran out. I had about an hour and a half to get to Long Island where the bus was leaving and I still had to go home to get my bag. But I heard Terry yelling, 'Naw, man you get a life and stop calling my house with your bullshit,' I didn't pay it any attention.

"I got to the apartment and it was dark. I didn't see that maniac's car, so I thought I would go in, grab my already packed bag, leave and catch up with him via phone on the road. You know, 'hi, honey, I'm in Chicago or Detroit or somewhere, miss you much, call you later, kiss, kiss…' "

Silence.

Talise could barely contain herself as she looked like she was on the edge of her seat.

"Humph." She nervously chuckled. "I was still wiping the chocolate we had used from parts of my inner thigh. So I strutted into the house thinking I could make good time if I hurried when the lights flipped on. Darius was sitting in the corner. He pounced on me like a panther. It was so fast, I can barely remember if he hit me with his fist or the two-by-four he was sitting there holding."

Gem began to hum, her only solace in time of crisis. Stephanie tapped Talise to be quiet and allow Gem her time. They waited. She continued to hum. They didn't much mind. Gem's voice was nothing short of being anointed. It was a total gift from God, protected by the angels in heaven. Her body swayed as her song became stronger. A tear formed in her eye as she smiled. Her smile reflected who and what she had been named for, Gemmia Grace Barnes. Her wise godmother named her as a prediction of brilliance for this gifted gem.

"You don't have to finish, honey. We understand," Stephanie sympathetically pleaded.

"I want to," she answered. "It's time."

"Good, because I want to hear," Talise said. Stephanie's head snapped back with another look.

"I think when I finally gained my composure, I had seen every color in the universe. He must have knocked me out cold for a minute 'cause when I woke up, I heard a pounding. I scrambled and tried to grab my bag to get out of there, but I was still dazed. I made my way to the front door where he stood aside and laughed. He had nailed it with the same board he must have hit me with. I then ran toward the back door and he was right on my heels with a cynical laugh as if I was in a house of horror.

"Where were you?"

"I told you I was at Terry's house. I needed to get some things for my trip."

"So why didn't you get on the phone when I called?"

"I probably left already. I just had to…"

He hit me again. *"I told you about hanging around that fucking dyke,"* he continued to yell. I was still on the floor trying to defend Terry, myself and anyone else. So like Tina Turner, I started to fight back. I got in one good kick before he punched me and got my head between his legs. He used his legs as a vice and my head as a ping-pong ball as he continued to slap my face back and forth. He then stripped me naked. He had poured lighter fluid on all of my clothes in the closet and threatened to strike a match all throughout the night. All the time, I was tied to the bed with the belts and he repeatedly held a knife to my throat between his threats of setting the place on fire. Needless to say I missed the bus."

"So how did you get out of there?" Stephanie questioned.

"At about six in the morning, I guess he was tired. He calmly untied me, threw me one of his shirts and told me to go call the police. I mean it was psychotic. I put the shirt on, bruised and beaten, ran down the street to the nearest pay phone and called the police. He calmly waited for them in the house as they came and arrested him. I called Terry, gathered my things and she took me to her house where I stayed for a month until I got myself together. I was just notified that he got three to five years for torturing me."

"The bastard should have gotten life," Stephanie said.

"Who are you telling? You know that when they searched the house, in the attic and basement, they found all this torturous paraphernalia. He had planned this torture for a long time."

Silence.

"I have to ask, I mean um, Gem, are you, um well…"

"No Talise, I'm not a lesbian," Gem answered solemnly.

Stephanie popped Talise on her almost sunburned thigh. "Ouch," Talise responded.

"Would you care for some ketchup or perhaps barbecue sauce with your leather?" Stephanie questioned.

"It's okay, Stephanie. I understand your concern," Gem said with caution.

"But, but…"

"Just leave it alone, Talise," Gem said. Stephanie gave Talise another implacable look.

The beachside waiter returned with their refills. Talise slurped the last of her Rumrunner before allowing him to take the glass.

"I wasn't going to pry in your sex life, Gem. I just wanted to know what happened with the tour. Why didn't you try to join Jade at a later date?"

"Too bruised, mentally and physically. I certainly couldn't show up with a bunch of black-and-blues all over my body, then wear some skimpy little costume and pray that no one noticed. Just too much." Gem sighed.

Silence.

"I don't know what to say."

"The psychologist is stunned? I'm marveled," Talise said sarcastically.

"There isn't much to say," Gem answered as she and the girls pulled their sunglasses from the tops of their heads and relaxed back into more sun.

A few minutes later, Talise popped up with a startling revelation. "I'm leaving. I'm not putting up with this crap anymore."

"You're serious, aren't you?" Stephanie questioned.

"Yes. Very," Talise affirmed.

"Well you have my support. If it's not right, don't keep trying to fix it."

"Well, ladies, to us!" Stephanie lifted her glass. The gloom had subsided and Stephanie rose and placed her smooth manicured toes in a new pair of white thongs and grabbed her towel. "I'm going to the lobby next door to peruse a few exotic picture frames. I'll meet you guys in the suite. Talise, you should probably start moving now. I'd prefer to be on time for dinner tonight, thank you."

Talise mimicked her by twisting her head. Gem laughed.

A few moments later, Gem and Talise, too, rose to the occasion. Stephanie was correct: They had been late every evening awaiting Talise to do something with her hair, which she would spend hours restyling, prior to dinner.

"You know, after listening to what you went through, I would be a fool to stay in this relationship with Maurice. I mean this is a brother who when we went to counseling to work out our problems, told the counselor that he shouldn't have to romance me because that's why he got married."

"Jerk," Gem chimed in.

"You got that right. I have the best friends in the world between the two of you, and I know I can make it. Hey, I'm really sorry for seeming so insensitive back there. I was just surprised, I mean shocked, I mean…" she babbled.

Gem placed her hand on Talise's shoulder. "You don't have to say another word. I know it was surprising to hear that your best friend had a lesbian affair. Note that it was an affair, and it doesn't mean I'm a lesbian. I just needed someone at that time, and she happened to be the best person for the job. It's not something I'm ashamed of but it's not something I'll freely admit either. I love men…."

"I'm really glad you guys decided to come. I couldn't imagine a better vacation," Talise said.

Bonk! Bonk! Bonk! The roaring engines startled Gem out of her thoughts. It was 11:38 exactly when Gem raced into the parking lot of the South Orange station. Fortunately for her, she wasn't the only one who was habitually late. The train hadn't come and looked to be nowhere in sight. At least when she got to the studio, she wouldn't be lying when she gave the excuse that the train was late. She didn't have to say which train.

Gem pulled herself up to the top of the platform and sat down. She retrieved her sheet music to review. Sadly she recalled several singers who had been fired and replaced. She desperately tried to help one girl, even stayed on in the mornings to help after the session was completed. That was until the girl started a rumor that Gem had her fired on purpose by teaching her the wrong notes. *The nerve of that girl,* she thought. *The bottom line was that it wasn't my responsibility to teach her anything. I was just trying to be helpful. But you can't help a person who got the job because of nepotism and couldn't hold it. Nepotism and no talent don't always work in this business. Just ask LaToya Jackson.*

Gem rustled her papers when the cell phone in her bag rang. "Hello," she said in a sing-songy voice.

"Hey, woman. It's me. I couldn't let the night go by without apologizing to you for my curtness earlier. You seemed a little on edge, and I should have been more understanding."

That was Stephanie's job. Always the one to console. She was always the glue.

"I'm sorry, too, girlfriend. I guess I was a little edgy. And the Talise thing set me off. I want to help but I felt bad, and I just want her to get herself together. She doesn't have to make the same mistakes I did by rushing in and out of relationships too soon. She's not even divorced yet."

The conversation had really opened up a wound that wasn't healing. The clever psychologist in Stephanie knew it but she restrained herself from prying. "I hear you but you have to allow her to travel the route she's on. We can't stop that. We can only be there for her when she falls."

"So you agree with me?"

"I didn't say that."

"Oh, come on, Steph, cut the psych stuff. It's okay to be our friend sometimes."

"Okay, I agree. I think she is setting herself up for a fall. She has little restraint when it comes to a man showing her a little attention, and I believe she is vulnerable right now. But again, all we can do is be there for her, just like we are here for you. No one is judging you, Gem, and one day soon, you got to let your defenses down."

Once again, her style had kicked in. She knew how to listen, and she knew how to call a spade a spade without being insulting. Friendship was always mixed with a little technique even when it wasn't requested. "Listen, I have to go. I'm expecting some company of my own tonight. I want to set a nice tone in the place, you know light a few candles and such…"

"You know I'm tired of hearing bits and pieces about this mystery guy. When are we going to get a chance to meet him?"

"You will. I'm just not ready to introduce him as my significant other yet. We still have some major ground to break, and I really don't want any outside pressures right now. I want some time to take it slow. You and Talise just bare with me. In time, okay?"

"Cool," Gem agreed. "Listen, the train is coming, so I'm gonna go. Have a good time tonight."

"Thanks. I will. Remember what I said. And remember Talise is on your side too. I'll tell her you're sorry, but you had to work," Stephanie said in her usual sweet tone.

Gem hung up the phone, smiled and boarded the train.

Stephanie pressed a button and watched the moon roof retract to reveal a perfectly set patio. She skipped down the first landing of her spiral staircase adorned in blush carpeting, setting the dimmers along the way.

She stopped and straightened her newly painted self-portrait. *Ahh,* she sighed. *Such an elaborate gift from an elaborate man,* Stephanie thought. He picked up this little trinket on his last excursion in Paris. He had slipped a photo from one of her albums without her knowledge. He hoped she didn't mind, he had said. She couldn't do anything but gasp.

She continued down the second landing of spirals, which led to the fully furnished basement, which included a small private wine cellar for each of the new condo owners of the private estates of Whispering Woods. She selected Bernaccio 1967. This was yet another trinket from his travels in Milan. It was too late for Moet and Chandon, part of her private stash. Besides the bubbles this late in the evening would render her hopeless to help her long-standing 11:30 A.M. appointment.

She trotted back up the stairs and grabbed her Mikasa wine cooler, the stand and a set of purple-stemmed crystal glasses. The cheese and crackers had been set earlier, resting at room temperature.

She was arranging some glassware and dishes around a fresh posy of lavender lilies when the bell chimed. She viewed one of the three small screens located on various panels throughout the house, including the master bedroom. It was Alec. Delightfully she buzzed him in as she awaited him at the top of the stairs.

"Good evening, sweetheart."

"What's that?" she questioned, eyeing yet another small package.

"Just a little something I picked up in the city. Just to let you know I was thinking of you."

"You are so sweet," she said, leading him to the roof.

He meticulously disrobed from his Brooks Brothers linen jacket. "You really should get a coat rack and place it in the corner over there."

"For the deck?" She laughed.

"I like to think of it more like a lanai," he said, placing a small brown bag on the table next to the neatly wrapped package. He grabbed her around the waist and pulled her toward him. His lips locked over hers as he caressed her buttocks. He pressed her soft full breasts closer to his chest. She melted in his arms.

"So what's this?" She pounced on his latest gift while he popped the cork and poured the wine. Inside the package was a mahogany leather-bound journal with her initials engraved in gold. Inside the gold-leafed pages read in script, PROPERTY OF STEPHANIE ALPHONSO. "This is exquisite! But Alec, I told you as much as I adore them, gifts every time you see me are not necessary."

"There's more. Keep looking."

She returned to the package fully tearing the box open. "Oh, these are beautiful! And my favorite color. You are so thoughtful." She pulled out one long-stemmed, royal-blue flute.

"It's Lalique," he said, sipping the wine. "Nice choice. Is it the 1964 or the vintage selection?"

"It's 1967. And I'm very familiar with Lalique. Besides I can read, Alec." She pointed to the box.

"Oh, I'm sorry, darling. I meant no harm. I just like to indulge myself by showing you that I only like to get you the finest. Join me," he said, patting the cushion of the swing. She poured herself a glass of wine and sat beside him. "I'm sorry if I've been condescending. I've had a rough day. I certainly didn't mean to take it out on you. Here you go," he said, handing her the brown bag with the ribbon around it.

"Okay, what flavor did you get?" She was confident that he had picked up scones from her favorite bakery in the city. "Oh, my, there are two in here. Alec," she said innocently, "you know I can't possibly indulge in two scones. Instead of my normal two miles a day, I'll be running six." She laughed.

"One is for me," he said, lovingly kissing the nape of her neck.

"But I have cheese and crackers and a dab of beluga over there," she responded.

"That's not for tonight. I was hoping we could enjoy those in the morning before work, after our showers," he said, rubbing her gently.

She pulled away and massaged the back of her neck. "Alec…" She grabbed his hand, placing herself at a safe distance with the table between them. "We're moving way too fast. I mean the gifts are lovely and…well…but…I'm just not ready to take this relationship farther, yet." She hesitated. "I mean no harm, but I'm just not ready. I thoroughly enjoy your company. Right now, I'd really like to leave it at that."

"Oh, come on Stephanie…" She felt the warmth of his breath. "It's not like we are total strangers to each other. I mean once I've had a taste, I mean you are insatiable and I really would like to go farther with this…" he pleaded.

"I know. I know. But one spontaneous night on the beach, well that's paradise. You know—sunsets, moons, stars, sand and water—I mean that's fantasy. But we are back in the real world. We need to be careful." She begged him to understand. "Besides, we both have a lot to do. I'm beginning my young teen's division with my practice, you know counseling young inner-city girls and you with your political campaign about to heat up. We just need to be careful and present ourselves when the time is right. We have to be patient."

Alec shuddered to admit her sound judgment. But he knew she was correct. As much as it frustrated him on one level, it fascinated him on the next. She was brilliant, poised, educated and a perfect match for him. Finally he had found the perfect woman he could uphold as Mrs. Alec Richards, and despite her resistance, he was determined not to allow her to slip from his grips.

"I can't believe you, Cal. You're headed for trouble. Haven't you had enough of high-maintenance women for a lifetime?"

"I know, I know, I know, but man, the time was right and, I have to say it was well worth it."

"Next!" the barber shouted. The place was packed. Calvin had found this barber when he first moved to Charlotte, and the man was in high demand. But Cal had given him a chance when the only clientele he had to show for his talent was his little brother. And that was in the barber's basement. Now he sported the largest complex in Charlotte with ten chairs. He worked on some of the top heads in the state including the Charlotte Hornets. No matter how long the wait, the shop didn't close until Cal was as sharp as a tack.

"Man, it's been a week. What can I do for you today?" the barber asked.

"You could shave some sense into this man's head," Cal's visiting best friend advised.

"Cool it, man. Just give me a shape-up on the fade," Cal advised.

"You got it." The buzz of the clippers felt good.

"Man, I don't care what you say. Pussy is pussy. And it probably ain't worth all that you're risking; I'm telling you. Hellooooo, does the name Nikki ring a bell?"

Not only did Nikki ring a bell, but this was the first time since their breakup five years ago that Cal had felt like something worth anything could be made out of an encounter. Candace was cool. She was attractive, not beautiful. Intelligent, well read, financially stable and independent. However, he lacked total passion for her. And her consistent noise of desiring two-point-five children, a picket fence and a dog was wearing thin. She even totally supported his quest for an independent business. But their passion just didn't match.

Nikki, however, was a different story. Nikki, a Whitley Gilbert of sorts, exemplified the true essence of what he wanted. She was gentle and very feminine, yet she could hold her own with astounding grace.

Her independence was well balanced with her allowing her man to be a man. Decisions made about the direction of their lives or the household were never in question. And as Cal often put it, Nikki no longer had to be all woman and half man. He wanted her to bear his children. Children from the combination of the two of them wouldn't be standing at the sidewall, waiting for the most popular girl or guy to choose them for the school dance. Children from the two of them wouldn't be the last chosen for a game of kickball on the playground. They would be prime and perfect.

He wouldn't have to worry about the family's pristine appearance. And he wouldn't have to fight with his wife to let her flowing hair fall gracefully upon her shoulders, rather than in a ratty ponytail. He despised ponytails, and they cut the chances of many women who approached him.

However, perfection had a price. The price was high—high maintenance.

Nikki came from a prominent family, born and bred of Atlanta's finest. She attended Spelman and he attended Morehouse, just across the road. She was the president of her chapter of Alpha Kappa Alpha Sorority and he an active member of the Me Phi Me Fraternity.

Shortly after graduation, one year prior to hers, he relocated in Charlotte, North Carolina, a then booming suburb that was to boast one of the most prestigious marketing firms in the southeast. He worked hard, climbing his way from trainee to junior exec to his current position, primed for partnership. Back and forth for five years they fought to thrive while he made his path in Charlotte and she in Atlanta.

Finally after her first layoff, he convinced her to start anew with them being closer than ever in Charlotte. "Leave your family. We'll be married and start our own family." He finally convinced her.

Shortly after their conversation, he met with a diamond designer to purchase a nearly flawless one-and-a-half carat, emerald-cut engagement ring. He was to place it on her finger the moment he carried her over the threshold of the newly purchased starter home in a nearby Charlotte suburb.

She moved into the house, which she immediately sought to redecorate. "It's so, so…I don't know. I'll do the best I can with the little space we have…" she said. Regardless, the plans for the grandest Atlanta wedding were in motion. Five hundred invitations had been sent out to a few of Nikki's parents' closest friends and Atlanta's elite, including the mayor. The ceremony would be a private candlelit one in the church Martin Luther King, Jr., pastored, followed by an elaborate four-hour reception at Atlanta's Peachtree Club. He objected as the bill grossly reached the $100,000 mark, but relented when her parents insisted that they would pay. He thought it best to put the money down on a larger house.

However, he couldn't argue with the beauty of the breathtaking reception hall draped in frosted glass, crystal chandeliers and bejeweled lights. High ceilings and marble floors led to a full bridal gazebo for the bride and groom. The twelve-course meal included international coffee served in sugar-rimmed champagne flutes. The final plans also included a classical eight-piece string ensemble.

This still wasn't enough to hold her. Her obsession with the ceremony quickly deteriorated. She was no longer the sweet, passionate lover he had grown to adore. Her lack of interest in their marriage beyond the wedding became more apparent as the days passed.

She called him at his place of business daily with details and changes. She shopped relentlessly until she had filled every closet in their new home. When he offered to lend some assistance with contacts for a corporate position, she became hysterical. And the house had been cleaned twenty times over. Finally he came home and told her that his plans to leave the firm to start his own marketing firm had heated up. He was not happy and he needed to spread his wings. She advised him that she was not in this relationship to struggle.

So after a series of high drama, disconnects and lack of support for his entrepreneurial spirit, Nikki decided she no longer wanted to be with Calvin. She hastily arose the Saturday before Memorial Day and decided that Calvin could not afford her, emotionally or financially. Feverishly and in a huff she packed her clothes into her car without informing him of her plans to abandon the relationship. He barely had thirty seconds to hop in the shower, grab his jeans, loafers, no socks and a wrinkled tee. He dressed, picked up his wallet and made the five-hour drive to take her home in complete silence.

When he finally reached her parents' cathedral-style home, he didn't bother to go inside for an offered glass of water. He dropped her bags at the front door. He used his cell phone while in the circular drive to call a cab and headed to the airport where he boarded the next flight back to Charlotte.

The official breakup was never fully discussed. However, he knew the end had come when six months later it was revealed that she was pregnant and about to marry a childhood beau. Her plans didn't miss a beat. She just plopped a new paper groom into them.

Calvin whored around like the world was coming to an end. His had. He hit the old, the new, the bold and beautiful with no remorse. He worked out the deposit return on the ring and used it toward the principal of the house.

Nikki finally called and asked why they separated. He still had no answers for her.

"I don't want another man's leftovers," he told his best friend.

"So what you gonna do now that you guys have taken this to another level?" his best friend asked as the barber brushed the excess hair from Cal's shoulders.

"I don't know. I got to ride it till the gas runs out. I mean it was that good. The feeling was unbelievable. I mean, man, we did shit, I didn't know she had in her. Her eyelashes were sweatin' man. I gotta go with it," Cal said.

"Well you gotta do what you gotta do," Grey said. "Even though I don't think either of you are being wise."

Cal shrugged. "Hey, man, here's a spare key, take care of your business and meet me at the house later," Calvin said. He was sure that Grey would get the hint to leave well enough alone.

Calvin clicked the alarm off, walked through the door of his house and placed his laptop on the counter. He strutted to his desk located in the office and pulled out his wallet. He picked up the phone and dialed. "Yes, I would like to use my frequent-flyer miles...yes...yes I understand the restrictions...I should be there for a week."

"Okay, sir, you are confirmed. You'll be arriving in Newark International Airport on next Friday at 7:30 P.M. departing the Friday after that at 10:00 A.M. Is there anything else I can do for you this evening?"

"Sure. Reserve me a midsize rental for the same dates."

"Okay, Mr. Jones. You're all set. Thank you for calling, and enjoy your week."

"I will. I definitely will," Calvin said before hanging up. He picked up the picture of Candace sitting on the desk, eyed it for a moment and took a long sigh. He dropped his head and placed the photo in the upper left-hand corner drawer.

Chapter 3

Gem took a sip of her Lemon Soother herb tea. She desperately needed to rest her vocal cords for the last stretch. It was 5:30 A.M. and everybody, including the producers were ready to leave.

"Gem, audio is almost done. We need you for one more piece," the engineer said. She nodded, placed her tea on the bench and proceeded to the booth.

She had just placed the large black earphones on when over the speaker she heard, "Okay, ladies and gentlemen, we need you to sing the hook over and over until we ask you to stop. It's just for background cutaways. Oh, and Gem please hang around after we're finished. The producers need to talk to you." Immediately everyone shot a look that made her want to crawl into the nearest small space.

What now? she thought. *I just want to finish this mess, get my check and go home. If I never have to see any one of these folks ever again anyway, it would be too soon.*

"Oops, sorry guys. We need you take fifteen. Something technical," the engineer said. Everyone soon filed out of the booth.

"Wow, Gem, what could they want with you? Well at least you know they can't be firing you. We're almost done, thank God." The deepest tenor voice was the boldest to speak.

"Yeah, I'm frustrated too. I'm ready to jet," Gem replied, returning to her tea.

"Not for nothing, but I know you, well, we all have had a rough time on this thang, girlfriend. But I want to tell ya that your voice is anointed. Y'all got it going on, girlfriend. Shoot, I'll never forget how you hit that note that time. What was that note again?" he asked with a hand on his hip.

She chuckled. "Thank you! Um, it was a high C," Gem chimed with genuine gratitude. "I really appreciate that. You just don't know."

"I'm sure I do know. That scant could not sing. And you a doll for tryin' to hep her. Hum. I ain't here to help nobody but myself. But I like you. You is good people."

"I wish everyone felt that way," Gem said, nodding towards two other singers who had isolated themselves since the beginning of the gig.

"Naaa, don't worry about them, 'cause they next. They just don't know it. But I know it, 'cause I spot true talent when I see it. You a fierce diva." They both laughed. "I'm Andre," he said, extending his hand.

"Thanks, Andre."

"Okay, people, let's punch this out so we can go home," the engineer said, rushing them into the booth again.

"You know I would love to keep in touch with you, diva. You going places," Andre said.

"Um, sure. Let's exchange cards afterward."

"Alright, move it, people. In a minute I'm going to have to use toothpicks to keep my eyelids open," the engineer said.

Normally Gem would have fallen fast asleep, but this morning, excitement kept her wide awake. Traffic was normally heavy riding across town from the Lower East Side to the producer's midtown West Forty-sixth Street office. The limo was extremely plush with its white exterior, dark tinted windows and plush leather seats. Even for a moment

Gem enjoyed the colored light show on the panels all around her. The driver offered her champagne. "No, thank you," she said. "It's way too early. I won't make it home."

"Oh, don't worry, they've offered the limo ride home for you as well. I'll be going to Jersey, right?"

The hairs sat straight up on the back of her neck. *What in the heck is going on? How do they know where I live and how do they know I want a ride home and why . . .* She took a deep breath. She wanted to relax, but her caution concerning her whereabouts flashed like a neon sign. She never knew when her abusive ex-husband might receive his get-out-jail free card. And she was afraid he would make a beeline straight past go to her. Even though he didn't know her place of residence now, it would not be that difficult for him to find out. Especially if she encountered careless people like these producers.

"Okay, Miss Gem. Their office is on the fifth floor. Sign in at the desk for WR Management. Your producers will radio me when they're done, and I'll be waiting to take you home."

"No, thanks. You don't have to wait. That won't be necessary," she said. She hopped out of the limo to a busy street. The building was magnificent with green marbled floors, live exotic plants and plenty of glass for the sun to shine in.

The fifth floor was less elaborate, with what looked like old construction. Borders were missing from peeled painted walls. As she knocked, the door opened. "Gem, glad you could make it." "Welcome to our humble abode. I'm Will," he said. "One half of an up-and-coming super producer team."

Humble *isn't the word. Where did you get this antiquated furniture from? The Salvation Army wouldn't accept this crap,* she thought of the stained fabric-covered chairs and broken-leg tables, secured with duct tape. "Remodeling?"

"Uh, no," he said.

Well you should be.

"Robb, may I present Gem. Gem, this is the mastermind Robb."

"Gem, welcome, welcome. Please, have a seat and thank you so much for coming. I know you're tired so we'll get right to the point. By the way, how was the limo ride?"

"Fine, thanks."

"Good, great, good, uh, shortly after we're done, it will be waiting for you downstairs to take you home to…South Orange, right?" he said, ruffling through the papers on the desk.

"I need to be frank with you," she said. They both took a seat. "First of all thank you for the opportunity to work on the jingle. It's been a, well…" She hesitated and thought carefully about her words. "…A pleasure. And thank you for the bonus in my check. However, I don't know why you have me here. And while I appreciate the limo ride, I don't appreciate my personal business being so open and free, particularly my home address. I am very careful about whom I trust. It has to be earned, and right about now, this relationship is a little lopsided. So what else do you want from me?" she asked, rubbing her temple. The windowless office started to make her feel claustrophobic.

"To make you a star!" Robb stood. "You're direct, and I like that. You'll find the same from us. You probably can tell you are in the building where deals and dealmakers are made. We have been searching for someone for a long time, and by God you're it."

"This all sounds great, but I've been doing okay without your help. I don't know that I need you," she said.

The negotiations were on. The duo was determined that Gemmia Barnes would be their brightest and best prospect yet. And they were willing to pull out all of the stops.

Erring on the side of caution, Gem decided against the free limo ride. No sense in taking liberties where she didn't have to. She clutched the fine-print, sixteen-page document close to her. "Excuse me," she said with attitude, fighting her way through the rush-hour crowd to get on the number two subway to Thirty-fourth Street. She only had one stop to go but if she didn't sit down immediately, she felt as if she was going to collapse.

"Excuse me," she said again as she stepped over blue sticky stuff. She moved beneath folks hanging on the metal overhead bars, bopping to their CD players. She finally reached a seat occupied by several large plastic bags. "Do you mind," Gem asked the obese woman in a semi-polite tone.

"As a matter of fact, I do," the woman said in a huff.

"Well your bags didn't pay for this seat. So either you move them or I will."

Gem sat down and smiled. Everything was happening so fast. Pretty soon, limo rides would be the norm. And the songs on the radio and people's CD players would be hers. It was finally happening. Despite all of her obstacles, her dreams to perform and secure a major record deal were coming true. She rested her head on the marked-up subway window. Her daydreams overcame her.

She vaguely heard the conductor announce, "Thirty-fourth Street. Change here for the A,C,E...Amtrak and New Jersey Transit trains on the lower level..." Her dream continued and so did the train.

"Well it's about damn time...I told you that I have to go back to the office."

"Don't curse at me, and I'm sorry," Stephanie said, hastily pulling out her seat. "I ran late with a new client. One of my teens. She's really a bright girl but she's confused, you know the streets or something better..."

Talise put her hand up to stop her friend from rambling. This was her moment and she couldn't wait to share it. "No offense, dear, but I'll hear about your new client later. You really need to order. I have to be back before three. I have a meeting with my boss. We have to work out a strategy to develop new agents. I need to grow the agent pool by forty percent, and I..."

"Now who's rambling?" Stephanie asked, eyeing her menu. "Man, I'm not in the mood for all of this heavy food today. It's pretty hot out. I think I could go for this fruit salad platter."

"Not me. I'm sorry. You don't come to Je's to have soup and salad. You come to Je's to eat homemade macaroni and cheese, to-die-for Granma's collards and stewed chicken that makes you wanna kick your mama," Talise said as she let out a loud laugh.

"Soooo. How was your weekend?" Stephanie asked.

Talise became anxious. "Well..." she said as she smoothed her napkin over her baby-pink cotton skirt. "It was wonderful!" She let out a scream. Stephanie gave her "the look," but the scream continued.

"Talise...calm down."

"That's not me." Talise defended herself. The waiter set down a rum and Coke before Talise and Je's famous homemade lemonade before Stephanie. When the waiter stepped away, a four-foot, nine-inch stick of dynamite named Anney Lewis revealed herself. She continued to scream and gave Talise a huge hug, forcing her to place her drink down quickly. Stephanie joined in the group hug.

"Talise, Stephanie. Ahhhhh. It's so great to see you guys. It's been, what ten, twelve years now?"

"Now you know you wrong trying to reveal our ages. But you're telling the trut. High school was a while ago. Green Bees, Green Bees, buzz a buzz a buzz buzz buzz, da, dat da dat."

"Oh, stop. Now you trying to go back to the cheerleading squad. I might be able to hit a back handspring for you," Talise said and they all laughed.

"Please, girl, don't go hurtin' nothin that might not be able to be fixed. But Stephanie, I heard you're a doctor, so you may be able to fix it," Anney said, laughing.

"Well if your heart is broken, I might be able to help, but not any bones. Anyway what are you doing here? I heard you moved to Florida. I looked you up when I was in school but maybe our timelines crossed," Stephanie said.

"Yeah. I was there for a while. I enjoyed it, but my husband and I had to come back to take care of some business. So we're back, but we hope to move again sometime."

The girls continued to reminisce. Anney asked about everything and everyone, constantly interjecting her many accomplishments. Anney was still perusing her list of credentials when she interrupted herself to change the subject—about herself.

I see much hasn't changed. Once a braggart, always a braggart, Stephanie thought.

"I'm so sorry to hear that your marriage didn't work out, Talise. I'm so blessed. I really enjoy marriage. It just works for me," Anney said, fondling the diamond pendant that hung about her neck. Stephanie's head bobbed like a Kewpie doll. "So do you think you'll ever do it a—speaking of wonderful husbands, here's mine now. Honey, honey, I'm over here." Anney ushered a bronze statue toward her. He was twice her height with a presence that could light any room.

Whoa. Absolute dream, Talise thought. *How in the world did she pull him?*

"Stephanie, Talise, this is the love of my life, Glenn. Honey, this is Talise and…" Stephanie and Glenn both cut her off.

"Stephanie." He coughed. "Um, how are you doing? Looking good," he said, seeming uncomfortable.

Stephanie mimicked that same agitation. Talise noticed it all as Anney continued to ramble. "You two know each other?"

"Um-hum. Uh yeah. College," Stephanie abruptly answered, all the time inspecting Glenn Barcliff.

"Get out. You went to Florida State? I tell you what a small world. Please don't tell me, did you pledge?" Stephanie and Glenn continued to stare. Talise continued to take everything in. "Hello, the pendant on your neck. You pledged brother-sister organizations. What a coincidence. I tell you…I personally didn't have time to pledge although my dream was to be a Delta but…"

"Doll, I believe our table is waiting, and it's getting crowded in here. We better go. Nice meeting you, Talise. Take care, Steph." Glenn yanked Anney's arm, and they walked away.

"Ah woo. What a dreamy, deep man. Now how do you suspect that Miss Thing landed him? You know, the average-looking sisters always end up with the finest men. I just don't understand it. I mean you look better than Anney, and I certainly do. Even though I'm busy right now. Don't you think?"

Stephanie had gulped down the last bit of Talise's rum and Coke. She was now snapping her fingers trying to get the attention of their waiter.

"Other than me, what else will you be having?" the waiter flirtatiously asked.

"Dark rum and Coke. In fact, make it a double, without the flirtation, thank you." He rolled his eyes and walked away.

"Okay, what is going on? We go from happy to sad and lemonade to a double dark rum and Coke. Stephanie, when you do drink, that's not your drink." Talise looked from Stephanie to Glenn, back to Glenn and then back to Stephanie. *Okay, college, fine, with a girl not so fine. Jealous? No. But maybe.* "Okay, Stephanie why are you jealous of Anney Lewis? I mean Glenn. What is going on?" Talise asked, frustrated.

The waiter came back with their drinks. He placed one before Talise as well. "Looks like you're going to need one too," he said, tipping his head toward Stephanie, rolling his eyes again and walking away. Another server brought the food. Talise dug in.

Silence.

More silence.

Stephanie twirled the cantaloupe on her fork. She took deep breath between small sips of her drink. "This cantaloupe isn't sweet."

"How would you know? You haven't taken a bite of it since he brought it out."

Silence.

"Well my chicken and macaroni are fantastic. Want some?"

More silence.

"Okaay. Um, my weekend was great. Calvin and I sucked and f—" Stephanie shot her a look, daring her to finish. "Thought that would get your attention. But Calvin and I did make mad, passionate love all day. He's also coming to see me this weekend. Something may be getting started here," Talise explained between bites. "What is going on with you? What is between you and Glenn that has altered your mood drastically… And don't take too long explaining. I told you I have to get back to work."

Stephanie remained motionless. Talise babbled to no avail. Whatever was eating her had bitten her in the worst way, and nothing seemed to shake it.

"Another drink, ladies?"

"Sure," Stephanie answered. Talise pointed to her drink to indicate that she wasn't finished with her first or her second one for that matter.

"…Anyway, just when I thought nothing was going to happen, everything did. I mean we were sleeping in the same bed. Not that that was anything new. We slept in the bed together when I visited him and once in college, and nothing happened. Anyway, it was cold and he didn't have any extra cover. The first night, he didn't notice me at all. I mean I was to' up from the flo' up." She giggled. "But the next night I was feeling this wonderful strange attraction to him. So I decided to sleep next to him again, but this time I was sexy. Lipstick, hair tossed just so and a cinnamon, very short nightie that accented every curve." She laughed at herself.

"I didn't expect anything to happen. I kinda hit a sore spot when I mentioned this girl he's seeing down there. He had her picture out on his desk, and I noticed her resemblance to the once love of his life. He got a little upset, corrected me and went to sleep."

"He's seeing someone?" Stephanie finally placed her fork down and pushed her plate away.

"Yeah, but it's not that serious. Anyway we went to sleep. The next morning when we woke up, we were sort of in each other's arms. We laughed and talked. Then we started comparing battle scars on our bodies. I noticed him looking, but in a different way. Then he kissed me. I mean my body is still tingling. Then he rolled over on top of me and that was all she wrote. We proceeded to have the best sex I've ever had in my entire life…girl, he sent me to the stratosphere…" Talise groaned.

Stephanie folded her arms and shook her head in disgust. She took another deep breath. She wanted to calm down. "Don't you think it's just a little too soon to get involved with someone on this level."

"No." Talise's tone now changed to match Stephanie's.

"You're not divorced yet! Do I need to remind you that you just moved out of your husband's house and you haven't unpacked all your boxes yet."

"So?"

"So when are you going to get tired of sharing other people's property?"

Talise sighed. "What are you talking about?"

"He has a girlfriend?"

"Well…yes…no…not really. I mean he can really be good for me right now. Why can't you just be happy for me, sometimes? Daag. I asked my friend to lunch, not my psychologist," Talise said, stabbing the remainder of her chicken.

Stephanie huffed then placed her hands in a prayer position in front of her face. She began to speak and stopped. She changed her mind. "Talise, trust me when I say I want to be happy for you. I really do. But I can't when I believe you are headed down the road of destruction. Let's look at this logically. You have been good friends with this man for years. He invites you down to his house as *just a friend,* cock-blocks you from another prospect, Banks whatever his name is and neglects to tell you or to emphasize the fact that he is in a relationship with another woman. You make mad, passionate love with him and now you are floating around as if you've found your Prince Charming. Talise, this stinks to high heaven. And unfortunately you are in a position of vulnerability, loneliness and horniness, and you want me to be happy. Sorry, no can do."

Talise squinted and checked her watch. She pulled out her corporate American Express and motioned for the waiter without another word. He retrieved the check and returned for her signature. She threw the card in her purse, removed the napkin from her lap and stood.

"Thank you, Dr. Alphonso. I'm sure my bill will be in the mail. In the future you might want to adhere to that old saying, if you can't say anything nice or productive, don't say anything at all. Furthermore, I'm tired of you and Gem taking things out on me when something is really going on inside of you. You need to check yourself." Talise turned and glanced toward Glenn. "And for the record, whatever is going on or has gone on between you and Anney Lewis' husband, I would suggest you resolve before it loses you a good friend and sacrifices any peace you may have with yourself. Yes, I read Susan Taylor and Dr. Gwendolyn Goldsby Grant too. Good day." With that Talise threw her cloth napkin on the table, slurped the last of her drink, bid Anney Lewis and her husband good-bye and walked out.

Stephanie remained, twirling her fruit and staring at Anney Lewis' husband.

Steffon rapped on the door before he walked in. He carefully looked around, becoming familiar with her new corner office.

"Well just make yourself at home. It's after eight. What in the world are you still doing here this late?"

"I had some clean-up work to do. You know since you are the big-time marketing rep around here, some of us little people had to take over your territory and finish out your policy renewals." He smiled. He put his feet up on the desk as he comfortably situated himself in the chair slated for guests.

"Chill out, Steff. K.J. is still around. I don't need him popping by my office and catching you with your feet up."

"Don't worry. He left. You're the only one around on this floor other than a few people in the claims department. They really got you burning the midnight oil, as you high execs say."

Talise listened as he continued talking. Her deadline was Tuesday for her first project. She had to reorganize each agent into the system. She needed to present a chart that showed activity and inactivity for every agent and an action plan recommendation. She was only on number eleven and she had 109 to go.

"You need to ask for more time. You can't get that done."

"I have to get it done. I don't want to miss my first deadline," she said, steadily typing.

"Well you got about fifteen more minutes before you're finished for the night anyway. The system is shutting down this weekend as of eight-thirty and nobody can get in it. They have to do some upgrades."

"Oh, man, what am I going to do? I have to get this done and the info can only be accessed on the system," Talise said, typing her data at a faster pace.

"I guess you'll have to go home and enjoy the weekend like the rest of us. Just let K.J. know Monday morning that the system was down this weekend. You couldn't do it."

Talise remained perplexed. It was her utmost goal to do well on this new job. She wanted to show herself and the rest of the world that it could be done, despite the naysayers' advice. *Humph. I don't know how I'm gonna get this done, but I've got to do something. There is no way I'm telling K.J. that the first project he assigned me to is a bust. Uh-uh. No way.* She continued to type.

"Not for nothing. But I'm telling you, Talise, you better watch yourself. I've seen how K.J. operates. He's slick. He wants you here for one reason and one reason only: You're the only black female on the management team, fine, got it going on but you ain't slick to his kind. I'm telling you watch yourself."

Eight-thirty came and as expected the system shut down. Talise grabbed a few papers and files and placed them into her briefcase as Steffon watched.

"Thanks, Steff, for hanging around to walk me to my car. I don't know what I'm going to do, but I'll think of something. Besides, I plan on having a glorious weekend," she said, fumbling with her keys in the lock.

"And why is that?"

"I have a friend from North Carolina meeting me at my place," she said with a smile.

"How come I haven't received an invitation?" he asked, placing her bags onto the backseat. "Dag, T. You just got this car a couple of weeks ago, and it's junky already. You need to clean this up. You don't want your clients to see this mess."

"I know, I know. Look, I gotta go. I want to make sure the doorman doesn't give my friend any problems with getting into my place. Hey, let's do lunch on Monday. My treat."

"You got it, baby girl. Check you."

"You too." With that she sped off.

Cal had finally fallen asleep. He should have. He was exhausted after five ferocious hours of lovemaking. But for some reason, Talise had more energy than he had bargained for. She turned the phone off in the bedroom. She didn't want any early-morning apologies from Stephanie waking him up. She put on a China-red-gold satin robe she had recently purchased and proceeded to the kitchen.

She stopped dead in her tracks by the obnoxious ringing of her phone in the living room. *Who in the world can be calling here at five in the morning? I know Steph can't be that crazy.* "Hello?" she questioned with exasperation.

"Finished?"

"Hello? What? Who is this?"

"I repeat, finished?"

"Who is this?"

"Now what is a brother supposed to do when his *wife* can't even recognize his voice."

"Maurice?"

"For the third time, I repeat, you finished?"

"Finished what?" Talise questioned still confused.

"Fucking that nigger you got holed up in your crib!"

Her breathing became shallow. "What are you talking about? Nobody's here."

He gave a sinister laugh. "Trust me, the motherfucker is there alright. And I'll be waiting right down here for him when he comes out. He has to go home sometime."

Talise put her fingers to her forehead. She remembered seeing a familiar-looking car in the lot not far from Calvin. *Dammit Red Dodge. Red Dodge. That's where I've seen that car. That's his mother's car. Oh, my gosh! Maurice has been sitting there since what, ten last night? Oh, my goodness.* "Look, Maurice, it's best you go home and we talk about this later. You don't want to start any trouble."

"Oh, I'm not only starting but I'm finishing…"

Talise hung up. She checked the door to make sure it was secure and checked the bedroom to make sure Calvin was still sound asleep. She drew the blinds and then she remembered Maurice couldn't see her because she was on the twelfth floor. The phone rang again, startling Talise.

"I'm back. I'm not going anywhere until that motherfucker comes out."

She hung up again.

The phone rang again. "Maurice, go home. We'll talk about this some other time. Nobody's here."

"You never were a good liar, Talise. Never."

Her heart pounded. "Look, liar or not, it's none of your business. I'm your wife in name only. Go home and stop ringing my phone." She hit the base so hard, she thought she might have broken the phone.

The phone rang again. She picked up the receiver and slammed it down without another word.

The phone rang again. This time she yanked the line out of the wall. She ran to the bedroom where Calvin remained sleeping. She retreated to the kitchen and started the coffeepot for a cup of brew. Her nerves needed the caffeine. She pulled the glass pot from the white base and retrieved her favorite oversized red ceramic mug. As she began to pour, the entire pot shattered before her feet and brown stains soaked her new robe and matching slippers.

Suddenly she heard Maurice pounding on the door.

Oh, my goodness. She tipped to the door. She checked the peephole and saw Maurice's square head dash to the side. "Maurice, go home."

"Let me in," he demanded.

"Maurice, go home."

He continued to bang on the door, this time louder. "Let me in."

"No."

"If nobody's there, then let me in."

"No."

"I have to go to the bathroom."

"Maurice, go home, now," she demanded.

He responded by pounding louder. "Let me in. I'll be waiting for that motherfucker as soon as his ass steps out this door." His voice grew louder and his pounding became harder.

"Maurice, if you don't go home I'm calling the police," she yelled in her loudest whisper.

"If nobody's in there, then let me in." He continued to pound.

She ran to the room once more. Calvin's snore grew louder. *I don't need a scene in here. I just moved in. This man is not getting me kicked out of my place.* She ran back to the kitchen phone and shoved the cord in the wall and dialed.

"Is this an emergency?"

"Yes ma'am, this is an emergency."

Maurice continued to scream and yell all the while pounding away.

"My name is Talise Grimes. I'm a new tenant in the 1185 Main Street high-rise. Right now, I'm separated from my husband and he is pounding away at my door trying to get in.... I don't know how he got through the front door. Maybe someone else buzzed him, but I assure you it wasn't me." She began to whimper. "Listen, I'm afraid. I don't know what he's going to do, and I need somebody to come here and strongly encourage him to go home."

She ran back to the door. He was still there. "Maurice, I have called the police. If you don't leave, you're going to be in big trouble. I'm telling you, just leave. Don't make this worse than it has to be."

"Let me in. Let me in this damn house!" he yelled.

At that moment Calvin entered the living room in nothing more than his royal-purple silk boxers. His bare chest still gleamed from the night before. He notice the shards of glass on her kitchen floor that once was Talise's coffeepot. "What's going on?"

Maurice still pounded on the door.

"Nothing, nothing," Talise answered frantically. "I've called the police."

"Who's at the door?" Calvin stared. "Your ex?"

Talise nodded.

Calvin proceeded toward the door. "I don't know what your problem is but you better go home."

"You motherfucker, my problem is *you!* Bring yo' ass out my wife's crib and I'll show you," Maurice shouted.

Talise remained frozen. She watched as Calvin briskly walked to the bedroom. He emerged momentarily in jeans, a T-shirt and sneakers. He grabbed a wooden stick that Talise had leaning against the wall and opened the door.

Immediately Maurice fell in, grabbing at Calvin and knocking him to the floor as well. They scuffled and the stick was pushed out of Calvin's hand.

Talise remained frozen as the slug fest got into full swing. Calvin regained his advantage, but Maurice remained steadfast on his heel. Calvin backed into the kitchen searching for his stick when Maurice plunged toward him, knocking Calvin into Talise's only piece of furniture. It was a small four-legged wooden table she borrowed from her parents' garage. It crashed to the floor along with her tears.

"Guys, please stop. Please," she finally pleaded. "Why are you doing this?" she screamed at Maurice between sobs. It wasn't until she heard a voice exclaim. "It's like the OK Corral in there," that Talise realized the door was still open. Without thinking, she ran straight into the line of fire. She was met with a force that knocked her out.

"What's her name, sir?" Talise heard someone say as she came to.

"Talise, Talise Grimes," she heard a somewhat familiar voice say.

"Miss Grimes? Miss Grimes, how do you feel?" the police questioned.

"Like I was hit by a mack truck," Talise said. She sat up too fast and the pounding in her head quickly forced her back down.

"Who hit you, ma'am?" one of the officers questioned.

"What?" Still dazed, Talise slowly rose again. Her place was a disaster. Her favorite and only piece of furniture was completely destroyed. She scanned the room and remembered the now broken coffeepot. The tornado had made its way into the kitchen where several cabinet doors dangled off the hinges. The few dishes left in the drainage bin also now found their way to the floor.

"I need to make a report. Which of these guys is responsible for this?" the officer asked, pointing to Calvin and Maurice who nursed their wounds.

"That motherfucker right there. He hit my wife. I want him outta here," Maurice yelled.

"Watch it, pal," the officer demanded. "Is that true, ma'am? Is he your husband?"

Talise held her head and nodded.

"Okay, sir, you need to come with us," the second officer said, grabbing Calvin's arm.

"Oh, hell no," Calvin asserted.

"Wait. He is my husband but we are separated. He does not live here, nor is he welcome," Talise said, now standing fully.

"Is that correct?" the first officer asked Maurice.

"Excuse me, would you like to check the lease? Only my name is on it. He's not welcome, so would you please escort him out of here," Talise said emphatically.

"Do you want to press charges, ma'am?" the second officer asked.

"No, just go," Talise said, as she staggered toward Calvin. She cupped his face in her hands and lightly kissed him on the forehead.

The officers opened a path for Maurice to walk.

"Oh, and Maurice—" Talise turned toward the door— "if you ever try anything like this again, I guarantee you that I will press charges. I don't want to ever see you again. Your final papers will be in the mail," she said, turning her back to Maurice. She walked behind the officers to close the door, when the second officer turned and handed her a card, she eyed it briefly and noticed a five-digit number. "What's this?" she questioned.

"That's my card should you need anything, and that's the file number your report will be under. It will be ready in three days. I suggest you get a restraining order," the officer concluded and walked out.

"I'm sorry," Talise said, closing the door.

Calvin remained silent.

"Please don't be mad at me. Maurice is not taking the divorce too well. It won't happen again," she said with angst. Her head still pounded from the blow.

"You can't guarantee that. It's not your fault but you should have gotten me up. You left me off guard," he said, cracking his knuckles.

"Well, if it's any consolation, it looks like you got the best of him," Talise said, joking.

Calvin didn't laugh. "As soon as you can, I want you to get a restraining order. I can't protect you when I'm not here."

She slid his jeans and boxers around his ankles. She groped and caressed his manhood as he moaned. She then placed her tongue around his long, strong organ and savored the flavor. He moaned some more. She slowly pulled him out of her mouth and noticed, "…ummmm some cream for this coffee?"

"Yeah," he replied stroking her hair, standing firm.

She touched the tip of his manhood with her finger and gathered some of his sensuous cream. She teased him with her finger. She then placed her finger in her mouth and sucked it like a lollipop. Calvin almost dropped to his knees right beside her.

With his knees still wobbly, she got up.

"Oh no. Uh-uh, you can't stop now," he pleaded in a raspy whisper.

"Who said anything about stopping? I'm just going to clean up the mess I've made." She walked away using her finger to guide him to follow her.

The next sound was that of the shower. He smiled, shook his head and joined her behind the vinyl curtain.

Chapter 4

Alec put on the newest Al Jarreau CD. He so adored the single by Al and Vanessa Williams. The new Audra McDonald was on the horizon for play next. "You see, darling, beautiful, beautiful music. Such a credit to the race," he said. He picked up his glass of wine and walked toward Stephanie, who was crumbling Gorgonzola cheese in a salad with orange vinagrette dressing.

"Some more wine?" she asked, picking up the bottle.

"No, no, no. Quite enough. What is this?" His expression was somewhat contorted.

"It's Merlot," she answered, checking on the caramelized walnuts roasting in the oven that would adorn the salad.

"I know that, darling. But what label? I mean it tastes as if you purchased it from the supermarket or something silly."

"Actually, I did. Well not really." She chuckled. "But I did get it from the store next door to the supermarket. I happen to like it. The brand is something domestic. I thought it was good," she responded, picking up the bottle.

"No, no no. It's cheap. Look at this." He walked around her marbled island. He slowly poured the wine, then held the glass upright. "You see. It bounces off the sides. It's thin. It's cheap. It's supposed to dance and flow off the side of the glass. That's the first test. The second is the bouquet. This one has vinegar or something. The third is the taste. Just a small sip should yield a mild, crisp and fruity flavor. This gives me a sort of rancid taste. I'll get us something decent from your cellar," he said, proceeding down the stairs.

"Alec, don't bother. I have nothing left. We've devoured a bottle every time you've come over, remember," she said now spreading the walnuts. She had practically ignored his entire wine-tasting lesson.

"Why didn't you tell me? I would have purchased a few bottles for you. Oh, darling—"

"It's okay, it's really not that heavy," she interrupted him. She took a deep breath to hide her annoyance.

"Of course it is. What a shame should you have company and not have an appropriate wine to serve."

Stephanie didn't have the strength to respond, so she continued chopping. "Where are you going?" She noticed him putting on his blazer and grabbing his keys.

"There's a gourmet shop in Princeton, opened late on the weekends. I'll go grab us a suitable bottle for dinner and a few to spare. It will only take a moment. I'll be right back." He kissed her on the forehead.

"But dinner is almost ready and…"

"Don't worry, it isn't far. I'll be right back," he reiterated. He dashed out the door and hopped into his brand-new silver Porsche.

She ran to grab the ringing phone. "Hello," she said abruptly.

"It's only been a week. What's the attitude for?" Gem asked.

"Oh, hey, girl. Nothing. Just a little annoyed. How are you doing?"

"Tired. How was your lunch with Talise yesterday? I tried to make it but I had an all-night session and ended up falling asleep on the train. Girl, I ended up in the last stop in Brooklyn. It was an abandoned yard where the trains go to rest. Girl…"

"How in the world did you do that?"

"I was tired and you know how New York is. Nobody thought to wake me up. I was sleeping so hard that maybe they thought I was dead or something. I'm lucky I didn't get robbed.

So how was lunch?"

"Disastrous."

"Why? I tried to call Talise but she's never home. The girl gets a new place and she's never there. I called her at work, too, but the voice mail keeps kicking in."

Stephanie sat down and poured herself another glass of her cheap wine. She gave an account of the entire scene at the restaurant. She conveniently left out the disturbance concerning Glenn.

"Well, I know it's no consolation prize but you told her right. I mean that girl will never learn. Now she's in love with Calvin Jones. Whatever…you gotta let her fall. That's it. Anyway…I have some great news!"

"Good, I can use it." She took another sip.

"I am closer than ever to landing a recording contract!"

"Oh, congratulations! You mean I'll be hearing my friend on the radio and visiting backstage at her concerts!" Stephanie said with glee.

Gem continued to explain how the producers of the commercial had a management company and were looking to sign her as one of its artist.

"So where do you go from here?" Stephanie asked, draining the bottle.

"Well I have to sign this sixteen-page book of a contract that I don't understand. Every time I try to read it, I fall asleep and I have nightmares of ending up in that abandoned yard." They laughed. "After that, they told me they have a series of clubs and showcases lined up. In fact they have a Sony showcase slated for me in two weeks. But they made it clear that all of it is a no-go without signing this contract."

"Don't do it without understanding it and getting a lawyer," Stephanie warned.

"I don't have time or money for a lawyer. I have until Monday to sign or they'll be looking at other talent."

"But, I'm telling you, it sounds shotgun to me and…" Stephanie heard Gem sigh. She refrained from finishing her statement. *She didn't ask your advice, Stephanie, so stop giving it voluntarily.* "I have some contacts with attorneys. They won't be able to meet with you over the weekend but perhaps you can stall for a few days," she offered.

"You're not listening. I don't have a few days, and frankly I'm not blowing another chance for me to do what I have always dreamed of doing," Gem replied anxiously.

"Okay. I have had my fill of catnip for the week. I'm not trying to pry, I just want to be an objective ear and encourage you to protect yourself, that's all," Stephanie insisted.

"I'm sorry for snapping. I just can taste success, and I really don't want to blow it. This chance has to be God-given, it just has to. I mean why else would I have met these guys at this time? They are practically dropping opportunity in my lap."

Yeah, if is sounds too good to be true, it probably is. "I understand. Oops, there's the doorbell, I gotta run. But I'll talk to you before the weekend is out, okay?"

"Who's at the door?"

"I'll talk to you later," Stephanie said as she hung up the phone. *Dag, she's becoming almost as intrusive as Talise. It's about time, Alec. I'm famished and that cheap wine as you call it is not helping me on an empty stomach,* she thought as she skipped across the room.

"It's about time, honey. You really didn't need to..." she said as she opened the door.

Glenn?"

"Hey, Steph."

"What in the hell are you doing here?" she asked.

"So how was your weekend, baby doll?"

"It was real cool. My friend just left this morning. We had a wonderful time," she said, frantically typing some information on the computer. She was in early after practically spending the entire evening with Calvin.

"Did you ever get that presentation finished for K.J.?" Steffon questioned. He sat down and placed his feet on her desk.

"Come on, don't do that. Dragon Breath might come by and see you and then I'll be walking in that Monday morning meeting explaining why an underwriter, specifically Steffon, was lounging in my office when I have plenty of work to do."

"So I take it you didn't finish."

She continued to type and rolled her eyes. "He put out the agenda over the weekend and I haven't had a chance to gather all of the information he will be looking for from me in fifteen minutes."

"Ooh. It is eight o'clock. Let me get to my desk. How about lunch today?" he questioned. She didn't answer. "Okay. You know I have some information for you that just might save your butt, but if you're not interested..." He proceeded out of the door.

"Wait, Steff, wait. Come on, I'm desperate. Whatcha got?" she pleaded.

Steffon sat back down and gave her some information on a brokerage firm expansion. One of his agents had tipped him that they would be coming into more than a million dollars worth of premium on prime business that was just Great Raritan's speed.

"Man, landing that account would exceed goal in just the first quarter alone. That would surely get K.J. off my back."

"What you need to do is present this information in the form of a strategy to land the account. Show him a preliminary plan and let him help you develop it. This will give him the right to the credit and save your butt from not getting the other project done. Talise, you got to learn how to play the game...."

Steffon hung around and helped her put together a plan to secure business that was sure to make her look like a star. Not only would it put her in great favor with the boss, but it might ease some of the tension with the other managers as well. They were no help and often conducted hazing sessions on her.

Just as Talise was printing the report and the strategy on her word program, Dragon Breath called. "Thanks, Steff. You better go. I have to get this. I probably won't be able to have lunch today, but I'll call you and tell you how everything went," she said. "This is Talise.... Yes...I have the agenda and reports from the weekend... Well I wasn't able to complete that because the system was down but...yes...I know but I do have some other information that will be just as important as...yes...okay, I'm coming right now..." She hung up the phone.

That woman is a doggone trip. Damn, she thought. She rustled through a few more papers. Her desk was cluttered with reports, files and Post-its with tidbits of important information. She took a deep breath and loosened her shoulders. She searched through the pile again. "Here it is." She retrieved the file and briskly walked toward K.J.'s secretary. "Here's the file. I'll be in my office if you need me."

"Um-hum," the secretary replied. "Oh, by the way, the Monday morning manager's meeting has been postponed until 11:30. K.J. is not in a good mood, and you better have everything he's asking for on the agenda. I would hate to see you embarrassed again."

Talise gritted her teeth and kept walking until Dragon Breath was a distant memory. Relieved that she had a little more time to get together her other presentation she sauntered off to the coffeepot. She retrieved a cup of Java and headed back to her office. Her colleague Vanee cut her path.

"Hey, girl, what's up? How was your weekend?"

"Absolutely wonderful. How are you doing?" she asked.

"Obviously not as good as you. But you can tell me all about it tonight."

"What is going on tonight?" she asked, taking another sip of coffee.

"We're all hanging out at Sequoia's. And from what I hear, K.J. is buying the first round. Knowing the management team, you all will probably be buying the rest. Anyway, I tried to call you all weekend but your phone was busy."

"Oh yeah. I had a little incident. Maurice came bangin' on my door, acting crazy." Talise recalled the entire event before sipping her coffee.

"Get used to it. You know how niggas get when they lose somethin' they shoulda been takin' care of. Don't sweat it," Vanee said. Talise just nodded in agreement. "Check it. So you in for tonight?"

"I don't know. I have too much work to do. Besides it's Monday, Vanee. What you gonna do with your little girl?" she questioned.

"It's her father's night to take care of her. I take whatever break I can," Vanee said, waving her hand in the air. "Ooh. Here comes Dragon. You better go. I hope to see you tonight. Even if you work late, come after, we'll be there for a while."

Talise nodded and met with Dragon Breath as she scurried toward her with the file in hand Talise had just dropped off.

"Wrong, wrong and wronger. This is not the file I asked you for, and this one needs work as well. Check your records and get me the correct ones please." Dragon Breath shoved the folder at her. "If you weren't so busy chatting at the coffee machine, you might be able to get something done," she said and scurried off.

Talise walked back to her desk, balancing the file and her coffee. Shaking her head, she sat down, realizing that now she had three things to complete. Those three things needed to be done before the meeting, and she now had less than two hours. She massaged her temples and wrote them in priority on yet another Post-it. She picked up the phone. "Come on, Steff. Please, please, please, help this one time. Analyze just two of these accounts for me and place the sheet inside. I'll take a look at them before the meeting…thanks I owe you one. Okay, lunch today.

It has to be a late lunch 'cause you know the meeting will probably last throughout the afternoon."

Now I can finish the two presentations and I'll be set for the meeting, she thought as she got to work. No sooner than the last, Dragon dropped yet another project on her desk, courtesy of K.J. She at least had a few days to get to that one. She placed it at the bottom of an already growing pile of junk and kept working.

"Gem, you won't regret this. Just sign on the dotted line, and we will get started on our quest of making you into a star!"

Nervously Gem grabbed the pen and signed. GEMMIA BARNES, she wrote placing her special insignia at the end. "I hope I'm not signing away my life," she joked. Will, Robb, their attorney and their assistant laughed along with her.

"I assure you, Gem, this is totally legit," the attorney said as he gathered the papers. "I'll be back in touch with you, but I must go. Enjoy the celebration without me."

The assistant re-entered the room with four glasses and a bottle of Asti Spumante. "You didn't give me enough for Korbel," she joked. Robb looking at her strangely, poured the bubbly and they tapped mugs, toasting their newest star.

"We're expecting big things for and from you, Gem. I hope you're ready," Robb said sternly. "Okay, let's get started."

"Can't we finish first?" Will questioned. Gem laughed as she noticed that Will had a Gomer Pyle appeal.

"No. We have much too much to do. Okay, Gem, how old are you?"

"I'm twenty-eight," she proudly answered. "In fact I turned twenty-eight on April 1."

"No you just turned twenty-two on April 1," Robb corrected.

"You're not serious, are you?"

"Very," he affirmed. "Twenty-eight just bursting onto the scene is way too old. The record companies won't be able to market you. You'll be too old for the younger crowd and too young for the older crowd. They won't know what to do with you. Okay, what's your name?"

"I like to use my full first name as my stage name. No last name."

"What's that?"

"Gemmia," she proudly asserted again.

"Hmmm. Gemmia. Gemmia. Pretty, but too close to Tamia, the R&B singer. Nah. We have to change that."

"I'm not changing my name, Robb." She noted that his brain seemed to work overtime. *I want to be a star and not have any problems, but I'm not changing my whole being.*

He spent the next few hours prepping her. He specified her weight, her hair, hair color, clothing, public appearances and anything else he could think of. "Oh yes, and make sure you get in touch with our assistant. She'll need to do a color analysis so we can determine the best colors to suit you," Robb continued.

"My favorite color is yellow, if it matters," she whispered.

"It doesn't," Robb added.

His assistant took notes and headed out the door. Immediately she was on the phone.

"Oh, we need a choreographer, we need new dancers, steps, the works. Let's go!" He snapped his fingers. The energy in the air was like static. And Gem felt like she was smack in the middle of a whirlwind.

Robb informed her that she had six weeks to lose twenty pounds, put together a good list of cover tunes and secure a band for an already prebooked gig. "If you have any problems, call me. I'll also be working on these things on my end. The place is Lola's, and it's hot. You can really cut your teeth, but you will not—you cannot—embarrass me." His voice elevated. "You gotta be sharp, chickie. With that all said and done, let's get to work." He dismissed her.

Can we say, Mr. Jekyll or Mr. Hyde, boys and girls, she thought as she walked out the door.

"Talise, you owe me. I can't hang out after work, I have something to do."

"I'm sorry, Steff, but the meeting lasted longer than everyone anticipated."

"How did the presentations go?"

"The one you helped me with went over well. Now K.J. assigned the project of me making the inroads in the agency. The others didn't go so well, but I'm still working. I'll be here until about eight or nine or so..."

"Well it's four, and I'm out. You owe me lunch tomorrow. Don't forget."

"It's a date, I won't."

K.J.'s secretary had entered before the conversation concluded. She eased herself into the guest chair, placed her hand on her chin and sat back. "You might want to work on your projects rather than dates," she said snidely while eyeing the mess in front of Talise.

"I wasn't working on a date," Talise defended. She still clinched her teeth, hoping one day she would get on this woman's good side. *Include her. Schmooze her,* the little voice said in her head. "As a matter of fact, I was just finishing the strategy for the new agent's business. I'm glad you stopped by. I was hoping to get your opinion," she said in a sweet voice.

"Well, I'm on my way out but…"

"Okay. Oh, don't worry. I'll place it on your desk before I leave and you can give your opinion to me tomorrow, if that's okay," she said.

"Well, no, I'll look at it now." Dragon Breath eyed the document ferociously. Eyebrows went up then down. She pursed her lips sideways and around. "Not bad," she murmured. She continued to read. "Yeah." She sighed. "Not bad. Could use a little work, but I'd say you're on the right track. It's going to be tough but get K.J. to help. He'll like that. He's in late tonight. Stop by his office later. He's anxious to hear your progress on the other projects as well," she said, rising from her chair. "Good night," she said, somewhat pleasantly.

Well that's a first, Talise thought. *Good, now with her off my back for a second, maybe I can breathe. Thanks, Steff. Don't know what I'd do without you…* she thought, remembering that the little voice to smooth her over was Steffon's. She continued to shuffle through her papers when the phone rang.

"…Yes. I do understand. Of course, I'll bring it right over, and K.J., I have something else I would like to discuss with you outside of the meeting today…great. I'll be right there," she said, hanging up the phone and retrieving her files.

Briskly she walked toward his door and immediately noticed the dark shadows looming behind the drawn shades. Cautiously she pushed the door open and knocked simultaneously. K.J. sat at his large cherry oak desk with a petite old English green lamp emitting less than a flicker.

"Ah, Talise. Come in," he said, barely lifting his head from his notes. "Have a seat. No, no. This is a quiet evening. Let's sit on the couch." She shrugged and complied. "Don't be so tense," he advised as he slid beside her. "I want you to know that I was pleased with your presentation today. You have a lot to learn but you're getting slightly better. I want you to know I have real high expectations but if you play your cards right, you'll be okay," he said.

"Thanks," she responded, with mixed gratitude and confusion. *Was that a compliment or a slap in the face?* "I have a few more ideas written down that I was hoping you would take a look at and give me some direction." She handed the files to him.

He studied them for what seemed an eternity. She tried to read his expressionless face. Finally he sighed and raised his head. "Looks good to me. Go with it," he said.

"But I don't really know where to go from here."

"Well, Talise, that's why I pay my marketing rep $40,000 a year. Figure it out."

Her eyes bulged in disbelief. *I hope you don't think I think that $40,000 is a lot of money.*

"Don't worry. Just stay focused, you'll be fine," he said as his large hand covered her neck. "You need to loosen up," he commanded now trying to massage her neck. "Why are you so stoic? I won't bite. Just trying to get you to loosen up a bit."

She rubbed her temples and assumed a grin. "No, I'm okay. I heard you're sponsoring a night at Sequoia's." She tried to change the subject. She eased a centimeter away, praying for a mile. He smiled. "Well, if you don't mind, I'm going to get some things done and I'll meet you and the rest of the guys over there," she said, easing herself from the couch.

"Sure. I don't want to keep you from your work. I'll expect an edited report on what we discussed tonight no later than tomorrow at three." She glanced at him with anguish. "I know you will handle it," he concluded.

Again she smiled and headed out the door. Before she turned the corner, he was hot on her heels, briefcase in hand. "I guess I'll see you there." She forged another smile and noticed that she was the only one left in the building.

"Okay, darling, I didn't mean to overstep my boundaries again. I just want to protect you and make sure you have the best, that's all. Please don't be angry with me for the rest of the evening. Let's just have a good time." Alec followed her up the spiral staircase to the roof.

"Hit the button, please," she requested while she balanced the dish of ginger-lime marinated salmon they were to grill. The glass panes retracted and a mini-tropical oasis stood before them. Stephanie took great pride in her newly refinished sky-top patio. She had handpicked almost every silk plant that mimicked her favorite Ocho Rios getaway.

"Why are you ignoring me? I said I was sorry," he said in a less congenial tone.

"I'm not ignoring you. I'm hungry, and I waited for you before I could finish preparing the meal. You know the flavor of this fish has a delicate balance. If I had waited any longer, the marinade would have started separating," she whined.

"I want to make it up to you. My father is taking the boat out this weekend. He wants to make sure everything is running well before my fund-raising campaign gets underway," Alec said as he arranged the crystal bowl filled with her favorite mixed green gourmet salad. "I thought perhaps you and I should take the yacht out alone and have some fun. Stephanie, you're not listening to me. Don't worry the fish can grill itself. Please come sit down," he said, pulling out her chair before pouring her a glass of Dom Perignon.

She obliged.

"You haven't answered me yet."

"What? Oh this weekend?" She grimaced. "I don't think that's a good idea, I mean I have jury duty on Monday bright and early. Oh, and I promised Talise I would come over and help her arrange some of her things in her new place, you know get rid of some of those boxes…" She made a mental note to call Talise and arrange it. "…Oh, and—"

"Why are you avoiding me?" he interrupted. "How much more can I apologize."

"Apology accepted but learn to be less demanding and less bossy. I keep telling you that you are not exposing me to anything I haven't seen already. I'm not from the slums, you know. I know a thing or two and if I choose, remember I said *choose* to drink wine from a store right next to the supermarket, it's okay. It doesn't mean I don't know better or can't have better or that I'm unaccustomed to better. It's just that that's my choice. You gotta learn to deal with me, not a creation of me," she said.

He held up his glass as a truce. She accepted.

"Now that we have that out of the way, perhaps you're in the mood to discuss platform strategy," he said.

She sighed before getting up to take the salmon off the grill. "I'm not in a bad mood, Alec, but I do have things on my mind."

He dismissed her outburst. "Anyway, we're quite pleased with the guest list so far. Mr. Kwesi Mfume has RSVPed. We are still waiting to hear from Jesse Jackson, Maxine Waters and others. I even thought about Colin Powell but Dad believes that crossing party lines is unwise," he concluded now biting into the succulent salmon. "Darling, this is excellent. I love the way you cook. It's so healthy. Unlike the heavy soul food dishes I've been accustomed to."

She tussled her hair. She was too weary to respond. "Well I agree with your dad. Inviting Colin Powell crosses party lines, and it will look too obvious," she added to focus her attention on the matter at hand.

"I'm surprised Dad is inviting Maxine Waters. I mean she is a viable voice, but her constituents are clear across the country. Other than Washington she has no real dealings on the East Coast. I mean we don't have gangs out here to deal with," he said casually.

"We do have gangs out here," she said, dabbing the corner of her mouth.

"Where?"

"You mean who. Trust me the police are gangs. Maxine Waters' constituency may not be in this vicinity but her issues are. Your father is a smart man. He knows what buttons to push. He should. He's created quite a name for himself in D.C."

"Darling, I beg to differ. The police aren't the gangs. They are trying to do a tough job in a ruthless community."

"Honey, let's just enjoy dinner. This conversation is going into an area I have no patience for tonight." *Hood Education 101. This man has no clue,* she thought. She continued to stab at her food.

"No these are conversations we must be free to have, especially if we are going to be successful with this relationship. I'm interested in your views."

"In the past you've called them diatribes." He glanced at her with a pleading look. She read it well. "Okay, okay. What I'm saying is that if you are going to be everybody's senator, you really have to be involved in everybody's issues. Not just those that are passionate to your heart."

He pondered her words for a moment. "So what are you saying, that I should start my acting lessons soon?"

"Find the commonality in the issues that you find less interest in. Place yourself in the position of a man, not a Black man, White man or

Asian man but a man being arrested because he's driving a fancy car in an area he has every right to be in. Or worse yet, picture yourself as a man having to experience your brother being shot forty-one times for holding up a wallet. And being shot because the presumption of guilt always looms in the mind of someone who sees color first. Or picture yourself having to bury your only brother because a cop with a history of racism has choked him to death because his football accidentally hit his police car. These are not just Black or Latino issues, these are human issues. And frankly, Blacks are tired of having to humanize ourselves to White America." Stephanie cleared their plates and poured another glass of champagne.

"I'm just surprised that it seems true that Black women always justify the inadequacies of their men."

"That is completely untrue," Stephanie defended.

"No, it's not. You stand behind them whether they are wrong or right."

"That's untrue," she emphatically stated. *I wish Black men felt that way,* she thought. She felt her temper rising. "Let's not go there again, Alec. I'm tired and I have a busy week ahead of me. I don't want to start an argument with you."

"Okay, okay. You know I don't think this way. I'm playing devil's advocate. I just want you prepared for the types of conversations and people we'll have to deal with. The press and the opposition will throw whatever they can your way. You are my love, you'll be on my arm, and I won't always be there to ward off silly notions people may throw your way."

"I can handle myself, Alec," she said. "And lady love? Don't I have a say in this love part?"

"No, you don't. My love for you is strictly between my heart and me. You just happen to be a casualty of that." He smiled, he grabbed her hand and kissed it.

His love was what she liked most about him after less than six months of dating. He was warm, sensitive and extremely protective. At times he was overbearing. But he was still very difficult for her to figure out. She didn't understand when he neglected to question her about very obvious things. She knew that if she were at his house and a lady emerged from his door upon her entrance, she would question it first. He bumped into Glenn leaving, the evening was almost over, and he still hadn't asked who Glenn was or what he was doing there.

Humph. Is it trust or is it just dumb luck that he chooses not to know? she thought as she returned his affection.

"Girl, this is my song. You better get on out here on this dance floor," Vanee said as she trailed off, leaving Talise standing at the bar. The beats played more like a migraine headache as opposed to music to her ears. Sequoia's with Great Raritan's finest was the last place she wanted to be tonight. K. J. had already chastised her for not being social enough. And after their meeting he was the last person she wanted in her face.

"Whew. I can't stand still when that song comes on. What is the matter with you tonight? Hell, you just got the best dick of your life, you claim, and you're walking 'round like you ain't had none since you and Maurice broke up. You should be happy. You have a great new position with the company, got your own place. Girl, you should be on top of the world," Vanee exclaimed still bopping to the beat.

"You're in a good mood. You act like you haven't been out in a while," Talise said, sipping her club soda. Drinking around K.J. and the company was the biggest mistake anyone could make. Alcohol told too much information—information that K.J. would use against her at any given time.

"I am. I don't get out much. You know how her daddy is. In fact, I better get my last groove on. The clock is about to strike twelve and Cinderella must be on her way."

"Vanee, it's only ten o'clock."

"Just a figure of speech. Lighten up! What's wrong with you?"

Talise thought long and hard about answering the question honestly. But she feared Vanee's sassy, no-nonsense personality might prompt her to take action. She just wasn't ready for action. *I mean, K.J. didn't mean anything. I wish he wouldn't put his hands on me though.* She shook her head as if to shake off the feeling. Suddenly her urge for honesty depleted.

"Nothing, girl. Nothing's wrong. Just tired. K.J. has me engrossed in three projects, and I need help. I'm making it though."

"Well good. Because I would hate to see our first black female marketing rep take a nosedive before she had time to get her feet wet. Hang in there, get yourself organized and you'll be fine."

"Yeah. I know."

"Just be careful. I've heard K.J. got a lot of stuff with him and he doesn't mind going after what he wants, especially if he wants you. I heard he got caught in his office by the cleaning lady."

"With who?"

"That new nineteen year-old clerk."

"Sarah?"

"Yep," Vanee confirmed.

"You know she's an underwriter now. She took my spot when I got moved up to marketing."

"I know. Isn't that special? From file clerk to underwriting in less than three months. I was here five years before they considered me for my supervisor's position. So just watch out. Look, I better catch that A train to Queens. I'll check you in the morning. Hey, lunch tomorrow?"

"Uh no, I promised Steff I would have lunch with him tomorrow. He really helped me out today. Hey, how is your negro treating you?"

"Same ole, same ole. That's why I'm rushing home, he's watching our daughter tonight."

"Well I'll rough him up for you when I see him," Talise said jovially.

"Cool. I'll call you then. Peace," Vanee said and headed off, leaving Talise lost and alone.

"Talise, having a good time?" K.J. questioned. The music had changed to techno and it grated on her nerves slightly less than K.J.

"As good as can be expected," she answered with reservation. She smiled graciously as several coworkers passed them on their way out of the door. "I guess I should be following them, I have an early day tomorrow," she hinted with a smile.

"Don't rush on my account," he said. His breath once again sprayed her neck.

She put safe distance between them, hoping the sweltering crowd would somewhat deter his actions. It didn't. She continued to inch away. She prayed his intentions wouldn't grow any bolder. Her prayers seemed as if they weren't being answered at that moment.

"Talise, K.J., what's going on?" someone asked, capturing Talise's grateful attention. Her soul let out a sigh. *Thank you, God,* she thought.

"Steff, what are you doing here? I thought you had something to do tonight," she exclaimed with glee.

"Yeah," he answered stiffly. "Hey, K.J., good to see ya."

K.J. gulped the last of his dry martini and placed the olive in his cheek. "You, too, Steffon. How are you doing? Oh, yeah, real good work on the Raymond account. Real good work. We should hear by next week whether we get it. If we do, it'll turn over a million in premium. Like I said, good work, real good work," K.J. concluded, placing his hands in his pocket.

Talise noticed K.J.'s discomfort.

"Anyway, I have to run. Steffon, keep up the good work. I'll be talking to you, and Talise, make sure your work is done tomorrow. No excuses," he asserted again and walked off.

"Once again you saved the day," Talise said, turning around toward Steffon.

"What were y'all talking 'bout. Y'all were so close, I almost decided not to walk over here."

"Nothing. Nothing important. So what are you doing here? I thought…"

"I know what you thought, but don't worry about that. It's late. Wanna ride home?"

"I appreciate that, Steff, but you don't have to take me all the way to Jersey. Besides Calvin should be at my place waiting. He was driving in tonight to meet with some clients over the next few days and he's staying with me." She ruffled through her purse to locate her monthly Path pass. "What was the grunt for?" she questioned still not looking up. She didn't wait for an answer. "Anyway I'll talk to you tomorrow and oh, thanks for your help today. Don't forget lunch on me tomorrow at the Seaport," she said and walked away.

Chapter 5

"I'm sorry, Ms. Alphonso, Dr. Kaplan is booked until the middle of October," the secretary emphatically repeated.

"But that's more than three weeks away and you could say it's an emergency, well somewhat of an emergency," she pleaded.

"I empathize with your dilemma. But technically it's not and I have to reserve space for true medical spur-of-the-moment emergencies. I can suggest someone else…"

Stephanie hung up before the woman could finish the sentence. She rubbed her temples feverishly. *She could fit me in if she wanted to,* she reasoned. She picked up the phone and hit redial. She heard the phone ring and immediately slammed it down.

Stephanie walked toward the fridge and retrieved the leftover chilled bottle of Chardonnay. She hadn't seen Alec in almost two weeks and she admitted she planned it that way. As of late he questioned her mood swings and lack of responsibility. For every event planned, she found a shaky reason to cancel or postpone. In some instances she felt like a heel because the cancellation had come so close to the date and time, but she couldn't face him or his suspicions right now.

"Hello." The phone disturbed her thoughts.

"Ms. Alphonso?" the familiar voice questioned.

"Yes."

"This is Dr. Kaplan's office."

Stephanie breathed a sigh of relief. *Good, they must've received an opening.* "Yes, yes…" she said, rumbling through junk drawer looking for her household calendar. *I have to get my housekeeper to straighten this drawer out,* she thought. "I'm ready, you have an opening?"

"Uh, no, Ms. Alphonso. I thought that perhaps you needed something else. Your number appeared on our Caller ID but when I picked up the phone I heard a dial tone."

Her face grew red. "Um no. No, I was just calling back to get, uh, the number from you for the other doctor, but my other line rang so I had to get it." *I guess lying is becoming second nature now.*

"Oh, sure. Her name is Dr. Baldwin, and her number is the same area code, 555-3820. Please tell her you come highly recommended, and she'll take great care of your needs. Is there anything else I can help you with?" the secretary asked in a singsongy voice.

"No, thanks. This will be enough," Stephanie said, hanging up without saying good-bye. *I know just how to rectify this,* she thought as she rustled her way back to the wine and fingered through her rolodex.

"Yes, this is Stephanie Alphonso. Please, do you have anything available for tomorrow?" She patiently waited. "You do? Great! As a matter of fact book me a spot for three. Yes…three. I really need your help. Thanks, see you then."

She hung up and took another full swig.

"I know, Robb, but I'm exhausted. No, tea isn't helping. I need sleep. If I don't get any, you can't expect me to perform. Lola's went well. Give me a break," she demanded through the large round microphone that covered her slender face. The soundproof Plexiglas was the only barrier between Gem wringing the necks of her managers, Robb and Will.

"This is a business for professionals, not spoiled babies. We have a demo to produce and it needs to be done in less than a month. So get it together and hit it again," Robb shouted. He pounded the button and shut her off from the conversation beyond the glass. She picked up the large black leather headphones and placed one over her right ear, leaving her left ear free. She sucked in a big breath and began to belt with the beat. She closed her eyes and began to fake her greatest climax. She was exhausted.

Since Gem had signed with them, Robb and Will had criticized everything she did. She was working overtime to perfect her voice, her hair and her makeup. In the mornings she noticed a stranger with dark circles under her eyes staring back at her as she brushed her teeth. Will and Robb had sheer determination behind their ever-growing investment, and they were destined to prevent any semblance of rest until she produced what she promised: her soul.

"I'm getting feedback. Hold up, Gem. I'm getting a ringing sound," Will said gently.

"Cut! Cut! Cut!" Robb shouted. Gem raised her eyes and shoulders as if to say what now?

"What is that feedback? What is it? Find it, now," Robb demanded of Will.

"Oh. Oops, I'm sorry," Gem said. She reached down and pulled her cell phone from her hip. She flipped the cover to the ringing phone and answered.

Robb was steaming. "Take a break." He pounded on the wall.

"Hello? Stephanie, hey, girl...yeah, you got me at a bad time but you saved me too," Gem answered, crawling out of the booth passed the engineers. "Oh, girl, don't apologize. It's okay. It's forgotten. That's what best friends do, look out for each other. I know you were just looking out for me." She paused. "Well you don't have to treat but I would love a day of beauty. I really could use it. Okay, if you insist. Cool, but I can't make it before noon. I have another session in the morning, providing this one finishes by then. Yeah...well I'll tell you about it tomorrow. Girlfriend alert is definitely in order. Look I gotta go. See you tomorrow."

"Now can we try this again without any interruptions this time. Gem, please put that damn thing on vibrate or throw it out of the fucking window," Robb enunciated. "On five, four, three, two..."

"Um, hello?"

"You sleep?"

She chuckled. "You could say that," she answered with more clarity.

"It's only 8:00 P.M."

"I know what time it is." She chuckled again.

"Anyway, listen, I called to apologize for our little tussle at the restaurant. I was hoping I could make it up to you tomorrow by inviting you to a day of beauty. My treat," Stephanie said cheerfully. She took another sip of wine.

"Honey, stop. Okay, I'm hurrying. Stephanie, that sounds cool, but you don't have to apologize and you don't have to put yourself through that type of expense," Talise answered while she enjoyed his affection. She placed her hand over the receiver. "Stop, honey. Why do you always wait until the phone rings? Okay, I'm back. Anyway, Steph, that sounds great but I have company and..."

"Calvin, I presume." Stephanie pursed her lips toward the glass and rolled her eyes.

"Well, yeah," Talise said, sitting up in the bed with defiance. "Besides, I can't take the day off tomorrow. I have too many deadlines at the end of the week." Calvin had made his way below the covers. "Umm," she groaned.

"Oh, please. Listen, I gotta go. I don't want to interrupt or participate in your escapade, so if you change your mind, Gem and I will be at..."

"Gem is going? Well I can't miss out on that...." Talise said, reneging.

Stephanie heard Calvin manipulating her into sticking to her original no. "If you're going to take the day off tomorrow, tell her you'll be spending it with me. I'll treat you to an even better massage," she heard him say.

"Steph, I'm sorry but..."

"No need to explain, Talise. But you might want to be careful about allowing that man to dictate your schedule. Especially when..."

"There you go again, Stephanie. See this is exactly why we got into it before. You apologize and then throw your apology back in my face by doing the exact same thing. I gotta go," Talise said and hung up. She put their conversation out of her mind and retreated between the sheets to join him. "Ummmm, 69 is my absolute favorite position," she said, sliding down.

Minutes passed when she heard the familiar voice on the answering machine once again, "Tal, I'm really sorry again. I just want the best and…anyway if you change your mind, meet us at Gazelle's on the East Side in the city at noon. The number is 212-555-8000. I miss you, and I really want to get together with you both. You don't even have to stay for the entire time, just half a day. I'm sure Calvin could stand to be away from you even for an hour or two. I hope to see you there." Talise heard the dial tone and the tape rewind to take another message.

"So what did she say?"

Stephanie took in a deep breath of the menthol, eucalyptus and lavender. She gently twisted her neck and relaxed her shoulders. She readjusted the pure-white fluffy towel that weighed heavy on her head.

"That was it, I told you. I really expected she would surprise us and come today. I called her job and there was no answer. I called her front desk to have a message delivered in person but the girl said Talise wasn't coming in today. She was sick."

"That man is going to be the cause of that girl losing her job," Gem said, retying her robe. She patted the only dry area on her face, feeling the skin cleanser harden against her skin.

"If you ask me, *she* is going to be the cause of her losing her job."

"I don't know when she'll ever learn. She's smart but she skips from one thing, man or whatever, to the next. I'm telling you, I love her dearly but you have to let her fall flat on her face or her results will be the same. She just—"

"What's up with you? Where were you when I called?" Stephanie tactfully changed the subject.

Gem stalled. She allowed herself to be taken by the exquisiteness of the holding room. She noticed the spider and snow plants that adorned the white walls. Peace lilies of all sizes danced along the corridor leading to the private facial rooms for which they awaited. Soft sounds by Gwen Molten, the renown opera singer, emitted from the speakers. Gem enjoyed the vast contrast to her own music.

"Earth to Gemmia," Stephanie said as she snapped her finger near Gem's head.

"Toodles." A loud voice came booming down the hall.

"Now that's her worst rendition of Regine, yet." Gem said, referring to the popular *Living Single* character.

"Yes, ma'am, I'm here to meet my two best friends. Of course I have an appointment. They're over there. Stephanie, Gem, please tell this woman I have an appointment." The woman glared trying to block her view.

Stephanie walked gracefully toward the concierge desk. "Lemure, I did make an appointment for three…"

"I know, ma'am, but she is more than an hour late and I'm supposed to…"

"I know. I know. Please excuse her this time. I gave her the wrong time and it really is my fault. Please," Stephanie pleaded. "I promise, I'll make it worth your while." Stephanie flashed her killer smile. She knew green spoke loud and clear.

"I know you will. You always do. Fine, I'll escort Ms. …"

"Grimes," Talise interjected and tilted her head with an air of superiority.

"Ms. Grimes to the powder room. I will start her on the underwater therapy massage that you had much earlier," the attendant said with a scowl. Talise returned it and followed.

"I'm so glad she made it. I really needed to see you girls today," Stephanie said as she sipped her herbal tea.

"What's wrong? You seem so solemn," Gem asked, sipping what tasted like peat moss.

Now it was Stephanie's turn. Talise's abrupt return disturbed the moment. She kissed them both generously on the cheek.

"Watch my facial," Gem commanded playfully.

"Ooh. I'm so glad to be here. I had to move mountains, but I made it and…"

"Late as usual," Gem interjected.

"…I'm so glad. Everything's been going so well, I can't wait to tell you guys what's been going on with my life and…"

"Slow down. This is not a marathon, Talise," Stephanie said, insisting on some tranquility. Talise's mouth was running a mile a minute.

Gem had put the drink down and was reading an article in her latest issue of *Essence*.

"So, ladies, let the girlfriend alert begin. So who wants to start?" No one answered. Talise ignored them. "Okay, let's start with the rules. Free and open, no secrets and no judging. Agreed?" They still ignored her. "Agreed," she repeated.

"I agree for you to stop talking through that bullhorn. In case you have forgotten, this is supposed to be relaxation," Gem said as she flipped another page.

"So you start, Talise. How are you and Calvin?" Stephanie asked, trying to be gracious.

Talise couldn't wait to spill the beans. Life had been going lovely for the two of them. She and Calvin communicated nearly every day. He was the consummate lover and friend, only having her best interest at heart.

"So is he still seeing that woman he's been seeing for oh, five or six years?" Gem questioned sarcastically.

"He's been seeing her off and on for five years, Miss Gem. And yes to answer your question, she is still around—for now," Talise said haughtily. "He's wonderful. We love and we laugh. Next week I'm meeting him in D.C. and the week after that we're going to some fantabulous formal affair in South Jersey. What more can a girl ask for?"

"Reality," Gem said.

"You're just jealous." Talise sipped the drink that had been set before her.

"Uugh. This is gross. What the heck is it?" she asked, practically spitting it out.

"Huh." Gem laughed. "So how did you manage to tear yourself away from lover boy and your job today?" she asked, flipping another page.

Again ignoring the comments, Talise explained that Calvin had several clients to see.

"That's what we're talking about," Stephanie said as Talise sucked her teeth in disgust. "You see. You were willing to miss out on a perfectly wonderful day for Calvin. You had no problems calling in sick and so forth but he was going to get done what he needed to get done, despite you."

Talise shrugged off the unsolicited advice. But she remembered rule numero uno of girlfriend alert: Feelings can be shared openly and honestly and each of them must listen with an open mind, was their creed. So she let them talk but it didn't mean she was listening.

The ladies had now applied the same plaster it seemed to Talise's face that had been settling on Gem's and Stephanie's. Each of them enjoyed the pampering.

"So, Gem, answer my question. Where were you last night?" Stephanie asked as warm moisturizers were massaged in her cheeks.

"I was at the studio. In fact I was there until about 10:30 this morning. I didn't even sleep. I came right here. I know I'm going to fall out after this but I have to go back. I won't be catching a ride in the limo you had arranged for us," Gem said, breathing in the lavender mask.

"Stephanie, you arranged for a limo?"

She nodded.

"Cool."

"So who are you working with in the studio this time, Rachelle or Oleta?" Stephanie asked.

"I'm working on my own stuff," Gem said in a less-than-convincing tone.

Talise and Stephanie sat straight up. "You're kidding, that's great!" they exclaimed in unison.

"Oh, I'm so happy for you, Gem. Why didn't you tell us?" Talise yelled. She followed the orders of the attendant who pressed her back down to the seat.

"I just did," Gem answered casually. "Besides, I talked to Stephanie earlier."

"Well tell us all about it. Is it an album or what?"

"It's a demo, and there isn't much more to tell. It's demanding, hard work."

"Well who was at the Sony party? How did you swing it?" Talise asked.

"You ask way too many questions."

"I would like to know too. How did it happen and with whom?" Stephanie asked less enthusiastically. She paused and thought. "Gem, did you sign with those guys?"

"What guys? Ouch!" Talise questioned. "Be careful, that hurt."

"Gem, did you sign with those guys?"

"Ouch!! What guys? Lady, if you pluck me one more time I'm going to bop you. Be careful. What guys? What are you all talking about?"

Stephanie explained her reservations about the men Gem had just met on her latest commercial. "I just wasn't impressed with their timing or their demands," she concluded.

"It's a good deal. Don't sweat it," Gem said, relaxing.

"I'm telling you that you would have been better off consulting with an attorney. You know what happens to those kids who just sign anything with anybody just to get a deal. They always end up with the short end of the stick. Look at what happened to Toni Braxton."

"I have this under control. And, yes, look at what happened to Toni Braxton, but at least she got there. Even if the road was rocky to the top."

"I'm just saying—"

"I know what you're just saying but I signed the papers and that's all to it. It's done. That's it. I don't want to talk about it anymore."

"Wow, Miss Perfect, has made a booboo," Talise said.

"Shut up, Talise."

"We're ready for you in the massage rooms now." The ladies followed the attendant.

"See you in a bit for our pedicures," Stephanie whispered as if she was entering a convent.

"Break it down," Steffon asserted between gritted teeth.

"What, what are you talking about?"

"Your voice. Step away from me yelling like that!" He raised his voice above hers.

She glanced around to see who might be lurking about their business. Even though she knew confronting him at his place of employment made everything fair game.

"Steffon, I'm sorry but I really need you to watch her tonight. I'm working really hard on this project. If I could stay later and do a little more research, this could be the straw that gets me a promotion," she whined.

"I told you I got bizness to take care of. I'm working on shit too. Now that's the fucking end of it. I'm meetin' with Romy Graham tonight and that's it. Step off!" He dismissed her. "Shit, I baby-sat for her ass Monday," he muttered under his breath as she stormed away.

"I heard that. Baby-sat, baby-sat? Have you noticed you are her daddy, not her baby-sitter."

"Don't act like I don't take care of my daughter, physically, mentally and financially. You looking to get your feelings hurt talkin' 'bout my daughter." His tone was severe.

"She's my daughter, too, and I just need you to help me out, just tonight," she pleaded "You probably ain't doin' nothin' but hangin' out. He ain't no good. Nothing but a crook wanna-be gangsta wanna-be crook," she snapped.

"I told you about speaking my bizness in the street…" He clasped his chin and squinted.

Silence.

His quiet furor spoke louder than anything he could say.

"I'm not telling you again, step off." He dismissed her with a low, monotonous voice.

She did. She was swollen like a bullfrog, but she stepped.

Talise re-entered the holding room feeling less than relaxed or fulfilled. The masseuse was way too rough for her taste and the music she played was less than exhilarating. She noticed the other ladies had not joined her as of yet.

A perfect time to call my baby, she thought. She flipped the top of her silver phone and quickly dialed her home number.

She allowed the phone to ring until she heard her own voice. *He probably doesn't want to answer my phone,* she reasoned. So she hung up and dialed his cell phone. No answer.

"Trying to track down lover boy…" Gem asked.

Talise picked up the nearest magazine. "No, no, just checking my messages at work. Surprisingly, everything's quiet."

"Um-hmm," Gem offered. She sat down in the reclining chaise and enjoyed the moment. "That was wonderful, wasn't it?"

"No. That woman felt like she was pounding ground beef," Talise said, flipping through to a magazine article of the latest Hollywood pregnancies. "I'll tell you what, that Jada Pinkett Smith grows more gorgeous with time, pregnant or not. She's incredible," Talise said still flipping.

"Money will do that for you," Gem said, trying to fall off to sleep.

"Her beauty is not dictated by money. Look at that killer smile and flawless body. And she's at least six months pregnant with her second child. Talking 'bout having a third," Talise defended.

"No, I'm not saying her beauty is tied to money. She's a beautiful woman, but money helps. If you could live in luxury every other day or every week or month for that matter, it would sure set my spirit straight."

"I'm not impressed," Talise said, suddenly stopping on one page. "I don't understand this. I just don't get it." She repeated in disgust. "You know what?"

"I'm sure you'll tell me."

"I'm so tired of brothers with White women," she said, referring to a feature on a popular athlete with his new interracial family. Look at this!" She shoved the magazine into Gem's face. "I'm saying. Why when brothers get a lot of money or status do they seem to appear color blind. They don't accept just any ol' thing from sisters. I'm so sick of seeing Black men with White women I don't know what to do. All of them. Money or prestige, and you know she's White. These White women wouldn't want them if they were any ol' Joe off the street. Or not off the street. Just average brothers don't get the same play."

"If they have a job and some potential," Stephanie said re-entering the room and the conversation. "The fact is the vast majority of professional Black men, entertainers and athletes marry Black women."

"Oh, I disagree with that," Gem said, suddenly alert. "The fact is the majority of interracial relationships come from Black men with White women, not the other way around. And the same brother that would date a White woman if he could, scowls at a sister with a White man."

"Oh, that is so untrue. Black men are much more accepting of Black women with White men, and we give them such a hard time," Stephanie defended.

"You are dreaming," Talise said. "You have been hanging around too many of your White office partners. Black men can't stand it. I can't blame them, I don't know what a Black woman would see in a White man anyway. They are just not that attractive. At least I don't find them attractive."

"That's you," Stephanie said.

"Ooh, touchy touchy," Gem said.

Just then the owner of Gazelle's interrupted their diatribe with a phone call.

"Hello?" Stephanie questioned. "Alec, um hey…sure…no, not tonight. Eight is fine. Okay, see you then…bye…" She started to hang up. "Oh, wait a minute. Alec what's the dress for to—Alec? Shoot," she said, placing the receiver back in the cradle.

"Would you like to make another call?" the petite cinnamon-colored woman asked.

"No, I'm okay, thank you."

"You're welcome," she said with a slight accent.

"Question. You're from France, aren't you?"

"Oui," she answered.

"What is your take as a person from another country on interracial relationships?"

The owner didn't ponder. "Love is love. Color doesn't matter. You Americans are way too obsessed with color. But…being here for the last five years, I do understand that your experience somewhat dictates that. But I just can't negate my experience that people are people. I guess I'm fortunate."

"I guess so," Talise murmured as she continued to flip through the magazine.

"I couldn't have said it better," Stephanie said, taking a sip of the drink placed before her. The owner sauntered off.

"So who's Alec?" Talise asked.

Stephanie choked. "A friend," she answered.

"A friend from where?" Talise asked.

"Oh, just a friend I met through some colleagues," she answered.

"And is there a reason you neglected to tell us about him?" Gem questioned.

"What would you like to know?" Stephanie batted her eyes.

"The five W's, of course. You know: who, what, when, where and why," Talise stated.

"Who…Alec. What…a friend…a local Newark politician. When…I answered that…Where…I answered that, and Why…because he's a nice guy with whom I enjoy good conversation and good company."

"Hmm. Evasive. So what really happened with you and Glenn at the restaurant?" Gem inquired.

Stephanie glared toward Talise who gave her most innocent shrug. Talise continued reading her magazine.

"Pedicures anyone?" the attendant asked.

"Naw, man, I gotta check you another day for our meetin'. I got some other bizness to take care of. I'll cut you in about it later. But keep your nights free next week. I got a deal goin' down that's hot. I'm talkin' to some folks tonight. They're record producers, so stay cool and low…peace," Steffon heard Romy Graham say as he hung up the phone.

Steffon now a lot calmer from his earlier encounter decided to take a break from his work. He hadn't seen Talise all day, and he was supposed to meet her for lunch.

He decided against taking the spiral staircase. Instead he approached her office from the fire stairs that sat adjacent to it. He walked upon an empty and dimly lit space. K.J.'s secretary was ruffling through the mess on her desk.

"Talise isn't in today?" he questioned almost making Dragon Breath jump.

"Oh. Hello, Steffon. No she's not here and she left her area a mess. I can't find a thing in here. Good job by the way. We got the account you worked so diligently on. K.J. is really noticing your work."

"Thanks. Talise helped me with the marketing plan." He stretched the truth.

"Really? Well you might want to talk to her, Steff. She's calling in a lot lately and she's not getting done what K.J. needs her to do. She continues to perform far below K.J.'s expectations. She's beginning a dangerous trend."

"I don't know that you should be discussing this with me. It's inappropriate," he said, quoting Talise.

"Maybe so. But she better get it together or get gone. She can't go back to underwriting. Her next move up is out. Here it is. Finally. Okay, gotta go. See you later, oh…" She turned back around. "…good job again. K.J. is going to announce it at the next manager's meeting and at the full staff meeting in front of everyone."

He blushed as she walked away. *That damn Talise. She's fuckin' up,* he thought. He pushed past several files to her phone and dialed her home number.

It rang four times.

"Hellooo," a deep voice resonated on the other end.

"I'm looking for Talise," a startled Steffon demanded.

"She's not here. How about a message, partner?" Calvin said.

"Naw. It's not necessary," Steffon slammed down the phone. *Damn.* He shook his head, picked up the receiver again and dialed another number. He was greeted with a sweeter voice.

"Policies?" she answered.

"Hey, babe," he sweetened.

She huffed. "What's up, Steffon."

"Look, I'm sorry a'ight. You know I don't like you confronting me at work. But kill all that noise. My plans changed. I'm free tonight."

"Thanks for fitting me into your schedule."

"Look, I said I'm free. Now you can act funky if you want to and all of a sudden I won't be. So what you wanna do?" he demanded.

She softened. "Good, thanks. I appreciate it."

"A'ight. Peace."

"Hey, Steff?"

"What?"

"Thanks…"

"You said that already."

"I know and…I love you…" She hesitated.

"Yeah, you too," he said and hung up the phone.

"Can we get off the subject already? Everyone doesn't have a problem with the interracial thing."

"I know but White men don't respect us, Stephanie. And the only reason there aren't more Black women married to White men is because White men on a whole won't marry us. Every other race of men for the most part hold their women in high esteem. I didn't say all or even most but a lot of Black men don't defend us the way we stand by them," Talise said now placing her magazine down in disgust.

"I have to admit, I do agree. You know, I was walking in the city just today and a man who happened to be White expected me to hold the door open for him. They don't treat you like a lady until you become famous and demand proper treatment. Look at Dorothy Dandridge and Josephine Baker," Gem said.

"First of all, ladies, just because Black men marry some woman from some other race doesn't mean they are putting us or all other Black women down. We can't take everything so personally, and secondly…Gem, you were in New York City. I don't know a whole lot of folks with manners in this city. You all need to lighten up…no pun intended." They all laughed.

Gem stepped in the studio ninety minutes early instead of her usual thirty minutes late. Since she had already been on the East Side enjoying her day of beauty, rather than go home she headed back to work to finish the latest track that was only introduced to her the day before.

She picked up the sheet music left there a few hours earlier. She hummed the melody. The ease of the lyrics hadn't clicked with her.

"You're not feeling it," a voice behind her advised.

"That's because there isn't much there to feel. The lyrics aren't real.

This 'I'll love you forever mess' is that, mess." She continued to hum, trying to ignore the visitor. *Get the hint, get the hint,* she sang in her mind.

He did. He placed his backpack on his console and pulled his massively cut arms from a thin brown leather jacket. His arms, attached to a medium but perfectly V-shaped torso grabbed excess papers and placed them in the corner of the room. His creamy midnight-black complexion was framed by a close-cut fade with a quarter of an inch of hair brushed toward the front. He sported a bright but modest diamond in one ear. On a good day, this would have been noticed and projected some sense of normalcy for Gem, but this wasn't any good or normal day. And her introduction to the muck and mire of the music industry as of late was no consolation. Flashy double-studded earlobes and large ornate figurines of a would-be Christ or zodiac sign were nowhere near her idea of normal or attractive.

She was determined to get this tune down but she had to admit she wasn't feeling it. She could fake it. She could create an orgasm out of the lame discovery of new love as the song described but she didn't want to. She knew what that felt like once but her days of making men climax by the sheer flicker of her tongue while she waited for her ship to come in were over.

So she hummed.

"That's definitely not it. You have to play."

"Unsolicited advice," she sang.

"Fine," he answered. Just like his body. He began playing with a few dials and checking levels on the sound.

She continued to hammer at the song. She started then she stopped and started again. Finally she let out a deep sigh in frustration. "So how would you do it?" she asked.

"Excuse me?" he asked, showing less interest.

"Any suggestions?" She struggled.

"Relax." He turned away still checking sound and beat levels.

"I am relaxed. Any suggestions about how I could start it off or finish it for that matter."

"Give me a second." He dropped the track. He played with the tone, added a different beat and put a spin on the background. Feverishly he worked for the next thirty minutes trying new things here and there. She hummed and accompanied whatever he dropped with ease.

"Listen to this," he would say.

"I like it. What about this with that?" she would ask.

"I like it," he would answer. So they played.

They played right up until the time Robb's annoying voice came screeching into the room. "Alrighty then. We have a lot of work to do. We have to finish tonight. Gem, I need to speak with you before we get started."

Her stomach did a belly flop. *He can't be firing me before the project gets finished. Shoot, he has to be flexible and give me a chance. I know I can deliver what he wants....*

"Next week I have a gig set up for you on the West Side. You, the piano and an audience filled with wanna-be fans and record execs. You will sing two songs from the demo and the rest of the evening will consist of cover tunes. I need stuff that you can wow the crowd with. You've sang background for Wincey, right?" She nodded. "Great, then you are familiar with her genre. Stick with that. Have a play list for me by the end of the day tomorrow. Also have two wardrobe changes and hairstyles you'd like to wear for approval to Will by the end of the week. That'll be all. Full details later. Okay, people, let's get moving. I don't have all night!" he said, cracking the whip.

Gem took her place in the booth. She allowed the melody that she and the engineer drummed up to entrance her. An orgasm was to be had tonight.

Robb let the entire production play without one interruption. That was a good sign. She held her breath for his decision. She watched through the glass now fogged with her sweat. He talked and tapped and talked. Finally a word came through.

"Gem." She acknowledged with a nod. "Love the passion but lose the other shit you added. I'm paying you to sing the fucking song as it's written. No one gave you permission to change it. Now do as you're told or don't do it all. Got it?"

"But…"

"Got it?" he repeated, his eyes bulging.

"Yes, Robb, I got it."

"Good. From the top and five, four, three, two…"

Disappointed, she hit the first note flawlessly. She looked over at her engineer friend who seemed just as puzzled and disappointed as she felt. She just sang the song.

Chapter 6

Here she was held up and cornered to entertain the oldest and stuffiest old White men chewing on old brown cigars. The place was one of the world's fanciest hotels, The Waldorf Astoria. The event was insurance night. And beaded gowns, coifed hairdos and penguin suits came in all sizes.

Talise traded her beads for a slinky, black satin, diamond-studded, spaghetti-strapped wonder. The foot-long train on the dress accented every curve on her delicate frame. And the thigh-high split revealed a sexy pair of matching strapped sling backs, which enhanced her muscle-toned calves.

The cigars dripped saliva every time her authentic Chanel perfume, courtesy of Stephanie, wafted passed their noses. Too bad her reaction wasn't the same. So after several hours of phony smiles, compliments and fake laughter, she grabbed her trail in one hand, a glass of Dom topped with a strawberry in the other and headed for the forbidden suite of Great Raritan's biggest competitor.

She stepped into an oasis. The worn wooden walls, antique chandeliers and oriental-like rugs jumped to the sounds of a seven-piece jazz band instead of Bach. The large suite held corners of Buppies grouped together sipping a colorful array of elixirs. Their fit shoulders and torsos put the T in their designer tuxedos. Now it was her turn to lick her lips. She did and so did they.

"Damn," she heard a group of them say. She headed toward the bar and ordered a topper.

"Topped with what? Would love for it to be me."

"Only topped with Dom. Thank you very much," she answered and turned. A piece of dark chocolate stood before her. She eyed him ferociously just as he did her. She liked what she saw. *Umm...eye candy,* she thought.

"Why don't we begin again? Garrett." He extended his hand.

She dropped her train and caught his hand. "Talise. Very nice to meet you," she offered.

His smile sparkled as they talked of the evening they were sure everyone found more of an obligation than an opportunity. Beguiled but destined to work the room she handed her card over and dared him to call her.

He did call. "Hello," Talise answered with a hangover lingering on her tongue. "Who? Who is this?" she asked twice. Finally frustrated, Garrett hung up the phone and Talise clutched her temples out of pain and embarrassment.

She shucked it off as a no-brainer until tonight. There Garrett stood talking to his comrades. She had done her research with Steffon of course and Garrett now stood between her and one of the biggest accounts of the year. Not only would it get K.J. off her back but also it would put the s in super marketing rep that she so craved.

"Garrett? Garrett, Talise Grimes. I'm not sure that you remember me but..."

"Umm, Talise Grimes," he pondered.

"Insurance night at the Waldorf," she graveled.

"Ohhh yeah. Talise. Of course I remember. You were running game and..."

"No. Just had a little too much champagne the night before, nothing more," she cut him off. *Time to eat crow.* "I just wondered if I could steal you away and talk to you for a minute."

"No time, baby girl, I'm 'bout to blow outta here," he said, turning back to his colleagues whose stares made her question if purple monkeys danced on her face.

"Excuse me," she said, boldly pulling him by the arm. "Listen, I'm really sorry about our last conversation. But can I talk to you for just a minute? We might be in a position to help each other," Talise pleaded.

He pulled out his electronic organizer, tapped around a bit and answered, "Thursday. I'll be here again at the Seaport. Maybe you can catch up with me then." He proceeded to walk away.

She stepped in front of him. "Thursday isn't good for me. In fact I'll be leaving for D.C. tomorrow and that's going to begin a string of travel. Please give me a chance. I'm sure it will benefit both of us. It's all business."

He looked her up and down with a sly attitude. She stood there like a puppy.

"Alright. I'm about to blow out to a spot in downtown Brooklyn called…"

"Dean Street," she replied.

"Smart cookie. I guess you know what's up, huh?"

"You could say that."

"Why don't you come with me? You have your car here?"

"I do but…"

"Don't worry about it. I'll drive and bring you back to your car. We can make a night of it."

Hesitantly she agreed. She excused herself to the ladies' room and agreed to meet him on the Water Street side of the building. He instructed her to look for a candy-apple-red Porsche.

Patiently she waited. And waited. And waited. Finally just as she resolved herself to being stood up, a noisy worn vehicle blew a sour horn in her face.

"Sorry for the wait. I had to start 'er up."

"You know I don't mind driving my car. It's right over—"

"Talise, let's not make this another insulting night. Hop in. We'll be fine."

She gave a reassuring smile.

They sped, with his prized possession chucking all the way. She tried to spark conversation concerning her true purpose but he politely let her know that this was not the time. *I hope some time tonight will be the right time. Shoot I have to go home and pack for tomorrow,* Talise thought.

He guided her by his arm into a jam-packed house full of R&B, catfish, collards and jerk chicken. He led her to a table near the front, much to the chagrin of other patrons already seated. *I guess he really does have pull.*

"I'll be right back. Do me a favor and order me a cold beer and something nice for yourself. Don't worry, the tab is on me." He stepped away.

She gave him a strange look and double-checked for her cash. She also made sure her credit card was in her wallet. *Just in case.*

The beer was cold and the rum was smooth. It was more than twenty minutes before she noticed his disappearance. Anxiously she continued to sip and enjoy the groove.

"Alright then. You started having a good time without me, I see," he said, obviously annoyed that her rum and Coke was almost depleted. "This beer is warm," he complained. He snapped for the waitress.

"If you hadn't taken so long in the bathroom, perhaps you would have caught it chilled," she said. She now noticed that his white Chinese-collared shirt was unbuttoned down to his navel. His wildly hairy chest did not turned her on.

"Where do you get these guys, Talise?" Calvin asked calling check on the board.

"Would you please listen to my story about last night? Checkmate."

"Damn," he said, rubbing his forehead.

"Anyway…" she said.

She tried to continue to enjoy the music. Two hours later she realized much wasn't to be accomplished in the area of work. So she sought to make the best of the evening.

The set had concluded when she intimated that she was hungry. "Uh, the kitchen is closed. They were closing the kitchen when I went to the bathroom," Garrett said.

"Then why is she seating that couple with two giant menus?"

He stuttered.

"It's okay. I'm ready to go. I have a long drive to D.C. tomorrow anyway."

The drive back over the bridge proved less fruitful than the drive there. Sensing her annoyance he took an unfamiliar detour toward the bridge skyline. He stopped the car, parked it and let a quiet storm of soft music continue to play.

"This is Brooklyn Heights."

She had to admit his voice was erotic.

"Uh, I know where we are. But I need you to take me back to my car."

He ignored her. He popped a tape into the dash. The Whispers sang out.

The Whispers? That's older than I even want to go back. Ugh. "This is really nice and all. And this is a great view, but I really don't want to have to tell you again to take me back to my car. I have family and friends in Brooklyn and I know where you work. Hit it, now," she snapped and popped the tape out of the dash.

He huffed and he puffed and tried to blow her house down, but she wasn't budging. She folded her arms and eyed the ignition with a vengeance.

He complied and the candy-apple-red wagon chugged along.

"I'm just curious," he said after five minutes of silence. "What did you need me for?"

She softened. She hoped she could still get in his good graces to at least secure a meeting with his boss for the major account she had been eyeing. "Honestly, Garrett, I was just hoping to meet your boss. You all have an account that I know my company could service well. I thought it would be a good opportunity for both of us."

He laughed.

"What's so funny?"

"You. I thought you were trying to hook me up with a gig. Please, I'm not even gonna be at my gig long. My boss hates me. I couldn't get a meeting for you, even if I wanted to." He laughed again as the Porsche stopped right on a dime, a block before her car. "This is it, darlin'. Peace," he said, motioning for her to get out.

She gladly obliged. Had the loud screeching noise he made not scared her to jump out of the way, she would have kissed the ground.

She walked toward her car with her key in hand. As she approached the blackbird as she affectionately called it, she heard a familiar sound. He had returned.

"Oh, and by the way, a date with you is like underwriting a bad risk!" he yelled and then screeched off again.

"It wasn't a date!" she yelled back through the smoke from his engine.

Calvin chuckled at Talise's story. "First of all, if the brother wanted to impress you he should have been turning a key into his place in Brooklyn Heights, not parked on some abandoned bridge overlooking it. Secondly, Talise, what were you thinking? Dates happen at night, not deals. If you weren't planning on giving up the goods, you should have made the *meeting* for a more reasonable time, like brunch, breakfast or lunch. God bless you." Calvin acknowledged her sneeze. He handed her his hanky. "Oh, let's go over here so I can whip you in backgammon." He led her to an oversize game table at the Grille Games restaurant.

"You didn't whip me at chess and you know BG is my game!" she shouted.

"BG?" he questioned.

"Backgammon. I just made it up. But it is my game."

"We'll see. God bless you. You getting a cold?"

"Either that or my allergies, I can't tell from one day to the next."

"Calvin Jones, party of two, your table is ready."

"I'll whip you later…" she flirted, kissing him on the cheek.

"I can't wait. Um-um."

"Cal. Cal Jones." The man's voice stopped them before they reached the table. "I thought that had to be you. Only one Cal Jones." The chubby short man greeted him. Calvin returned the greeting. "This is my wife." The man introduced an equally chubby woman. "Honey, this is Calvin. We went to Morehouse together." She smiled politely. The man extended his hand to Talise.

She tucked the soiled hanky in her purse. "Hi, I'm Talise." I would shake your hand but I think I'm coming down with a slight cold, and I would hate to spread my germs."

"I understand. Hey, are you all sitting there all by yourselves? Come on. Why don't you join us."

"Uh, that's okay. We'll just leave you two lovebirds by yourself, besides…"

"No, Cal, I insist. Besides you can't get enough food on that little table they gave you."

Humph. You two probably should try your best to fit into that table.

Talise could tell that Calvin was reading her mind. He smirked.

They graciously slid into the booth large enough for eight with barely enough room. But by the end of the evening, Talise was glad they joined Cal's buddies. They were a delightful couple with a great sense of humor.

"Girl, I have just the thing for that cold."

"I can't take anything hot. It's warm outside," Talise answered.

"No. This concoction is cool. Miss, may I have a large blue Hawaiian for me and a brandy Alexander for my friend. You guys want anything else?"

The drink was milky smooth and felt like silk on her throat. The brandy gave Talise a sense of security as she snuggled slightly closer to Calvin's arm. She now felt lightheaded and sleepy all at the same time. "I'm sorry to cut this short, but this concoction my new friend ordered for me is not keeping me awake," she said still clinging to his arm.

"Yeah, it's about that time," Calvin said, checking his watch. "Well good to see you, man. Nice meeting you. I'm gonna get her back home."

"So I'll see you at Silas' and Martha's affair next week?"

"Yep." Calvin shook his hand.

"Talise, will we be seeing you as well?" he innocently asked.

"Uh, uh…"

"Yes, she'll be there," Calvin answered.

"Great. See you guys there."

"Thanks for everything, Mary." *Aachoo.*

Mary winked. And the two couples walked off in separate directions.

"They were really nice," Talise said, swinging his arm as they walked hand in hand.

"Yeah. He was always cool in college. I know one thing though. He and his wife better stay away from that cake."

Talise cracked up. "I'm honored."

"About what?" he asked, placing the key in the lock and helping her into the car.

"That you have decided to let me escort you to your shindig, next week. I have to go find something to wear. I wasn't planning on it."

"Oh, oh yeah. Cool. I just need you to pick me up from the airport and we'll go straight from there. We can get changed in the hotel room. Don't be late. I'm a board member. Oh, and dress really nicely. This is a very formal affair," he said, closing her door. She continued to sneeze all way back to the room.

Jury's was a wonderful hotel right in the center of D.C.'s Dupont Circle. Calvin had the suite on the sixth floor, fit for a president. He headed straight for the shower, revealing his ever-so-sexy washboard torso. It never failed to send her soaring. Bared down, he disappeared behind the door, leaving his scent and sexy silk boxers.

She took in a deep breath and coughed. She stripped to her matching black lace bra and panties barely covering her hips and lay across the bed. The last sound she heard was the droplets of water behind the mirrored door.

What seemed like hours later, Calvin stepped into the room with a just a fluffy white towel draped across his waist. His glistening silhouette dripping in sensuality would have been all she needed to make her moist on a good day.

However, this was not a good day. Talise felt herself getting sicker. She was burning with fever, he noticed as he touched her damp forehead. And all she did was toss and turn across the bed. Instead of waking her, he grabbed a glass from the bar and retrieved a Tylenol packet from his briefcase. *This should break her fever.* He crushed the pills in the glass and ran cold sparkling water with a twist of lime in it. He gently shook her.

"No, no thanks. I don't want any," she mumbled.

"Drink this. You'll feel better. Trust me."

She did.

He then removed the remainder of her clothing and wrapped her in the kelly-green silk pajamas he brought everywhere. She barely noticed his movement. He grabbed extra blankets from the closet. After nestling her between them, he gently placed the extra comforter on top and tucked her in. She wrestled slightly. He dropped the towel and crawled in with her. He wrapped her in his arms, reached over, cut off the light and proceeded to hold her until the deep sleep caught them both.

"Steph, please pick up. I'm sorry. Please please pick up. I didn't mean any harm. It's just a matter of opinion, my opinion. No harm was meant."

She stood still listening to his message as Alec groveled on the phone.

"Come on. I know you're there. Please pick up. Okay, I really need to know if you are going to be able to make the fundraiser on the yacht."

"It's voice mail, silly. I can't hear when you're leaving a message," she said to herself. She cut off the groveling.

Just as she placed the phone down, it rang again. She decided to put him out of his misery.

"Hello," she answered with an air of sarcasm expecting Alec on the other end.

"Ms. Alphonso, please."

"This is she," she said with question in her voice.

"This is Dr. Baldwin's office…"

Her heart skipped a beat and landed straight in her toes. "Is this Dr. Baldwin?"

"Yes," she politely answered.

Oh, shit, the doctor only calls when there is a problem.

"Are you there, Ms. Alphonso?"

"Yes, yes, I'm here. There is a problem, isn't there? What is it?"

"I need for you to come into my office as soon as possible."

"No, tell me now. I want to know now. What is the problem, doctor? Am I sick? Just tell me," she screamed.

"You're a psychiatrist yourself, Ms. Alphonso, and you know that it's not wise for me to discuss your condition on the phone. I need you to come in as soon as possible. Do you have time today?"

"Don't give me that bullshit, just give it to me straight. Am I sick, dammit?"

"We don't know," the doctor said.

"What the hell do you mean you don't know. You took nearly a damn gallon of blood and you don't know!"

"The tests are inconclusive. We need to take more blood and run a few other tests. In fact we need to hospitalize you for observation. Can you come in today?"

"It's six o'clock at night. No, I can't come in today. I have to finish my jury duty out this week and I have to counsel a family of four on Friday. No, no, no. If you aren't sure, it can't be that bad," she reasoned.

"It might be and it might not be. But we need to discuss this in person, and we need to run more tests. Time is of the essence. The sooner we know, the better we can help you. Ms. Alphonso, be reasonable. Don't tie our hands here. You need to come in so we can…"

Stephanie didn't hear the end of the sentence because she hung up.

The phone rang again, and she yanked the cord out of the wall.

Her cell phone rang moments later. Without thinking she picked it up.

"Yes!" she demanded.

"Dr. Alphonso?"

"Yes!"

"This is Kanesha. I'm sorry to bother you on your day off, but I have an emergency here at the office. One of the other doctor's clients is in bad shape and the doctor is out of town on vacation and…"

"I'm not on call, Kanesha. Call someone else in the office or refer him to Greystone emergency staff."

"I tried that, but he's demanding that if he can't talk to her he wants to talk to someone else in the office and he specifically named you. He's threatening to kill his wife, children and himself if he doesn't talk to someone soon…I'm really sorry to bother you but…"

"Okay, okay, I'll be there." Stephanie wiped her forehead and noticed her eyes were soaked. "Get the file ready for me to review. Pull out the observation points and give me his number so I get him on the phone while I'm driving there. Got it?"

"Got it. How soon do you think you'll be here?"

"I'm about an hour away. I'll call you if I can." She snapped the phone closed. She ran to her open office and tore her desk apart looking for her micro tape recorder. She stuffed it in her bag, moving other necessary items including her stethoscope and syringes.

She grabbed everything and ran out the door straight into Alec.

"I can't talk to you right now, I have an emergency." She stormed passed him.

"Okay, I understand. Call me when you get back please."

"It might be late but I'll try." She slammed the door and sped off.

"So what are you going to wear?"

"Probably the black silk number I wore last year."

"Oh yes, that is nice. In fact come over, I have the perfect wrap. It's black lama faux fur."

"Why can't I wear your mink?"

"Because it's the end of October, I haven't even taken it from storage yet."

"Oh."

"So are you staying overnight?"

"Yes."

"Separate rooms, of course?"

"Of course."

"Good. You two have been friends for too long to mess it up. Don't go messing with that, Talise. It's not worth it."

"Yes, Mother."

"Don't 'yes, Mother' me. How's the job?"

"Yeah, how's my Wall Street executive doing?" Talise's father said in the background.

"Tell Daddy I said fine. You know a job is a job."

"You've taken a lot of time off lately. Don't blow that good job with those good benefits, Talise."

"Yes, Mother."

"Okay, darling. When are you coming to get the wrap?"

"Sometime this week. Leave it out in case you're not home, please."

"Just make sure you return it right away."

"Ma, don't I always?"

"No."

"Talk to you later."

"Love you."

"Love you too."

"And take care of that cold. You sound awful."

"I will."

"What are you still doing here?" Stephanie asked.

"Waiting for you. You have some dinner on the stove. I saved it for you," Alec answered.

She dropped everything at the front door and placed her shoes to the side. Not saying a word she sauntered over to the stove where an array of silver trays and white tops sat. "You cooked or you ordered?" she questioned, peeking into the pans. "Milano's." She answered her own question.

"Monica said to tell you hi. She's had your favorite Tiramisu coffee, hot and ready but she said you haven't been in the shop in the last few days."

"I'm on jury duty, remember," she said, picking at the cold veal piccota.

"Let me fix you a real plate." He led her back to the sofa. She didn't argue. She really didn't want to see him. She might have to look at the ever-widening differences between them.

"I missed you last week. I was hoping I didn't have to miss you Saturday as well," he said, pulling the cork on the Glass Mountain Chardonnay.

"I'd rather have the Merlot."

"Of course. So I was saying…"

"Alec, I'm not going to be able to make it Saturday. I'm just not feeling up to it," she said, wiping her brow. "Thank you." She accepted the glass of wine.

"Stephanie, we can't let this fester, and I really need you there. I'm sorry."

"Alec, you don't have to apologize for your feelings. But I want you to know that your view is sordid." She shifted her right leg underneath her. "My view is that, especially in the inner-city areas where you find defendants are usually people of color, a concerted effort should be made by people of color to accept jury-duty assignments. You are leaving the fate of these sometimes innocent victims in the hands of middle-class, self-absorbed America that believe they are supposed to fix people. These are self-righteous, pompous idiots who believe serving their country is by getting rid of the riff-raff out of the community. They use unfair stereotypes that can only be combated with diverse pools of jurors. For example on my panel, a non-English speaking gentleman is up on charges for allegedly fondling his grandchild.

"Now while I feel for the families because this has torn them apart, there is no concrete evidence of such. No doctor's reports of penetration or irritation. And the prosecutor is clearly trying to get a conviction based on emotion. We get back in the room and the deadlock comes from a man who says something happened so someone has to pay. He has now convinced four other jurors of the same theory, and we have to go back to somehow break the deadlock. The only other person on my side is another woman of color who agrees that you can't convict someone on the basis that something may have happened. Needless to say, I will not be voting guilty on this one. I don't care if we're deadlocked for a week." She finished her glass and got up to pour another one.

"Voila," he said, presenting her with a now hot veal piccota, warm bread and a side of seafood linguine. "I'm not saying you're wrong on the issue of diverse jury pools. I disagree with why people should serve.

Not to wrong some perceived blanket injustices but because as citizens it is our duty. Please sit. Let me serve you," he said, pulling her chair out.

"Now who is that?" she asked, getting up to answer the door. "It's after 11:30."

"Glenn. What in the hell are you doing back here? I told you never to come by here again," she said, trying to keep her voice low.

"We have to talk, Stephanie. I'm not leaving this time until we talk."

"Who's at the door, darling?" His breath was now on her neck. "Ahh, this is the gentleman I saw leaving here once before, isn't it? What business do you have here? You're upsetting her."

"Who is this?" Glenn questioned indignantly.

"Don't worry about who I am. Who are you?" Alec asked.

"No, you don't worry about who I am, White boy, yo you better step off before I…"

"Before you what? Use some brut force in a situation where you are clearly not wanted. Just try it, pal, and the only place you'll be communicating with my fiancée will be from the county jail."

"Fiancée?" they both questioned.

"Yes. You heard what I said, now you better leave before this goes farther than you are prepared to handle."

"Steph, I'm not trying to air your business, but I need to talk to you."

She raised her hand to bring some control to her day. "Glenn, I've said it once and I'll say it again. I don't know how you got my address but lose it. Don't ever come back here again!" she yelled and slammed the door.

"So when did I become your fiancée? Huh? Wanna clue me in?" Her eloquent vernacular was dropped.

The battle raged for about an hour. It was so hot neighbors knocked asking if they should call the police. Stephanie beckoned them off and the heat was on again.

"Don't tell me what I do and don't do. I have backup," he said, rustling through the inner pocket of his sport jacket. He tossed a small navy blue velvet box her way. Inside was the most brilliant solitaire in an antique engraved platinum setting she had ever seen. "I wanted to do this Saturday, but you've been avoiding me, and I can't lose this. It's more than three carats," he bragged.

"I'm not property, Alec!"

"When I say this, I mean what we have. I'm not referring to you as property."

"Yes, you were."

"Oh, I say black, you say white, I say tomato you say tomatoe. Why are you so contrary?"

"Don't you get it? That's the problem!"

The doorbell rang.

Here we go again. As if this night couldn't get any worse. Then she heard the voice.

"Stephanie, everything alright in there? I know you're here, I heard your voice. "Stephanie, everything alright." She banged on the door.

"Talise, I can't talk to you right now. I'm busy."

"Who's in there? Let me in. I need to talk to you."

"Talise, it's after midnight. It has to wait until the morning," she answered.

"Stephanie Alphonso, if you don't let me in this instant, you'll regret it. I'm not going anywhere. I said I need to talk to you." She banged.

"Alec, you have to go."

"What?" he asked incredulously.

"Please, we'll talk about this later but I can't leave her out there. I'm not ready for this, please. You have to go." She placed the box on the dining room table, grabbed his jacket and ushered him out the back door. He was stunned.

Talise still banged on the front door.

"Is there a full moon or what?" Stephanie asked herself.

"Thanks for all of your help," Gem said as she and the engineer from the studio walked out toward Broadway.

"How are you getting home?" he questioned.

"Subway to NJ Transit."

"Oh, you live in Jersey?" She nodded. "So do I. I have my car. Why don't I drop you off?"

"Where do you live in Jersey?"

"Weehawken."

"Near the Lincoln?"

He affirmed.

"Oh, thanks. I'm in South Orange. You would have to pass your house to get to mine. I wouldn't put you out of the way like that. There is nothing worse than passing your home on a late night like this and then having to backtrack."

"Actually I'm going to work in Orange so it wouldn't be a problem."

She recalled the last time she refused a car ride after a late session and how she ended up reaching the overnight train yard. So cautiously she agreed. They dodged the traffic across Forty-sixth to the garage. She noticed how well he must have tipped the guys in the garage to get their car before the line of other waiting patrons. They brought up a cobalt-blue, plush, lambskin-leathered Ford Explorer.

"Nice."

"One of my recent gifts to me."

"Always pays to treat yourself well."

He agreed.

The ride was so comfortable that Gem fell asleep before they hit the turnpike.

Her next memory was that of a family of squirrels meeting her at her front door.

"Whew. Thanks so much. Wow, you listen to instructions well. Sorry I nodded out on you."

"Yeah, you were drooling and everything, I hope you didn't ruin my seats," he joked.

"Ooh. I'm sorry. Send me the bill for cleaning. I'll be glad to pay for it."

"I was kidding, Gem. It really is okay. Have a good night," he said, coming around to open her door.

"Thanks again. And oh um, Vaughan, right?"

"Right."

"Will I be seeing you next week? Will and Robb set up a gig for me in the city. Are you part of the band?"

"How do you know I play?" he asked curiously.

"I can tell sexy saxophone lips from across the room," she said.

He blushed. "I would love to, but sorry you won't catch me on that gig. No offense, but studio time is more than I can handle with that management team of yours. Somebody is liable to get hurt with me hanging around them, and trust me it wouldn't be me." He subconsciously flexed his broad shoulders.

"Oh. Okay. Then take care. Maybe some other time then." She lumbered toward her front door.

"Gem, can I talk to you?"

"Depends on what you have to say."

"I don't know you that well and you certainly don't know me. You don't owe me anything. But you are incredible with a lot of talent. More than what I've seen since Gladys or Anita or Wincey, but…"

"But…look I'm not for constructive criticism tonight…"

"No. Just listen. Be careful with Will and Robb. I mean I'm not so sure if you know who or what you're mixed up with. I don't really know for sure, but I've seen some things. It makes me wonder why you are the fifth act in the last six months those cats have tried to groom."

"They're just building their repertoire. They told me about the other girls on the roster," she stated defensively.

"Yeah, but they are not on the roster anymore. Makes you wonder. Just be careful. Peace." He got back in his truck and pulled off.

CHAPTER 7

"You are going to look mahvelous!" They laughed as Talise danced in front of the mirror. "Oops, I'll be right back. Make yourself at home," Vanee said, obviously pleased with her work.

Talise continued to dance around in the shawl and shoes that were a perfect match for the dress she was to wear on Friday evening. She had practically lost all support in her quest to make her and Calvin an item. Stephanie disapproved with an iron fist. Gem promised not to hear anymore. Her parents suspected something but backed off with minimal old-time wisdom. And Vanee, her only friend on the subject, encouraged her to keep getting the best of it.

"You're gonna look great," Vanee added, re-entering the room with her daughter in tow. "What is this affair, anyway?"

"It's a formal celebration for one of Calvin's business partners, I think."

"You think?"

"Yeah." She twirled around.

"Don't you think you should know?" Vanee said.

"No. Why do I have to know? The most important thing is that Calvin and I will be there together. That's all I care about. What about accessories?"

"You really can get away with nothing on the neckline because of the diamond straps. Keep it simple. Just add some really nice diamond studs. How did you wear it last year?"

"Plain."

"Yeah, but you got a lot of compliments I heard. It was all over the office about how you stole the show. I'll be glad when I'm able to hang out for the company."

"Really? What are your plans?"

"I want to get into marketing, your end of the world. But my boss insists that I continue with these classes every other weeknight to prepare. The problem is her daddy ain't never around at night so that I can get done what I need to get done."

"But he's working hard on your behalf, right?"

Vanee thought before she answered. "Let's not talk about that. How is working for K.J.?"

"Okay, let's make a deal, I won't bring up your man and your woes and you don't bring up mine. Let me change out of this stuff before I mess it up. I'll give it back to you on Monday after the affair, I promise."

"Cool. I trust you. Besides I know where you live and work." They both laughed. "But seriously…"

Talise continued to undress.

"You know how my boss tells us everything."

"Yeah. He always keeps you in the loop."

"Yeah, he does. Well, you're not doing so hot in K.J.'s eyes. In fact, my boss is grooming me to take your spot in a year or so, if not sooner. I told him that I wanted to work with you, not take over but he says it doesn't matter because you aren't going to be there long enough at the rate you're going."

Talise sat in shock. She felt anger rising in her heart, partially because one of her dearest friends was telling her she was almost out of a new job and partly because she had been the topic of discussion at their clandestine supervisor's meetings. "So what are you saying, Vanee?"

"I'm saying this as a friend. My boss pulled me aside and told me in so many words to disassociate myself with you at work. He said for me not to be caught hanging out in your office because Dragon Breath reports everything. He said you are unorganized, sloppy and you haven't got a clue. He also said that since you aren't giving it up, you don't have a chance. I'm not trying to hurt you but I can't lie and deceive you about what's going on. You have to learn to work smarter and harder. No offense, I'm happy about you and Calvin, but you need less energy into Calvin and more into work or you are going to find yourself out."

Talise was speechless. In a daze she rolled the black dress up and placed it in the bag. She took the shoes, earrings and shawl she originally planned to borrow and handed them back to her friend.

"Now I'm not as well spoken as you but I'm gonna say this the best way I know how. If you want this job, you gotta fight for it. That's the bottom line. Name your terms and fight on your turf. I'm telling you or you gonna be eaten alive. Clean up your act. Organize yourself. Set goals, write them down and get 'em done, one by one. It's the only way. Now, take this stuff, give it to me when you're done and have a good time Friday."

Talise knew everything Vanee and everyone else had been saying was true. But in all honesty she knew that she didn't know how or where to go from there. She placed everything she had back in the bag with the dress and hugged Vanee tenderly for her friendship, honesty and integrity.

"Cut the mushy stuff. Now you go on home. I'll see you at work tomorrow with a new attitude. Got it?

"Got it!" Talise affirmed. "Ooh yeah. How do I get out of here?"

All Vanee could do was laugh.

Stephanie listened to the phone ring off the hook. At first it was her office who she thought finally got the hint. Then Gem and Talise picked up where the office left off. Finally it was Alec, and he wasn't getting the hint or taking no for an answer.

He practically banged her door down several nights in a row. She just sat there, practically held prisoner by her own woes. She had no energy to fix anyone else's.

The phone rang again. She noticed an unfamiliar number on the Caller ID. Just as she decided to pick it up, she reasoned that someone, particularly Alec, got smart and called from a different phone. He always knew how to get to her. So she let it ring. Silence. The silence that had been driving her mad finally prompted her to listen.

She picked up the receiver to a sound of several beeps that meant she had messages. When she accessed her special code, the ever-so-friendly recording advised her that she had thirteen new messages.

She sighed and followed the familiar prompts to retrieve her calls. She cut each one off until a voice pleaded for her contact. "Dr. Alphonso, this is no playing matter now. We need you to come in and discuss your condition immediately. This is not a game. I pray that you will not force me to send someone to your house. If I must I will discuss it with you over the phone. That is not my ideal option but you are leaving me no choice. I have beckoned your office to get in touch with you, and you are not returning any calls. Please, it is imperative that I speak with you today." The woman sighed and continued to reason with the answering service. "I don't normally do this, but this situation calls for drastic measures. My home phone number is…" Stephanie hung up the phone once again before she allowed the doctor to finish.

Damn that Glenn. Damn him for ever stepping to my stoop and damn him for stepping into my life. I can't believe there was ever a time that I worshipped the ground that man walked on, she thought shaking her head vigorously. She hoped to stop the impeding flood from her eyes. It didn't work. Sentimentally she retrieved her college yearbook from a desk drawer. She rubbed her fingers across the brass circles on the hardened leather cover. She opened the book and gasped at the signatures and well wishes for the smartest, wittiest and prettiest girl that roamed the campus in four years. She smiled at the candid photos of her and her friends, on the set chilling in their bright sorority colors. She smiled at a candid of Glenn and herself, the sweetheart couple of the year after he was pinned for his fraternity. It was an honor achieved only because she stood by his side. She frowned at the faces lurking in the background that waited for the utmost opportunity to capture her pride and joy. They were successful.

In the back of her mind she knew Glenn wasn't faithful. And even though she wasn't a trained psychologist at the time, she knew the term projection extremely well. Glenn embarrassed her in the middle of the yard. He had called her a degenerative whore of sorts. He promised to never step foot inside her door again or that "rancid pussy" she tried to call womanhood. She was so devastated that she couldn't put up a fight that ultimately her sorority sisters had to finish. Her sorors denied the entrance of a potential candidate for her. Even though in the end it was worth it, she promised to never revisit it again until now.

It started as an innocent trip to the campus clinic. She had been experiencing discharge and irritation for a week. "Why did it take you so long to see us, Stephanie?" the nurse practitioner asked as she viewed her chart.

"My schedule is extremely heavy. I'm carrying twenty-one credits this semester. I need to graduate on time," Stephanie proudly announced.

"Well your tight schedule has allowed your chlamydia to advance. How many partners do you have?" the plump lady in the white coat adjusted her bifocals and boldly questioned.

Indignantly Stephanie answered, "One. I have had only one for the last three years."

"Do the two of you use condoms?"

"Of course not. We are strictly monogamous. We talk about it all the time."

The woman sighed deeply. She wrote the prescription and handed it to Stephanie who was gathering her things to go. "I think you two should do a little more talking and for your sake, sweetheart, use condoms, always. You can't ever be too safe. You should also have him come in," she advised and proceeded to her next victim.

Stephanie decided against taking the campus bus down the hill to her dorm room. So along her trail she met with fourteen guys dressed in fatigues, marching to a familiar beat in full syncopation. They stopped short when they saw her.

"Greetings, most honored queen of..." She held up her hand to thwart the mandatory greeting she received from pledges.

"No greet. Please relax, fellas."

"Glenn, I need to talk to you. I can't talk here in front of your line brothers but I'll see you in calculus later. Oh, by the way, I left some food for all you in the trunk of your car. Don't miss class because we're having a test next week and it'll be too much for you to catch up on. I'll bring my tape recorder so you can review."

He nodded, fell back in line and trotted off with his future fraternity brothers.

"Skee-Oop." She heard the sound of the inter-sorority call from her dearest friend. Even though they had pledged separate organizations, the bond they created from the first day they stepped on the yard together had not changed.

"Where are you going, Miss Thing?"

"The pharmacy. You see the pledges up there."

"Yeah, I'm not going to mess with them today. I'm tired. Girl, did you see that review Dr. Proctor has for us? That test is going to be a mother of all mothers."

"I know. I told Glenn he better not miss class. He's getting carried away with this pledging thing. He has to put more effort into his work rather than becoming a brother."

"I'll say," her friend Dana said.

"Okay what is the sarcasm for?"

"Oh, nothing. Nothing. I'll walk with you to the pharmacy."

"Don't 'nothing, nothing' me. What's up?"

"You know I can't keep a secret from you, but you might want to start thinking about cutting Glenn loose. He's a cannon, girl."

"Dana, I'm not for gossip today…"

"This isn't gossip. Girl, Glenn is too wild for even the brothers. You know how they tell them to do things just to see if they'll do it?"

"Yeah."

"Well they started calling Glenn Mr. Do Right Anythang, because he does whatever they tell him even when they don't really mean it."

"What are you talking about?" Stephanie asked, handing her prescription over to the lady at the pharmacy counter.

"What's that prescription for?" Dana asked.

"Nunya."

"Please don't confirm that it's for some STD."

"Why would you assume that?" Stephanie asked.

"Anyway, last month, the bros had some visiting bros from another campus. They decided to throw a little party and it got real wild. It got so wild that our brothers had to break it up. You know that so-called sweetheart, the slut of all sluts? I think they call her Mo."

"Yeah. She's been after Glenn since we started here."

"Well apparently she got him. The brothers asked old girl to put on a show. And show she did. They convinced her to dance naked before everybody."

"Now I don't believe that," Stephanie said, taking the bag from the pharmacist. They proceeded toward Robeson Hall, named for the famed Paul Robeson.

"Believe it. Guess how they got her to do it? They told her to put a paper bag over her head so that no one would recognize her. When she finished her dance they dared the young pledges, Glenn included, to handle their business. Guess who was first?"

"Come on, Dana. Don't tell me."

"You got it. Now it's going around that the slut gave all the pledges and bros that bumped her an STD and they passed it on to their honeys. Lo and behold I see my best girl going to the pharmacy. You know I wasn't tryin' to be quiet about this one."

"Dana, I'm not listening to anymore of this filth. I'm not going to let you down Glenn like this. Now cut it out."

"You better start listening and you better start opening your eyes. Remember, I don't want him."

Stephanie had to admit that what Dana was saying could have some truth to it. She knew the pledge process and the off-campus brothers Dana spoke of. Not only that, the fact that she contracted anything, she knew had to have come from Glenn. She had been practically celibate since he started pledging with the exception of one night where she kidnapped him and gave him some for sustenance's sake.

It was a bright sunny day on the yard that all of Dana's revelations came true. Blatant and in the open Stephanie came upon Glenn slobbing down the very slut everyone rumored about. When she confronted them, Glenn didn't bother to budge. Names flew and tempers grew as she proceeded to school him about him not even making it on line if it were not for her. He retaliated by openly accusing her of giving him the STD they had to go to the clinic and have cured. The "we" stung the most as he referred to himself and the slut rather than his long union with Stephanie. Several brothers from the other campus who saw Stephanie creeping when she should have been sleeping, also confirmed this.

Dana, her boyfriend, Lance, as well as several of Stephanie's other sorors broke up the horror and escorted a devastated and distraught Stephanie back to her dorm room.

Lance reassured her that Glenn was just talking out of the side of his mouth, and by no means did anyone else in the brotherhood or on campus feel the way Glenn displayed. "He's sowing his oats right now. Give him time, he'll settle down," he said.

It wasn't a year after the incident that Glenn had come to his senses and a love struck Stephanie had taken him back. They lasted for some time after that, with Glenn following Stephanie up to New Jersey to start a better life.

But the final outcome was that Glenn and Stephanie were long gone.

Glenn hadn't graduated and had moved back to the Florida area. She painfully graduated and tried not think twice about him until she saw him once again, in a place and space she wasn't prepared to face.

"Damn that Glenn Barcliffe. Damn him." She grit her teeth and slammed the yearbook closed.

"I'm at Newark airport waiting for his plane to come in," Talise answered. "I know but this is the weekend and I'm going to enjoy it. We're going to some affair in South Jersey that we now have less than two hours to get to. I told you what she told me. Vanee said that her boss is after me. For whatever reason, he's grooming her to take my job, and she told me to cross every *t* and dot every *i*. Only my girl, would bother to tell me something like that. So if it's a fight her boss wants, it's a fight he's going to get. He's trying to sign a new agent to the roster but I'm voting no on the agency because they show no potential for new business. That should cool his heels for a minute. Ooh, look, Steff, I have to go, the police are out here ticketing folks for standing in the three-minute zone and Calvin hasn't come out yet, so I have to circle…yeah, I'll talk to you when I get back."

She hung up the bulky company phone and threw it on the backseat. Just as the police siren beckoned her to move on, she spotted Calvin.

"Cal, over here. She hit the automatic windows and beeped her horn." He spotted her, smiled and trotted her way.

"What happened? You were supposed to be here an hour ago."

"I know," he said, placing his garment bag in the back on top of the bulky phone. "I missed my first flight. Had business to take care of. Let's go," he said, positioning himself forward as if to give her directions.

She put the pedal to the metal and not long after, they were speeding down I-73.

They pulled up in front of a modest hotel. They entered the slightly more elaborate suite, which was adorned with plush crimson carpet and a king-size bed with sheers across the canopy and a royal-purple spread. The bedroom stood off the small living room, which had a fully stocked bar and big-screen television. *Not that we'll be watching much of this,* she thought. She slowly sauntered to the kitchenette, opened the refrigerator to reveal a bucket filled with a cold bottle of champagne adorned with a silk rose. COMPLIMENTS OF YOUR HOTEL STAFF, the placard read. "You don't have time for the grand tour," he advised, slapping her on the butt. "We don't have more than a half hour, and I'm not trying to be late so let's shower and change."

He practically had to fight her off him as she tried to forgo the evening for a night of passion. She didn't really care about the affair, but he did. After all, it was another opportunity for business. She finally got the hint and finished her shower, bathing herself in her luxurious Red by Giorgio perfumed shower gel.

She lavishly spread the matching body lotion all over, hoping to ignite a spark. Finally she added the body talc, sprinkling her most private areas to be explored later that night. He really approved.

Just as she finished putting the last touches on the soft big curls that lay across her forehead, they heard a knock on the door. "I'll get that and you finish dressing. It's probably my friend," Cal said. It was.

"So you gonna introduce me to the fine honey you been talking about?" she heard the strange voice ask.

She beamed. *So he's been talking about me,* she thought.

"She's finishing up now. You know how women are," Calvin answered.

"No, how are we?" Talise asked seductively, appearing behind him. "How are you? I'm Talise," she said, extending her hand.

"And I am pleased," the gentleman said, making her blush.

"Alright, alright stop slobbering all over my date." Calvin broke them up. She looked shocked at his description. "Y'all ready?" he asked, leading them out.

They followed Calvin's friend to the main ballroom several levels below their suite. What the outside may have lacked in grandeur, the inside of the main ballroom made up for. It was decorated like a Winter Wonderland. It was spectacular. There were floor-to-ceiling beveled mirrors, modern chandeliers and large tables with linen tablecloths. On each table sat grand antique candelabras laced with fragrant white roses, lilies and gardenias. The circular pattern of tables surrounded a dance floor that reminded Talise of a glass bottom boat. The transparent groove magnet revealed a band that seemed to have fun with or without an audience. She was impressed. *Now this is where you have a dream wedding,* she thought as she made her way toward one of the many waiters in red coats serving strawberry-topped flutes filled with bubbly and gigantic chilled shrimp.

"There you are," Cal said, making up for the fact that he had slipped away from her. She fed him her strawberry.

He caught the juice with his handkerchief. "Talise, this is Silas and his lovely wife, Margaret. They are the people responsible for this lovely affair and two of my dearest friends." Silas gave her a hug filled with warmth. Margaret stood back and studied Talise intently.

"Lovely gown. Versace original?" Margaret asked.

"No. Off-the-rack duplicate." Calvin, Silas and Talise were the only ones who got the joke.

"Darling, I need to mingle with a few other guests. Calvin, always a pleasure. I'll see you throughout the night. Tarveese…"

"It's Talise."

"Oh yes, of course, Tarzaneese, charmed I'm sure."

Well helloooo, crabby, Talise thought. She watched Margaret saunter off and greet some of her friends. Talise turned her attention back to Calvin and Silas.

"Yep, twenty years in the making, Cal. I feel like we made it. A lot of hard work and perseverance. I tell you, Margaret is some lady."

"Yeah, some lady," Talise sarcastically added, gulping down her last sip of champagne and trading her old glass for a new one.

"You know, she could have used her Harvard degree at some major firm, making a lot more money, but she chose to put her stake in this brother. It paid off, man. I couldn't ask for a better woman."

Yeah, you couldn't have asked for a better bitch, Talise thought as Silas led them around the room.

"Oh, Calvin, there are a few more clients here that I want you to make contact with. "Excuse us, Talise. I hope you don't mind."

"Of course she doesn't. Talise knows that nothing comes before business. Don't worry, she can handle her own," Calvin answered for her.

Actually I'd prefer you not to leave me with the vultures circling, she thought, eyeing Margaret and her obviously catty friends. "No, I don't mind," she lied. "I'll just go hang with your boy, that is if you don't mind, Calvin."

"No, just tell my man to keep his fingers tickling those ivories over there in the corner and make sure they don't land on you," Calvin playfully added before walking off.

"So what are you and Candace up to?"

Calvin was stunned at the question. It jolted his memory for the first time since he started these clandestine visits to New Jersey. But this group of friends knew the entire story. "Same ole. Same ole."

"So then what's up with you and Talise, from your end? I can tell what's on her end."

"What do you mean?"

"Man, her nose is wide open. Now what about yours?" Silas dug deeper.

"Same ole, same ole. I dig her. She has it going on but you know I can't take that next step with her yet. She still has some issues that I don't have the energy to solve. But you know she's not lacking by any means in areas Candace is…"

"I know Margaret and I were responsible for introducing you and Candace, but I like Talise. She has a lot of style and class. But don't mess over Candace, man. At some point you are going to have to choose. Two women are always too much work!" Silas said.

Talise made her way into the palatial ladies' room. Its dim lights reflected gold marble from the vanity mirror to the toilet and to the wash sink basin. Different fragrances, hair sprays and designer perfumed lotions adorned the countertop. The washroom attendant even had an assortment of products for the lady who may have forgotten an item.

"Well who knows what I may say when I see Candy next month during homecoming. Especially after I've had a few sips of champagne. Girl, this is some affair." Talise heard ladies speaking through the crack of the stall.

"I know what you mean. Humph, you know they have a suite together upstairs. Friend, my behind. She had the nerve to give me dirty looks. I wouldn't have been so nice had she not been with one of Silas' best friends. She don't know who she's dealing with."

"Y'all are worse than a bunch of hens," a voice reasoned.

"Come on, Dana, you know like I know, Cal ain't right."

"I'm not saying he is, but neither are we standing here talking about it. It's not like you all are Candace's friends, right?"

Silence.

"Yeah, because if you were, you would have to abide by the same principle. Let's see. How did Calvin and Candace meet? Hum. Your boy was cheating on his wife with Candace's sister, and we all happened to be at the same affair. Remember?"

"That's because we couldn't stand the witch and she got what she deserved. She cheated on him first," Margaret defended.

"Two wrongs don't make a right. And you all are not right. I'm not participating in this crap anymore tonight. I'm going to join my husband." The woman exited.

"All hail righteous Dana!" The two ladies laughed. "You know we called her big sister Holy, Holy, Holy…behind her back of course. She was always encouraging us to take the high road."

"I'm sure."

"I don't care what she says, I'm going to make sure that that little slut does not work her way into Cal's grips whether he's with Candace or not. There's just somethin' 'bout her. Can't put my finger on it but somethin' 'bout her…"

"Excuse me, ladies." Talise stepped out of the stall. She washed her hands. The attendant stood silently, picking up on what was going on. She handed Talise a cloth to dry her hands. Talise picked up her miniature beaded purse, and turned, "…you ladies do have a lovely evening. Oh, and Margaret, you and Silas have put together a lovely affair." Talise allowed the bag's long straps to extend, and she slung it over her shoulder, tipped her head and stepped out.

"Talise, is Margaret in there? They're beginning the meal and requesting our presence on the dais."

"Oh, she's in there alright. I'm sure she'll be out momentarily." With that she captured Calvin's arm and he led her to their table.

"There you are. We're starting. What's wrong? You look like you swallowed a mouse," Silas said, escorting Margaret to the front. She continued to smile for the arousing crowd.

"Trust me I did. I'll explain later." She continued to smile.

He hugged her generously as the tribute began.

Talise joined Calvin in the center and gave a sinister smirk barely affording a decent applause.

Gem had taken her final bow on her third encore. She wowed the audience so that one woman approached her almost in tears before she could retreat to her dressing room. "I was feeling so down before I came here. I wasn't supposed to come, but that voice, you just lifted me up. God bless you, my sister. Much success to you," the woman said, leaving Gem in a state of gratitude.

Gem opened the door to her makeshift dressing room. Slowly she relished in taking off the heavy stage makeup which felt like paste under the hot lights. She tossed her hair for a wild natural look, unlike the Toni Braxton short style her managers had paid so dearly for. Her solace wasn't to last for long. Just as she peeled the last layer of makeup away, Will burst through the door without knocking.

"I have someone you need to meet."

"I hope it's that A&R from one of the three major record labels you promised," she said, angry at herself for not addressing his intrusion.

"You could say that, dahling. May I present Mr. Steffon Bryant, A&R for Honey Graham records."

"Nice to meet you. You tore that stage up, babygirl."

"Thanks." Gem hesitantly shook his hand. She viewed him from the tip of his head to almost the sole of his feet. "S-Steffon?" she stuttered.

"Yes. That's me. I'm here to represent Mr. Jerome "Romy" Graham. I know he'll be pleased when you sing for him in person." He handed her his card.

"Excuse me? Sing for him in person?"

"Yeah. Will here promised that you wouldn't have a problem auditioning for Romy in person."

"Auditioning. Will, what is he talking about?" Gem asked.

Will cleared his throat. "Well, Romy couldn't make it tonight. I told Steffon here, that if you passed his approval he could present you before Romy in his office. This is a new startup label. Romy could rival the next P. Diddy and you could be his Faith," Will said, focusing his attention on Steffon.

Steffon stroked his goatee. "Like I said, I like your style. Gotta couple of things we could work on but all in all…"

She completely cut him off. "Mr. Bryant? That's what you said your name is, right?" He nodded. "Do you have any experience in the music business?"

"What's your point?"

"My point is that I don't need a wanna-be music exec who doesn't know the difference between a treble and clef much less a record label that doesn't exist, telling me how he needs to work on things. I have been doing this for my entire life. Probably longer than you've been off your mama's milk. Thanks but no thanks…" she said, handing his card back.

Steffon started to go old school on her but he was traveling a different route. He knew Romy wouldn't be pleased with him bringing his old gang tactics into this new business situation. He shrugged, stroked his goatee one last time and said, "Cool. If that's how you livin', playa." He turned and gave Will a handshake and stepped off. "You know how to contact us if you change your mind." He stepped out of the dressing room.

"What is your problem? Why are you trying to sabotage everything we've worked for?"

"First of all I told you about using that tone with me. Don't you ever speak that way to me again. I'm tired, Will. I'm tired of your demands and you and Robb acting like you are the only ones making sacrifices here. I have been with you for months now. Half a year to be exact and have yet to see the fruits of my labor. You got me playing in these half-behind clubs with no potential and no dressing room and nothing you say comes true. This person is going to see me tonight and that person is coming to see me another night, and it never happens. I'm starting to think that you really don't have any contacts. Then you show up with this makeshift wanna-be record exec who's not much older than me and still has his mama's milk on his breath as a representative for a record company that doesn't even have a valid address. I said it once, and I will say it no more, don't ever, ever use that language with me again, and I guarantee with all my heart, if something doesn't change you'll be finding another dynamite singer with potential that you can go places with."

"Don't threaten me, you little—"

"Watch it. I'm warning you. Watch it."

"Success doesn't come overnight. Don't think I—we haven't risked a healthy sum of money on you, Miss Diva. It takes time. You have to produce the right sound at the right time in front of the right people. And I—" his voice escalated—"I am making that happen!"

"I know that it takes time, but you aren't doing anything for me I hadn't been doing for myself. I can book my own gigs in these dinner clubs and places. I have been doing it for more than five years now." She stood. "Now you are playing by my rules, either you get things going or I'm gone."

"Are you threatening me?"

"Oh, trust me, Will, dahling, it's not a threat, it's a promise. You have six months to get this thing off the ground with a legitimate record company and representation. Legitimate. I'm not stupid. I know what's happening in the streets. You got a bunch of thugs like Romy Graham trying to become legit and funnel their drug and gang money into something or someone else. I'm not the one. I'm not taking your language or your abuse any longer. I'm not working my butt off for you to trash me rather than support me. That's it. Now leave."

"What?"

"You heard me. Leave." She sat and resumed taking off her makeup.

Furious, he obliged.

"So how did you enjoy the evening?" Calvin questioned.

"Dreamy. Thank you so much."

"For what?" he asked, pressing the elevator button to go up.

"An absolutely wonderful evening. I felt like Cindy…" She twirled.

"Who in the hell is Cindy, Tal?"

"Cinderella, silly. With a soul twist." She snapped her fingers in a Z formation. "I need to go to the ladies' room."

"Can't it wait?" he asked under his breath.

"No." She darted off. She entered the bathroom to the sounds of sniffles and a whimper. "Hello, anyone in here?" The sound grew silent. Talise walked upon the same woman who had been in the bathroom earlier. "Ooh. It can't be this bad. What's wrong?" she questioned as she handed her a wad of tissue.

"Thanks."

"Dana?"

"Yes. How do you know my name?" she asked, patting her now swollen eyes in the mirror.

"Not for anything, I saw you in the bathroom earlier when Margaret and that other woman were actin' like a bunch of cackling hens, to quote your words exactly. I just wanted to say thanks for standing up for me like that."

Dana turned around like a dart shooting the most venomous of arrows. "Standing up for you like what?"

"You know, telling them they needed to mind their business and all. I really appreciate it. I wish more sisters would stand up for one another rather than tearing one another down."

"Well I wish more of us sisters would respect ourselves and other people's property."

"I was just saying..."

"Save it, sister. I know what you were saying. Don't you know that men will only treat you the way you demand to be treated? Men only do what we allow. They don't cheat unless they have someone to cheat with. Let me tell you something. I don't know you and frankly after this conversation won't ever care to. I wasn't standing up for you, I was standing up for the situation. They had no right to talk about either of you or Candace like that because they didn't have the other woman's best interest at heart. They were just gossiping, which doesn't serve anyone. Personally, I don't endorse or condone your behavior. Calvin may not be married to Candace but he is in a relationship with her and has been for years—good, bad or indifferent. But they don't need you coming along to help with the decision process. So please don't give me that sister bull. Until we learn the true meaning of sisterhood and that it is not just a bunch of rhetoric we won't be able to promote healing in our communities and most importantly with ourselves. You remember that, sista." In one swift mood, Dana scooped up her belongings, placed them in her purse and walked out.

Talise started to tell her that only half of her lipstick had been applied but then she thought, *let the heifer go out looking like a clown. I think I just got told off.*

The washroom attendant appeared from nowhere and handed her a towel. She gave her a look of agreement. It was as if she said, you did get told off, lady, and real good at that. Talise snatched the towel and didn't bother to leave a tip.

"You okay?" Calvin asked, seeing her frazzled.

"Yeah, let's just go." She punched the up elevator button.

"What's wrong with you?"

"Nothing, just nothing." She stood tapping her foot with her arms crossed. The elevator couldn't have come a second sooner. She pressed the close-door button before anyone else could enter.

"That was rude."

"Yeah, whatever."

With fierce passion Calvin pulled her toward him. He squeezed her breasts and worked her dress up to her curvaceous but compact hips. He reached underneath her dress and had no problem finding her wet spot.

"Very nice garter..." he said as she moaned. He fondled and entered her with his finger. He pressed his body against hers and lifted her legs. He set her on top of his hips as he unzipped his pants. He entered with hard thrusts and then teased her slightly until the elevator alarm startled them. Accidentally, the stop button had been hit. The elevator moved again quickly, and she hopped down off his hips to fix her clothing.

He could barely place his manhood back in his shorts so he tried to cover his trousers with his hands as they ran toward their room. But the moment the door was opened, anything and everything that remotely resembled fabric hit the floor. They kissed, they groped, and he led her to the bed.

She reversed the position by flipping herself on top. She then pulled her overnight bag from under the bed and pulled out a small bottle of Hershey's chocolate syrup. *Ooh, boy, you don't know what I'm about to do to you,* she thought. She poured chocolate all over his body, slowly and deliberately. She then licked every inch.

He rolled her over and smeared her body. He also had a few tricks up his sleeve. He reached under the other side of the bed and pulled out a small bottle of red gel. It smelled like strawberry. He poured it over each nipple and tasted each one. After exploring her body, he gently turned her over and massaged her round buttocks with his smooth large palms. He continued to massage her with his tongue as well until he reached her backside and the tip of her spine. She screamed in ecstasy. He then gently penetrated her from the back and rocked her into desire. He flipped her over exploring her from the front. He rocked and rocked and rocked and rocked. From midnight until nine the next morning, they rocked and rolled, only taking brief intervals for rest.

The next morning the two woke to blissful exhaustion.

"Where are you going?" she questioned as she rolled over to the empty side of the bed. The silhouette of Calvin's sleek brown body beckoned her to the shower where the passion began all over again. That very moment she declared love. She was in love with him, and by his very actions she knew he was in love with her.

Chapter 8

"Who are you calling?" Steffon questioned as he headed toward the Long Island suburb of Hempstead.

"Calvin. I haven't talked to him in weeks."

"Not on my phone."

"Steff," she whined.

"I'm not playing. Put it down, Talise. Besides we got other business to take of. That's your problem: you focusing on that nigga's dick rather than handling your business."

"Thank you for your concern."

"I'm serious," he said, picking up speed. He dipped and dodged his way around cars.

"How did you find these guys, anyway." She hit the end button on the phone.

"I got connections. You lucky I'm passing them onto you. They're a good firm. And I'm not going to be around much longer to help you out, so take heed," he said, watching his mirrors. He sped up once again trying his best to take her company-issued blackbird passed the legal limit.

"Where are you going?" she asked.

"Between me and you?" He eyed her suspiciously.

"Always," she confirmed. Outside of her love for Calvin, Steffon had now inched his way up as her utmost confidant. Their friendship was blossoming during Calvin's mysterious disappearance.

"I'm working on this deal. I've been checking this singer out that this company is trying to sign. She's bad and if we can get her signed with a bunch of other folks, the record company will be on its way and Great Raritan will be history." He dodged a red Viper taking up road space on his way to the exit. "Pull out the map so I can see where we need to go."

"Oh, the office is on the main street. So you say we would be this office's first major account, huh?"

"Yep. They're a group of sharp young brothers looking to place some profitable business all over New York, but particularly the Black community, an area I know K.J. is trying to penetrate."

"How do you know so much?"

"Because I listen and I read."

Still disinterested she began to map their local route. "I know a great singer who would be good for your company."

"Everybody knows a singer, Talise. Where you know her from? Your mamma's best friend's church choir?" He laughed and maneuvered them into more traffic he couldn't shake. He rested at the light.

"No. She's really good. She's done commercial jingles and everything," Talise said. "Her name is Gem."

"Did you say Gem?"

"What the heck is your problem?" she asked, calming herself after almost going through the window. He slowed the car to an almost haunting stop. "Yeah, I said Gem. She's one of my best friends."

"Oh, snap! Talise, you gotta get me in," he said excitedly.

"Green means go, Steff," she reminded him as cars honked behind them. "Get you in what? Oh, there it is." She pointed out the office building. "Good sign, it's not a storefront."

He pulled into the parking lot. "They even have their own spaces. Steff, you have found me a gold mine," she said, showing interest for the first time since their journey began. He turned off the ignition.

"Talise, I been there for you. Now you gotta help me."

"Whatever you want, shoot," she said, removing her seat belt. She pulled her briefcase from the backseat.

"Tal, now I'm hooking you up with this agent who I know will put you in K.J.'s good graces. You have to promise me that you'll hook me up with Gem. She's the singer I been scoping. We tryin' to get her signed. She's a tough nut to crack."

"Oh, that's easy. I can hook you up. I can almost promise that she'll sign with you too. That's her dream to have a deal."

"Tal, that'll be cool. When you think you can come through?" he questioned anxiously.

"Easily by the end of the week. This deal is putty," she assured.

"Cool. Cool," he said, calming down. "I love you, girl!" He grabbed her and kissed her. "Now let's go show them Great Raritan's finest," he said, making no mention of his action. She followed him, stunned.

Stephanie's three-plus carats held her gaze almost the entire night. She still hadn't given Alec an answer but he assumed she had. She walked around the yacht, which provided a spectacular view of the private Catalina Islands of Jamaica all evening long, courtesy of his dad and their Friends to Elect Alec campaign. He was caught politicking in every corner while she smiled and made nice.

"Stephanie, meet this one. Stephanie, meet that one." Her face was tired from grinning. She really didn't know what to say at this point. She thought it best to keep making nice.

The cool breeze and Bordeaux made her shiver, so she stepped below to catch a break. "A warmed cognac to soothe the bones?" the bartender asked.

"No thanks. If I drink any of that, I'm not sure I'll make it back to shore with or without the boat." She smiled again. This time it was genuine. "But thanks for asking."

"I have something special, if you'd like. You look cold."

"I am but alcohol, particularly strong alcohol, gives one a false sense of security and I've had enough of that for the evening. Besides I'm not feeling well." She pulled her wrap closer.

"Then this will really warm those bones. Don't worry, it's an Old Irish recipe. I'll have ya fixed up in no time flat," the bartender added with an accent straight from Ireland. "Try this." He handed her the snifter full of the deep purple liquid. It seemed to warm her the moment it graced her tongue.

"Whoa. This is nice. What's in this?" she asked, looking at it admirably.

"Now if I told you, I'd have to kill you. And considering the security in this place, I'm not sure it would be such a good idea." He chuckled and returned to rinsing his glassware. "So what brings you aboard, other than the fact that you must have substantial voting clout or funds to back it up?"

"I'm here in support of a friend," she said, casually, enjoying his concoction.

"There you are, darling. What is this you're drinking?" Alec grabbed her unfinished glass and placed it on the bar. "Come, my father has an announcement." He grabbed her off her comfortable high chair with its full leatherback cushion and led her to the other side of the large room.

"Stephanie, Alec, front and center please," Alec's father called. The white-coated waiter handed them each a glass of bubbly. "I'd like to propose a toast," he began. Stephanie, now tipsy from her drink, tried to remain focused and poised. "I must say, when this all began, I was a little skeptical. A parent only wants the best for his child. Well you can't imagine how pleased Alec's mom—God rest her soul—and I were when he announced his contingency for candidacy in New Jersey. I thought, *he's following in my footsteps*. Well after undergrad woes and post-grad bills..."

The crowd shared a laugh.

"...I started to wonder. Frankly, taking after his mom, I started to worry that Alec hadn't yet picked the caliber of wife we knew to be a help-mate of sorts..."

Oh, get on with it please, Stephanie thought as she prepared herself to double over from the waves and the bull.

"Anyway, I'm getting off the beaten track as usual. When I met and married my wife some forty-five years prior and had our only beloved son, it was our prayer that Alec stood for what he believed and that he found a mate to help propel that belief. Well friends, colleagues and family, I believe that prayer has been answered. Please welcome the soon-to-be newest addition to our legacy, Dr. Stephanie Alphonso. Alec and Stephanie will be wed in the most elaborate ceremony some six months from now. Please, ladies and gentlemen, welcome her kindly."

Applause and flashes of light flew before her brow. The next time she heard the sound of someone's voice was when Alec was placing a damp rag over her head, begging her to wake up and be okay.

"What were you drinking that made you pass out like that?" he asked.

"What? What are you talking about?" she asked, propping herself up to the best of her ability. Her pounding headache forced her back down. "I wasn't drinking much. I nursed that one glass of wine for about two hours."

"But you were drinking something else when I found you." He continued to fan.

Oh, that's right. Oh, she thought as she grabbed her head. She prayed that the engagement announcement she had heard was only a dream. She looked down at her hand to see the glistening of the rock that made her know that not only what transpired was not a dream but a nightmare.

"Alec, we need to talk about this. I'm not sure we're ready…"

He fanned faster. "Not now, darling, we'll talk about this when you're well." He spoke in a condescending tone. "No more pictures please. She's fine. Dad, Dad, please escort these reporters out of here. She needs air."

"Reporters, what?" She coughed. "Alec, I'm going home. This is too much."

"Don't worry, darling. I'll have arrangements made. You'll be flown off of the island on the jet tomorrow."

"No, Alec. I'm not feeling well and I want to go home tonight!" she demanded.

"Quarrel in paradise. Can't wait for the television headlines, Alec, *Fiancée Faints at Announcement of Engagement…Details at Eleven.*"

"Okay enough. You print one word of that trash, and I'll make sure that you are not deemed credible enough to carry it much less report on it," his father announced. The reporter left in a huff.

"Thank you so kindly, Mr. …" Stephanie said.

"Oh, you can call me Dad," Alec's father said.

Stephanie grunted not knowing what to say next. "I'm not feeling well at all, and I really need to go home. Is there any way you can arrange for my flight tonight?" She overrode Alec, for once.

"Sure, if it's mandatory, I mean…"

"Trust me, it is. Besides I have a few clients that I must tend to."

Just slightly after midnight Stephanie found herself stretched out in the plush leather sleeper seats of a private jet on her way home. The sole flight attendant on board asked her to sit back, relax and enjoy her four-hour nonstop ride to Jersey. "Do you need anything?" the flight attendant questioned.

Stephanie answered, "A reason." *And I have less than four hours to think of one,* she thought. "May I use the telephone?"

"As soon as we're airborne, I'll bring it to you." The flight attendant strapped herself in her seat. The attendant then gave her a sympathetic look.

"No, Talise. Not even for you. I'm not doing it."

"But this is your chance to get everything you've ever wanted. A deal, Gem, a deal."

"Not with that thug wanna-be record exec. No and stop questioning me. That's my final answer."

Talise stopped leafing through her dresses. She wanted to look stunned but Gem wasn't paying her any attention. She couldn't believe that Gem of all people was about to let an ideal situation slip through her fingertips.

"But Gem…" She still fought to convince her.

"You know, you are pressing me harder than Will and Robb."

"Your managers, right? How is that working out?"

"Yeah. It's not. In fact I haven't heard from them in weeks. Not since my last blowout at the concert with Will who introduced me to your thug friend Steffon Brian."

"He's not a thug, and his name is Bryant. He's a good guy, Gem, and he helps me all the time. You need to rethink his offer."

"I said it once, I said it twice. They are not the type of representation I'm looking for. I'm not the next ghetto diva. I want a classy label with some producers with a track record. Now either you're here to help me find some suitable outfits for my next gig or you are welcome to leave."

Talise just rolled her eyes and continued looking at dresses. She really wanted to help Steffon. She promised him, and he always came through for her. *Oh, well, I tried.* "Hey, what about this one?"

"Now you're talking. Hand it over."

"Can I use your phone?" Talise asked. Gem nodded and pointed her toward the white slimline phone.

"It's on the other side of the vanity," Gem declared.

It rang and rang and rang. Finally the disturbed look on her face revealed that the other party obviously wasn't answering. "Cal, this is Talise again. We keep missing each other. I'm at my girlfriend Gem's house for a while. You can give me a call here for the next few hours. Otherwise call me at home. Miss you. Talk to you later. T."

"I know you have lost your ever-living mind now."

"What? What?" she questioned, resuming her search for Gem's perfect outfit.

"Talise, you know better than that, and if you don't I'm about to school you. Sit down.

"Whenever you find a man playing phone tag that is a definite sign. He knows how to find you if he needs to and giving him your every move, like giving him the option to call you here is not smart."

"It's not like that. He calls me in the office and at home, but I've been working on this account with Steff and..."

"When was the last time you two actually spoke, at length?"

It wasn't long before Talise realized that they hadn't had a real conversation in weeks—since the affair in South Jersey. She also remembered that Calvin acted quite odd the morning after and just before she dropped him off at the airport. Almost preoccupied. And he had the nerve to call Candace to tell her that he was on his way home and to please pick him up. She had to admit something was strange but she wasn't giving up on her new chance at happiness.

"A couple of weeks," she finally answered.

"You told him you love him, didn't you?"

"No," she lied.

"Okay. I'm just saying, Talise, that man is not losing it for you the way you've lost it for him. And what's up with Steffon?"

"Okay, Dr. Stephanie, full of questions tonight. Ain't nothin' up with me and Steffon."

"Steffon and me."

"Whatever. We're just friends. He helps me out."

"Um-hum. He'll be collecting on that soon too. Just wait," Gem said. She parted the white sheers over her bed and jumped through to the other side to get her ringing phone.

Talise had completed her scanning of the closet and moved to the rack of shoes. *She must have 150 pairs in here.* "Who was that?" she asked Gem after she hung up.

"Speak of the angel, and she shall appear..."

"Who?"

"Stephanie. She appeared on the phone anyway."

"Speaking of that buzzard, I've called her for the last few days and she hasn't returned my calls either. Where is she?" Talise asked.

"Right now she's on a private jet on her way home."

"Huh? Ooh, Gem these are the shoes, girl."

"Yeah, yeah, yeah. She needs to meet with us as soon as possible. She wants us to meet her for lunch at Je's tomorrow. She said this is the most serious girlfriend alert yet."

"What's wrong with you?" Talise asked, trying Gem's slightly larger shoe on her foot.

"She didn't sound good at all. Something's wrong."

"It's okay, we'll see tomor—oh, wait a minute," she stopped herself. "I can't meet tomorrow. That agency that Steffon hooked me up with is coming to meet the management panel at the job. I have to be there. I can't meet tomorrow. At all. You'll just have to pass the info on to me later. And where is she coming from? Who's jet? I didn't know her clientele escalated to that point."

"Jamaica."

"Jamaica what?" Talise asked, still not paying full attention.

"That's where she's coming from, silly, and she said she'll explain everything tomorrow. So you better find a way to be there. If not for lunch then we'll meet at her place tomorrow night. Got it? And take your crusty foot out of my shoe. You're right though, these are some bad shoes and they'll go perfect with my outfit. I knew you were good for something...."

"Man, you better start making some better choices. I'm telling you the more time you spend with a woman, the more dangerously she becomes attached, no matter what she's saying on the outside. You playing with fire, Cal, and man, you 'bout to hit thirty, you getting too old for these games. Now I'm not telling you whom to choose, 'cause you got a heavy one but you better choose something or you will be the loser, mark my words."

Silas' speech trailed in his mind.

"Hennessy on the rocks with the lemon spread around the rim, sir." The redhead with a complexion as sweet as cane sugar handed him the glass.

He had spent a week in the Northeast and didn't bother to call Talise. He needed some space to breathe and sort out what everyone seemed to be saying, including his own conscience.

"Whoa, I'm not finished with that." He placed his hand over the rim.

"I'm sorry, sir, I'll be sure to give you a fresh one in flight. We're about to take off."

He took a final swallow, noticing her very tall, slender frame and long, sensual fingers. Her dusty-red hair was cropped very short. Her matching red freckles danced like diamonds on her face.

The first Hennessy had taken its toll. The words *high maintenance* ran through his mind as the plane safely ascended beyond the clouds. He didn't notice that the redhead stood before him with his freshly made drink.

"Aren't you deep in thought? Is there anything else I can get you?"

"Uh, no. I'm okay. Thanks."

"Are you sure you're okay? You seem troubled?"

"No. I'm not okay." Calvin was shocked at his own candor.

"Oh, what can I get you?"

"An answer."

"Female problems, huh?"

"How can you tell?"

"Just always can. Listen, let me finish serving the rest of my passengers their drinks and you can come and talk to me in the galley area while I set up."

"Okay," he said as she walked off, giving that sparkling smile away to the others. He pulled out his notebook computer to review his strategy for his upcoming sessions in New Orleans.

She noticed him typing away. "You type pretty fast for a guy."

"Actually I do. I was up to about eighty words a minute at one time. You ready for me?"

"Sure am," she said, beckoning him to follow her.

He slipped out of his seat, leaving his laptop resting on his tray table. He propped himself against the flight-deck door.

"I'm Diamond, by the way." She extended her left hand.

"As in the ice on that finger of yours?"

"You could say that. So is that little filly you're going to see in Atlanta?"

"Oh no. Actually Jersey and well Charlotte. I'm going to Atlanta on business. There's a commerce fair going on in Buckhead."

"I'll be there as well for my fiancé."

"Businessman, huh?"

"You could say that. He's expanding. The new flux of business there is tremendous, with the record industry and all. Everyone is there now from LaFace to Elton John."

"You can say that again, Hotlanta is happening. You don't only have the music scene but the sports folk, general entertainers, movie industry and politicians moving into the area. Plus the industry that is generated just from average folks is booming as well. Hotlanta is the best move."

"You seem to know a lot about the area," she said, popping some bread in the oven. "It's the place to be. Money attracts money, my fiancé always says." Another flight attendant joined her. "This is my friend…"

"Calvin." He helped her out and extended his hand.

"Nice to meet you," the attendant said.

"So being a stewardess must be synonymous with being gorgeous," Calvin said, flirting.

"Now you were making points until you made that comment."

He tried to figure out how he made a mistake. It was his business to market. And marketing himself first was almost instinctual.

Diamond passed the trays out to the returning flight attendant to deliver.

"So what does your husband do?"

"Mistake number two, not listening. I see why you're having problems. Here you go, sweetie," she said, handing over the wine for delivery.

"Okay, help me out. I'm lost."

"I can tell. Number one, the correct term is flight attendant. Personally I appreciate flight service manager but I'll let you slide with attendant. Number two, if you were listening I said fiancé. I did not say husband. But I'll let you slide on that one too. Sack has been like my husband for the last five years. So what do you do?"

He handed her a card with grainy taupe background and navy blue embossed lettering. She studied it carefully.

"The Jones Group. We're market consultants. We're independent consultants."

"Hmm. Not bad."

"So…?"

"Yes," she said, continuing with her service.

"What does your hus—fiancé do?"

"Smart of you to get back on the subject. He owns a limousine corporation."

He rubbed his forehead, recalling her mentioning a familiar name. "Sa…Sack…St. Clair Hughes. Diamond, St. Clair better known as Sack

Hughes, is your fiancé?" he asked. "He's trying to penetrate a marketplace I know well and already have contacts in industry and commerce as well as the mayor's office. I would love an opportunity to speak with him about it."

She passed out the last tray of food. "Wouldn't you like to eat first?"

"Trust me, this conversation is like food to my soul. Let me show you what I'm working on. It'll give you a little confidence in my ability to sell St. Clair on the Jones Group."

"Calm down. I'll do my best to make your meeting happen on one condition."

"Almost anything. I'll bear your firstborn if it's humanly possible."

"It's not." She laughed. "But you have to tell me what was aching you earlier."

"Well, Diamond…I have this friend…two friends…" he began. Candidly he told her everything. He told her about Candace and her character but their extreme lack of sexual and emotional compatibility. He then told her about Talise's compatibility in the bedroom but lack of security emotionally. He tried his best not to present himself as a player but he knew if he acted too cool, as smart as Diamond had already proved herself to be, she would pick up on it. So he went for the subtle route. She seemed to buy it because she listened intently.

She was the perfect sounding board. She didn't utter a word, occasionally raising her brow at critical points and nodding. It was almost twenty minutes later when he finished.

"I admit, you're right."

"About Talise not handling her emotions properly?" he asked, now sipping a beer.

"No, about you crossing the line and making a mess. You led her on, Calvin." She began cleaning up the galley in preparation for landing. "You've spent valuable time with her, and contrary to what men believe, actions speak louder than words. Now you have major damage control. Can I be straight?"

"Please."

"You seem rare. I mean you're young but you seem to need to be involved with women on some level. Nothing wrong with that. I don't know what I'd do without my Sack. But sincerely you have to figure out what you want. If you want Talise, go full speed ahead and stop holding back but let the other chick go. Actually you need to let the other chick go completely. She can't hold your interest, but if you don't want the energy Talise requires, let her go. But be gentle. There is no need to break her down after everything she's been through. Look, I need you to take your seat so I can finish serving. Wonderful talking to you, Mr. Jones. I can't promise you anything but I will do my best to secure a meeting for you with Sack." She shook his hand.

As she followed him to his seat she questioned, "Where did you go to school?"

"Atlanta. I'm a Morehouse Man," he proudly announced.

"Oh, did you pledge?" He shook his head. "Oh, well I will tell you this, Sack bleeds the orange and green from the Rattlers. Then he bleeds purple and gold for the Omegas. Either one of those affiliations help, but you seem like good people so I'll do my best."

"I appreciate that."

"Cool. Give me a couple of days. If you don't hear from me, his assistant or Sack himself, give us a call and reference this conversation. Hey don't forget, choose wisely, my friend, choose wisely and quickly."

In a flash, Diamond sat down out of sight as the plane took what almost felt like a nosedive into Atlanta airport.

I will. I will.

Talise paced around the entire desk. She couldn't believe his tone and his refusal to accept her dilemma. *What's the big deal? She said no,* she thought. True, Steffon came through for her at every angle. He helped her to sign her latest agent for Great Raritan. True, he was always there to talk or listen, especially now that Calvin made himself scarce. But what in the heck did he mean by "you better make it happen. Don't blow this, Talise. You don't want to mess with me." She had never seen the seriousness he displayed.

Oh, well, I'll have to deal with him later. She packed her briefcase full with five of the eighteen files K.J. had her to research. Instead of going home, she was going straight to Stephanie's for their big girl-friend alert meeting. Just as she turned to catch her breath, Dragon Breath disturbed her moment.

"Going home so soon, are we?"

"Yes. I have a life."

"We're being sarcastic, are we? Well, Miss Sarcasm, you know you are responsible for inputting the data for all of our agents. And you have to get it done before the holidays. It takes at least a month to process all of their checks, and K.J. likes to have it all done before the holidays."

"So, that's a couple of months away."

"And you think you'll be able to calculate all the data, input it and file these forms for all 120 agents in a couple of months." Dragon laughed. "Good luck because you're going to need it," she said and exited.

Talise shrugged off Dragon Breath's comments and headed out the door.

She ran smack into Steffon. "Did you drive today?"

"No. And I have to go." She pushed passed him.

"Wait, I'm sorry."

"You should be. I don't appreciate you threatening me."

"I said I'm sorry."

"Accepted. Gotta go." She raced toward the elevator to beat the rush. She pressed the button several times.

"You know pressing the button more than once doesn't make it come any faster," he said in her ear. He grabbed her bags. "Let me take you home. We can talk about this."

"Steff, I…"

"Come on. I said I'm sorry. I didn't mean to flex on you like that."

"I'm not going home. I'm meeting my girls and…"

"Gem?"

"Yes, and Steff, she said no a thousand times. She's not interested. I can't talk her into it."

The elevator finally came and they got on.

"Then let me take you wherever you need to go. We don't have to talk about this anymore. Agreed?"

She thought. She could use the ride all the way to Stephanie's Whispering Woods condo, which was near the Princeton line. If she refused his offer, she would have to take two trains home, get her car and ride another forty-five to ninety minutes depending on traffic. She could always get Gem to drop her off.

"Agreed."

"Cool. Let me just call my girl." He dialed the number as the elevator let them out to the street. She waited in the front of the building as she watched him mouth something about having business to take care of.

The ride to Stephanie's was smooth. Laden with anticipation of the news Stephanie was to bestow, Talise tried to have a conversation with Steffon. She thwarted every attempt he made to divert her attention to her convincing Gem to sign with Honey Graham records. He was relentless.

"She said she wants a classy, upscale company with a reputation she can recognize. I have to admit, I've never heard of Honey Graham either," she said, changing the radio station.

"Then why is she hooked up with Will and Robb? Where do I turn?" he asked, squinting. The area grew dark quickly around the vast country area. "It's so deserted out here that I'm not sure we're still in Jersey."

"I know. It's country down here. Oh, there it is. It's beyond this set of trees. Don't even try to breeze over that one. What's up with Will and Robb?"

"Nothing. Make a right here?"

"Yes. Now answer my question."

"This is phat. All condos through here?"

"Yes. Now answer my question," she said impatiently.

"Don't ever raise your voice at me, Talise." His tone grew tense.

"I didn't mean anything by it," she said, whining. "I just wish you would stop avoiding my question."

He swerved the car around the winding road into the elaborate Whispering Woods. He seemed to marvel at the quiet calm that enveloped them. He turned the radio down as if it was disturbing an unwavering peace.

"Right there. You see the blue Beamer. That's her place." It was well lit. She noticed Gem's car right next to Stephanie's. The curtains were drawn as if they were waiting.

"Thanks, Steff. I owe you one. I hope I didn't get you in any trouble."

"I own stuff in my house," he said, patiently waiting for her to exit. She kissed him on the cheek. Just as she pulled away, he pulled her back toward him and landed his luscious lips on hers. This time longer and more passionate than before. She didn't resist.

"What was that all about?" she asked, feeling a tingle down her spine.

"You tell me," he said sexily.

"So are you going to tell me or what?" she begged.

"I don't play my hand like that, babydoll, even if you do have the prettiest baby browns I've ever seen."

"How do you know what I was talking about?"

"Because I know you. I've learned you. It's not hard. That's what you do when you want something or someone. Remember that," he said, stroking his bald head and bringing his hands down to rest on his connecting goatee.

"You're avoiding again."

"Talise, you have to go. I don't repeat myself but I will break it down for you. I'm not giving you a bit of information to help out Goldilocks when she can't trust me or my partner. You don't get something for nothing. Now I will let you in on a little secret and take it or leave it. Tell her to watch herself carefully. I haven't been dealin' with those cats long but the more I see, the more I know what they're really about."

"That's it?" she questioned incredulously.

"That's it. Now scat. I gotta go. Remember what I said about wanting and learning something and someone."

"I thought you don't repeat yourself," she said, closing the car door.

He let down the window. "Be safe. Call me when you get in the office tomorrow."

She watched him drive off. She turned to walk up the stone staircase leading to Stephanie's door. It opened before she could knock.

"Now you're sleeping with that thug?" Gem snapped.

"Spare me please." Talise sauntered passed her. "What's going on?" she asked, approaching Stephanie and planting a kiss on her forehead. "Welcome home, even though we didn't know you were away." She placed her jacket and briefcase on an adjacent chair and found a comfortable spot on the floor.

The doorbell rang again. Neither Stephanie nor Talise moved.

"I guess the maid will get it. What is this, a block party tonight?" Gem looked at Stephanie for an answer.

Stephanie just sat there quietly.

Before Gem could get the door fully open, a tall lanky dark-haired White man whisked through the door. "Darling, are you okay? I came as soon as the plane landed."

"Well who are you?" Gem questioned as Talise stood.

Stephanie finally gave introductions.

"Gem, Talise, this is Alec. Alec, this is Gem and Talise." Stephanie retreated to her corner.

"Well. It's wonderful to finally meet you. I've heard so much about the two of you. You are well thought of in my darling's heart."

"Your darling?" Talise asked with a snarl.

"Yes, my darling. Oh, I guess Stephanie hasn't broken the news yet. We're engaged. Show them your ring. Where's your ring?"

Chapter 9

An unseasonably warm January had roared in like a lamb, and Calvin was officially missing in action. His calls had become so infrequent that Talise barely recognized his voice when he did call. His excuse was always he hadn't been to visit since their last encounter in South Jersey. He had been working on a marketing plan for a perspective client.

"I don't understand. You've been at this for months. It's obvious the flight attendant was just trying to be nice. Pullin' the wool over your eyes. Get over it and develop a plan for someone else," she whined. "Are you coming up for my birthday or what?" He would try to get a word in edgewise, but it never worked when she was in this state.

"This is my business. This is my livelihood. And it comes first. If you haven't learned that about me then you haven't learned anything. Business always, always comes before pleasure. Especially when things aren't so pleasurable. See that's the damn problem, Talise.

You're supposed to act like a New York executive now. My woman would understand that. And that's exactly why you couldn't be."

Sting. A queen bee couldn't have been worse, and Talise was allergic to bees. *I thought I was your woman.*

"I said I'll try my best to get up for your birthday. But no promises. Look, I have to go. I'll talk to you later." He didn't wait for a response.

She barely wanted to believe her ears. But the fact that she was stuck in Philadelphia for a two-day convention on her actual birthday and had an hour-and-a-half exhausting ride home, parked reality right in her face.

If Dragon Breath had been anywhere near her, Talise could have strangled her. It was Dragon's suggestion that Great Raritan's presence was imperative. Not only did she convince K.J. that this was a perfect opportunity for Talise, she neglected to tell Talise that all of her arrangements for her hotel accommodations were up to her. So when Talise trudged into the town, not a hotel in sight had availability. Some convention had taken up every room within a sixty-mile radius. So reluctantly she decided a cold birthday night at home was her ticket. Hopefully it would be balanced by a visit over the weekend that she had to practically beg for.

It was well after five and she was still in Philadelphia. She packed up her things, shook a few more hands and checked her voice mail. K.J.'s message was for her to give him details about the convention. His secretary questioned several files that of course needed her immediate attention. Vanee wanted to know when she was back in town so she could take her out for her birthday and Stephanie…

She had not faced Stephanie since she announced her engagement to a man she and Gem weren't aware she was seeing. She still had extreme difficulty getting over the fact that her best friend was engaged to a man she hardly knew, they hardly knew about and they still wouldn't have known about had she not feared some tabloid scandal surrounding their impending nuptials. Gem practically refused to acknowledge the situation, and Talise didn't know what to say, so she acted as if Stephanie's message had been deleted by mistake and ignored it. The final message was from Gem, first extending warm wishes for a happy birthday and secondly inviting her to another show happening in the city the following week.

She pulled out her new electronic organizer, courtesy of Steffon, and jotted the date down with the long plastic stick attached to the side. *I need the outlet*, she thought. *It's not like I'll be overly busy. I'm sure Calvin won't be making it,* she thought, recalling their last unfeeling, cold-hearted conversation, which left her desiring him even more.

Why do we always want what we can't have? she thought as she rolled toward the Ben Franklin Bridge. She passed the very hotel where they shared a wonderful time at the affair. The car phone disturbed her out of her thought, saving her from almost missing her next turn.

"This is Talise," she said, untangling the monstrosity of a cord attached to a dinosaur the company called a car phone. She had hoped for another voice when she remembered Calvin didn't have this number.

"Hey, Steff…yeah, I'm on my way home…. It'll be at least an hour and half, I'm in the middle of Philly rush-hour traffic, the bridge is as bad as New York….I don't know when her next gig is….Steff, honestly you and that Romy—Jerome or whatever his name is—needs to give it up, Gem is not interested, and I can't do anything about it….Yeah, I understand….Okay, do what you must….No, I'm not in the mood tonight….I have to get ready to come back here tomorrow, so I'll talk to you later….Yeah …Cool…No, I'm okay. I'm not down, just tired….Yeah, look I have to go….I'll call you when I get home….Yeah…Talk to you then." She put the car in cruise mode as she sped off.

"Hello? Yes, I know I've spoken with you a few times and—"

The woman completely cut him off.

"I know Mr. Hughes is busy but Diamond said specifically for me to call her in a few days for a discussion. In fact she advised that she, Sack or Sack's assistant would be getting back to me in days. It's been weeks…." He tried to continue.

"I'm Sack's assistant, and I don't know anything about this meeting or encounter but I would be happy to give Mr. Hughes a message that…"

"Ma'am," he said, calming himself. "I'm going to be in the area soon, and I was hoping that I could perhaps meet with Diamond again or set up a phone conversation or meeting with Sack. Is there a better time I would be able to speak with either one of them?" *Like when you aren't around.*

The assistant wouldn't budge.

"Great. Listen, I'll be in the Northeast soon. Would you please give either Diamond or Mr. Hughes my number and name. Please reference the conversation I had with Diamond on a flight to Atlanta. I would greatly appreciate it….Thank you…Have a good day, ma'am." *Another dead end.* He sighed.

He picked up the phone again and redialed. He heard the familiar voice he had heard so many times over the past week, but as usual he did not know what to say, considering the nature of their last conversation. This time was no different. "This is Talise. I'm unavailable at the moment but…" He hung up, avoiding the routine once again. Just as he placed the receiver down, it rang off the hook. He prayed that it was someone he longed to hear from.

"Hello? Calvin? Are you there?"

Talise! He sighed. "Finally, nice to hear your voice," he said sexily.

"You've been calling? Oh, well I've missed you too."

His heart dropped. "Oh, Candace." His tone changed. "Hey, what's up?" He quickly tried to divert any unmerited attention.

"I'm surprised you're home. I'm having an early Monday and since it seems like you are, too, maybe we can get together. I need to go to the mall."

He pondered for a split second and decided that a breath of fresh air might do him some good. "Sure. Just give me a chance to shower and change. I'll pick you up in a bit."

He pulled the Gray Ghost into a modest graveled driveway and blew the horn. Candace appeared atop her red-brick steps in an eggnog-colored wool suit and matching swing coat. Her hair flowed effortlessly around her shoulders, and her Gucci handbag accented her outfit perfectly. She eased into the front seat and pecked him on the cheek.

"Hey, I brought something that might be of some interest," she said, pulling out a familiar magazine. "I don't know what this means, but I know you've been working tirelessly on this account, and I thought this might give you some insight," she said, showing him the cover entitled *Sack and Di: An Affair Fit for a King and His Queen.* The photo was a gorgeous display of the very woman who had given him advice not too long ago. She stood regally as her groom seemed to melt into her glow. The article chronicled a lavish fall wonderland for Sack Hughes, the owner of the largest limousine corporation in the country and his debutante bride, Miss Diamond M. Ferguson. The couple had exchanged their vows before fifteen hundred of their closest friends and relatives.

"Of course it will help. Please read it to me."

"…The fabulous Plaza wedding in New York City culminated with an enchanted white-horse carriage ride for the couple to Sack's brand-new state-of-the-art Hollywood styled hotrod. The latest craze in stretch limos accommodates a party of up to twenty-eight people with a fully retractable roof and movable platform for those Hollywood types getting a last glance of their adoring fans…This bulletproof fancy could be rented or purchased fully equipped with a bar, full entertainment system and a state-of-the-art resting facility for those who choose to ride alone…"

"That's why I haven't been able to get in touch with them," he said aloud, coasting down the highway. "Read some more."

"The grandiose affair was topped off with the couple being whisked away to a private honeymoon in an undisclosed location for three months aboard their new jet, parked in Teterboro, New Jersey….

"I just thought it was something you might need to know," she said.

"See you still got it," he said, thinking aloud. He continued to drive along.

"You seem pensive," she said, putting the magazine back into her purse.

"Just pondering my next move," he said. He pressed the automatic dial on his car-mounted phone. He neglected to take it off speaker.

"This is Talise. I'm unavailable at the moment…."

"Damn." He hit the end button. "Where the hell is she?"

"Client?" she questioned.

"What? Who?" he said, swerving around a car blocking access to a parking space.

"Talise."

He barely avoided the wreck. "Uh, yeah. Oh yeah." He laughed uncomfortably. *Cal, you just fucked up. Get it together.* "Um. I need to make my way up North again soon. I need to try and contact Sack. At the writing of this article, their three months should be about up," he reasoned.

"Yeah," she added. "Well like I was telling you, Cleon is in love again. He wants us to meet her. He claims he's serious this time."

"Your brother is serious every other month…." He laughed.

"You're right about that." She joined in and carried the conversation. "Hello. I'm talking to you. You haven't heard a word I've been saying."

"I'm sorry, baby." He felt obliged to call her baby. Besides, she had given him the best news he'd had in weeks.

"I'm glad we're spending this time together, Cal. I miss you."

"Yeah. Yeah. You too," he said.

"So how did the convention go? Did you learn a lot?"

"Yeah, it was cool today. I have to go back tomorrow. I have a meeting with other reps from the corporate offices, but I should be finished early."

"Cool. You comin' back to the office? If so, we could go to lunch or something and celebrate your birthday."

"I thought you were coming with me to hear my friend sing."

"I know, Talise, but I have class this week, and you know how hard it is for me to get a baby-sitter, especially on such short notice."

"Baby-sitter? The baby has a daddy."

"I know but he's so bent on what he's got going on that I haven't seen much of him lately. Anyway enough about that. I probably won't be able to make your girlfriend's concert, but there's a hot spot out here in Queens. Maybe we can hit. Knight Gallery. I heard it's hot."

"We'll talk, Vanee. Ooh, look, I'm almost home. I'll talk to you later okay," Talise said, getting off the phone abruptly. "And thanks for thinking of me."

"Always. You know you my peeps."

"I know," she said as she hung up the phone. A familiar car sat in her space. As she pulled toward it, she recognized the goatee from a mile away. She smiled, too, glad she had company for what could turned out to be a cold, lonely night.

"What are you doing here?" She smiled. She turned off the ignition and directed Steffon to the trunk to help her with her belongings.

"Why don't you leave the stuff you don't need tonight in the car? This way you don't have to lug it downstairs by yourself tomorrow."

"Makes sense, Mr. Bryant." She complied.

He grabbed her from behind. He gently eased her bags out of her hand. "What are you doing?"

"We are about to celebrate your birthday, Ms. Grimes, in style."

She allowed him to take control. He placed a soft purple silk scarf in front of her face. The next thing she knew, blackness surrounded her. She heard him rattling in his car. *Wine, champagne maybe.* She thought she heard what sounded like a paper bag rustle.

He led her into the lobby past the glass doors.

"Steffon, this is really sweet but I prefer that you not see my place like it is. I don't even have a place for you to sit…."

"Ssh…" He touched her lips.

She allowed him to lead her toward her door. She directed him to her side pocket where her keys rested. He retrieved them and opened the door. He led her into her place and left the lights off. She stood while he maneuvered himself around as if he lived there.

Even in the darkness, something was different. Her bare, open space felt filled somehow. The linoleum floor no longer squeaked under her heels. Something cushy lay beneath the tiredness of her day.

Finally through the scarf, dim light bounced before her closed lids. She heard the clink of glasses. Steffon led her to what she assumed was the middle of the room.

Slowly he unraveled the beautiful scented scarf that she prayed was part of her gift. When she was able to open her eyes, she blinked to make sure she was in the same place. Bewildered she ran back toward the door, opened and rechecked the apartment number on the other side. It was hers. But the apartment was totally unlike what she had seen that morning.

"You like?" he said proudly.

Silence.

She was overwhelmed. She drifted toward the plush leather love seat that sat in the corner. It felt heavenly beneath her touch. She crawled toward the full-size matching couch so as not to bump the modern glass-and-brass coffee table that sat in the center.

"I wasn't sure how you wanted to arrange it. I did the best I could." He continued to pour the wine. "Oh, that's a full-size sleeper in there."

She allowed her body to roll into the crease of the chair, taking in all of the room's glory. The cold floor now held a corner-to-corner purple rug, which held pictures of African ladies who did a celebratory dance throughout the floor covering. All she could do was dance in delight.

She walked around the now fully furnished room several times, making sure this wasn't a dream. She kicked off her shoes and dropped her stockings, enjoying the feel of the rug between her toes.

"I guess you like it. Come 'ere," he said, placing the long-stem black crystal glasses on her new table."

"I beg your pardon. There are coasters for that, I'm sure. Where are they?" she questioned, feeling somewhat strange in her own home.

He pointed toward an oriental oblong pot. She used both hands to remove the lid.

"The glassware was comped by the store," he added, not waiting for her as he sipped in delight.

She kneeled beside him. Her head rested comfortably on his thigh. She looked above. "Why? How? Why?" she quietly asked. Her voice quivered, and she fought back tears.

"Don't worry about how. I love you, Talise." He bent down and supplied her with her own taste of his wine.

"Steffon, this is…we, we can't do this. What about…"

He stopped her with his kiss. She pulled him down to the floor and let all the passion she held for everyone and everything explode from within.

"I know but it's not every day that you hear that your best friend is about to be married to a White senatorial candidate who we had no idea you were even dating. Our feelings are just hurt."

"I'm not avoiding you guys, and I really want to come to your show, but Alec has a fundraiser for us to attend and I'm not feeling all that well. My energy is low."

"Not too low to play guess who's coming to dinner."

Silence.

"I'm sorry, girl. Low blow. Look bring Alec with you. If you're serious about being with this guy, give us a chance to get used to him, like him even. How was dinner at your parents'?"

"World War III. My mom's upset but she'll eventually cope, she says, but my dad hit the roof, but eventually he'll be okay too. No mater what, I'm always Daddy's little girl. Anyway attending your show will be awkward enough. You know I haven't heard from Talise since I told you guys."

"I know," Gem said.

"What has she said?"

"She just doesn't understand. And you know her feelings on interracial relationships. We don't have to rehash that. Besides she's got her own demons to deal with."

"Demons like what?" Stephanie questioned. She balanced the phone between her ear and shoulder, trying to get her appointments for the next day in order.

"She asked me not to talk to you about it. She said she'll talk to you when she's ready."

"She's really upset with me, isn't she?" Stephanie prayed for a different answer. She didn't get it. She placed the pen down.

"Don't worry about it. She'll get over it. I'm starting to worry about Talise again," Gem said.

"Why?" Stephanie asked, resuming organizing her details for an upcoming psychology session.

"Did you notice who dropped her off at your house last week?" Gem asked.

"Not really. I was so concerned about my news that—" Stephanie said.

"Steffon," Gem interrupted.

Stephanie sighed. She thought it best not to comment, but considering what she knew about Talise's track record, Stephanie agreed there was cause to worry.

"So, whatcha doing? Gem asked. "You're at your office kind of late."

I'm working on my outline and trip proposal. I have a troubled teen I'm counseling and I want to take her to my alma mater. My colleagues and senior psychologists are opposing me."

"Why?" Gem asked.

"Well my theory is that this young girl is smart but needs guidance. She's in love with this older thug, and I'm desperately trying to prevent her from getting pregnant before it's too late. It's my contention that the streets are a big influence now, and I want to be a bigger influence by showing her a different side of life, a better side," Stephanie explained.

"That's where you're making your mistake. I think what you're trying to do is noble but don't take that girl's choice away from her. Show her options but don't put her way of life down," Gem said.

Stephanie huffed. Her listening skills for Gem's lecture were fading. Her goal was to get this hands-on treatment approved and her field trip solidified.

"I'm going to call my dad when I'm done," Stephanie said.

"Stephanie, you're not listening to a word I've said."

"What?"

"Never mind. Look I have to go. I have a studio session tonight. Anyway, if you and Alec can, I would love for you to be at my show," Gem said.

"Listen, I can't promise but I'll try. My other line is ringing. I'll call you later," Stephanie rushed.

Okay, girl, I'll check you, and Stephanie…"

"Yes."

"I love you, girlfriend," Gem said.

"I love you too."

Talise rested snuggly under the covers. Steffon had lifted and carried her to bed after he put her to sleep like a newborn baby. His words enthralled her as he ripped her very underwear from her with his bare teeth. *I can't believe we're here. I always say, if you're patient, whatever it is, you'll get it. I thought about you a lot, girl. I never thought we'd be right here. Just a year ago, you were married, and today I'm inside of you....* She moaned. He felt like a dream. He wasn't large like Calvin or as smooth but he knew what to do. His panty trick made her so moist that she couldn't think of denying him or being denied, regardless of the circumstances.

"Everything went well." Steffon's voice was low. He stepped farther away from the door to make sure he wasn't heard. Just then his pager went off with a 911 attached to it. He stumbled slightly in the dark while he thought Talise remained sound asleep.

"I think it'll work like a charm," Steffon said.

"I don't know what made me let you talk me into this, man. I'm about to move on and find another singer," the voice on the phone said.

"No, I'm telling you, they are closer than sisters. Gem'll do anythang to get her girl out of this jam. I'm telling you, it was the right move."

"Yeah, the right move for you to get in that ass," Romy Graham of Honey Graham records replied. "Well she better come through, I'm telling you it was risky and if this don't work, this will be the most expensive piece of pussy you ever bought. And Steff, I don't collect in payments, you got me?"

"I got you, Romy. She's my boo. She'll be alright," he said, checking on her. "I gotta run. My pager's blowing up. Peace."

He picked up the pager as the second signal came through. He rustled through his bag and retrieved his cell phone. He found Talises's keys on the new end table closest to the door and stepped out. The last thing he wanted to do was to get locked out of her self-locking apartment in the middle of the night.

He finished his brief conversation with sarcasm and used the key for re-entry. She was sitting up when he returned.

"Where were you? I rolled over and got scared. I thought you left me." He took off his pants and neatly laid them across the foot of her bed. He crawled back between the sheets.

"You don't have to ever worry about me leaving you. You understand?" He looked in her eyes and tapped her chin.

His firmness made her blush. She felt protected. She felt loved. She wrapped herself completely around him so that once more, he could have his way. She owed him and she didn't mind having to repay.

Talise jerked with the onset of the morning sun. They had forgotten to close the blinds the night before as the moon and clear sky provided the perfect backdrop for the consummation of their friendship.

Steffon was still there. She smiled and stroked his goatee. Her moderate-length fingernails ran across his stubble, and her smile widened. She eased out of bed so that she wouldn't disturb him. She assumed he had time to shower and leave for work. It was only 5:30. She rummaged through her vanity in search of any leftover razors for Steffon to use. *He can use my toothbrush,* she thought. She skipped toward the kitchen but she ran back into the room to grab her slippers. "Where are you going? You can go to work from here. I found a razor and you can use my…"

"Slow down, babygirl. I gotta roll. I shouldn't have stayed this long. You know the sun ain't supposed to catch you going in. Gotta make my tracks outta this one," he said, casually putting on his socks and Timberlands.

"But, Steff, it's only…"

"I know what time it is. Don't sweat me, okay. We had a good night, and don't worry it won't be the last. But I have to be careful." He tapped her on the butt.

She tried to ignore her disappointment. She stood and watched him prepare to leave.

"Don't look so sad. I stayed here a lot longer than I should've and that was because you were having nightmares all night. I stayed here to protect you. Besides she was blowing my beeper up all night."

"You didn't call her from my phone, did you?" she questioned with a panic.

"And if I did?" he shot back. His coat was now draped over his shoulders, his shoes were partially unlaced and his pants were rolled up past his ankles.

"Because my number might appear on your ID. How would you explain that? Besides where's your suit? You had on your suit last night."

"You make a good point. Don't worry, I didn't call her back from your phone and I never will. I left my suit in your room. Do me a favor, clean my shirt and pants with your stuff and leave it here. I'll get it another time when I stay. Next time, I like my eggs scrambled hard with cheese, turkey bacon, wheat toast and O.J. I don't do that coffee thang. Peace. I'll call you later," he said, letting himself out.

She grabbed her robe and tied it tightly around her waist. "Wait, you're not coming to work today?"

"Naw. Got some stuff to take care of. I'll call you later. Hey, do yo' thang in that meeting today. Take no prisoners. Promise?"

She stood in the doorway looking like a lost child.

He repeated. "Promise?" He waited for the elevator.

She perked up and answered, "Promise." Once again she felt protected and loved.

The bells rang and the doors opened as people shuffled out of the Forty-second Street station. Once again, Gem squeezed her way in past the men reading their half-folded papers. She managed to grab a seat in the corner, lodged between the wall and a man who appeared to be homeless. She allowed her body to relax only slightly, when a tinklng noise kicked her alertness into high gear. Immediately with the wave of the crowd Gem jumped up, stumbling into people to get away from the homeless man. "Is he pissing on the train?" Gem heard another passenger say.

Gem fought her way back through the crowd, realizing she jumped up without her bag. She noticed that the man was laughing. She also noticed him crinkling a piece of plastic. He popped the peppermint candy in his mouth and continued to laugh.

Gem laughed as well as she took her place back in her seat.

After tonight, I won't be fighting these crowds and bags. Limos will take me everywhere I go. She secretly dreamed that Robb and Will would finally come through on their promise of several legitimate prospective record companies. They had showed her the RSVPs. Everything was almost in place. They had one more song to complete on the demo. But she planned to be in rare form tonight. Her belief was that an incomplete demo would be the least of their worries once they heard her knockout voice.

The window seat became a demon for sleep as it had been so many times before. She was unable to contend with her own morning breath that even peppermints couldn't cure. Her feet burned as she kicked herself for wearing shoes that offered more style than comfort. She wasn't surprised when she noticed she missed her stop to Penn Station once again.

She stepped off the train and forced her way through the crowd, mimicking the suit-and-tie-wearing torpedoes that had emerged from a sticky, stuffy subway cannon. She noticed she was extremely close to Talise's job and contemplated a visit. But she was so tired, she barely fought her way toward another train.

She was now on the Path train to New Jersey where she heard the familiar voice of her favorite conductor who always ended with "Have a good journey." She allowed her body to relax against the glass once again, comfortable that she had at least twenty minutes to escape into dreamland. As soon as the train emerged from the underground tunnel, her pager disturbed all of her honorable intentions. She hit the silence button without a second thought. But whoever was paging her was persistent.

Just as she dialed the persistent number from her cell phone a sharp pain filled her stomach.

She patted her face to wake herself up as she waited for the person who paged her to pick up. "Oh, come on.

"Hello?"

"Someone paged me?"

"And this is?"

"Gem. Gemmia Barnes."

"Oh. Yes, one moment please."

"Gem…"

"Will?"

"Uh, yeah, look Gem…"

"Where have you been? I haven't heard from you guys in a while. I was surprised I didn't see you in the studio all night. What's up and what's so important that you couldn't wait until I got home. I'm exhausted…"

"I know, listen…I'm really sorry about this but…."

"Will, this doesn't sound too good." She held her breath.

"It's not. Listen, the deal fell through. The show is cancelled for tonight and right now you're going to be on hold for any more showcases for a while."

"For a while. What, you guys are dropping me?" she asked hysterically.

"No. No we're not dropping you but—"

"But what? Just give it to me straight, Will…"

"Well, Robb feels that we're not getting anywhere and we need to concentrate on some other areas. The execs that were supposed to show up backed out at the last minute and it doesn't make sense to put you through another night of disappointment…."

"But my friends and family were planning on being there tonight. I picked out a really nice wardrobe for you guys to check over before the show. I went to that expensive hairdresser you guys recommended. She charged me $250. I can't wear my hair around town like this normally, and I hired that makeup artist you guys have been pushing on me for the longest. What's the deal?" She clutched her stomach. She wiped her wet face. She couldn't determine if the dampness was from perspiration or tears.

"I'm sorry, Gem. It's not over. We're just taking a little break from each other. Give us a call in a few weeks and come into the office so we can devise another game plan. Oh, and Gem, you're okay by your contract to perform and make a few things happen. My suggestion: keep working. I'm sorry," he said and hung up.

She doubled over as the deep-seated pain grew stronger. There was more to this situation than Will was telling. But she was too embarrassed and too weak to figure it out.

The conductor said, "Next stop, Frank E. Rogers Boulevard. Have a good journey."

"I'm starving. Please do me a favor and stop here. Wait for me please. I'll be right back." She stepped around back where the sign beckoned her to have the best barbecue this side of Orange, New Jersey. The neon lights indicated the place was open, but the locked door and lack of patrons said differently.

She turned around and noticed the Burger King directly across the street. She contemplated a burger as the now cold air whipped between her sexy thighs.

"Lady, whatcha gonna do? I have another pickup," the cab driver barked.

"One second. Just keep your meter running," she said, clutching her coat closed.

"Miss, you trying to get to the café in the back?" a voice that sounded vaguely familiar questioned.

Gem turned and noticed strong bowed legs holding up a sternly built torso attached to massively appealing arms. "Yes. I'm trying to get a…Vaughan?"

"You're trying to get a Vaughan?" he responded.

"No, silly. Vaughan? Is your name Vaughan?"

"Yes."

"Oh, my gosh. This is where you work?"

"Oh, shoot, Gem," he said with excitement. "Girl, I'm sorry, I didn't recognize you in your disguise. I've been jammin' all night here and my eyes are shot. How ya doin'?" he asked, embracing her.

"Hangin' in there. I was at an all-night rehearsal. Was supposed to be getting ready for a set tonight in the city when Will paged me and cancelled."

"Lady, please, I need to go," the driver yelled out of the window and honked the horn.

"Well go then," she shot back.

"Not without my money." He started to climb out of the car.

"How much? You're rude. Don't you see me talking," she said, digging into her bag, which she called the brown abyss.

"Twenty-three and climbing."

She handed him twenty-five dollars. "Change please."

He rolled his eyes and handed her two soggy and worn bills.

"He probably did that on purpose," she said aloud.

"I'm getting off in a few minutes, I'll drive you home. Come inside and wait. I won't be long," Vaughan said.

He led her inside. The room was still dark and smoky from the night before. She sat at the black lacquer bar with red sparkles. She looked on as the bartenders still dressed in their shiny red vests and black bow ties scurried about. They were obviously cleaning up. She made her way through the maze of red-and-white tables scattered about the stage. The microphone drew her in.

It sat on a tall black stand that resembled that of the olden days when the oversized metal with black lines and grooves captured some of the world's greatest sounds. Sounds like Gladys Knight and the Pips, Diana Ross and the Supremes and the Temptations. She loved them all. She cupped the cold, hard steel.

"Hmm…" She retrieved her note. "Keep on hanging on…" Her

voice filled the room so powerfully that all movement stopped. She fell into a zone and sang the most sultry rendition of Donny Hathaway's "Someday We'll All Be Free."

When she completed the song, acapella, everyone gave her a standing ovation. Their claps awakened her zone entranced state.

She gave them a gracious smile and stepped off the stage, back to the bar where Vaughan had left her.

"See, she should have been on the stage last night for amateur night," she heard one of the girls say before the woman resumed her cleaning.

"You have some voice there, lady." A middle-aged man with a full salt-and-pepper beard sat before her.

"Gem, this is the owner of The Peppermint Lounge. He'd like to talk to you about a unique opportunity. What would you like to drink with your meal?" Vaughan asked, positioning himself behind the bar.

"On me of course. Wine, beer, cocktail?" the owner said.

"Too early. Cranberry and orange juice would be great. Thanks, Vaughan," she said, stuffing the succulent chopped barbecue in her mouth. "So how can I help you?"

"I don't have a lot of time to go into detail, but I'd love to have a voice like that showcased here."

"I appreciate your interest in my talent, but I've just been dumped by my management, I think, and I really don't have the energy to talk about new prospects. Besides, with no offense intended, your establishment is quaint, but right now, Orange is not where I intended for my career to go."

"Oh no, dear, I'm not talking about management, I'm talking about winning a chance to host amateur night."

"Excuse me? Winning a chance to host amateur night? You mean participating as an amateur and winning a chance to what?"

"Come back every week for the next six weeks and host. If everything works out, six weeks can turn into a contract for six months, providing you bring in enough people to pay your salary and tips of course."

"And that salary would be?" she asked.

"Three hundred dollars every two weeks."

She smiled and took a deep breath, casually gazed over at Vaughan who was obviously interested in the deal as well. "It was only by chance that I walked in here in the first place. I was looking for something to eat and I ran into Vaughan." She bit her bottom lip to pause. She didn't want to offend anyone. "So like I was saying, I'm flattered and I really appreciate the gesture, but no thanks. My résumé affords me a much better financial opportunity and exposure for that matter. Sorry."

"I understand. You're a great talent. If you change your mind, please take my card and give me a call." He threw on his black suede fedora and matching cashmere coat and left.

"Vaughan, I'm really tired. If you can't leave, I understand. I'll call a cab."

"No, I'm ready."

He drove her home as she outlined the day's events.

"Sounds like you're better off without them. Why don't you take my boss up on his offer? It's a steady gig and I wouldn't mind having to look at that pretty face a little more often."

"No thanks, but I appreciate you listening to me, Vaughan. Oh, and thanks for the ride home," she said, exiting the car. She bent over and rode the window down with her elbows as he lowered it.

"So can I call you?"

"I would like that." She flashed her killer smile. She dug deeper into the brown abyss and pulled out a wrinkled card. She scribbled her home phone number and pager on the back.

"I hope to hear from you soon," she said, handing the card to him.

"You will," he said and backed out of her driveway and sped off.

In the darkness she entered the house, which seemed emptier than when she left the night before. The only light broke through the drawn curtains in the far corner of the living room. The small flashing red signal on her phone acted like a beacon.

She put the phone on speaker, hit a few codes and listened to the messages as she stripped in the middle of the floor.

"Gem, it's Talise. Girlfriend alert. Girlfriend alert, and it's not me this time. It's Stephanie, and it's an emergency. Meet us at Je's as soon as you can." She heard the dial tone.

"What now? Is there a full sun out or what?"

Chapter 10

"Where were you?" she screamed following him around the apartment.

He casually entered the kitchen, picked up a chicken wing, grabbed a root beer out of the fridge and sat before the television with remote in hand. "I told you. I had business to take care of," he said, popping the can.

"What business, Steffon?"

"I had business with Romy."

"You a lie, 'cause Romy called here looking for you again. I gave him your new cell number and pager. I'm sick of your shit, Steffon. I know you were with some ho! Don't you know that I know how you sound when you roll outta bed with another bitch, motherfucker," she yelled, looming over him as he laughed at the cartoon he had flipped to.

"Vanee, I'm not in the mood today for your shit. You feel me?" he said with intensity.

"Who is it now, Steffon. I'm sicka this. You ain't home no more, you ain't spending no time with me or your child. Who is this bitch that's got you so wide open now?" she screamed.

"I told you, I'm not for your shit today." He threw the remote at the window. Vanee screamed, their child cried and Steffon retreated to the bedroom, slamming the door behind him. She dropped to the floor in horror, trying to control herself before she could tend to their little one.

She was still on the floor when Steffon finally came out of the bedroom, fully dressed.

"Where are you going now?" she asked hysterically.

"I told you about gettin' in my business, didn't I? I got shit to do, and you and nobody else is holding me back. Now get your shit together and take care of my daughter," he said and walked out without another word. She remained on the floor.

"So have you told them how you feel?"

Stephanie stood from the cocoa leather couch with its deep grooves before the floor-to-ceiling glass panes that gave her a painstaking view across one of America's most intriguing cities, all from the fifteenth floor.

She gazed at the bridges and tunnels that connected this city to some of New Jersey's streets. The Empire State building stood tall in her view. She then gazed at the green-and-brown mass some people tried to mask as "heaven on the Hudson," wondering how many secrets it claimed. She turned around and laughed at herself.

"You know from what it sounds like, you have taken on too much of their problems and made it your goal to solve them. I don't know how wise that is. You have to be honest with them. It hurt. You needed their attention and their care and when you called this girlfriend alert meeting and they weren't there to meet you, you had every right to be upset. But you don't have every right to keep it to yourself. You need to talk to them."

"Do you think we'd be friends if it were not for this professional arrangement?"

"It's okay to admit you are in counseling, Stephanie. We all need it sometimes. I often utilize the services of colleagues as well. We all need an outlet to get ourselves straight," the doctor offered.

"You didn't answer my question."

"I'm not going to. It's not the issue. So if your friends had shown up for girlfriend alert, what would you have told them?"

She massaged her neck vigorously as she stood silently.

"Stephanie, you have to face this. I'm not telling you anything you don't know."

"I know what you're telling me. For three months now, I've struggled with going back to the doctor. For three months, I've struggled with whether I should talk to anyone. I mean, Alec, Talise, Gem or my parents. I keep telling Alec to be very careful about this smut campaign he has going. He's going to make the camp of his opponent dig deeper than Alec might be willing to face." She plopped back into the chair.

"But you don't know what's going on, Stephanie," her colleague said compassionately. She pulled her chair closer to the couch. "You haven't been back to the doctor about your condition, you've only surmised. But you need to face what's going on with your body, your mind and your soul. You don't know if you're ill. You're keeping secrets from your friends, your family and most importantly your fiancée and yourself. Every argument centers around surface issues—the differences in your race, his campaign, your role in his life and whether you're just a trophy. But the real issue is what is going on inside of you and how committed you are to resolution and your own peace. You know that you can't begin any treatment or healing until you find out what's going on…."

"Stop telling me what I know. I'm not here for that, I'm here for help," Stephanie snapped.

"And that's exactly what I'm trying to do."

"Is this Talise?"

"Yes. How may I help you?"

"Talise, you don't know me. I'm a friend of Vanee's."

Immediately Talise's heart began palpitating. She recalled her last night of passion with Steffon. Incredibly he had taken Calvin's place like a thief in the night. She braced herself. *Vanee probably found out and called one of her Queens homey,* she thought with fear. She turned the small volume button to mute and took a deep breath.

"Anyway…" The woman hadn't stopped talking about some sister support group they had formed. She called to tell her how she among a few select and dear friends were invited to join. They would meet monthly at one another's houses. Their meetings would be their waiting to exhale moments. "I'm sure we can all use the support. It's a close- knit group, girrrl, so you don't have to worry. I'm sure it'll do you some good, like the rest of us. Vanee told me your situation at the job. I work in corporate America, too, so I know whatchoo going through."

"Oh, are you in marketing as well?" Talise added nervously.

"Oh no. I'm a executive seckkkerritery. So we about go through the same stuff."

"I'm sure," Talise said, relieved that this woman had no clue. "Um, sure, I'm interested. I'm just surprised that Vanee didn't tell me herself. We work just a staircase apart."

"I'm the coordinator, you know 'til we have elections and all. We gon' make it strictly prafeshnal. You know what I'm sayin'?" The stranger sounded as if she had a mouthful of food.

"Well alrighty then. Um, sure. Just give me a call with the details, considering you already have my number at work. Of course you can always relay the messages to Vanee. I'm sure I'll get them."

"Oh yeah. I need your home number too. I'm trying to put together a list of you know numbers like a um..."

"A roster, perhaps?"

"Yeeh girrrl, that's it. Well okay, welcome, and we'll be seeing you soon, and I'll be talking to you soon. Oh, and this is esssclusive, so nobody else should be informed, okay?"

"Okay. No problem." Talise chuckled and hung up the phone.

She continued working.

"Hey, babygirl," Steffon said as he walked through the glass door.

She smiled.

"Any luck today?"

"Not really. I made a few calls, but I haven't been able to get through. But I have to keep trying."

"Well why don't you let me cheer you up."

"Thanks, Candace, but I have a lot of work to do. I'm going up to Jersey this weekend and I'm going to New Orleans next week. I have to make sure my finances are straight and make sure all of my paperwork is in order," he said solemnly.

"Calvin, I have tickets to *Carmen* starring Kathleen Battle. Other than

The National Black Theater Festival, it is very difficult to obtain prime-time shows with bona fide stars in the Carolinas. So I'm not taking no for an answer. You're in town and I intend to make the best of it," she asserted.

"Okay, you got me. I'll go."

"I'll pick you up at seven sharp. Your Hugo Boss or Armani will do."

"Okay, don't get carried away. I know how to dress for the opera. And you're driving too? I can't wait."

"Me too, Cal. Me too."

"I'll drive," he said, taking her keys.

"Wasn't that just lovely. Oh, she was in rare, rare voice. The costumes were magnificent. You know it reminded me of the beauty of the *Harlem Nutcracker Suite* with the Dance Theater of Harlem. That, too, was magnificent. It was a beautiful love story," Candace said, clutching Calvin's arm in the crisp night air.

"A love story?" he inquired, opening her door and placing her long Venetian-styled gown underneath her legs.

"Yes. A love story. You've never seen the *Nutcracker*?"

"Actually as a child my mom took me and my cousins to see it. We had to be culturally aware," she said. Calvin laughed with fond memories of his mom. "I just went along, afraid I would miss out on something. Needless to say I was bored to tears and mad at myself for not hanging out with the boys. I'm still lying about why I never showed up for that street game." They both laughed.

"No, see you're talking about the *Nutcracker Suite,* which is a masterpiece in itself, but *The Harlem Nutcracker Suite* is a magical experience that I bet you would enjoy. In fact the next time they come to town, I'll be sure to get tickets."

"I'd like that. Where to next?"

"Chez Josephine's," Candace said.

"So you were able to get reservations?" he asked with excitement.

"Oui, oui."

"Okay." He tipped his head and sped off.

They laughed like school kids. Instead of going directly to the car to continue their good time, they ventured off to downtown Charlotte admiring the progress going on in the town.

"I don't care what you say. Yeah, the food was tasty but I'm still hungry. French restaurants aren't known to feed a brother real well." He laughed.

"You didn't like the escargot?"

"It was okay, if you enjoy the slugs of the earth drenched in butter." He laughed some more.

"Well if you're that hungry, I know where you can be well fed," Candace said seductively. She stopped him in the middle of the street, planted a wet, sloppy kiss on him, and rubbed her thigh up and down his leg.

He moaned but he dared not tell her that he could barely feel her gesture through her gown. Nevertheless, he returned her sweet kiss and led her back to the car without another word.

They entered her house where he aggressively attempted to follow up on the their stirred passion. She stopped him cold, led him to the couch and bid him to cool his heels for what she promised only to be a moment.

He plopped himself on the couch and rubbed his hardness to maintain the momentum.

He waited.

And waited.

Finally she emerged in a white satin body suit trimmed in feathers, panty hose and white sandals.

He smiled as she sat next to him and continued stroking his manhood. She kissed, moaned and rubbed some more. With each stroke she became bolder. Finally she reached over to cut off the light.

He took her upstairs where he stripped her of first her body suit. He then peeled away her bra as he nibbled his way past her belly button and rolled off her panty hose. She moaned in ecstasy. She smelled sweet as he slid down toward her inner thigh.

After his erection once again stood proud, he moved toward her head. Her eyes opened widely as he stroked himself and moaned for her to pleasure him.

She opened her mouth and allowed him entry. He begged her to clasp her tongue around it but she instead clasped her jaw. "Ouch!!!" he yelled in his raspiest voice as he clenched his legs and rolled to the side. "No teeth, baby! No teeth."

She begged his forgiveness and massaged him until once again, he stood proud. She begged for his entry inside of her. He obliged.

She smiled pleasantly as she got up and retreated to the bathroom.

"Why are you walking like that?" His face was contorted with angst.

"Oh yes. Just a lot of stuff coming out of me and I want to wash it off. It's not very pleasant as it becomes hard and sticky," she said with a frown.

"Most ladies would die for the pleasure of having my stuff roll down their thighs," he mumbled.

"What did you say?"

"Nothing important." He laughed. He took a deep breath and pulled the covers under his chin. When she finally returned, she rolled him over so she could lie comfortably in his arms. He allowed her that comfort until he was sure she had fallen into a deep sleep.

He kissed her face, her forehead and her lips. He slipped out from under her, down the stairs and sat gingerly on the couch. He dared not to disturb her by turning on the lights. He grabbed a cold brew from her fridge, turned on the television and sighed.

"Have you talked to her again? You know Romy upped the deal," Steffon said as Talise basked in their latest escapade.

"Why do you keep pressing me about this, Calvin? I told you she was adamant about not signing. In fact, I haven't heard from her in the last week. I haven't heard from her since her gig was cancelled. She seems to be a little depressed and signing with Honey Graham records doesn't seem like it's going to be the cure."

She rolled back over and began sucking his bare chest. She made her way downtown to entice him one more time before she knew he had to go home. Her busy day was to be filled with explaining to K.J. why all of the agents had been over-commissioned due to her latest mistakes.

Steffon grabbed her hair and violently jerked her head. She thought perhaps he was getting excited again, so she went with the flow as he guided her head up and down.

What the hell is he doing? He knows I hate when he grabs my head like that and shows me how to suck him. It makes me feel like a whore, she thought still going with the flow.

Finally, his body jerked.

"What is wrong with you? Since when did you start cumming in my mouth," she said half out of breath. "I almost choked. You know I can't stand that stuff."

Without a word he got up, put his stained underwear on and walked into the bathroom. She pulled the covers near her head trying to figure out his drastic mood swing while she listened to him gargle. He re-entered her bedroom, searched for his pants and shirt and continued to dress without a word.

"Steffon, what is wrong? I'm sorry about Gem, but there isn't much I can do. You have to stop putting all this pressure on me about her signing," she whined.

He said nothing.

"I'm sorry. You're just going to leave like this?" She followed him to the door wearing nothing more than a sheet. "Steffon? Steffon?" she shouted down the hall.

He turned around, looked at her with a furor and stepped in the elevator without saying a word.

"Damn," she said, having allowed the self-locking door to shut behind her.

"It's cold today. The winter started out nicely but it's ending up really cold. I have to purchase a new pair of gloves."

"So what have we chosen since our last meeting?"

"That I need to buy a pair of gloves."

"Stephanie, I think you need to extend your leave of absence."

"That's the best idea since I've been coming to you. You know Alec provided the jet for me to go away for a few days of solace. I flew to the Cayman Islands. Almost two years ago, my girls and I flew there. That's where I met Alec, you know. He was a little upset."

"About you taking the jet?"

"About my destination. He wanted us to return together for our honeymoon."

"So that's why you're wearing your ring," the doctor said. "What are you planning to do about the wedding date? The last time we spoke, Alec seemed to really be pressuring you."

"I know. But I've led him to believe that I'm not feeling well and until I can figure out what's going on with my body, I can't commit anytime to a stressful event like wedding." Stephanie returned to her favorite view in front of the glass.

"What if he decides to forgo the pomp and circumstance for a quiet private ceremony along the beach."

"You're good, doctor. Very good. He already did."

"And you said?"

"His father and I convinced him that he could get better coverage off this image Alec and his father are trying to build. Our marriage is a testament to him embracing all people."

"Sounds like a platform more than a commitment for life to me."

"And what's wrong with that? We all want security."

"What's wrong with it is that as a passionately suppressed person, for you this won't last. Men, and particularly Alec, have a survival instinct that women don't possess. He'll outlast you, Stephanie, and you won't be happy."

"What is this, How to Date and Marry White Men 101? I know what I'm doing."

"Okay, I'm going to give it to you straight, as you say." She twirled a strand of her strawberry-blond hair, took her glasses off and placed her pen down. "You are paying me $225 an hour to tell you what you don't want to hear. Alec and his father sound like they have an agenda you haven't discovered. You don't love him, you are walking around possibly fatally ill and you won't face yourself. This has got to stop. For the three months you've been seeing me, we've achieved little progress. We don't have time for baby steps, Stephanie. You don't have a choice, you have to make a step toward healing or you'll be stuck for the rest of your life spending excess time and money to talk about things you already know."

"I always have a choice, doctor."

"Yes, you do, but not choosing is not an option. Take responsibility for yourself. Now, your prescription is as follows: You are to see a medical doctor for a checkup. Once we've determined your condition we'll work on a game plan from there. You are barred from practicing for three months until we are able to further assess your capabilities."

"But..."

"Trust me, Stephanie. Don't fight me on this. I will go to the board and have your license revoked if I have to. You have to face this stuff. You have to face this situation with your ex-boyfriend, Alec, your health and your heart. You're falling apart, and your life is depending on it." She turned softer. The doctor grabbed Stephanie under the chin and lifted her head. "You know, I'm only doing this to help you...but your help has to come in the form of action now. It's time." The doctor cupped Stephanie's wet chin. She rolled her chair back to her desk and wrote on her tiny notepad. "Here, this will help you relax. I expect to hear from you tomorrow with your appointment for the doctor of your choice made."

Stephanie rose, put on her jacket, grabbed her bag and proceeded to leave.

"Oh, and Stephanie, trust me, I will follow up with your physician of choice. Don't let yourself down."

She finally spoke. "I thought you were going to say don't let me down, meaning you. That would have been better motivation."

"That is the problem. Your well-being should be motivation enough. I look forward to hearing from you tomorrow and seeing you next week."

"Is this an emergency, Miss Alphonso?"

"Yes."

"Okay, the doctor has an opening at 2:00 P.M.

"I'll be there."

Stephanie rang the worn bell. Its shiny white surface was now gray. *Dr. Kaplan hasn't changed,* she thought. She remembered as a child dreading ringing the bell and walking through the open door. The brown paneling once refurbished in the seventies remained the same and the walls retained that familiar old smell. The magazine rack held together by a rusted screw still boasted the magazines *Life, National Geographic, Reader's Digest* and the *Medical Journal*. She allowed her fingers to rub the worn metal, which surprisingly didn't have a speck of dust.

With a faint smile she sat on the same brown pleather couch that hadn't cracked in twenty-plus years. Even though Dr. Kaplan didn't allow smoking before it was in style to do so, she wondered why he maintained the ashtray.

The room still held an air of darkness. Even as a doctor she still shuddered at the idea that no matter what the illness, Dr. Kaplan always gave her a needle in her backside. She cried and cried at the pain but never admitted to the almost instant relief from the annual bouts with tonsillitis, strep throat and pneumonia.

She laughed to herself at the picture that still hung on the far wall of a doctor caricature with syringes around his neck like a necklace, stethoscopes in one hand and his magical black bag in the other.

"Stephanie, it's been a long time. You're a little thin there." The once chubby man was now lean himself with hair color that matched his lab coat. He invited her behind the double doors. "So what brings you here today?" Stephanie looked at him across the steel desk. Between them stood his antique quail pen and a desk full of papers.

He pulled her chart from the matching steel cabinet just in arm's reach. "Okay, let's see, you haven't been here in two years."

"Haven't had a need to."

"I see. Every two years, it was either the tonsils acting up or the flu or a viral infection. So what's going on today?"

"You know, Dr. Kaplan, it's amazing to me how you keep records so well and you've relied on nothing more than your answering service and your trusty pen. My parents always said your impeccable records always kept us healthy."

"Yes, yes. Stephanie Alphonso. Born August 27 at 12:01 A.M., five pounds, six ounces. I left out the year on purpose."

"Thanks." She chuckled.

"How are your parents doing? I haven't seen your father much at the latest fund-raiser balls. Your mom always looks so good."

"They're doing well. Dad's practice is booming."

"I'm aware. That's wonderful. So what brings you here? Tonsils? Feeling under the weather?"

"Yes, well no, well yes. Doctor Kaplan, I need a complete physical checkup. Everything, including blood work," she said solemnly.

"Well don't worry. I'm sure you're in perfect health. I caught you coming into this world, remember."

"Of course I remember. Well I don't actually but you know what I mean."

"So let's get started." He led her into the examining room.

"So how did you get back into your house?" Gem asked, laughing.

"It's not funny. Thank God my neighbor across the hall let me stay on her couch until the doorman reported for duty. He let me in."

"So are you going in to work today?"

"I have to. I've been summoned. I'm just going in late. I told his secretary that I had a personal problem."

"Yeah, like you could only show up for work in a sheet." She chuckled some more.

"Gem, this is not funny. And Steffon is not talking to me. I tried calling him today but he's not in the office and he's not answering my pages or his cell phone."

"Talise, you are messing with fire. What are you going to do when his girlfriend, your friend Vanee finds out, and trust me she will find out?"

"I'm not doing anything!"

"Don't give me that crap. Talise, it's all in your voice when you talk about him. It's all in your eyes and your conversation. You're running a dangerous game, girl. I don't care how good he is to you right now in 'your time of need,' " Gem emphasized. "He's not good for you."

"But…"

"But nothing. And no, my answer is final. I'm not signing with those guys. I don't have a good feeling about it."

"So what are you going to do?" Talise sucked in her stomach. She held the phone between her ear and her shoulder while she tried to fasten the back of her skirt.

"The same thing I've been doing. I'm not taking that gig at the Peppermint, I know that much. I've come too far for that. I have some feelers out for a few more jingles. Nobody's biting except for a few background gigs. I'm not interested in that either."

"Picky, picky. Ooh, hold on, that's my other line. It's probably Steff." She clicked over.

Gem waited impatiently only because she really had nothing else to do.

"Okay, I'm back."

"Was that Steffon?"

"No."

"Oh, the job?"

"No."

"Then who?"

"Calvin."

"What? I thought that was done."

"Apparently not. He's coming up this weekend. He wanted to know if it was okay for him to stay here."

"For what?"

"Since he missed my actual birthday, maybe he's making up.

"Did he say he was coming up specifically for your birthday?"

"No."

"Then why assume?"

" 'Cause. Why else would he be coming up here? I haven't heard from him in so long, maybe he's trying to make amends."

"You know what they say when you assume, don't you?"

"I'm not making an ass of myself. There would be no other reason for him to come up here. He chose to stay with me when he could be staying in a hotel. Don't get jealous."

"Please. Why would I be jealous of you and your thug men? So what are you going to do about Steffon?"

"Speaking of which, you know Vanee and her friends are starting a sister support group. They invited me to attend."

Gem began to file her nails. "I know you declined."

"No."

"No. Girl, what are you trying to get yourself in? That's just stupid. Just crazy. You have done some really stupid stuff but this takes the cake. I can't help you out of this one. We need Stephanie for this."

"Have you spoken to her?"

"Not really. I've called a couple of times. She's taken some time off from work. She hasn't been feeling well recently. I think it's just stress. Alec is really pressing her for a wedding date. Girl, did you see that rock!"

"Yeah, yeah. She'll never be happy. She's not in love with that guy. I don't really like him. He's arrogant."

"Well the pot speaks."

"Huh?"

"Well if that's not the pot calling the skillet a pan."

"Yeah whatever. Look, I have to go. I have a meeting with K.J. this evening and I better be prepared."

"Good luck."

"Thanks, I'm going to need it."

Gem immediately dialed Stephanie's home number. Once again she got her machine. She didn't bother to leave a message. Still undressed with no plans of changing she sauntered to the kitchen and pulled out her *Backstage* newspaper and scanned it for entertainment gigs. She passed over the cruise ships looking for singers. *Oh no, not another* My Grandma Prayed for Me, Part 12...she thought as she bypassed those auditions clips as well.

She flipped through the seventeen pages of what she deemed as nothingness and proceeded to pour herself a cup of chamomile tea from her whistling kettle. She stumbled across an ad that caught her eye:

SINGER WANTED FOR NEW MANAGEMENT PROSPECTS...RECORD DEAL IN PROGRESS MUST HAVE A STRONG R&B WINCEY QUALITY, ABLE TO BELT, ORIGINAL MATERIAL DESIRED BUT NOT REQUIRED. ALL EXPENSES PAID PLUS SALARY AND SIGNING BONUS...PLEASE CALL...

It's fate, she thought as she picked up the phone and dialed. *Shoot, I know I can sound as good as my favorite singer.* Immediately she heard an intriguing voice. "W&R Enterprises, please hold."

Gem held as the sounds of several Motown sixties music soothed her ears.

"Yes, how may I help you," the bubbly voice said when it returned.

"I'm responding to your ad in *Backstage*."

"Do you have original material?"

"Well I have a demo."

"Great. Would you be willing to come to our offices, play it and audition live for our managers?"

"Who are your managers?"

"I'm not at liberty to give that information over the phone. Are you interested or not, because if not, please do not waste my time, I have loads of other callers who are."

"I am. And trust me once you hear me sing, you won't have to look any further."

"Confidence. They like that. Okay, what's your name?"

"Gem. Gemmia actually."

"Which one is it?"

She's snippy. "It's Gemmia. Gemmia Barnes."

"Okay, Gemmia. Send us a copy of your demo along with a recent headshot and résumé. If we like the demo we'll call you in, and you'll have to audition for us in person. There are a lot of kooks out there who would send demos of someone else."

"Don't I know it."

"Anyway, get that to us as quickly as possible, preferably by messenger and we'll get back to you once we've heard it, either way."

Gem eagerly took down the address noticing it was close to Will and Robb's office on Forty-sixth and Broadway. Will and Robb still had all of her materials, demo, headshots and résumé. She would pick them up, hand-deliver them herself and force a live audition out of the deal.

For the first time in weeks, she felt excited and invigorated. She hadn't felt hope since her last gig was cancelled and Will and Robb dropped her as well. She decided to celebrate.

She closed every curtain in the house. She dimmed all of the lights, ran bath water and lit candles. She pulled out her bible and began to read. The running water sounded like music to her ears. She began to hum one of her favorite Yolanda Adams spirituals.

She picked up her bible again and read aloud from Mark 11:24 *"What things soever ye desire when you pray. Believe that ye receive them. And ye shall have them."*

She then read another favorite verse, Philippians 4:6, *Be careful for nothing; but in every thing by prayer and supplication with thanksgiving let your requests be made known unto God.* She read all the way through to 4:13, *I can do all things through Christ which strengtheneth me.*

At that moment she felt she got the message. *This new opportunity must be my destiny*, she thought. So she eased into the now full tub of warm water filled with lavender-scented bubbles. She immediately began to pray out loud: "Lord, I want to thank You today, for watching over me while I slept and waking me in my right mind with activity in all of my limbs. I want to thank You for your love and guidance through those situations that I sometimes wondered if You were with me. In the end You've always shown me that You are always with me as you told Joshua. I'm coming to You today with a special request. I know You want me to excel and use the gift that You have given me—my voice. I want the world to hear me. I want this deal and I know You've sent me signs. The paper with the ad, the reference to my favorite singer and the conversation that I had on the phone. Please God, I want this and because I am your child I know I deserve it. Amen. P.S. God just as You instructed, I am standing on the belief that You will grant these things unto me. Amen."

Gem submerged herself even farther, relaxed and smiled. *Watch out world, here I come.*

"Okay, Stephanie, you're all done. Your blood work will be back in three days. I need you to call me or come in as soon as I call you. Do you understand?"

"Yes, Dr. Kaplan. I understand. And Dr. Kaplan?"

"Yes."

"You will be honest with me?"

"I know no other way."

She nodded knowing the answer. He walked her out of the door leaving her with a big bear hug and a kiss on the forehead.

She hopped into her car and sped off for home. She clicked her cell phone on speaker and hit the number one button. She had recently re-programmed it in order of priority.

"This is Stephanie. I just finished my full physical including blood work. I'm okay. I'll call you tomorrow with my follow-up and my next appointment. I'm tired and weak, so I'm going home. Don't call me, I'll call you. Oh the doctor's number is 555-7283. His name is Dr. Kaplan, and he's been my doctor since birth, if you need to verify." She hung up the phone and gassed the engine harder.

CHAPTER 11

Long time, no see. I thought you were coming in earlier," she said. She continued stirring her famous salmon alla vodka with penne and peas.

"It smells good in here. Looks nice too. You didn't tell me you got new furniture," he said, placing his garment bag down on the couch. He grabbed his tote and started to place a few items on the shelf she reserved for him in the bathroom.

Talise followed him with a heaping spoonful of pasta, cheese and the pink vodka sauce. "Taste this," she said.

"I'd rather taste you," Calvin said, pulling her close.

"Plenty of time for that. Taste it." She played. She shoved the spoon between his pearly whites. He kissed her with the noodle sticking out of his mouth.

She grabbed hold of it. "Um. This is good," she admitted.

"So are you," he said, hugging her.

"I'm glad you came."

"I told you no promises, that I would try my best to get up here. So here I am," he said as he turned and continued to place his things in the cabinet and around the basin.

Talise ran back to a pot just about to boil over. She turned down the flame and stirred. "So what are your plans for tomorrow?"

"I have a chance to meet with Diamond and Sack Hughes tomorrow at a charity event. I should be here until Tuesday and from there I'm off to New Orleans for a big sales conference." He entered the bathroom leaving the door slightly ajar.

She heard the shower run. She imagined how the water must have danced off his shoulders. At that moment it didn't matter that he'd been away for what seemed like eternity. She placed the spoon down and followed him into the bathroom.

Talise stood for moments, sneaking a peek at his lather-covered body. At that moment she longed for him like she once did in the initial stages of their now fleeted escapade.

"You mind if I join you?" she asked.

"Yes." He turned and faced the water.

"Yes, you want me to join, or yes, you mind?"

"Talise, don't ask silly questions. Do whatever you feel like doing," he said. He returned to the running water.

That was a helluva invitation. Wounded she walked back to the stove where her salmon was now burned and the pasta was stuck. "Dammit. Dammit. Dammit." She slammed the spoon down, breaking her ceramic spoon rest. "Dammit." She scrambled, placing the scorched pan under cold running water. The steam from the two extremes created a gray hue in the air accompanied by the burned smell.

"I thought you were coming in with me," Calvin said seductively, standing before her wrapped only in a towel, drenched from the water

"It didn't sound like you wanted me to," she said with her back to him, still tending to her ruined meal.

"What did you do in here?" he asked as he walked toward her.

"What does it look like?" she tried to remain calm but she remembered she had spent her last bit of disposable income on this meal and already it hadn't yielded the results she craved. "If you give me a minute, I'll throw a few steaks on. This is overdone."

"Fine. I'll be in the bedroom." He walked off. "Oh, and if you don't mind, I'm in the mood for onions tonight. A lot of onions."

She turned to hear the door to her bedroom close. She gazed at his jacket that lay on the couch next to his garment bag, which was also draped over his tote. "What is this? I left work early to clean up for his butt and he just drops his shit all over my couch." She flung his jacket over her shoulder and hung it in the closet. She threw his shoes that she had almost tripped over in the closet as well and placed his tote on the side of the loveseat out of harm's way. She made her way back to the kitchen where she proceeded to cut up two large spanish onions. This was feeling far from the birthday weekend she had planned.

A pleasant but light dusting of snow had fallen on the ground. Still grateful for what she felt to be a breakthrough, she donned her suede mustard-colored high-heeled boots and her navy-and-mustard suede skirt suit. It was revival week at her church.

"Why does the phone always ring when I'm about to leave?" she asked aloud. She grabbed her keys and purse and caught the phone on the final ring before the call entered the voice mail of oblivion.

"Speak quickly, I don't have a lot of time."

"What a pleasant greeting…"

"You're right. Hello." She paused. "Now speak quickly because I have less time…"

"That's better." He laughed. "Now tell me this, how is it that you tell a brother to call but never seem to return his call? Is it my breath or what? A brother could always get an Altoid…"

"Funny. Who is this?"

"Wow. This conversation is a real boost to my ego."

"Vaughan. I'm sorry."

"What made you catch on?"

"You are the only brother I've met that can go toe-to-toe with my sarcasm and come out unscathed. Listen, I hate to do this to you but I'm on my way out, I'm running late and…"

"You'll call me back," he answered.

"Yeah."

"Gem, I don't appreciate the runaround. If you don't want to be bothered, that's cool. Pretty soon your actions are gonna speak louder than your words."

"I'm sorry but actually…hey, why don't you come with me."

"Where are you going?"

"To church."

"It's not Sunday."

"My church is having revival. It's young adult week. The messages are geared toward the young adults of the community. Messages to inspire us."

"Thanks but no thanks."

"Why not? It's not like you have to work tonight."

"How do you know?" he answered defensively.

"Because you wouldn't be calling me asking why I haven't called you possibly leading to what are you doing tonight and how about we get together. I just saved you several steps," Gem said, checking her watch.

He sighed. "Confident, aren't you?"

"When it comes to you," she said.

"Me and the church thing. You know, I don't know."

"Okay. Let's cut to the chase. You like me. You'd like to get to know me better. Cool. I like you too. I love God, music and life. And in that order because the former fuels the latter. Now we already know we have one thing in common, music. If we don't have the first one in common we have nothing to talk about."

"Why are you so hard? You trying to be a hard rock when you really are a gem, Gemmia…"

She sighed and rubbed her temples. "Vaughan, I'm going to church. You're welcome to meet me there. But I have to go. I'm already late."

"As usual."

"Whatever."

She gave him the address and the time of the service.

"It doesn't sound like much of an invitation."

"Vaughan, I hate to break it to you. I'm not in the business of begging. I hope to see you there, but if not, I'll catch you another time. Now I gotta go." She hung up the phone, wrapped her head, threw her bag on her shoulder, and headed out the door.

"Yes, sit down, sister. Don't worry, you're not late. You're here at God's appropriate time. Because God is always an on-time God. Can I hear an amen?" the fervent minister advised.

"For those of you just joining us, we are speaking about the Holy Spirit as opposed to other spirits. Tonight our topic is fornication and the spirit of lust. Now turn with me if you will to…"

Fornication? This message isn't for me. I'm celibate, God. What's up with this? Gem thought as she sat down in the back pew. Immediately she flipped her bible open. She was ready for scripture.

"Now I know some of you young people are saying, 'What does this have to do with me? I'm married or I'm seeing a man or woman in the church and we don't have sex outside of God's sanctions.' But you know how we as humans allow ourselves to be in situations that God would not have us to be in."

"Preach, Reverend," Gem heard many of the congregation say. Reverend Joanne Newell was the preacher of the evening. The reverend had stepped from the pulpit and continued to converse without the microphone as she walked down the aisle.

"…But I want you to know that no matter what situation we get in, God always gives us a window or a door to walk out of. It is up to us to use it. Remember He will never trample on our free will. That's why our will should be God's will. You know, Our Father which art in heaven…" The congregation joined in.

"Now we think that God's will or commandments are too hard or come with a lot of rules, don't we?"

No one answered.

"Sister Carol. This is my friend, my brothers and sisters. And you all know that if you sit in the front row and I know you just a little bit, I'm probably going to ask God to allow me to use you. And we don't mind because we are always saying, 'God, please use me.' Amen, everybody. Yes amen." The congregation loved her. In fact she was requested more often than any other preacher.

"Now my sister in Christ, Carol is a stewardess. Am I right, Carol?"

"Flight attendant." The petite woman in the front row corrected the reverend.

"I'm sorry, flight attendant. Now my friend is a flight attendant, and she is always complaining that folks want to give her a hard time when they fly, particularly about their bags in front of their feet. And what my friend has said to me is that people think we are just trying to tell them what to do just for the heck of it. What they don't understand is that we are advising them for their own safety. We're not just telling them what to do. We have their safety at stake. But you must remember, my brothers and sisters that God has our salvation at stake."

A chill ran through Gem's spine.

"Now, my brothers and sisters, God says that intercourse without the benefit of marriage is not sanctioned in His sight. And our goal, we agree, is to please God. Now let's examine the word *intercourse. Inter* according to *Webster's* means in and out of one another, thing or person. The word *course* means path or road. Intercourse then means you are entering the path or road with one another. But God says to worship him in spirit and in truth. Can I get an amen, somebody?" All in the congregation gave an amen, whether it was with the clapping of their hands, standing on their feet or waving their arms in the air.

"Now let's take fornication, because we have to call it what it is, fornication. Now let's take the act of fornication.

"It is said that when you have intercourse or we fornicate, if we do not use protection in the form of a condom, whomever you have intercourse with, you are doing so with every person that person has had intercourse with and vice versa. So the world encourages us to use protection."

"Now there is one thing that condoms will not, cannot or have not protected us from, praise God, and that is a spirit. You see my bretheren there is the Holy Spirit and there are other spirits. Alcohol is a spirit. Drugs are a spirit. Addiction of any kind is a spirit. There is a spirit of lust. There is a spirit of despair, destruction and depression. Are you a shopaholic? That is a spirit. Are you a workaholic? That is a spirit. Are you a gossip? That is a spirit. Do you get where I'm going?" Amens and hand claps emerged all over the sanctuary.

"Now when you have intercourse, you must know that your spirit is entering the course of another spirit. Whatever spirit, including the Holy Spirit lingers with that human being that your spirit is entering the course of, so are you rolling the dice to acquire that spirit. Let me make it simple: You don't drink or drink socially. You meet a new someone special in your life and this person must be sent by God, he or she is perfect, this person drinks more than what you consider to be a little. Or you meet someone and this person seems to always have something going on, some kind of strife in his or her life. Or this person dabbles in a bit of weed as you young folks call it. Anyway, you look up one day and all of a sudden, that social drink you used to take becomes a common occurrence. That strife and gossip you so desperately tried to avoid seem to have entered into your life like a ball of fire. That weed you puffed in college now becomes cocaine, acid or something worse. That pull at the slots becomes blackjack tables that cause you to lose your house. The little thing that you picked up at the mall becomes mounds of credit-card debt that you still can't understand how it got out of control. These things are all spirits. And then what happens is when you get to the core of the problem you have allowed your spirit to enter into the course of things other than the Holy Spirit. This includes but is not limited to fornication or sex. You ever heard of toxic relationships? All of a sudden you are burning candles and saying chants and believing more in the power of the candle than that of Jesus Christ, and you wonder…" She paused and looked around.

"…You wonder where is God? Now here is where the lesson comes in that I brought up about my friend Carol the flight attendant. You think we make up rules just to make up rules. You think God makes up rules to bind us when he makes up rules to set us free. You see, God has not sanctioned this relationship that you are in and remember what we spoke about before, He will not trample on your free will. So you have allowed your spirit to enter into the course with another spirit and God's will is not being done because you've sacrificed His will for yours. Again the window or the door to which you can exit from any sin is that of Jesus Christ who died on the cross for your sins and mine so that your spirit may enter the course with the Holy Spirit."

She paused again and looked around. So the next time you decide to have intercourse, you think about whether you are allowing your spirit to enter the right course. Think about what spirits are lingering with that person that you know nothing about. Ask God. He'll tell you…"

Gem was floored as she walked toward the front of the pulpit to shake the reverend's hand.

"Wonderful message, sister. Thank you," Gem heard many people before her say.

"No, thank God," was always the minister's response.

"Your message was wonderful, Reverend. I really enjoyed you," Gem said as she shook Reverend Newell's hand.

The reverend returned her handshake by grasping both of her hands politely. "You have a gift, my sister. There is a light around you. Make sure God is guiding it. You are entering into some deep water. There are a number of relationships around you. Some mean you no good, just what you can offer them. You must be very careful. Always ask God for His help. Be careful, my sister, and remember even when it seems like

He's not, God is always with you just like He commanded Joshua, be strong and courageous, be strong and courageous. Have I not commanded you, be strong and courageous? For I am the Lord thy God and I am always with you just like I was with Moses..." With that the reverend kissed Gem's hand. Once again Gem felt another chill up her spine.

"Reverend Newell, this is Gem. Her voice is like that of angels. She's a God-sent talent. We pray for her daily and we know that she will be blessed with the opportunity to reach everyone with her melodic voice," Gem's own minister said.

"Oh, she will. Just keep focused on God," Reverend Newell said never letting go of Gem's hand. "I wish you would serenade us with song, my sister."

Before she could answer, Gem's minister bade everyone to be seated as the benediction would be followed in praise with a song by their own Gemmia Barnes.

Gem's rendition of "Never Alone," The Clark Sisters' "You Brought the Sunshine" and "This Battle's The Lord's" sparked the beginning of an all-night gospel jam session. Word spread all over town as Gem was joined by many of the greatest musicians and singers in the state of New Jersey and the world—Gloria Parker, Louberta Byrd, Darryl Williams, Frank and Fred Frierson, Mr. Fryer and much to her great joy and tears, Mr. Vaughan Winters himself.

She sat on the bench as the dust of snow covered every bare spot around her. It had grown cold throughout the night. But she licked on her ice cream cone as if it were the middle of summer. The words rang as a piercing pain throughout her mind.

"*I won't give you a timetable on your life, Stephanie, but I will confirm that you have full- blown AIDS. Your T cell count is critically low...it's the part of the cell that fights infection. At this point we can offer pain-control medication.*" The candid words of Dr. Kaplan whispered by her ears like a sharp wind. "*If you need help in informing your family, please let me...*"

She hadn't heard him finish before her mind gave her relief in the form of blackness. When Stephanie awakened some brief moments later, she realized she was on the same cold bench with the snow falling around. Only now she wasn't alone.

"So who are you going to tell first, your fiancée or your best friends?" The man she loved so hard that she couldn't fathom loving anyone near to that capacity sat down. "You know I'm sorry that you had to suffer because of my stupid mistakes. I want you to know that I've always loved you. I never felt good enough for you. I tried to tell you but you wouldn't listen. I made you leave me the best way I knew how. But even though I continued to fuck up and hurt you time and time again, you never listened. That bitch didn't mean anything to me. I just used her to get you away from me. I didn't want to hurt you any more than I had. I made a decision, fucked up and wanted to live with it. But you didn't want to listen. You just wanted to love me. I didn't know what to do. That's why when I found out—I made it my business to find you—to tell you face-to-face that I'm sorry. The only consolation prize is that I, too, am suffering. I'm in my final stages of this disease, and I don't know how much time I have either…"

"Do you love Anney Lewis?"

"Of course I love my wife. I met her just as my life began to change. She, like you, is forgiving and kind. But more than that she loves me with all of her heart. No pretense with her. She's patient and she helps me. She's suffering too. I wish I could take her pain away, just like yours, but I can't. This is the consequence for my actions. I'm sorry."

"Well you sure have a damn funny way of showing it! I loved you with everything I had. And now because of you, I'm dying! Do you hear me, bastard, I have died a thousand deaths because of you, and like always, you have to have the last word."

She raised her hand in extreme anger and swung with all of her might. Her swing never reached Glenn. All of a sudden he was gone. It was just Stephanie and the ice cream cone just as she had been before her mind drifted off on the cold park bench where she sat alone.

Talise continued to pick up all around the apartment. Calvin left early that morning. And she labeled their evening the night before a deflated balloon. There was still some air but no helium. Disappointment proved to be her only sentiment.

"Thanks, girl. I'm all done," she said in her neighbor's doorway.

"I told you to keep it until the morning. I did my cleaning yesterday."

"No. I just wanted to go over my rug a little bit."

"You have company, huh?"

"How did you know?"

"Because that's the only time I've seen you clean your place so ferociously. I felt sorry for that guy when he had that furniture delivered. When the doorman opened your door without you being home, I said to myself, y'all better be careful. You don't know what you're walking into. No offense, girl, but I've seen your place on a good day. It's good you live alone."

"Scherrie, I asked for your vacuum, not your advice," Talise said, noticing her neighbor always kept a meticulous household, even with two small children. "You were around when my furniture was delivered?"

"Yeah. I came home when the little sexy man was bribing the doorman to let him in. Don't worry, I told him that I don't care what kind of cash somebody brings, don't you ever let anyone into my apartment when I'm not there. I will have your hide and make sure personally that you are prosecuted in court. The doorman knows better than to play that mess with me," Scherrie said as she leaned against her own door frame. "I've seen the furniture wrapped in plastic. You mind if I take a look at your place now?"

"Sure, come on over." Talise led Scherrie on a tour. She was glad that the place had defied the insult the neighbor had just laid on her even though the insult reeked with truth.

"So where is your friend now?"

"Well it's not the friend that gave me the furniture that's visiting. My visitor is another friend. Someone a little more important for lack of a better word," Talise answered with a smile.

"So where is he?"

"Hopefully buying my birthday present." She smiled wider.

"Ooh, girl, happy birthday! Why didn't you tell me? I could have arranged a night for you and my girls. There is a new hot spot in Roselle. We would have had a good time. Some real fine eye candy out that way."

Talise laughed. She always enjoyed her neighbor's company and wished they could hang out a little more. "I have all the eye candy I need. Trust me, Calvin's got it going on."

"Well I'm not mad at cha. Your place looks nice. Real nice. My girl on the fourth floor is moving in with her man and selling some stuff. She has brand-new vertical blinds if you're interested. They'll give your living room a nice touch."

"Thanks. I'll think about it. Well look, I don't mean to rush you off but Cal should be coming back soon, and I want to get ready. I'm sure we'll be going out tonight. At least we better be."

"Cool. I'll talk to you later. Happy birthday again."

"Thanks. I'll talk to you later." Talise closed the door behind her and proceeded to get ready.

Six o'clock came and went. Seven o'clock ticked like torture and eight passed even slower. Talise was fully dressed in a royal-blue-and-black satin skirt that hugged her hips. The matching top with oriental appliques danced on a chest that out of upset heaved up and down with disgust. Calvin hadn't even called.

Talise called an overly jubilant Gem.

"Well he said he had an important brunch, right?"

"Yes. Technically brunch lasts from oh, let's say eleven until about two in the afternoon. It's 8:30 P.M." she emphasized. "…and he's nowhere to be found. I thought he was going out to get my gift but—"

"Maybe he still is. I hope he wouldn't be that callous and forget your special day. I told you we should have gotten together."

"I'm telling you, Gem, he better be. He better make this one up real good. I'm not taking this shit anymore. I'm telling you. Calvin is going to let me know where we stand, birthday or not. I'm tired of this back and forth."

"Don't ask questions if you are not ready for the answers, Talise. You might get your feelings hurt. As a good friend recently said to me, actions speak louder than words."

"Is Stephanie on the phone? I didn't ask for your commentary," Talise snapped.

"No Stephanie isn't on the phone. Okay. I'm just trying to help."

"Well aren't you Miss Mellow. What's up with you?" Talise asked, still checking her watch. She cradled the phone between her shoulder and ear and began to undress. Any decent restaurant would not be available without a reservation during this late hour.

"Well since you asked…"

"Oh, hold up wait a minute. That's my doorbell. Hang on. It must be Calvin buzzing up."

Gem waited patiently as she heard the conversation on Talise's intercom.

"Yes?"

"Miss Talise, Steffon Bryant is here to see you," the doorman said.

"Steffon? Steffon?"

"Should I send him up?"

Talise hesitated. "Um, of course. Of course you should send him up," she said faintly. She ran back to the phone. "Gem, I have to call you back. I'm in deep shit right now."

"I'm sure," Gem said sarcastically. "And watch your mouth with me."

"I'll call you back."

Gem heard a dial tone.

Talise shook her head in disbelief. She threw on her top. Without a thought she ran across the hall to Scherrie whom had saved her earlier.

"Girl, why are you pounding on my door like a maniac?"

"Scherrie, I don't have time to explain," she said out of breath. "But, I told you earlier, that I have company who should have been on his way back here hours ago. Instead, you know the cutie who gave me the furniture?"

"Yes," Scherrie said calmly.

"Well he's on his way up, and I don't know what to do. Calvin will be here any minute. Steffon knows about Calvin but Calvin doesn't know about Steffon, and if these two meet, you want to say World War III?"

"Okay, calm down. What does Calvin look like?" Scherrie asked. Talise described her chocolate wonder. "Ooh, girl, I might have to keep him here for myself."

"Please don't play with me now. I really need help," Talise said almost on the verge of tears."

"Okay, just leave it up to me. I'll head lover boy off while you get rid of sexy. But be quick or Cal as you describe him won't have a reason to come back across the hall."

Just as she finished her sentence, Steffon walked off the elevator. He barely nodded and walked straight into Talise's apartment without expressed permission.

"Ooh, girl. Too much for me. Handle your business." Scherrie waved, pointing toward the storm that had just entered Talise's apartment.

"You got my back?"

"I said don't worry, didn't I? But you need to get baby boy's attitude straight."

Talise nodded with gratitude and left Scherrie.

She entered her apartment with caution. "Hey. What brings you to Jersey tonight?"

"It's your birthday, remember?" Steffon said, flipping on the television. His feet were perched on the ottoman.

"Yeah. You already gave me my present, um...Steffon, what's wrong. The last time we ended up here you walked out without so much as kissing me good-bye. What's wrong? You haven't been at work the last few days either. Please don't tell me Vanee found out," she said as she eased down beside him.

"Talise, you really pissed me off."

"Why? What did I do?" she questioned still looking at the door.

"You look nice. Going out?"

"Yeah. But what did I do?"

"You called me Calvin the last time we were in bed, Talise."

"Steffon, you are hallucinating. I never called you Calvin. Besides, if I did, what's the big deal? That's your middle name. I thought about that being my nickname for you anyway, so that Vanee doesn't find out who I'm talking about..."

"My name is Steffon Calvin Bryant. You don't call me Calvin. Nobody does. I'm telling you don't fuck with me," he said, pointing in her face.

"Steffon, if I did, I'm sorry, I didn't mean anything by it. You know that Calvin and I are over, finished," she said wiping the beads of sweat from her forehead. Just then someone knocked at the door.

She was dead. She hesitated.

"What you waitin' for? Answer the door." Steffon continued to turn the channels.

Talise walked cautiously toward the door..

"Hey, girl, you ready?" Scherrie had pushed her way into the apartment. "Oh, my bad, you still have company. Hi, I'm Scherrie." She extended her hand.

"Scherrie, this is Steffon." Talise sighed a breath of relief.

"Nice to meet you." Steffon tried to sound proper.

"Girl, I just came over to see if you were ready. Val, Gayle and the girls are all waiting downstairs. It's party time." They laughed and slapped hands.

"Y'all going out?" Steffon questioned.

"Yeah, we trying to hang out a little bit. We tried to surprise my girl but she's so nosy that she found out. I would invite you but it's a girl thang. You know what I mean."

"Definitely. Just don't have my girl out all night." Steffon rose from the chair and turned the television off. "Hit me on my hip," he said as he clipped Talise's chin. "I'm not playing, Talise, no later than 2:00 A.M. Don't make me come out here and find you. It won't be pretty." He planted a sloppy kiss on her Ruby Woo lipstick.

"Okay."

"Steffon, right?" He nodded. Scherrie pulled him to the side. She whispered, "We have a really big night planned for her. I doubt that we'll have her back by two. Cut her some slack for the night." She batted her eyes.

"I feel you. Alright, T, call me tomorrow. Don't get carried away. Remember my name," Steffon said as he headed out the door. He kissed her hungrily, gave his good-byes and disappeared beyond the elevator.

"Girl, I owe you one."

"No you owe me two thousand. You better watch that brother. He ain't cool. Where he come off holding tabs on you like that? That's some stuff. Girl, you better be careful. I'm telling you, it took everything in me to keep my cool but—"

"Thanks, Scherrie. Where is Calvin?"

"I don't know. I tried to head him off but he never came upstairs. I heard you and little man in your place talking so I figured you needed a little help with getting him out."

"Thanks."

"You're welcome. You know, not for nothing, me and my girls are hanging out tonight. That place we told you about in Roselle. You're welcome to come with us."

Talise plopped herself on the couch. "Thanks, but no thanks. I better wait for Calvin."

"Don't wait too long. Trust me, life will past you by. I've been there, Talise. Trust me and when life does keep going, you can't get it back. I'm out," Scherrie said, making her exit.

Talise's self-locking door made a loud clicking noise as she exited. Just then the buzzer rang.

What did Steffon forget? I get out of one situation and get pulled right into another, she thought as she made her way to the intercom.

"A Mr. Jones is here for you, Miss Talise," the doorman offered.

"Please send him up."

It was now eleven o'clock. For some reason, no hope lingered in her soul that her birthday would turn out the way she had dreamed.

"So what happened. Did he bring you a fabulous gift?"

"No. He didn't even say happy birthday. He didn't even give me a card."

"Is he still there?"

"No. He was disappointed that he couldn't meet with his client. He met up with an ex-girlfriend instead and spent the day with her."

"How do you know?" Gem asked in a shocked voice.

"Because he told me."

"He had the nerve to tell you?"

"Yes."

"Talise, I don't care what you say. This man is not in love with you. Actions speak louder than words, my friend. Let's sum this up. He comes up to see you on your birthday weekend. He neglects to spend that time with you. He doesn't bring a card, a present or any form of acknowledgement. You give up two offers to spend time with people who love you—me and Stephanie and your neighbor and her friends—and this negro comes back to your house like you are Motel 6, barely greets you and goes to sleep and leaves you hanging in that fabulous outfit we spent tireless hours picking out? Talise, smell the coffee, sweetheart. Before you dump him for good, you need to tell him how you feel. Oh, and the classic one, he spends the rest of his afternoon with an ex-girlfriend he's still friends with and takes her to brunch. Talise, give him up before I have to come over there and raise my blood pressure."

"Don't worry. He's gone. He said he needed to get back, and I gladly sent him on his way. Oh, hold on that's my phone." Talise clicked over to her other line. "Hello."

"Talise, it's me. You seemed upset when I left so I called to talk."

"Calvin?"

"Yeah."

"Hold on."

She clicked back to Gem on the other line, advised her that she had business to take care of and that she would call her back.

"Be honest, Talise. Tell him how you feel…." Gem's voice trailed off as Talise clicked back.

Calvin was still on the line. She spilled her guts. She poured out everything and anything she could ever feel about him, her birthday and most of all how he had treated her.

"Talise, I'm sorry. My real reason for coming up there was to explain why we had to end this."

She cried and whimpered without the success of holding all her emotions back.

He said, "You are gorgeous, beautiful and a wonderful woman. You don't know this and I don't have time to teach you. It's just more work than I'm willing to take on right now. You have some things to work out within you. I can't help you right now…I'm sorry…I love you but…"

Those were the last words before she regained emotional consciousness. And it was at that moment, Talise knew their love was over.

Chapter 12

So my girl said you called. Did you want to see me? What's up?"

"You mean you were home long enough to get the message. What happened? That Jersey pussy dried up?"

"Romy, this ain't about my home life or who I'm fucking at night," Steffon yelled over Wu Tang Clan pumping loudly in the background.

Romy's bodyguards pulled out the chair directly in front of him and indicated for Steffon to sit. The night was black, the music was perfect and the new club that Romy had opened in honor of his old gang was the hottest ticket in Queens. Romy, of course, sat in the very special VIP section on the upper level, encased in bulletproof glass. It featured a view of the entire club. The hidden zones like the bathrooms, cashier's rooms and closets were stocked with state-of-the-art cameras that gave Romy eyes behind his head.

"I'm calling in your $5,000 marker, boss." Romy remained calm and collected. He twirled the porcelain dominoes between his fingers. "The Knight Gallery cost me a lot of money, partner. That furniture was supposed to buy me a bona fide singer. So far ain't nothin' happenin'. I warned you."

"Romy, I just need more time."

"I ain't got it, Steff. What is it 'bout this pussy that you willing to risk life and limb. You got a sweet sister at home. Cooks, cleans, takes good care of yo' seed and you fucking around wit' shit way out yo' league."

"I told you he wasn't shit, Romy. Let me smoke this motherfucka," one of the guards said.

Steffon immediately grabbed under his belt. He grasped the cold hard metal he called his American Express because he never left home without it.

"I wouldn't try it if I were you." He stared the brother down. That was signal numero uno that Steffon may have left the streets but the streets hadn't left him. "Romy, man, this shit don't happen overnight. If we go strong-arming this situation, you gon' lose all the legitimate shit we trying to build. In the corporate world shit don't happen yesterday. You have to be patient or you can kiss your label good-bye. I know you want Gem. I want her, too, but I've been scoping some other shit that will suffice until she comes through. She ain't the only babe in town. I'm telling you. I was in Jersey at this club in Roselle. A babe named Hope was rocking the place. I'ma tell you she ain't no Gem but she close. We gotta start rockin' other avenues."

Romy paused. He slammed the domino on the table and told the brother to pay up.

"Steff, I got nothin' but love for you. You my partner. We been in and outta some shit. I'll hear this Hope babe. That'll buy you some time but not much. I want Gem. So you keep working. And don't ask for no mo' cash to handle it, you on your own. You got fo'teen days, two weeks, to show me something wit' Gem. In the meantime, get me this Hope tape. I'll see what I can do."

"Cool, Romy. Thanks, man."

"Don't thank me. Take care of yo' bizness, man. Take care of home too. I'm telling you, you keep fucking around and Vanee ain't gon' be nowhere to be found."

"I hear you, man."

"Nothin' but love for you, baby." Romy stood, and he and Steffon exchanged pounds.

Romy's bodyguard escorted Steffon out of the VIP section and out to the door.

Steffon laughed as they reached the street. "What's up wit' that. We used to be boys. Now you gon' try and smoke me?"

"Just doin' my job, Steff. You ain't down no mo'. You Mr. Big Exec now. Can't count on you like we used to."

"Yeah, well I'm just doing mine too. Whatever that is, I'm out."

"Peace."

"Peace," Steff ended. The valet brought his car around, and he sped off.

She coughed vigorously between laughter and joy. "I'm happy for you, Gem. Vaughan sounds like a good guy."

"We're putting together a show for me. Vaughan is overseeing everything. God is good."

"Yes, he is."

"What's up with you and Alec?"

"The same ole, same ole. His campaigning is taking up much of his time. His opponent is tough. He has a track record with the city that Alec just can't match. I'm trying to be as enthusiastic as possible, but if you want my honest opinion, the other guy is better for the job."

"Yikes. Stephanie, be careful of that opinion. This man is going to be your husband. The public can sniff out lack of loyalty."

"I know."

"What's really going on? You don't sound like yourself."

"Just tired, girl. So where is your show going to be?"

"We're trying to secure Euphoria Café. It's tough but Vaughan has a few connections, so we'll see. I know you'll be there, with or without Alec."

"Yeah, God willing. So what's up with your managers? Are they helping?"

"Girl, they are MIA. I'm still on contract but pursuing other venues. In fact I auditioned for a group of guys in the city the other day. They seemed to like me, but they want my demo. I've tried calling Will and Robb but they've seemed to change their number, and they're not returning my calls."

"They might be doing that on purpose. I'm sure they don't want you to sign with anyone else."

"Will told me to pursue other avenues with his own lips. So that's what I'm doing. If another offer comes up, I'll have to work my way around it."

"Just be careful." Stephanie coughed again. She checked her watch and noticed she was ten minutes late taking her medicine. "Oops, hold on. That's my other line." She clicked over and caught the other call.

"Stephanie, it's Mom."

She had hoped it was Alec. "Yeah, Mommy, I got Gem on the other line."

"Yeah? Stephanie, you're a college graduate with her master's as well. You really should do better with your grammar."

"Yes, Mother."

"That's better. Anyway. Have you taken your medicine for this evening?"

"Mom, the medicine, the medicine ain't gonna matter."

"Isn't, dear. Isn't."

"Mom!" Stephanie shouted.

"Stephanie, you listen to me. We can beat this thing. But you need to stay focused and keep steady."

Stephanie slammed her arm down on the phone in frustration. Her parents had been working her nerves ever since Stephanie broke down and revealed her illness to them.

"Mommy, you think that I will beat this thing with medication. I have AIDS, Mommy, not HIV, AIDS. There is nothing I can do except manage my impending pain. Do you understand that!" she yelled.

"Stephanie, Stephanie!" Gem scream. "You have AIDS?"

Calvin stepped off the plane to smell the warm and welcomed eighty-five degrees. He walked down the long corridor with a smile. He gazed at the many large lithographs in the art galley of the Louis Armstrong Airport of New Orleans, Louisiana.

Carousel number three held his rolling leather duffel, and he squeezed his way through annoyed passengers whose bags hadn't come up on the belt yet.

"St. Charles Place, Patsy's," Calvin informed the driver upon sliding into the black leather seat of the cab. The dashboard held the driver's cross, which hung by rosary beads and several statues of saints. It always amazed Calvin how New Orleans bordered a mix of sin and saints. No matter which way you stepped you could have it either way in this city, which was what he loved about it.

The driver zoomed past the historical graveyards and the Superdome, to the heart of zydeko and the best gumbo a man could have. Shortly Calvin was in front of his favorite hotel, Patsy's, where Patsy the owner greeted him personally.

"Hey, Calvin. It's good to have you back with us again." Patsy was a grandmother of four who looked like somebody's granddaughter instead of the other way around. She was a proud mawmaw as she would say, who didn't look a day over thirty. Her skin sparkled with that tawny complexion only reserved for N'awlins beauties. Her hair color of mixed golds lay bright against her flawless skin.

"Here's your itinerary. The convention center had it faxed a few days ago. I saved your favorite suite. Here's your key and your tour package. Call me if you need anything." She smiled.

"Patsy, you always take good care of me. I 'preciate it."

"Next time you tell those Black MBAs they ought to have their conference here. I just remodeled a state-of-the-art conference center off the garden. Take a look at it when you get a chance."

"I will, Patsy. I will." He smiled and headed up for his room.

Marble greeted him in the foyer and led him through to the gargantuous bathroom with a separate Jacuzzi and shower. Clear sky panels in the ceiling provided perfect sunlight during the day and erotic moonlight at night.

Calvin threw his suit jacket on the round king-size bed. He ran his fingers along the crackled white headboard.

He stripped off his airplane duds and placed them in the valet bag for servicing. "I might as well take advantage of it," he thought aloud, referring to the complimentary cleaning service Patsy offered exclusively for patrons who booked the penthouse suite.

The open shower was surrounded by plush greenery. He stepped into the lukewarm rain that poured from the twelve-setting showerhead. He lathered with the custom soap that flowed from the built-in wall dispensers. He used Patsy's signature Calvin Klein shampoo on his beard and hair and basked in its luxury.

Calvin stepped out of the shower and wrapped the huge luxurious white towel around his lower torso and stepped down a level into the living area, which held a fully stocked bar of premium liquors and other delights.

I might as well get this party started right, he thought as he poured himself a snifter of Courvesier V.S.O.P. He grasped the remote and laughed. *You need a Ph.D. to work this thing,* he thought. He hit the audio button and instantly Nancy Wilson emerged from the surround-sound Bose speakers hidden throughout the suite. He sat in the plush chaise and savored the moment.

"I can't leave right now. Is it that serious?"

"Yes," Gem said firmly. "I wouldn't be calling you on the cell if it weren't that serious. Tell Vanee and those newfound friends of yours that you have a family emergency and meet me at Stephanie's pronto." Gem clicked her cell and continued to speed toward Whispering Woods.

"Are you okay?" Vanee asked, walking into her kitchen to retrieve some more hor d'oeuvres.

"I don't know. My two best girlfriends—I've told you about them." Vanee nodded for consent. "Well something seems to be going on. Gem won't tell me over the phone. She's really upset and said I better get to Stephanie's house fast."

"Well it's only the first meeting and you've been here for most of it, so go ahead. Just know that we are all here for if you need us." Vanee reached over and grabbed her friend. She extended the warmest hug. Talise almost broke down in tears. "Let it out, girlfriend. That's what we're here for. I know exactly what you're going through. You know it's going to take some time for you to really start healing from your divorce with Maurice, your relationship with Calvin and the shit K.J. is putting you through on the job. But remember, this is what it's all about."

Vanee continued to rub her back. "You know things aren't so hot with me and Steffon either. He's staying out all the time, later and later. He's not paying attention to home. I'm lonely and I'm tired. Tired of waiting, girl. You know I want to get married, have a family. I want to do better with my career…I want so many things too…"

Tears had welled in Vanee's eyes, too, but she didn't let them fall. Talise felt a major lump in her throat and sweat drove down her forehead like a car on the Audubon.

"Let's go back inside with the others. Get yourself together and then get on the road to see about your friend," Vanee said as Talise led her back to the living room.

Vanee ran back to the kitchen to get the veggie puffs she left earlier. Talise resumed her spot on the eggplant-colored carpet in front of the faux fireplace that blazed with light. She picked up a dinner cloth and wiped her forehead. The ladies still conversed.

All of a sudden, it was quiet. The joyful noise that captured the room had grown dense like a fog. The momentum shifted quickly as Steffon stepped through the door without speaking. He eyed each and every intruder in his living space, proceeded to the back room and slammed the door.

"Who was that?" Vanee asked, peeking out of the kitchen.

"You mean what was that?" Vanee's cousin said.

"It was a shitload of testosterone," someone said. The other ladies laughed and agreed.

"You got that right. You notice how everything changed the moment he walked in here?" another voice from the crowd chimed in.

Talise sat quietly. This was the perfect time for her to make her move. "Well, ladies, it's been real. I appreciate your hospitality but an emergency just came up so I have to run," she said, bouncing up. She walked briskly toward the large double closet doors. Steffon met her. They both stood there, she in awkward silence.

His eyes caused hers to well. Her patent-leather shoes reflected a glare of guilt.

Silence.

"Steffon, I need to see you," Vanee said, piercing the standoff. She pushed past Talise.

Talise released her breath as Vanee led Steffon a few feet away.

"What is your problem? You don't come home this early on any other night and all of a sudden on a Friday no doubt, you have to make your presence known. You knew I was having a girls-only get-together. You just messed up the mood."

"I told you I ain't want all them bitches up in my crib, no way," he said, leafing through the sweaters Vanee so meticulously cared for.

"Steffon, that's not fair. You plan on stayin'?"

"Actually no. I'm out."

"Good," she said, folding her arms.

"You don't say that shit any other night. Any other time, you forever begging me to come home."

Vanee sucked her teeth. Talise continued to listen.

"Steffon, just go somewhere, anywhere. I'm having a good time with my friends, and I don't need you disturbing the groove up in here," Vanee said less than politely and walked out of the room.

"Are you okay to drive?" she asked Talise who was standing in the threshold.

"Yeah. I'll call you when I get there," Talise said.

Steffon pushed through the ladies, eyed Talise and stomped toward the kitchen.

"What's wrong with him?" Talise asked nervously.

"Nothing. He's just ornery. Take care of yourself. Call as soon as you get there too." Vanee hugged her friend again.

"I will. Ladies, take care. Let me know when the next one is. I'll be there with bells on. Thanks."

The other ladies waved and said good-bye in unison. Steffon briskly walked out of the kitchen munching chips and drinking from a plastic cup. He barely grunted before he shuffled out behind Talise.

"And good-bye to you too," Vanee said as the door shut behind him. "Anyone for champagne and strawberries?" They all laughed as their peace resumed.

Calvin was feeling nice and relaxed. He had changed into his linen vanilla shorts and topped them off with a sage Egyptian cotton collared golf shirt. He coordinated his black leather belt specifically purchased from Milan and his black Cole Haan leather sandals.

His stroll took him from the outskirts of the French Quarter to the outskirts of Bourbon Street where the fun would begin. His first stop was Café Dumonde. The outside cafe with its tall orange pillars and green trim sat on the tip of where the entertainment would soon commence.

It was only 12:30 so Calvin sat down with his *Wall Street Journal* and ordered a trio of beignets and café au lait. Just as the barely English-speaking Asian woman smiled and asked for $5.50, a trumpeteer stepped up and began a sultry rendition of Billie Holiday's "Strange Fruit." He recognized the tune anywhere.

He swayed as he bit into the fluffy powdered delight. A slight breeze blew the powder everywhere. He took a soft swig of the coffee and chickory mix. It slid down his throat like velvet. He continued to brush the white powder that now freckled his attire.

"Somebody has yet to learn how to eat a beignet, I see. Takes a little practice, but you'll get the hang of it." She laughed as she lifted another napkin from his table toward his face.

"I guess it is an art," he said, continuing to brush his clothes. He accepted the napkin from the pleasant woman with medium build who stood before him. She sported a straight ponytail which from what Calvin could tell was hers. Her brown complexion bore very little makeup. She twirled her simple gold hoop earring and smiled. He caught the hint and stood. "Would you care to join me?" he politely asked after his three-second assessment.

"Thanks. I might have to take you up on that later. I'm here with my friends." She pointed to two other ladies at the table across from him. "But you are welcome to join us…that is if you are here alone," she said as she glanced around the table.

He tipped his coffee cup toward the ladies who casually gazed over. "Sure, I'd love to," he said neatly folding his paper.

"I'll help you move," she offered. She picked up his plate and led him to the table where her friends had pulled up a fourth chair.

"Good afternoon, ladies."

"Good afternoon," they chimed in like giddy school girls.

"I'm Calvin," he said, placing his cup down and extending his hand.

"Oh, I'm sorry," the woman who escorted him said. "I'm Chynna. These are my sorors Dawn and Beverlyn."

"Are you all here for the convention?" he asked.

"Well sort of. Not for the sorority but the Black MBAs convention," Chynna said. She hadn't taken her eyes off him. "What scent is that, Calvin. It's lovely."

"Cartier for men. Yeah, the convention is what brings me here as well. Here to do a little networking myself," he said, sipping on his café, which had now gone cold. A different waitress made her way to the table. "A dozen beignets please and three café au laits?" he ordered, looking at the women for approval.

They nodded.

"So are you going to the brunch tomorrow?" Chynna questioned.

"I haven't had a chance to look at my package. I had it faxed to the hotel," he answered.

"Oh, where are you staying?"

"Patsy's," he casually answered.

"On St. Charles?"

"Yes."

"Whew, you must have it like that. That place is exquisite!" Chynna beamed.

"Yeah, it's a nice place," Calvin added casually.

The waitress brought the order. The ladies began digging in their purses when Calvin kindly extended his arm, indicating that it was his treat. He pulled out a twenty and placed it on the woman's tray. Chynna nodded with silent admiration.

"So tell me about the brunch tomorrow," he said. He took delight in watching the ladies watch him.

"It's going to be fabulous. A good friend of mine is the keynote speaker. She's pretty dynamic. She's spearheading the entire convention this year. Her company is the main sponsor," Chynna said, digging into her pastry. "I love these things. They don't love my hips, but I love them." All of the ladies agreed. "Oh, shoot," Chynna said, catching the powder in her mouth

He noticed her glance at her Timex. "What's wrong? Late for something?" he asked.

"No, but you are," she said. He just stared. "If you don't get over to the Superdome and register, you won't be able to attend the brunch or anything else. You said you hadn't looked in your packet yet, right?"

"Right." he said.

"Yes, well it's slightly different this year. Registration is all taking place at the sign-in desk. It closes at two, and it's already 1:30. You have to hurry and catch a cab to the Superdome or space may not be available at some of the events," Chynna said.

"Thanks. I'm glad you told me. I better get going," he said, wiping his mouth one final time. "Ladies, it was a pleasure. I'm sure I'll see you again this week." He gathered his things and proceeded to walk off.

"Calvin, hey." Chynna caught up with him as he hailed the first cab to whiz by Decatur. "Here's my card. If you're not busy after registration, maybe we can meet for a drink before the festivities tonight."

"Cool. I'll give you a call," he said, grabbing her card and placing it in his left breast pocket. "The Superdome, sir, and fast," he said as the cab sped off.

"I'm so sorry. I got here as soon as I could. Traffic was horrible," Calvin said, heading toward the main table. Everyone, including this

Halle Berry look-alike, was packing up.

"Well it looks like you made it just in time," she said with mild pleasantry. She unpacked her leather attache and pulled out a manila folder full of forms. She grabbed a navy blue goody bag from the box in the back of her.

"Now this is going to cost you," she said, warming a little.

"As long as the cost isn't too high," he said, wiping the sweat from his brow. Five seconds out of the cab the dome proved brutal.

"Never something for nothing. Choice always comes with a price. Now here are the forms for some of the events you might be interested in."

"I already know what I'm interested in," he said, looking at the stunning beauty. Her hue was that native only to Louisiana. Her hair was cropped short. Her magnificent features glowed like the blazing sun. She had strong midnight-black eyebrows that curved her bright, sensuous eyes. Her nose peaked above full lips that were dressed with the prettiest peach glaze.

Her tiny torso was accented by perfectly toned buttocks and dancer legs. Her arms were no stranger to hydraulics as the cuts reminded him of Angela Basset in her rendition of Tina Turner.

"Your name please." The woman pulled out a form.

"Calvin. Calvin Jones," he said. *Ahh, a leftie,* he noticed. He always liked lefties. "And your name?" he asked, extending his hand.

"Tracee," she said as she continued.

"Humph," he grunted, taking his hand back after she failed to embrace it.

"I'm sorry. I'm just trying to get you registered and get this paperwork over to the center for processing before my deadline," she offered apologetically. "Calvin, what's your company affiliation?"

"Self-employed. I'm here representing TJG, The Jones Group," he answered, offering her his card.

"Nice. Entrepreneur, huh?"

"You could say that," he answered.

"Interesting. Market research and representation…interesting," Tracee said, placing the pen down and studying the card.

"What's so interesting?" he questioned.

"Based out of Charlotte, huh?"

"What's so interesting?" he repeated.

"Well our theme and focus this year is entrepreneurship. Corporations are great but our societies will be sustained by the X generation, which promotes their own growth through a well-maintained balance of corporate affiliations and corporate competition. We must include our own businesses into the fold. We need to make our graduate degrees work for us, not just for major corporate America, which doesn't always have our best interests at heart." She placed the card down and continued writing.

"I couldn't have said it better myself. I'm impressed."

"Well good because that's the crux of my conversation tomorrow at the brunch."

"Are you giving the main speech?" Calvin asked. He pulled a vacant chair up to the table.

"I like to call it a conversation rather than a speech. A conversation calls for dialogue and participation. I think people like to speak with rather than be spoken to," she said as she continued her writing.

"I like your style, Tracee."

"Thanks. So I guess I can mark you down for the brunch?" She cupped her chin and placed her elbow on the table.

"Wouldn't miss it for the world." He smiled.

"What else are you interested in, Mr. Jones?"

"Dinner and perhaps drinks with you. I like your style, Tracee."

"Thanks, I'm flattered but this isn't the time. I have too much to do—"

"Then sign me up for the golf tournament and I've written down the evening affair, I'm interested in," he said, interrupting her. He knew when to cut his losses as well.

Tracee continued writing and the silence between them remained.

He glanced at his watch and raked his fingers through his black wavy, bushy hair.

"I'm almost done," she said, writing quickly. "So Calvin, tell me, have you worked with food corporations in your area?" Her eyes remained glued to the paper.

"Sure. In fact I've worked with and maintain a contract with an number of food corporations in the area."

"My biggest contract is Allynt Foods. It specializes in airline catering," Calvin said casually.

"I know. That airline contract is on my list to get for my company," Tracee said confidently.

"I'm good, Tracee. So I hope you're ready for a fight," Calvin said, slightly amused.

"And so am I," Tracee said as she stared into his eyes.

"I always love a challenge," Calvin said, adding seduction to his tone.

"And I never back down from a fight, Mr. Jones. Now, here is your badge, your ID for special VIP entrance to all events throughout the convention week. This is your registration for the tournament. Good luck because we have some heavy hitters registered this year, and this is your ticket for the brunch tomorrow."

Tracee began to repack her boxes and things while Calvin remained bewildered. He couldn't seem to score. He pondered the various pieces of papers that she had placed in his hands. "Looks like you have a lot of stuff. Can I at least help you to your car?" he asked.

"Instead of what?" Tracee questioned, placing the last of her manila folders into her attaché.

"What do you mean?" he asked.

"Well, you asked could you at least help me. The 'at least' means that perhaps there was an alternative to something."

"You don't miss a beat, do you?"

"I try not to." She smiled. "Please. I would be honored if you would help me to the car. I would also be honored if you would let me drive you back to your hotel because you, my friend, are about to work your ass off." Tracee laughed.

"Tracee, one box does not constitute me working my ass off." He accepted her softening. He grabbed his papers, placed them on top of the lightweight box and picked it up. "Just lead the way, little lady." He followed her through a maze of prefabricated booths. "What the hell is all of this?" he asked, referring to the sea of other cardboard boxes before him.

"I told you, man. You are going to work your ass off. Since you've made me late, you are going to have to help me get all of this to my car and then some. "Do you have a license?" she asked. He nodded. "Good...you have to drive."

"Really?" he said as his eyes widened.

"Really," she affirmed.

"What were you going to do if I hadn't showed up?"

"I guess we don't have to worry about that, do we? You're here," Tracee said. She grabbed a box and lead the way.

One more time, Calvin thought as she parked the car in front of his hotel. Her teeth were too beautiful for him to quit. "So what about dinner tonight?" he questioned as he leaned against her car door.

"Sorry, meeting with some sorors of mine and then we're going out on the town."

"What about a hurricane after the reception tomorrow?"

"Tennis date," she said, looking at the clock on her dash.

"Well it was nice talking to you, Tracee," Calvin said, finally giving up. *No need to chase,* he thought. "Look me up when you get to the Charlotte area."

"Maybe I will. I'm up for a promotion that would have me based in Atlanta, so I won't be far away."

"Where are you based now?"

"Kentucky. So it'll be nice to be around some folks."

"Well, nice talking to you, Cal. Don't get so drunk tonight that you miss the brunch tomorrow." She laughed, released the clutch and sped off.

"Why you leaving so soon?" Steffon asked as he caught up with Talise at her car.

"You didn't have anything to say to me inside. Why say anything now?"

"I been calling. Where you been?"

"Trying to hold my own, Steff. You know we can't continue with this."

"With what?" He leaned against her door, crossed his arms and cupped his hand under his chin, stroking his goatee.

"You know with what. Us. We can't continue with this. I mean you're good to me, Steff, and I appreciate everything that you've done but this ain't right. Vanee's friendship is way too important to me to fuck it up 'cause I'm fucking her man." She tried to shove him aside to get into her car.

"Whoa." He held his hands up. "Nobody forced you, you know. I thought I was what you needed. I thought I was there for you when everything else wasn't goin' right."

"I didn't say you forced me to do anything. But this just ain't right. It's been going on way too long. I love you and I love Vanee. She's a good friend to me as well. We happened and we shouldn't have."

"So I guess your boy Calvin is back in the picture, huh?"

"Steffon, don't make this harder than what it has to be. Let's just give this a rest and be friends. It's not Calvin or you, it's just me. I can't get myself together if I'm constantly stirring in shit. I gotta go." Her eyes pleaded with him to step aside.

He complied.

"So you choosing your friendship with Vanee over me?" he asked in a deep voice.

"If that's how you want to look at it."

"Yeah, that's fucked up, Talise. You just remember what I told you. You see that up there?" He pointed toward the window. "I control that shit. Everything that goes on or doesn't go on is me. You can walk away but you just kissed yo' so-called friendship with Vanee good-bye too. Remember when I told you at the drop of a dime, I can fix it so that Vanee will hate you. But me, my shit will always be intact." Talise's eyes grew wild and furious. "Consider it done. Oh, by the way as for the furniture, I'll expect my cash in full. You got ten days, bitch."

His coldness left her heated. He slid away from her car and hopped into his. He gassed his engine all the while emitting a stare that could break through anti-freeze. Tears of fear welled up Talise's eyes and her chest heaved with heaviness. He winked and pulled off.

The worst of her night was yet to come, Talise feared, and it had just begun. She didn't look back. She didn't notice that the window from the apartment from which she had just left contained a shadow. Vanee remained until Talise pulled off leaving nothing more than a trail of dust.

Dusk had hit and the party atmosphere in New Orleans began. Slowly but surely the night sky became stronger and the lights went up like flames. Soon the streets would be so crowded that everyone would have to walk at a snail's pace. He didn't mind though. His thoughts aimed at nothing, he savored the congestion lurking behind the dark alleys as he passed under the swinging gas lanterns that hung below almost every balcony.

The chairs that occupied the second floors of the some of the world's most vintage architecture were being pulled inside. The workers were making room for the hoards of people that were to crowd their second-floor balconies. Soon, women would be adorned with the famous colorful beads that hung about people's necks as a reward for showing their boobs.

Calvin's first stop was a restaurant with a variety of cuisines as only native N'awlins folk could muster. The menu boasted French and native Louisiana Creole. *Game plan: meet with Chynna and a few of her friends for pre-dinner drinks. If that flows okay then maybe we will venture upstairs to dine, dutch-style of course and the rest of the evening will play out with adventures in some of New Orleans best-kept back-alley secrets full of Zydeco, jazz and the blues. She can hang if she's cool but if not her cord gets cut with a quickness and without regret,* he thought as he walked through the dark wood double doors with a hint of stained glass on the front.

"Reservations, sir?" the woman adorned in wench-style attire questioned with a deep drawl.

"Uh yes, but first I'm meeting a friend for drinks at the bar."

"Is the lady's name Ms. Chynna Griffin?" the hostess questioned.

He nodded in shock. "I guess so," he said with angst. He wanted to make sure this wasn't construed as a date, but casual acquaintances meeting for a drink.

"Don't be alarmed. She just left word at the desk here to make sure you found each other. We're quite crowded tonight." Her drawl continued to linger. She seemed to pick up immediately on his disquieted aura. Her secret smile revealed that she knew of the hypnotism of her city, which made even the most skeptic weak at the knees when it came to two bodies intertwining in the land of crawfish and alligator sausage.

"Right this waaaay, sir," she said as she led him to invariably different woman from the one he had met over sumptuous pastries earlier.

"Calvin, great, I'm glad you made it. I got worried for a second," Chynna called out.

Her ponytail turned into an elegant upsweep. Her Timex was replaced by rhinestones and her pumpkin-seed-like sneakers had been transformed to black leopard strapped open sandals that showcased neat muscle-toned legs.

"You look dreamy," she said, patting the stool. "Isn't this great?" She referred to the live band on the stage before them. "Wait until we hit the next place. That band is incredible." She continued to bounce to the beat of the music.

Normally this would have been prime time for Calvin to let someone know of his minimal interest. But instead he took a deep breath and chose to enjoy the moment.

"So how did registration go? Everything set?" she yelled, trying to hear herself over the music and the crowd.

"Yeah, everything's set. Thanks for the tip."

"You're welcome." She raised her half-full glass, noticing that he had nothing to toast with. "I'm sorry. Excuse me, bartender, may I have another hurricane please," Chynna asserted.

"Chynna, calm down. I appreciate the gesture but I can order my own drinks," Calvin said.

"Oh. No harm meant. I just wanted to toast."

Within moments, the drink was placed before them and Calvin obliged. He reached in his pocket to pay when Chynna politely advised him that she had a tab going and that it was all but paid for. "Just think of it as a payback for the beignets," she said with pleading eyes.

He accepted.

"So how is the city treating you?" Chynna asked with a smile. She sipped her hurricane slowly.

"This city always treats me right. It's one of my favorites," Calvin said. He took gulps of the drink he considered lightweight compared to his usual Hennessey.

"I love this city. Its dynamics amaze me. The city is a flirtation between good and evil. It's like everything around here is centered on one or the other, God or voodoo. The poverty still gets to me too. It's amazing that with so many colleges in the area, including black colleges like Southern and Xavier that you find blacks stricken in poverty, despair and so uneducated." Chynna took another sip. "Black MBAs could do well in a city like this. So where did you get your MBA from?"

"Didn't. No need to," he said, now switching to his usual. He sipped. The brown liquid made a warm stinging sensation down his throat.

"Oh," Chynna said. She placed her drink down and twirled the bracelet. "Well that's okay," she offered with a singsongy voice. "I mean, I guess. What do you mean no need to." She fidgeted.

"I'm running a successful business of my own. To a large degree, I'm my own boss. My promotion comes from me generating more business and reaping the reward of expansion. I have to work twice as hard, but it's worth it. An advanced degree wouldn't put me in a better place with my own business right now."

"Oh, so you're here to…" she questioned with slight indignation.

"To meet and greet. Always great to make contacts. Now that helps my business."

"And what is your business, if you don't mind me asking?"

"Marketing and sales. I run The Jones Group out of Charlotte."

"Well good for you. A man who forges his own path is courageous. Me on the other hand, I need the stability that comes with a major corporation. And in those circles, education is the key. No advanced degree leaves one with nothing to bargain with." She continued to sip. "I work for a major oil firm in Jersey."

"I have a lot of friends in Jersey. I'm there a lot. Well, used to be. I still have a few clients I see from time to time," Calvin said, placing the empty glass down.

"Well, Calvin, here's to new friends that you might want to look up whenever you come back to town. Oh, I guess you have nothing left to toast with," she said.

He smiled.

"Listen, I'm really hungry but I'd rather get some down-home gumbo from this wonderful place off Bourbon. It's a nice spot called Divas and a few friends are meeting there. Care to come with?"

"What the hell? Why not." The last bit of Hennessey spoke. "I hope you don't mind a third wheel."

"Try a twentieth wheel. There's a bunch of us." She laughed.

"Well lead the way." Calvin helped her off her stool and placed a light trench on her shoulders.

"Thanks, Calvin. It's always nice to meet people," she said as they walked out of the door.

"Yeah. This is cool," he said. They strolled into the street where everything was now in full swing. The city was now like a pot whose water had just hit the boiling point.

She grabbed Calvin's hand as they made their way through the crowd. Her holding his hand didn't keep a woman from stopping them short in their tracks and flashing him with some of the largest and perkiest bare breasts he had ever seen.

"Oh. Nice," he said, not apologizing for looking. "I'm sorry I don't have any beads for you."

"No, he isn't," Chynna said, glaring at the woman.

He laughed and they continued to stroll into what appeared to be a makeshift garage down a dark back alley.

"Chynna, you seem like a nice girl and all but I don't know about following you down no dark alleys. For all I know, you might be trying to jack me." He laughed.

She punched him on the arm playfully. "You've never been to Divas

I guess." He shook his head. "Well you're in for a treat. This place serves the best gumbo and hurricanes in town. It also serves the hottest blues."

They entered the vast blackness where they were barely able to see their hands in front of their faces. Shortly thereafter, they approached a threshold decorated with long colorful plastic beads that swayed with the music. When they stepped inside, a sign that pictured five robust faces informed them that the original divas were appearing tonight, including the grand diva herself, Miss Red.

"Ooh, see, I told you that you are in for a treat. Oh, there are my friends."

"Chynna, girl, over here." She almost left Calvin in the dust.

He scoped his surroundings. The place had flavor. What seemed to be dark and dingy turned out to be sort of an oasis. The makeshift garage commanded character with its old oak bar, neon lights and wooden boxes for stools. He followed Chynna's dust toward a cluster of tables and chairs that looked as if they were borrowed from every garage sale in the country.

He finally caught up with Chynna as she introduced her new friend to the crowd of at least twenty people. "The more the merrier…" one bubbly voice said from the crowd.

Calvin made his way around the table, extending handshakes to as many people as he could before the Diva, Miss Red aka Kim bade everyone to sit. The crowd went wild. "They love her here in New Orleans…" he heard a person in the crowd say.

One after another these divas rocked. Miss Red, Sahira, then Saunja with her pretty rendition of "At Last," Hassie, Michelle and a really weird chick named Marty. All could sing in their own right. The ladies really put on a dynamic show culminating with a heartfelt rendition of Tina Turner and the Ikettes' "Proud Mary." The finale really blew the crowd away with a spectacle of lights and fake fireworks while the ladies belted Sylvester's "Love and Tender." They finished to a standing ovation.

"That was some show, wasn't it?" the Halle Berry look-alike said, approaching the table.

"So where were you, Miss Thing. You missed a great show."

"No, I didn't. I was in the back. You know Miss Red does not play when it comes to her guests being late and making their way to the front." Tracee sparkled with laughter.

"It sounds like you come here a great deal," Calvin said, standing and offering her his seat.

"Calvin, nice to see you. I warned you about hanging out and drinking and missing the brunch tomorrow," she said casually.

"Don't worry, I won't be missing your speech. In fact I'm looking forward to it," he said.

"Thank you." She took his seat.

"You two know each other?" Chynna questioned.

"Nope. Just met today. Hey, Lipton," Tracee answered and then greeted the bartender.

"Hello, Miss Tracee. I suspect everyone is having a grand time just like you planned. Miss Red and the girls put on a fine show." He placed a napkin before her. "A round of gumbo for everyone and something to drink to cool the palette?"

"Since there are so many of us, why don't you make up a few pitchers and set them on the table," Tracee said.

Chynna stared incessantly as she watched Tracee take her place on the throne.

"That'll be just fine. Wait around, too, the girls still have three more sets tonight. The party's just beginning," Lipton said.

"I can't wait," Tracee said with glee. She seemed pleased that the evening she planned for several of the convention goers turned out to be a success.

"So, Tracee, is everything set for tomorrow? Is there anything I can do?"

"Thanks, Chynna but everything is set. I put the finishing touches on my conversation for the brunch tomorrow, and the hall is set up. I checked before I left. I just like to be sure. I just want everyone to come and enjoy themselves," Tracee said as she sipped the soothing, cool drink. "Lipton has outdone himself."

"So Calvin where will you be seated? Perhaps I'll have my seat rearranged to keep you company," Chynna said.

Calvin still gazed at Tracee. "Well I don't know where I'll be seated, Chynna. Tracee is the boss."

"Actually, I've reserved a spot for you on the dais. As I said earlier, my focus is putting innovative ideas to work for us collectively and individually. As MBAs our power must extend far beyond old corporations that are not working for us. We're being pimped with fake dollars and not building our futures."

"I agree, Tracee. You're right on target. This should be good," another gentleman among the group chimed in.

"But the focus is MBAs, right?" Chynna asked.

"Yes. This is the Black MBAs conference."

"But Calvin doesn't have an MBA," Chynna interjected smugly. "I mean shouldn't your dais contain some of our best and brightest climbers."

"Exactly, and that's why Calvin is going to be upfront. He's a self-starter. He's built a major conglomerate conquering corporations all over town. He's established himself in the Southeast metropolitan area as a leader for marketing. He's also established himself among several area corporations, including Pitney Bowes, and to say the least Allynt Foods. The Jones Group is a force to be reckoned with. And because he's his own man, he's free to consistently blaze new trails for himself despite the downsizing or restructuring of major corporations." Tracee leaned over slightly. "I've been doing my homework as well," she said as she glazed at Calvin who by now had forgotten the rejection. "So, Chynna, Calvin is the perfect candidate for the dais. He is one of our brightest and best."

"You mean at the registration table?" Tracee asked as they walked down the cobblestone path together. At four in the morning, the atmosphere on the street claimed the city's unique festive flavor. Street vendors peddled their wares and acrobats tumbled before them.

"Yes, at the table. You were totally about business."

"That was the business hour, Calvin. I don't usually mix the two. Well, we're here. So I'll see you in the morning," she said as she placed her hand on the pearly decorative gates that stood before them.

"Usually. So what are you saying?" Calvin asked.

"You're perceptive. I don't usually mix the two but I certainly wouldn't mind spending more time with you," Tracee said, as her eyes seemed to sparkle.

Calvin grabbed her at the waist. He gently pecked her forehead and slid his lips toward her temple, her cheek, finally landing squarely on the cloud that covered her teeth.

"Let's be clear from the beginning. I don't start things I can't finish. I don't mess with other people's property, and I don't deal with two and three people at one time. Are you married, divorced, committed or with child?" she asked lightly.

"Tracee, hold up, I'm not asking you to marry me."

"You're correct. I don't start anything I can't finish. I'd like to spend more time with you but I will keep this relationship strictly business if you are attached with any of the above."

He maintained a hold on her waist. "No, no and no. I'm single."

"That was three no's. I asked you four questions. I guess you're not as smart as I thought." She smiled. She returned his kiss.

"No." He obliged between breaths. "But since we're being so forward, I guess you became interested when you saw that your girl was trying to hit it real hard."

"Who, Chynna?"

"Yes, Chynna." He wrapped her tighter.

"Well, if you're interested in Chynna, I know how to back off quickly," she said, pulling away.

"No. Chynna is cool, but she really isn't my flavor. You are."

"Chynna is good people. She's really a bright woman. I would love to work with her if I get the promotion but she's not interested in Atlanta. Listen, it's getting late and the brunch starts bright and early for me, so I gotta go. I'll see you tomorrow? You're welcome to come out to the tennis tournament after the brunch. I'm playing doubles." She walked toward her front door.

"I'll be at the brunch. Won't be able to make the tennis tournament, though."

"Oh, that's right, you've signed up for the golf tournament. Good luck."

"You certainly know how to make sure your guests are well taken care of."

"Just keeping abreast of what's current. Good night, Calvin. And good luck, again."

"Won't need it."

"Oh, that's right. You're the NAACP's latest and greatest golf champion."

"You really do your homework, don't you?"

"Always. Good night, Calvin."

"Good night, Miss Tracee." His voice commanded his deepest southern charm.

She shifted her weight from one leg to the other. "Calvin, if I let you come in for a nightcap, you promise you won't keep me up all night. I need to be fresh so I can break out a can of whup ass on the court."

"A charity event, right? Who are you playing?"

"The ladies of pink and green will tame the ladies of crimson and cream. Are you Greek?" She laughed and nodded for him to follow her inside.

He threw his coat down on the red velvet couch and matching round king-size bed in full view of the wide open French white double doors.

"I'm surprised you didn't request a different room, considering all this red in here." he said, making his way to the bar to pour himself a nightcap. "What can I pour you?" he yelled toward the back.

She emerged in a pink satin oriental lounger decorated with silver butterflies. Her royal purple laced body suit underneath clung to her ebony curves. "Normally I'd take tequila, but I need to be on my best behavior. How about a B-52?" she said, sitting on the couch.

"What's a B-52?" he asked, pouring his Courvoisier.

"It's Frangelico, Baileys and Amaretto. A shot of each," she said now standing near the glass cart filled with premium liquors. She lifted the port wineglass and helped him pour. "To a great convention week," she said as she held up the glass.

"To a great week," he answered, sipped and seductively kissed her lips.

"Chynna just wasn't on her game today," Tracee said, relieving herself of her racket.

"But you did your thing. That's all you can do. Your part," Calvin said, surprising her by attending her game.

"But it's my job to motivate people. But I just couldn't do it today."

"Maybe Chynna's agenda was not winning today," Calvin said, wiping her face with her towel.

"Yeah, I know. Anyway, that doesn't matter. We raised a lot of money for the graduate school fund. Thanks for showing up today. It meant the world to me. I can't believe you missed your tournament for mine."

"Yeah. I thought, why not let someone else take home another trophy." He grabbed her around her waist and they walked off.

"Tracee! Excellent, girl. Good work with the convention too."

"Thanks." Tracee offered her opponents a hug. "You make sure you bring that baby back next year. I plan on seeing it on my shelf," she said, referring to the trophy.

"You got it."

"Tracee!" another voice yelled from the crowd now exiting the stadium. She stopped short in front of them. "I'm sorry about today. Just lost track. Hello, Calvin," Chynna offered with pursed lips. "We'll get them next year, huh?" She turned back to Tracee.

"Yeah. We'll get them next year," Tracee agreed.

"Oh, great speech this morning. It was really inspiring. You did good work."

"Thanks. See you later?"

"Yeah, later. Have a good day, Calvin," Chynna said, walking away.

"You too," he said. He placed his arm on Tracee's shoulder, cupped her chin and kissed her lovingly.

Tracee smiled.

Chapter 13

Who is blowing up your pager like that?" Gem yelled to Talise as she marched across the room to find the gadget that had annoyed her all day.

Talise eased her way down the stairs from the bedroom. "Stop yelling. She's asleep again. Where's the cat?"

"Hopefully nowhere near me," Gem said, now making her way to the kitchen to pour some tea. "How about we order some goodies from Milano's. She'll love that by the time she wakes up."

"Good idea," Talise said, grabbing her pager and turning it off. She placed it back in her purse.

"Who is that?" Gem questioned again.

"Steffon," Talise answered.

"Calling like that?" Talise nodded. "I hope you didn't tell him you were hanging out with us. Talise, don't start that crap about signing me with him. This is not Steffon's time. It's Stephanie's," Gem commanded.

"I know. I know," Talise answered solemnly. She threw herself into the plush white pillows on the couch. Her eyes welled once again. She thought she had successfully drained them the night before when Gem shared the dreadful news of Stephanie's condition. "It's not fair. It's just not fair. That's a good woman up there, and she's being ripped from us without warning."

"She's not gone yet. We have to pray, be strong and have faith. Always God's will be done," Gem said, clutching Talise.

"But how could God allow something like this to happen to her? This girl doesn't sleep around. She's not promiscuous like some hoochie mamas I know. Nobody's straighter than she is. She doesn't use drugs. Why? Why her?" Talise's voice had grown shallow and raspy.

"God says for us to lean not to our own understanding. His way is not our way." Gem held Talise's face as if she were a child.

"Now that's your phone blowing up, not my pager," Talise said, sniffling. They laughed as Gem climbed over her to get it.

"Hello…Vaughan, hey…yeah, something came up…I'm sorry I didn't get to call you back…but I have a family emergency going on…well we're going to have to postpone it…I know Euphoria is hard to get, but Vaughan, trust me it must really be an emergency if I am willing to cancel—postpone, I stand corrected—what could be the biggest night of my life. We'll just have to make another biggest night of my life."

Gem sighed. She noticed that Stephanie had awakened from her brief rest. She watched her friend's astute descent down the stairs. If it were not for her drastic and sudden weight loss and the deep, dark circles that now occupied the once firm and supple skin below her eyes, she wouldn't have known that one of her best friends was dying.

"Look, Vaughan, we'll talk about this, okay? But I gotta go. Okay, thanks for understanding." She hung up the phone. "Good afternoon, sleepyhead. We were just about to order from Milano's for us."

"Actually I could do well with some General Tso's chicken," Stephanie said, making her way into the kitchen.

"Chinese it is then," Gem conceded.

"Sorry, I do not do cat," Talise responded, leafing through the paper.

"Is ignorance a prerequisite in your book? It's not about you all the time. We're ordering Chinese."

"Yeah, Talise. This is my illness, my disease and my death. Why are y'all being so selfish?" Stephanie chided the two of them. "I didn't plan on telling you guys…I didn't know when I was going to tell you. But now that you know, you all have to help me heal, not help me to the grave." She grew silent.

"Talise has always been selfish. Why should she change now? I wouldn't know how to handle it. You, Gem, don't postpone your concert for me. I need something to lift me up. We have to keep on living. It's the only thing that will keep me alive." She sat at the breakfast bar in their full view. "So let's order Chinese and Milano's. How about that?"

They all cracked a smile. "I'll do the honors," Talise said, rushing to the phone. "In fact, it's my treat." She rustled through her purse for her wallet and stumbled across her pager. It immediately chimed.

"I'll order. Talise, please call that fool back so he can stop blowing your pager off the hook," Gem said, picking up the phone. She was faintly heard in the background ordering from the local Chinese restaurant.

Talise deleted the number that appeared succinctly on her pager. It was Steffon's cell phone.

"Why he is so desperately trying to track you down?" Stephanie asking, scaring Talise, as she seemed to sneak up behind her.

"I cut him off. I told him I wasn't swingin' with him anymore," she answered barely above a whisper.

Gem overheard the conversation and pranced over to the other side of the room. She held three glasses of fresh berry juice that they happily relieved her of. "Thank God! You didn't need that loser anyway," Gem said as she sat down carefully.

"He's not a loser, Gem. He's just trying to make his way."

"Yeah, make his way into your panties, which he so successfully entered, owned and sealed."

"Whatever. Anyway, he's upset because I called it off. That relationship was going nowhere for me, and I know I was just using him to help me to feel better. I just feel like I owed him." She became solemn. "And now he's telling me I owe him for the furniture I thought was a gift. Turns out he was just using me too." She uncrossed her legs and stepped in the kitchen to refill her glass.

"Is he threatening you?" Gem asked compassionately.

"Yeah," Talise answered. "He left a message on my machine saying that if I don't get him, you or the $5,000 for the furniture in his hands in ten days, I'm going to suffer serious consequences. You know he has serious gang ties. He threatened to tell Vanee about us. That's going to make things difficult for me at work and at home, but I can't quit my job. I really won't have any recourse to start paying that money. And he doesn't want payments. He wants this money in full. I don't know what to do." Her voice trembled.

"Well let's figure this out. I have $3,500 that I can get to you by Monday. I can borrow the rest from my parents, it's not like they'll turn me down and…"

"No, no, no. This is bribery and extortion. We're not taking this crap," Gem said, making her way back to the phone.

"Gem," Talise pleaded. "Steffon has told me things about his past that could put all of us in danger. He's dangerous, just like you said. He used to be part of one of the worst gangs in Queens. He and Romy still have ties, and when people don't do what he wants, they force them to. Gem, Stephanie, I gotta do this by myself. Don't get involved."

"You want us involved," Gem yelled. "If you didn't, you wouldn't have jeopardized yourself like this. When will you get that we are a part of one another? We don't want to see anything happen to you. Now you see what I was talking about? Dick ain't worth all of this. I'm telling you, Talise, Steffon will not get away with this crap. He won't."

"What are you going to do? You're not signing with them. They're just like you said," Talise said as Gem ignored her.

"I'm doing what I knew I should've done a long time ago. Here I was trying to let you be an adult," Gem said as she waited patiently for the phone to ring. "Hey, I'm sorry to call so late but I really need your help…"

"Gem, what are you…"

Stephanie pulled Talise away from the phone. "Let her handle it. She knows what she's doing."

"Thanks."

"No thanks needed. This is what family does. Talise, you have to start knowing that your choices have consequences. Nothing happens by chance, Talise, but everything, everything—past, present and future—happens by choice. Remember that. You don't owe him or anyone anything, especially a piece of yourself."

Gem got off the phone. "Talise, don't worry about it. It's taken care of. Stay away from Steffon for good. Whether you planned to or not. Stay away from him. You hear us." They gathered and gave one another hugs of joy, as much as they could muster at a time like this.

"So how was your trip? I'm surprised you didn't call me when you got back," Candace said.

"It was excellent. Just what I needed," Calvin answered as he sorted papers and mail he hadn't seen in a week. "Hold on, that's my other line. Helloo," he answered still shuffling.

"Hey, babe. What's up?" Tracee's voice was a breath of sunshine for him. "Still coming down this weekend?

"You know it." He smiled.

"I have a little surprise for you."

"I'm not surprised. You got the promotion."

"Slow down. You're correct, I am taking the promotion, and I will need your help but this surprise is all you," she said joyfully.

"Well what is it?" he asked as he sat behind the desk.

"If I told you, it wouldn't be a surprise. You just can't fink out on me this weekend. This surprise is time sensitive, and I know it will benefit you tremendously but I'm putting my reputation on the line, needless to say a long-time friendship, so you have to promise me that you're coming down."

"Tracee, don't ask again. I said I'll be there and that's it."

"Cool," she said.

"Cool. Oh shoot, hold on, I have somebody—a client—on the other end," he said, popping up in his chair.

"No. Cal call me at home later. I'm on my way to a meeting. I'll talk to you later, babe."

"Alright. Later, babe." He laughed and clicked back over. "Candace, Candace?"

"Yes," she said with a long, drawn-out twang.

"I'm sorry. Important business," he said, sitting back in his chair.

"That's okay. So are you available this week?" she asked impatiently.

"Candy, I doubt it. I have a lot of work to do. I landed another account while I was in New Orleans, and I'm going to Atlanta this weekend. I'm going to need to check you out some other time."

Candy, Candy? she pondered. *Where did that come from?* "But Cal, my reunion is this weekend. I already paid for the tickets, $150 apiece because you said you were attending with me. This isn't fair. And this isn't like you. What's going on with you?"

Calvin scratched the back of his head. Beads of sweat popped up across his forehead. "Candace, I'm sorry. I forgot. Listen, I'll see what I can do. If I can't attend, I'll pay for the tickets. Let me see what I can do."

"Thanks. I guess I'll speak to you in a couple of days, then," she said with an air of disappointment.

"Yeah. Listen, Candy, I gotta run. I'll call you in a couple of days, okay?" He continued cleaning papers off his desk. He began organizing a new file with the contacts he had just made in New Orleans.

Quickly he dialed another number.

"Got a minute?" he asked.

"Always for you playa, shoot." Grey would be able to help him out as always. Grey was his best friend, and Calvin could count on him for his candor and honesty. "How was the conference?"

"You missed a good one. The honeys were hot," Calvin answered.

"So which one's fire did you light." Grey laughed.

"Yeah, there is one."

"As usual. So what's the dilemma?"

"How you know there's a dilemma?" Calvin frowned.

"How long have I known you? Damn near your entire life," Grey answered his own question.

"Yeah, yeah, yeah. Anyway I met a hottie."

"Name?"

"Tracee."

"Age?"

"Ours."

"Occupation?"

"Comptroller on her way to CFO for a major food corporation."

"Stats?"

"I'd say 31-24-32 and maybe a C cup."

"Damn, just your speed. I don't need to ask if you hit it or not, Mr. C cup. I'll guess you'll be hitting Vickie Secret for a few gifts?"

"Yeah, as a matter of fact, I probably will."

"That means it's worth keeping around. Must have been off the hook."

"Better," Calvin affirmed.

"Damn, playa, then what's the dilemma?"

"Candace."

"Come on, Cal. How long you gonna string that—"

Calvin tried to interrupt.

"Naw, man, listen. Candace is a sweet woman. She has a lot going on, but after five years if you haven't realized that you ain't feeling that, you don't deserve a Tracee. Okay, let's go through the routine." Grey sighed.

"Man, I ain't saying that I'm ready to walk down the aisle."

"Let's go through the routine," Grey asserted. "What is it about Tracee that you like?"

"Man, she's gorgeous, number one. She's athletic and outgoing. She's assertive but not aggressive…"

"Examples please. Specifics, stay away from the general."

"Alright. When I first met her, I thought she wasn't feeling me. It was cool. I met up with her later through some friends. One of her friends was diggin' me and invited me to hang out with them at a bar. I wasn't diggin' her friend even though she was kinda nice…"

"The friend?" Grey interjected.

"Yeah. But I ended up hanging out with them, and Tracee joined us later. When she did she blew my mind. Within hours from me meeting her this girl had my entire career outlined in her mental Rolodex. I was impressed, not just with the facts but her take on it. From a business standpoint, we think alike."

"More details, please. You know I'm writing down the pros and cons of this situation."

"Yeah, yeah, anyway, her girl tried to flex on me. She tried to dig when she announced to the entire table that I didn't have my MBA. She was salty 'cause I wasn't diggin' her the way I was diggin' Tracee. But before I could say anything, Tracee defended me with hardcore facts about my choices in business and talked about how we need to take similar approaches to secure our futures. Man, she blew me away." For the first time this morning he noticed his face seemed to light up when he spoke of Tracee.

"So let's review this: she's gorgeous—eye candy we could say—intelligent, supportive, assertive but not aggressive and does her thing in bed? Right?"

"Right!"

"Then what is the problem? Oh, I know."

"Candace," Calvin repeated with a hollow void in his voice.

"That's been the problem all along. Nothing's changed, Cal. I haven't met Tracee, but she sounds ideal, so don't gamble, man. You'll lose. Candace is a wonderful person but she's not the one you can build something with. Chose or lose, man, and to me, you've already chosen."

"Yeah, man, but I'm not tryin' to hurt Candace's feelings," Calvin said.

"I know. You'd rather hurt her feelings by fakin' it and hangin' with other women on a consistent basis."

"You made your point."

"Man, I would love to keep shootin' the breeze but I have to bounce. Hey, we still on for the end of the month?"

"And you know that. The investment club will commence this month."

"Cool. I'll be there. Hey, how's Talise doing? I'm glad y'all ain't kickin' it no more. That arrangement wasn't cool. We all been friends too long to mess that up," Grey said.

"Yeah, you right again. Hey, do me a favor and give Talise a call, just make sure she's alright," Calvin said with sincerity.

"I will, dawg. Look, peace out."

"Peace," Calvin said. He took a deep breath and dialed another seven digits. The phone rang five times before the machine answered.

"Candace…" He tried to sound cavalier. "…It's Cal, listen I'm sorry to disappoint you. I can't make it this weekend. Some stuff has come up, and I need to handle it. I'll pay for the tickets. Um, we'll talk when I get back. We need to talk," he said as voice deepened. "Try to have a good time this weekend. I'm sorry." He hung up the phone.

Feeling somewhat relieved he resumed the task of organizing his papers. The phone rang shortly after that. He knew it was Candace.

"This is Calvin," he answered in his most professional tone.

"Calvin, hey, babe. This is Tracee."

"Hey, girlie. What's up?" he said with a smile in his voice.

"Listen, small change of plans. I hope you don't mind," she said.

"My best friend and her husband are going to be in the Charlotte area this weekend. I haven't seen them in a while, since their wedding actually. Anyway I thought I would move the surprise to your place this weekend and meet you up there. Whatcha think?"

"Cool. Is everybody trying to stay in my crib?"

"Well of course I am but no they already have their arrangements made," Tracee answered.

"Cool, it works for me," he said with another smile.

"Okay. I'm leaving here about three in the afternoon. So I should be at your place no later than eight. Then we'll all get together and swing it from there."

"What about my surprise?" he asked.

"Don't worry, babe, got it covered. See you then?"

"See you then."

Two seconds after his smile slightly faded the phone rang again. Confident that it wasn't Tracee, he turned the ringer off mid-ring. All of a sudden he had a new direction for sorting everything.

It was 8:12 A.M. and Talise had three minutes to cross the major intersection against the light, catch the elevator to the fifth floor and make it to her desk on time, where only God knew what would be waiting for her. She hadn't been to work in three days, ever since Steffon threatened to shatter her world.

Immediately in the crisp air, Talise's palms began to sweat. Her armpits put a wet spot in her freshly pressed navy blue dress. Vanee was ahead of her, and Talise was scared stiff as to what Steffon may have told her. *Oh, well, face the music,* she thought as she noticed an exceptionally cuddly Steffon grab Vanee at the waist and escort her through the glass revolving doors.

She took the elevator to the second floor and made her way to the fifth by way of the emergency stairs. Now drenched, she made it safely to her desk where an eerie calm seemed to loom. Her phone light message indicator acted like it was going to blow in her face and send the phone soaring.

Talise took a deep breath and dialed the voice mail. "You have seventeen messages..." the friendly automated operator announced. "...Press 1 to play, 3 to delete and 7 to skip to the next message. Talise plowed through the plethora of messages when she came across the first to make her day. "Talise, K.J. and I are both out of the office. We're in Philadelphia today and tomorrow. Be prepared to go over the agenda, it's in your e-mail. If you have any problems or questions, leave them on my voice mail and we'll get back to you," Dragon breath said. Talise sighed with joy. *At least my next two days should be light,* Talise thought as she pressed on.

"Talise, it's Gem. We're meeting at Stephanie's tonight again. She's gonna need support. I think she's gonna try and tell Alec soon, so be available. Oh, and don't worry about that office problem. Trust me, it's taken care of. See ya. And don't be late." Talise heard the dial tone. She hit the pause button on the phone and decided to breathe a minute before resuming message catch-up. She sat back in the chair and threw her jacket on the empty guest chaise in front of her.

"Any reason why you've been avoiding my calls?" His voice was tight.

"Steffon, please leave me alone. I'm not in the mood for you today," she said defiantly.

"Just answer my question," he said.

"Talise. Oh, hey..." Vanee said peeking her head in at Steffon and Talise. Both looked as if they were deer caught in headlights.

"Hey, girl. Come on in. Steffon, excuse us please."

"No problem." He obliged.

"So, what's up?" Talise asked, feeling relieved that Steffon hadn't followed through on his bluff. She blushed with gladness. The weekend made her realize how much she regretted jeopardizing her friendship with Vanee out of her own selfish gain.

"I know that K.J. and his secretary are in Philly. I'm running the high school project today."

"High school project?" Talise questioned.

"Yeah. You know we sponsor the career day when the kids from the local high school come and hear about careers in insurance."

"Oh yeah," Talise said, rearing back in her seat.

"Well anyway, I figured it would be a nice break for you to speak for twenty minutes about what you do. Plus, it would be nice for them to see a sister in the position you're in. I have you scheduled for 11:30 and then afterward I figured we could do lunch."

"Well since you're twisting my arm, I guess I have no choice."

"You're right. You don't. So I'll see you later in the media room," Vanee said.

"Yes. Hey..." Talise said, stopping her at the door.

"Yeah?" Vanee turned around. She leaned against the door.

"You two doing okay?"

"Better than normal. These last few days...I don't know what's come over Steffon but I like it. He's been around, and we've been having a good time. I guess my all-girl get-togethers somehow jarred him into reality. I don't know. I'm not trying to figure it out, just enjoying it."

"Good," Talise said, picking up her pen. "I'll see you later."

Vanee waved and left.

"This is Steffon. Romy, what's up? Today? Man I'm at work. I understand...yeah...of course...Fine, I'll be there about 12:30. I won't be late." He hung up the phone, exasperated. *What the fuck is going on?* he thought.

The phone rang again. He picked it up with a vengeance. "What?" He forgot he was at work.

"Steffon, this Gemmia Barnes."

"Who," he asked.

"Gemmia..." She huffed. "Gem. Talise's friend."

"Gem. Oh shoot, Gem. I'm glad you called but I told Talise not to mix my business. Let me give you another number to call me on and perhaps we can meet," Steffon said confidently. *That's what Romy wants to see me on,* he thought.

"No. No need for small talk. My position hasn't changed," Gem added curtly.

"So then why you ringing my phone?"

"I take it you received your visitor?" she questioned, matching his confidence.

"What visitor you talking about?"

"Okay, your cuteness doesn't work with me. I'll make this sweet and simple. My girl has enough pressure on her without any added stress from you. You don't know what she's going through. Just put it this way, I'm not the one to mess with. Trust me."

"Oh, really," he said, looking around with a smirk.

"Really. I'm not the one. You can strong-arm her but it ends here with me. Now I just called to let you know your visitor is courtesy of me. And trust me, if you don't leave Talise alone, it won't be the last time you'll be paid a visit, and it won't be pretty. Got me?"

"Are you threatening me? I don't think you know who you fuckin' with!" Steffon said.

"Expand your vocabulary, Steffon. That language doesn't move me. Anyway, no need to cause a scene. Just remember: Leave Talise alone. She deserves better than you. Make no mistake, your visitor is courtesy of me, not Talise."

Steffon raced through the side streets of Manhattan on his way to the Brooklyn-Queens Expressway. As usual he dodged traffic like a bat out of hell. His pedal hit the metal as he scoured onto the bumpiest road in America on his way toward The Knight Gallery in Queens for this urgent emergency meeting with Romy.

As he pulled up, he noticed the funeral-like procession of cars, including Romy's customized purple Navigator parked in front of the entrance door. Romy's driver remained in the car.

Steffon bolted through the door. "Romy, what's up, I'm here," he yelled. Three of Romy's henchmen appeared and surrounded Steffon.

"You know the drill," one of them said in the darkness.

Steffon lifted his hands in the air while the second guy lifted the cold, hard steel from his hip.

"He got the nerve to be packing, rolling up in here," the one guarding Steffon's hands said. They all laughed.

"Chill out." Romy seemed to appear from nowhere. "Steffon, my man. Whatchu doin', man. You bringing heat?" he asked, indicating for Steffon to sit before him. "Don't worry 'bout your piece. It's safe until you leave here."

"Rome, man, what's up? What's going on? You know I don't go nowhere without my piece. Now you giving me heat? I thought we was down."

Romy lit the slender brown cigarlike cigarette. He took a deep puff and sent circles through the air. "I've been practicing."

"And you getting good, Romy." One of his henchmen laughed.

"Steff," Romy said, placing his cigar down in the glass ashtray before him. "I don't know what you did or are doing. I'm not questioning your way, I'm just saying do what you have to do it without bringing heat. I'm telling you I ain't going down for no petty bullshit over no $5,000. I can make that easily in one night, and it ain't worth it."

"You talking in riddles, man. What are you saying?" Steffon said, waving the smoke out of his face.

"I'll make it simple. I was paid a visit today, DEA Agent Brevard. He said for us to lay off one Talise E. Grimes. That's Jersey pussy, ain't I correct?" Romy picked up his cigar again.

"Yeah," Steffon answered.

"Now Mr. DEA agent advised us that we will be shut down immediately if we don't. Now I don't know what kind of pull this bitch got, but I ain't trying to handle it. Now I called the marker in on you, not her. It's up to you to straighten this mess out. It's not up to her. Got me?"

"But Rome…"

"Steffon, kill it. Leave Gem, Talise and the rest of them alone. Got me? Or, partner, you on your own. I'll drop yo' ass like a baad habit with a quickness. Got me?" Romy leaned in.

"So what you want to do about the label? About Gem?" Steffon asked.

Romy stretched. He placed his hands behind his head and clasped his fingers. He picked up his suede fedora off the table and twirled it.

"Steffon, I'm telling you, if you wasn't my peeps from way back, this situation wouldn't be pretty. But since you are, I'm gonna let you handle it. You still on the A&R tip but the five g's, it's up to you to get it back to me. I don't care how? You got thirty days. But I want you to stay away from Talise, got it?"

"I got it, man. I got it."

"Cool. Now I know you got to get back to that Wall Street thang, so I'll check you later," Romy said and sat back.

Steffon picked up his piece and strutted out the door. Great Raritan wouldn't see him for the rest of the day.

"To a great day," Vanee said as she lifted her glass of ice water with lemon. Talise did the same.

"It was a good day, wasn't it?" Talise smiled in the sunshine as the ladies sat at the table on the pier waiting for their lunch.

"Yes, it was. The kids really enjoyed you. I have to admit your speech went well. Good idea to get them involved like that. How did you come up with that?"

"Honestly, girl, I was winging it. It came from the top of my head. I'm creative when I want to be, I just wish I had the room to be here," Talise said.

"Well it was good. So what's up for the rest of the day, taking it easy?" Vanee allowed the waitress to place a veggie pizza with whole-wheat crust in front of her.

"No, I'm going to skip out after we finish."

"Talise, is that wise? I know K.J. is out but you've been out the last three days and…"

"Vanee, thanks for the concern. I have some serious problems at home."

"You want to talk about it?" Vanee asked.

"I really can't. It's real private," Talise said.

"Well if you need to talk, you know I'm here for you, girl," Vanee said as she placed her hand over Talise's. "Speaking of support. We pulled names after you left the sisterhood meeting…and your place was picked for our next meeting. Is that okay?"

Talise hesitated. *You need to can that sisterhood group, you can't be honest,* she heard Gem and Stephanie say. "Um, Vanee, I don't know, I mean, I'm really not equipped to entertain yet…"

"I thought you got new furniture and all," Vanee continued to eat without looking up.

Talise almost choked. "Yeah, I did but…" She wasn't quick enough.

"Then it's settled. Your place. We want to start earlier too, like six instead of nine."

"Okay…don't forget to give me the date."

"Don't let me twist your arm." Vanee's street sense kicked in.

"I'm sorry. I just have a lot on my mind," Talise said, and they finished eating in silence.

"Well this was wonderful. I'm going to have to cut out, though. My boss is in and while today was successful, he won't go for me taking the rest of the day off. No rest for the weary. Hey, you know where to find me if you need me."

"That I do." Talise stood and gave her a big hug. Talise sat back down and finished her meal.

"You done?" the waitress asked sometime after Vanee left.

"Yes, thanks. You can just take it all away."

"I'll bring the check right over," the lady said.

Check? Vanee was supposed to… she thought and laughed to herself. She pulled out her credit card and laid it down on the table.

Her transaction was complete, so before heading toward Whispering Woods for another emotional round she decided to walk around the wooden planks that surrounded Water Street.

Her reflection in the water showed a person who now found herself in a world of trouble with no reprieve. She was losing people out of her life left and right in every literal and physical sense of the word. Her world seemed to be going into a downward spiral, and she didn't know how to pull herself out of it. She didn't know where to begin.

She continued to walk a little farther, heading toward her building of doom. She wanted to pick up her things before she left. She headed toward the back of the building that met the cobblestone and led to all of downtown's trendiest shops.

She stopped short when she noticed that one of the benches contained her once friend, lover and confidant.

"Steffon, listen, I don't know what happened between us, but I'm sorry."

He didn't say a word. He gave her a look as if she was discarded trash. At that moment that was exactly how she felt. He continued to stare.

"Steffon, are you going to say anything?"

No response.

"Well, I'm sorry…for everything," she said as she headed through the back door. She waited briefly for the elevator. When it opened, Vanee stepped out.

"Girl, I thought you were going home. You still here," Vanee said, barely halting her long-legged stride.

"I'm leaving now, just getting my stuff. Where you headed?" Talise questioned. She placed her hand between the doors to prevent their closing.

"Steffon called. He asked me to meet him outside. Got some stuff he needs to talk about. I'm on my break. I'll talk to you later."

Talise let the door close. She didn't want to be anywhere near the explosion that she was about to be the center of. She reached her office and quickly gathered her things, turned off the lights and headed back to the elevators. Her heart felt like it was going to explode. She held her chest tightly, praying that she would avoid seeing either one of them.

The door to the main level opened. She sighed. She practically ran out of the front doors and up the hill toward the Path train to take her home.

The train doors opened and she grabbed a seat with no real struggle. It wasn't until the third stop that she realized she had driven into work.

Chapter 14

Gem scurried about. All afternoon she avoided the phone to preserve her voice for this evening's show. Just as she stepped into the shower, the doorbell rang.

"Doggone it," she said aloud. She wrapped the oversized fluffy towel around her body. She held it close to her skin to avoid the excess water being soaked into the new plush carpet she had just purchased with an unexpected jingle commission check.

"Vaughan, I thought we were meeting in the city. Come in, I'm cold," she said, ushering him through the door.

"I thought we agreed that you were supposed to contain your voice." He grabbed her about the waist and savored her sensuously wet lips.

Reluctantly she pulled away. "Vaughan, I told you I'm not ready for this. I'm trying to stay focused." She backed away.

He twisted his lips and shook his head.

"What? We've had this conversation several times. I'm celibate, and if you can't respect that then not only will we have to discontinue our friendship, but our business relationship will cease as well."

"Okay, okay. I'm sorry. I didn't come over for this. I came over thinking we could ride into the city together. I just want you to remain focused."

"Well how am I supposed to remain focused when you come over here looking good, smelling fine and being as sweet as you always are."

His smile told her he understood. He always did. "I'll be ready in thirty minutes," she said, trotting back to a running shower.

"You don't have thirty minutes, Gem. You have fifteen," he yelled.

"Okay, okay," she shouted back.

She emerged from the bathroom with a thick terry robe covering her.

"How did that situation work out with Talise? My cousin said he made his way to Queens and met with Romy a few weeks ago."

"Apparently it worked. Talise hasn't said anything else about Steffon harassing her about the money or me signing with them. She's just bummed out because she said Steffon hasn't said a word to her at work since the incident and she's still drowning with that tyrant of a boss of hers," she yelled down from her bedroom. "Well, I'm ready. How do I look?"

"Wow." His eyes grew large. "You look fabulous and in, whoa—" he checked his watch—and in only twenty-three minutes. You're getting better," he said as he led her out to his car. "I want you to take this time to relax, focus and warm up. Don't mind me, just act like I'm not here." He started the car and allowed the engine to roar. "That's it, baby," he said aloud. "That's it. You're in good form tonight. I hear it. I want you to dance like nobody's watching tonight. You understand me?"

Vaughan always made her feel like he had her back. And in her book that was the quickest way to her heart. She grabbed him on the arm as she finished her latest crescendo. "That's it! That's it!" she yelled mostly out of breath.

"What, what?" He laughed. "You're supposed to be warming up."

"Vaughan, the song. That's a great title for the song! I Danced Like Nobody's Watching." She squealed. "It's perfect."

He gave her a swift nod. "I like it. I like it a lot. I don't want you singing it tonight though. I don't think it's ready."

"Vaughan, I appreciate everything you've done and are doing for me, but you don't run me or my career. What I do is my decision," she said.

"I was just giving my opinion and a word of advice. We have a lot of people showing up tonight. Some you know, some you don't. The song isn't copyrighted, remember?"

"I know. I understand. But please do me a favor. You stick to the engineering and producing and I'll handle the show."

"You going to the show tonight?" Talise asked as she began cleaning up files. "I figured I would stay in the city and just go over from work. I'm sure Gem will understand if you're not feeling well. But make sure it's because you're not feeling well physically and that you're not hiding from Alec.

She plopped back into the chair as she noticed the blue sky that now had turned black. She rolled her eyes and held her breath as she said, "You know if you want, I'll pick you up. It'll take some time because I have to go home and get the car, then I'd have to drive down to you and…" Talise said.

"Release your breath. You don't have to pick me up," Stephanie said, praying Talise would insist.

Oh, thank goodness, I'm tired, Talise thought.

"…I'm really not feeling well enough to hang out tonight, anyway. I'm really weak," Stephanie said.

"Have you told Alec yet?" Talise asked as she continued to close up shop.

"Not yet. He seems to avoid any serious conversation outside of the election or the wedding. I know he suspects something but he always avoids everything. He said something about my weight the other day…"

"Um-hum." Talise chimed in.

"He said I looked great and he was happy I was taking steps to lose weight. Can you believe that?" Stephanie said as she noticed her flaky nail polish was peeling away. She patted her hand and looked to the sky.

"Well, Stephanie, hasn't your relationship been built on shallowness from the beginning? It seems that way to me," Talise said, realizing that she should have exercised some caution. Placing her foot in her mouth had become and was maintained as her specialty. Suddenly her second line rang, and Talise felt thankful she had some reprieve. "Hold on, Stephanie. This is Talise."

"Good I'm glad you're still there. Talise, I need to see you immediately," K.J. said.

"I didn't plan on being here long, I was just about to…"

"It won't be long. I expect you over here in the next five minutes," he barked.

"Should I bring any files?" she asked.

"Not necessary," K.J. said without fanfare. The next thing she heard was the dial tone.

She clicked back to her previous call.

"Hello."

"Girl, I was about to hang up on you. I have to go take my medicine."

"Yeah, well, I have to go. The boss is beckoning," Talise said.

"Girl, you need to hurry up and get out of there. The sheer mention of that man's name or that company brings you down. Maybe you're not supposed to be there."

"You're right but for right now this is where I am so until then, feel better, and I'll talk to you first thing tomorrow and let you know how everything went."

"Have a good time. Tell Gem to break a leg," Stephanie said.

"I will. Love you, girl."

"Love you too. And hey…"

"Yeah?" Talise said.

"Put that man in his place once and for all. You don't need the crap he's dishing out to you there."

"I know you're right," Talise said. She dimmed the lights for her departure and headed toward K.J.'s office of doom. *What could it be now?* she thought as she turned the corner.

Sound engineers bustled about as Gem watched Vaughan orchestrate the production. She took a minute and procured the aura that the empty room emitted. She could barely contain herself with the thoughts of the fire that would blaze the moment the dark chairs were filled with warm bodies, all there just to hear her melodic voice.

"Gem, you ready for a sound check?" a voice from the sound booth asked.

"Sure," she said. Her voice for the first time was shaky. "Oh, are we going through a few songs for the lighting too?"

"Of course," Vaughan said as he stepped into the light.

"This is your night, baby." He smiled, which warmed the fright from her bones.

"You're right, it is my night. And I'm going to make the best of it." They embraced and he planted a sloppy wet kiss on her lips.

"Alright kids. We have a show to put on in fifty-five, and I want to run through a few things before Gem heads to the back," the same voice commanded.

"Okay, do your thing, baby. I have some last-minute details to work out at the door. Remember, I want you to dance like nobody's watching, baby," Vaughan said as he planted one last kiss on her lips.

"Okay, okay. Vaughan, out. We have to pop like popcorn, kids," the voice continued. "Gem, find your light and let's go."

She obeyed. The hired pianist planted himself on stage behind her. The remainder of the band took their places in the pit below. Vaughan had spared no expense. One by one they ran through a series of songs, with the lights highlighting certain points. Thirty minutes later Gem felt fatigue mixed with anxiety. She knew it was time to retreat to the upper room she had created in the back. She informed Vaughan who was more than supportive of her preparing for the evening the way she needed to.

"Oh, where is your friend Talise. I got a great idea," Vaughan said.

"I don't know. I'm surprised. She said she would be here by now," Gem said, checking her watch. "What's your great idea?" she asked.

"Well I thought it would be a nice idea for Talise to introduce you tonight."

"Oh, Vaughan, that's a wonderful idea. She would love that."

"Good. It's settled. As soon as she gets here, make sure she sees me."

Gem glided off the stage and disappeared behind a sea of lights and sound as the musicians completed their last rehearsals. Amid the noise, Gem knew the stage was where she belonged. She unfolded her burlap cloth, which lay in the corner of her dressing area. She lit and placed a simple white candle at the edge of the cloth. She took in several deep breaths as she kneeled. She placed her forehead on the floor leaving her hands in a position of receiving.

"Father God, in the precious name of Jesus, Your son who died on the cross for a sinner like me, I thank You. I thank You for the breath of life. I thank You for the many blessings and opportunities You have bestowed upon me. I know I don't deserve Your love but because of Your mercy and

Your grace You continue to sustain me. You continue to bless me with Your presence. You continue to show me the way, even when I for whatever reason seem to go in the opposite direction. I ask for Your guidance and Your continued love and blessings. Father God, I come before You tonight asking Your blessings on this evening of song. I ask that You allow my love, my light and my voice to soar with Your angels as You have done so many times before. I ask that in all things Your will be done, may I be in Your perfect grace, dear Lord, and bless this evening so that all is well and ends well.

"*Our Father, which art in heaven, hallowed be thy name, thy kingdom come, thy will be done on earth as it is in heaven.* Just then she was joined with a familiar and much-needed voice, and they continued in unison…*Give us this day our daily bread and forgive us our trespasses as we forgive those who trespass against us. Lead us not into temptation but deliver us from evil. For thine is the kingdom and the power and the Glory, forever and ever. Amen.*"

"Girl, where you been. You had us worried. What's wrong? Are you okay?" Gem asked, hugging Talise and speaking in the baby voice she knew always made Talise laugh.

"Yeah, girl. I'm okay. Don't worry about me. It's your night."

"Yeah," Gem agreed.

"And a grand night it's going to be. Vaughan told me he wants me to introduce you."

"Are you going to do it?" Gem asked.

"Now you know you don't have to ask me that. Of course. I'm honored. I'm sorry to tell you Stephanie can't make it tonight. She really wasn't feeling well. She sends her regrets, of course, and said for you to break a leg."

"Yeah." Gem's energy seemed to drop again.

"Anyway, no time for sadness. This is your night, and the house is packed, girl. You ready?"

"As ready as I'll ever be. Are you okay? You seem off-center," Gem said as she glanced in the mirror and placed the last bit of powder on her face.

"Yeah. I'm fine. I had a brief conversation with K.J. and literally was threatened ferociously with my job. So…" Talise thought for a moment. "…let's not worry about that. This is your night. I want you to go out there and be fabulous. You have some real lookers out there."

"Yeah. Like who?"

"Come on, Gem, don't force me to rat. Vaughan made me promise I wouldn't tell." Talise tried to change the subject. She sauntered over to her well-lit dressing table. She glanced at her Mac line of products strewn across the vanity.

Gem pulled her away from the mirror. "If you don't tell me, I will tickle you to death, and you'll be too out of breath to introduce anyone. You will embarrass yourself, and I'll be in the back laughing," Gem said as she prepared to attack.

"Okay, okay," Talise relented. "Okay. You have several execs in the audience, from Sony, a rep from LaFace, Sylvia Rhone's assistant and..." Talise made a drum roll with her fingers.

"And?" Gem waited anxiously.

"And, Gem..." she hesitated.

"Spit it out." Gem was about to burst with excitement.

"Wincey is in the house!" Talise squealed.

"Girl, get out of here. Wincey is here, at my show?"

"You got it. Girl, you have to blow it out."

"Okay, don't put any more pressure on me," Gem snapped.

"Gem, you asked me to tell you. Vaughan didn't want me to because he wants you to do well and be yourself. I'm sorry. I really didn't mean to spoil it for you."

Gem sat still for a moment. She allowed Talise to remove the blush brush from her hand and place it in the clear plastic bin before the mirror.

"You're beautiful," Talise said sincerely.

Gem relaxed. Tears welled in her eyes as she gazed in the mirror and saw the reflection of God's creation and where He had brought her. "Yes, you're right. I'm sorry. I'm just a little nervous, I guess."

"Well, Vaughan, told me to remind you to dance like nobody's watching. I don't know what it means but, hey, it works for me."

Gem smiled and grabbed a tissue from the box.

"Baby, you ready?" Vaughan came knocking on the door.

Talise released the bear hug from her friend's shoulders. "Baby?...ummmmmmm," Talise said with pleasure.

"Shut up, girl. Yeah, boo, I'm ready," Gem said as she unwrapped her silk robe and revealed a spectacular pure-white jumpsuit adorned in gold trim. She placed her feet into three-inch-high pumps.

They formed a circle and prayed together.

Talise kissed her on the cheek just as Vaughan handed her the mike. The spotlight followed her onstage.

"No, I'm not Gem but you can keep clapping. I kinda like it," Talise said into the mike, turning on the charm. Gem laughed along with the audience and waited in the wings. This was her time and she was ready to take it.

"Steffon, good evening."

"Talise," he returned as cool as a cucumber.

"So…the first set was great, wasn't it?" she said.

"Hey, girl. What's up?" Vanee entered with an unusually bright voice. "Ooh, what the heck is wrong with the two of you? You could cut the tension with a knife," she said, planting a friendly hug and kiss on Talise.

"Hey, woman. What are you doing here?" Talise asked as Steffon slipped away.

"Well, Steffon asked me if I wanted to come out with him. So I found a baby-sitter and we're here. I'm having a good time. He didn't tell me you knew Gem," Vanee said, looking around.

"Yeah. Gem is one of my best friends. Remember I told you," Talise said nervously.

"Oh yeah. Is everything okay? You didn't forget about the sisterhood this week, did you? I'm sure you need it after what happened with you and K.J. tonight. My boss told me what happened."

"News travels fast, huh?"

"Like lightning when it comes to you. K.J. is watching you like a hawk. Talise, he is hell-bent on getting you out of that position," Vanee said.

"Thanks." Talise lowered her voice. "Look I have to go and help Gem get ready for the second set. I'll talk to you tomorrow, and I'll see you at my place, six sharp?"

"Yeah. Be strong, girl," Vanee said.

Talise turned without a word and headed straight for the dressing room. She found Gem ready.

"Where's Vaughan?" Gem asked nervously.

"He's talking to Wincey. Why, you need him? I'll get him," Talise said.

"No, no," Gem whispered. She grabbed the back of Talise's royal-blue silk dress, almost tearing it. "Stay cool. I wonder what they're talking about…"

"Once again, ladies and gentlemen, please welcome Gem...," the deep, sultry voice called out.

Gem took a deep breath, grabbed her mike and glided onstage. The powder-blue light accented the silver sparkles on her new costume. Vaughan helped her pick out a platinum form-fitted "giving him something he can feel" gown from Prada. She had added stunning elbow-length gloves in soft white and a white gardenia in her hair.

"Woooooo..." she heard the crowd whisper as the light followed her everywhere she roamed.

She felt the approval swell in her torso. She suppressed and allowed the first note of Roberta Flack's "The First Time" to slide from her lips. The crowd went wild. She acknowledged them with a nod and a smile. She continued to soar when she noticed the movement of a dark shadow in the crowd.

Gem continued, all the while with her eyes fixated on the tall, slender shadow who now had reached the door. It was Wincey. Gem watched as Wincey turned around before leaving. She gave a sweet smile toward the stage, nodded and disappeared.

Gem fought the devastation with all of her might. Her next songs, a melodic tribute to some more of her favorite divas like Chaka Khan, Gladys Knight and Patti Labelle brought the crowd to its feet. After her finale the crowd called for three encores.

"You hear that? That is all for you!" Talise said with glee. She helped Gem out of her shoes.

Gem rolled her eyes and sighed.

"Why are you allowing Wincey leaving in the middle of the show to upset you like this? She is a major star! Maybe she had something to do," Talise reasoned as Gem held her head in her hands.

"Then why couldn't she leave during the intermission? That was rude, Talise, and you know it," Gem said, slamming down a tissue. And I noticed that she and Vaughan talked at the door before she left."

"You sure noticed a lot for someone focused on the task at hand. Maybe Vaughan was trying to put something together. You don't know. Stop obsessing over this stuff. Get ready. You have to go out and meet the executives from the other companies. Come on," Talise said, trying to motivate her friend.

Just as Talise began gathering some of her things, Vaughan stepped in with a purpose. "Okay, babe, you ready? Sylvia Rhone's assistant has to leave soon and..."

"So what were you talking to Wincey about?" Gem snapped around in the chair.

"Huh? Baby, what's wrong? What are you talking about?" Vaughan looked stunned.

"She's just upset right now, Vaughan. She saw Wincey leaving during the middle of her second set and…" Talise interjected.

"I can speak for myself, thank you very much." Gem jumped up and found herself in Vaughan's face. "So what's up with you and Wincey. You didn't tell me you knew her personally and you didn't tell me she was coming to my show. So what's up?"

"I don't know what's gotten into you but you better back off before more than your feelings get hurt. That's straight up. I'm not taking your crap, Gem. I have worked my ass off for you, and you've done nothing except turn your butt up at me. I'm tired of it, Gem. We're friends. I'm not your man, remember? You made that clear, now you want to flex on me about business that I'm trying to make come through for you. You know what, after tonight, call me ghost. You got everything under control. It's all yours, right back at you, baby." Vaughan turned to storm out of the dressing room.

"Wait, Vaughan. No please don't go. Tension is high. It's been a stressful but successful night. Come on. Y'all cool down. Don't go," Talise said, tugging on his arm.

He turned for a word from Gem, who turned to her mirror.

Silence.

"Gem?" Talise said, standing next to Vaughan who waited patiently. "Gem?"

"If he wants to go, let him go. I don't take idle threats from anyone," she said with an eerie calm. She rose from the vanity and proceeded to the rack that held her garments. She continued to bag them up.

"I'm out." Vaughan left a without another word.

"What the hell is wrong with you?" Talise yanked Gem's arm.

"Don't you dare curse at me," Gem said.

"Gem." Talise flailed her arms in the air and clenched her fist to regain her composure. "Is your ego that important to you? You have literally pushed out the best thing in your life without a whim. What the hell is wrong with you? This man stands by you through thick and thin. He put together this whole evening for you without an ounce of gratitude from you. Are you crazy?" Talise's voice escalated with every syllable. "I don't get it. You talk about me. Finally when things seem to be working out, you push people away and expect them to grovel to be back into your life. Gem, you are a wonderful person with a wonderful talent but you can't keep taking advantage of people and situations. You can't."

"Are you finished?" Gem asked.

"I'm done," Talise said.

"Great. I'll see you out front in a few minutes."

"No, thanks. I got myself here. Trust me I'll get myself home," Talise said.

Gem shrugged as she watched Talise walk out.

Talise stomped off the stage, through the crowd waiting to see their star. She managed to bump into Vaughan in the process of loading his equipment in the truck.

"Hey, Vaughan. I'm sorry for everything. I don't know what's gotten in to her."

"No need for you to apologize. I'm through, Talise. She's becoming impossible, and I'm not dealing with it," he said, placing his amplifier in the truck.

"Vaughan, she's very independent, and it's very hard for her to lean on people. She's just scared. Don't hold it against her. Please give her another chance."

"Talise, I appreciate everything you're trying to do. But it's not your place. This situation can't be solved with kind words and understanding from you. Gem better get it together. I hope she does for her sake. Can I drop you home?" he questioned.

"Um, no. You're really going to leave all these people in there?" Talise asked.

"I'm out," he said as he made his way around to the driver's side of the truck.

"Hold up. Just let me get my things. Sure, I need a ride home." She made her way back through the crowd. Gem had emerged from her dressing room and was the making the rounds.

Gem and Talise made eye contact without another word. Talise grabbed her things and marched back to Vaughan's truck.

"Talise, Talise, where you going?" Vanee appeared from the crowd.

"Home, girl. See you tomorrow?"

"Yeah. Hey, cheer up. Your girl put on a great show. She's over there now talking to Steffon's and Romy's partners, Will and Robb. Sounds like things may start jumpin' off."

“Whaat?” Talise questioned. “Vanee, I can’t talk about this now. Too much is going on. I’ll talk to you later, okay?”

“Yeah, girl, tomorrow,” Vanee said as Talise walked out of the door.

Chapter 15

It was not a good day. Stephanie's once voluptuous thighs had become mere toothpicks. She raked her finger through her hair, which now stood like loose limp noodles. She made her way to the bathroom where she almost broke down in tears from the sight of her grayish, clammy skin.

The disease was taking its toll, and there was no way to stop it. Alec was coming by, and she decided this was the day of revelation no matter what. She could only hope that his love would endure this tragedy, for she decided that she did not want to die alone.

She hadn't seen him in three weeks. Surprisingly when they spoke, often briefly right before bedtime he commented on her weakened voice. She passed it off as fatigue and anxiety from planning their upcoming nuptials, which he had insisted they push up. He wanted her to bear his name prior to the election.

Stephanie gingerly made her way down the stairs. Blue, her cat, scurried about. He rubbed his tail against her leg before heading toward the kitchen area. Stephanie followed him, searching her Rolodex for the number to her hairdresser.

"Hey, girl, this is Stephanie. I was hoping he could fit me in today…no, I don't need a relaxer, just a wash and roller set. I have a really important appointment today and…yes…I understand…thanks…" She sighed "…for nothing," she exclaimed after hanging up.

She dialed another number. A thought dawned on her. *My hairdresser always made time for me no matter what. Now all of a sudden he can't accommodate me because he's too busy. Something's not right.*

Stephanie, receiving energy from the anger that brewed inside of her, grabbed her purse and pulled out her cell phone. *They don't have this number*, she thought. She hit speed dial number 12. At one time her beautician was so vital to her 'do that it was necessary for the shop to be listed in case of an emergency like this one.

"Hello, my name is Danna Jefferies and I was referred to Mr. Andreas by a trusted friend who happens to be a long-time client of his. I have an extremely high-post affair occurring this evening and well, I know it's extremely short notice but I was wondering if he could accommodate me with a simple wash and roller set sometime today. Yes, my hair is medium length and rather thin. The most he would need to do is bump it after he sets it. Today at 3:00 P.M.? Oh, that would be wonderful. I will see you then," Stephanie said in her sweetest voice. "Good-bye…oh, surely my telephone number is."

"This number sounds familiar," the receptionist on the other end said. "I can't place it right now. Are you sure you haven't been here before?" she asked.

"I'm positive. Like I said I was referred by a friend who swears by Mr. Andreas…"

"Well, he is good. It don't matter whatcho head look like, he make it shine like new money by da time you walk outta here. Okay, we'll see you at three. And don't worry we'll have you outta here no later than five 'cuz he ain't that busy."

Stephanie was stunned. Her instincts were dead on but she had reserved no energy for confrontation today. She hung up the phone without finishing the conversation.

Gem's phone rang off the hook. *Either she's on the other line and just not picking up or she's on the computer. But her voice mail isn't picking up either,* Stephanie thought as she depressed the lever.

Immediately she hit speed dial on the home phone to call Talise.

"Hello." Talise sounded almost out of breath.

"Ooh, girl, I'm glad you're home. I meant to dial your office but anyway…what are you doing home?"

"I took the day off. I've been having an even worst time at the office of late, so I took Friday off. I didn't feel like dealing with anybody today. Besides I'm holding the second sisterhood meeting at my house tonight and I wanted to tidy up a bit."

"Talise, no. Why are you still a part of that group? It's false…"

"I know, Steph." She cut her off. Talise just sighed. "You sound stressed. What's up?"

"Well, I'm a little upset."

"Yeah," Talise said.

"Oh, how was the show?" Stephanie remembered before she became lost in her own reverie.

"The show went extremely well. It was afterward that was really the show."

"Why, what happened? Did you and Gem get into it again?" Stephanie asked as she sat at her breakfast nook table.

"No. Well sort of. Anyway it's a long story. I'll tell you about it if we have time after you tell me what has you so stressed and upset.

"I think I've been dumped," Stephanie revealed.

"Oh, Steph, I'm sorry. You told Alec, and he's not accepting the situation," Talise said.

"No. I'm talking to him this evening. But I think my hairdresser has dumped me. I don't how he must have found out, but I don't think he wants to work on my head anymore."

"Maybe you're just paranoid."

"No, I'm not. I had a gut feeling so…" Stephanie told Talise about her phone calls.

"So, maybe the guy didn't have any room."

"Talise, I'm not that dumb. I called him back on my cell phone and disguised my voice. The ghetto receptionist made an appointment for me. And she had the nerve to tell me that he had plenty of openings. Do you realize that I've been patronizing that shop almost every week for the last seven years? Come on. I still can't imagine how he found out. My feelings are hurt, Tal. He has some nerve to discriminate. He certainly didn't discriminate with my money and overly large tips for seven years. Shoot, and he has the nerve to be gay."

"Stephanie, baby, I think you're jumping the gun. Don't be so unforgiving before you know the facts. It's not healthy for you. You have to remain calm. You want me to come over? I have some time before the girls are scheduled to show up."

"No, continue with your plans. I just wanted to talk this thing out."

"So talk, girl, I have time...."

Gem noticed her message light flashed fiercely. She neglected to take her windbreaker off before heading straight for the phone and dialing into the voice mail.

"You have fourteen messages," the automated attendant announced.

After last night Will and Robb promised to make a better go of their relationship. She pledged to do the same, with or without the help of Vaughan. Against her intuition and better judgment Gem mailed a recently assembled unfinished demo that she and Vaughan had been working on.

She deleted most of the messages from well wishers, all the while secretly praying that Vaughan had called. But she was out of luck.

Even more shocking was the fact that none of the messages were from Talise. She thought for sure that she would have called to explain and apologize about why she had driven off with her man. *I'm not your man, remember. You wanted it that way,* a voice rang loudly in her head.

Instantly Gem cut it off. It was not convenient for her to think of it right now. She had too much to do. She hung her windbreaker in the closet and began to sort her mail. Just as she leafed through what she surmised to be all bills, the phone rang.

She jumped for the phone. Her private smile reserved only for the confines of her personal space revealed the hope that Vaughan was calling for them to talk.

"Hello." She quickly cleared her throat hoping to suppress any lingering excitement.

"Hey, woman. Congratulations on the show last night. Sorry I couldn't be there but I heard you brought the house down," Stephanie said.

"Oh, hey, girl. Thanks. How are you feeling?" Gem asked with a mild air of disappointment.

"Expecting me to be someone else," Stephanie asked?

"No, no not really."

"Gem, what's going on? Talise just told me everything. She's really upset with you. What happened?"

"She's upset? She has some nerve, she's the one who drove off with Vaughan before the after-show concluded," Gem confessed.

"They left? Together?" Stephanie questioned.

"Yes. Left me high and dry," Gem said. "I guess sleeping with her friend's man is just in her nature."

"Low blow. Real low. Now we know that girl wouldn't do anything like that to either one of us," Stephanie defended Talise.

"Why not? She did it to her so-called friend Vanee."

"Gemmie, stop it. What is wrong with you? Vanee is her acquaintance, first of all, and I'm not excusing her behavior but that girl is in pain, too, and she's trying tirelessly to make amends with that situation. Gem, she would not do that to hurt you. What happened?"

Gem recalled the events as she knew them to be. All the while with Stephanie fielding questions to interject some objectivity.

"So why didn't you just ask Vaughan what he and the superstar were talking about rather than accusing him? I mean I wouldn't be surprised if he was working on your behalf. It's what you've been praying for, right?" Stephanie reasoned.

"Right." Gem remained speechless.

"Then why are you pushing him away? What are you scared of, Gemmie?"

"Hmm?" Stephanie heard Gem whimper.

"What are you scared of?"

"I don't know. I really don't know." Gem paused. "I'm feeling Vaughan. I enjoy being around him. He's fun, he's level and he's a man. You know what I mean?"

"Yes."

"I feel protected. You know whenever anything occurs and when everything is good I know I can always look to Vaughan to make it right or keep it right. We have a lot in common, and the physical attraction is off the Richter scale. But..."

"But?" Stephanie asked.

"Well you know our first issue is my celibacy. I'm not breaking my vow to God. I'm living right this time, Steph, and I'm not trying to blow it."

"Has he ever expressed a problem with it?"

"Not really. He admits that he wants us to be together in that way but he respects my views. Remember that time he showed up at my church?"

"Yeah."

"Well he said he really got the message. You know, spirits entering the course with other spirits in situations that are not sanctioned by God?"

"Yes, I remember. I found that sermon interesting as well. Don't forget I have the tape. I want to return it," Stephanie said. She cradled the phone between her shoulder and ear and began her search through a sea of tapes near the stereo.

"So I mean there is some tension with that but he respects me and my view," Gem said.

"So what are you scared of?"

"This is not a psychological session, Steph. You're trying to give U.A. and I'm not feeling it right now."

"U.A.?"

"Unsolicited advice," Gem answered.

"Okay, defense, now let's get on the offense." Stephanie heard Gem sigh. "No, really. Let's take a look at this situation." Stephanie knew Gem was being stubborn but sometimes the best form of therapy and breakthrough came from people who weren't willing to take it on the surface. She knew her friend well enough to recognize she was crying out. *We recognize in others what is usually present in ourselves,* Stephanie remembered a colleague telling her. *Psychology 101. To help others, we must be able to help ourselves.* She also heard her say.

"You care deeply for Vaughan. He has great qualities and he has your best interest at heart. But Gem, he's a smart guy. He has his best interest at heart too. You can't expect that man to keep deflecting your insecurities and your controlling behavior. From your account of the events, you sound like you were out of line and focus was shifted from your performance to aspects that could have really hampered you. And this issue with Talise, please, that's nothing more than a smoke screen. You're not upset with her, you're upset with yourself. You should have been in that car with him riding off into the sunset of your success, but instead you chose to sabotage it."

"I didn't choose any…"

"I repeat, you chose…" Stephanie emphasized, "…you chose to sabotage it. Now my advice: It's cleanup time. Come to grips with your reality and what and whom you want. If you want Vaughan and you want a relationship with this man, please for the love of God, admit it and in your words, step out on faith. You can't or you won't have the privileges of a girlfriend or wife or partner without the commitment. It's not that type of party."

"Well who have you been talking to? It's not that type of party? You been watching too much *Queen Latifah*." Gem chuckled.

"You get the point."

"Well taken."

"Good. I expect that you'll be calling Talise immediately and apologizing and…"

"Yes, I will," Gem said.

"…And what about Vaughan?" Stephanie questioned.

"I have to pray and meditate on that one. I'm on overload. One friend at a time, okay?" Gem said.

"Okay. Listen, woman, I have to bounce…"

Gem gave a hearty laugh. "I don't know what has gotten into you."

"Seriously, I need to go. I'm getting tired, and Alec will be here soon. I need to take some medicine and get ready. I'm telling him tonight."

"Oh, girl, I'll be home for the rest of the night, and I'll rush right over if you need me."

"Thanks. I'll call you later," Stephanie said.

"Later," Gem said.

Gem retreated to her bath where she lit various scented candles and ran a steamy hot bath. Bubbles merged with the ceramic over the sides of the Jacuzzi tub and onto the floor. She stuck her hand in to test the water.

"Perfect," she said.

Immediately she dropped to her knees and thanked God for all things great and small.

The bumpiness of the road below was eased by the comfort of the Lincoln Continental stretch limousine. Candace's Escada gown lightly brushed the floor of the extremely plush carpeting. She was forced to enter the halls of her ten-year high school reunion alone. Several last-ditch efforts proved vain, as her only alternative to sheer embarrassment couldn't even alter his plans. Her brother also had a previous commitment and Candace couldn't bear to place someone in the position Calvin had placed her in.

"Ma'am, is this okay?" the driver asked.

"This is just fine. Your card contains your pager number, so I can call you when I'm ready?"

"Yes ma'am."

"Great."

"Have a great time," he said as he opened her door and assisted her out of the car.

"Thanks, I'll try," she said as she made the slow walk down the red carpet to the awaiting doorman. She nodded, took a deep breath and walked through the door. She prepared herself for the usual who, where, what, whens and why nots. *I would have been better asking the chauffeur to be my date for the evening,* she thought as she donned her plastic smile.

"Babe, you ready? I told my friends we'd meet them there in fifteen minutes. The restaurant isn't far, is it?"

"Nope, practically around the corner. Just let me grab my cell," Calvin said.

Tracee took the opportunity to place her things in his bedroom on the lower level. She brushed up on her light application of makeup and swished her mouth with his special alcohol-free mouthwash.

She replanted herself in the living room. Soon Calvin emerged looking casually chic as always. Tracee planted a monstrous kiss on his lips.

"I see someone's been dipping in the mouthwash," he said. She smiled, and he said, "Um, I think I need another kiss." He returned the passion.

"Okay, enough of that, let's go. We have plenty of time for that later," she teased.

"I'm looking forward to it," he said as he led her out the door.

Calvin and Tracee were led to a modest table in the far corner of one of the best-kept secrets in the south.

"How did you find this place?" Calvin asked as they worked their way through the maze of people waiting to be seated. "You sure your friends are going to be okay with this?"

"Ooh yeah. Just wait. My friends are really down to earth. I know you'll like one another," Tracee said as she slid into the red leathered booth.

"May I offer you two some drinks?"

"Sure. I'll take a glass of Lem-Tea," Tracee said with a smile.

"Lem-Tea?" Calvin questioned.

"Yeah, it's real brewed iced tea mixed with lemonade," she explained

"Um." He turned up his lips. "What brews do you have?"

"The usual on tap and in the bottle," the waitress answered impatiently.

"Okay, how about Amstel Light?" Calvin returned the attitude.

"We don't have that."

"Well what do you have?" Calvin questioned.

"Um, do you have MGD?" Tracee asked. The woman nodded. "Your coldest MGD in a bottle, please. Thanks," Tracee said, dismissing the woman.

"Tracee, don't do that," Calvin said firmly.

"Do what?" she asked innocently.

"Take over like that. I can handle myself. The woman is here to serve us not give us attitude."

"I know, honey. I just want everything to be perfect," she said, stroking his face. "I didn't mean anything. Ooh, there they are," Tracee called out.

As the couple approached, Tracee and her best friend embraced with a scream.

"Girl, I'm so glad to see you. Sit, sit…oh, I'm sorry, Calvin this is…"

"Oh, my what a small world!" Tracee's best friend said, noticing the young gentleman.

"Yes, it is." Calvin said, standing. He took her hand.

"You two know each other?" Tracee inquired.

"Not really. We met briefly on a flight. Honey, remember the young guy I told you about that we were supposed to meet. Well this is him. Calvin, Calvin Jones, right?" Diamond confirmed. "Calvin, this is my husband, St. Clair Hughes."

"A friend of Tracee's and my wife's is a friend of mine." His raspy voice sounded as if he gasped for air. "My friends call me Sack. Please do the same," he said, shaking one hand and embracing him with the other. "Are you frat? You got some grip there."

"No, I'm not. I did the independent thing at Morehouse."

"A Morehouse man, huh? I'm FAMU myself. I'm also an Omega man."

"Yeah, yeah, yeah. We know. We all know," Diamond chided. "Let's sit, please."

"May I take your order?" The waitress returned having not shed her previous attitude. She set Calvin's beer on the table.

Calvin grasped the bottle. "This is not cold." He returned it to her by pushing it to the end of the table. "May I have another one please?"

"Babe," Tracee whined.

"Tracee, please, I'll handle it." He looked back at the waitress. "Again, do you have any cold beer available?"

"Yes, sir," the woman said as she turned on her heels.

"I'm glad to finally meet you guys. Congratulations on your recent nuptials," Calvin said. The waitress brought back another beer accompanied with a frosted glass.

The group continued with light bantering and ordered. Calvin and Sack hit it off immediately, while Tracee and Diamond caught up.

"Barbecue with hush puppies?" The waitress began placing the plates before everyone. Tracee accepted hers with glee. "Blackened redfish?" Diamond accepted hers. "And two chicken Caesars with mixed greens." She placed the plates before Sack and Calvin. Calvin frowned.

"Excuse me, this is not what I ordered," Calvin said.

"Yes, it is." The waitress looked at her order pad. "Two CC's, it's right there. I don't miss on orders."

"No, this was supposed to have mixed greens. This is nothing but iceberg—and the worst part of the iceberg at that."

The woman sighed. "Would you like to see the manager?"

"By all means," Calvin said. The remainder of the group sat in silence.

The manager entered quickly. "My best waitress tells me there is a problem at this table." The waitress stood behind him with her arms folded across her double D chest.

"Well your best waitress just served warm beer and a mixed green salad with iceberg lettuce and maybe a strip of chicken. Your best waitress is correct, there is a problem."

"Well, sir, that's what you ordered? Am I correct?"

"Yes, that's what I ordered but it's not what I received. I ordered mixed greens, per your menu and you, or I should say your best waitress, brought out a salad full of iceberg and the worst part of the lettuce at that," Calvin said, placing his fork and linen napkin down on the table.

"Well, sir, that's the dish. What would you like it mixed with?"

At this point Calvin was steaming. *If I were White, this conversation wouldn't occur. My meal would have been replaced immediately.* "Um, let's see. Mixed greens, a little red leaf, green leaf even romaine would do."

"Well I'm sorry we don't do it that way. Would you care for me to give you something else? It'll take a few minutes though, we are very full tonight."

"No, no. Just take this, please." Calvin looked to Sack, Diamond and Tracee. "I'm really sorry for this poor hospitality but I can't stay another minute in here. Would you guys mind if we go somewhere our business is wanted and respected?" Calvin questioned.

"Not at all," Sack said, leaving the table.

"Well my fish wasn't that tasty anyway," Diamond said, following.

Tracee politely advised the manager that she was the comptroller for the restaurant's distributor, and this would be a topic of conversation with the firm on Monday.

The manager's facial expression by now had grown crimson.

"Hello?"

"Hey, Tal," she answered in a somewhat syrupy voice. "What you doing?"

"Getting ready for the sisterhood meeting. The girls should be here any minute. What's up? And Gem, I'm not in the mood for a lecture about how I shouldn't be involved in the group." Talise was on the defensive.

"I'm not calling to lecture. I called to apologize. I don't really know what happened or how it all happened but my behavior last night was uncalled for and mean-spirited. I'm sorry."

Silence.

"No need to be. I understand you were stressed and under a lot of pressure. It's okay," Talise offered. She dragged the phone around, trying to pick up last-minute items hidden in various corners of the apartment.

"No, I'm taking responsibility, and I'm really sorry," Gem repeated.

"I appreciate that but I'm not the one you should be apologizing to.

Gem, Vaughan is really in your corner but you keep pushing him out at every turn. It's not cool, and I'm afraid you're going to push him out for good if you don't make amends."

"Aren't you the one to lecture on relationships, Talise? What, this revelation came across to you during your little drive last night? Now you're an expert?"

"So much for that apology. You're right, I'm sorry I was insensitive about riding home with Vaughan. He's a good guy with a good heart..."

"You don't have to tell me," Gem snapped.

"Like I said, he's a good guy with a good heart, and he's in love with you, Gem. And just by the way you're acting, you're in love with him. So you ought to get yourself together and be true to your feelings for him or someone else will. And no it won't be me," Talise said. "I gotta go, the girls are at my door. I love you dearly," Talise said.

Gem softened. "I love you, too, and hey..."

"Yes," Talise asked cautiously.

"Nothing. Just be careful, okay?" Gem said and hung up.

"Welcome, ladies. Welcome," Talise said as the eight women who trailed one another filed past her.

"Oh, this is nice. Wow, great view," several of the women offered.

"Hey, girl. I brought you a little something." Vanee brought up the rear. She made herself comfortable first.

"Ladies, you are no guests in my home. *Mi casa es su casa.* Take your shoes off, relax, hang your own jackets and get your grub on," Talise said with laughter.

The ladies milled about. Some gathered plates of lasagna and green salad that Talise spent most of the day preparing. Others found their way into the wine bottles that Vanee so graciously provided. Still others made their way outside onto the patio and gazed at the exceptionally bright moon.

"Okay, ladies, eat and drink up. We need to get this meeting started," Vanee said.

The ladies acknowledged with nods and faint sounds of agreement "Talise, you put your foot in this food, girl," one woman said.

"She sure did," another agreed.

Talise was in her glory. She gave her thanks and continued pouring glasses of wine and fresh berry juice.

"This is some nice furniture, girl. Is this new?" One of the ladies sat in the center of plushness.

Talise almost choked.

"How much did you pay or you bought it on credit?" the girl continued.

"That is rude." Vanee saved Talise. "You don't be asking stuff like that. You wanna know, go to the store."

Talise disappeared into the kitchen behind the guise of needing to get extra supplies.

The ladies continued to mill about all the while with Talise attempting to be the perfect hostess.

Vanee met her in the kitchen. "Whoever thought eight women could be so loud. Oops," Vanee said, grabbing her hip. "That's my pager. Steffon, what do you want, now?" she said with a playful voice.

"So I take it you two are doing okay?"

"Yeah. Since a few weeks ago, we've been better than ever. We've been hanging out like we used to. A lot of stuff has changed. He's even watching the baby tonight, and I didn't have to fight with him. Let me call him. It's kinda loud in here," Vanee said, looking around for an alternative.

"Oh, use the phone in the bedroom," Talise offered.

"Cool," Vanee said. She walked from the kitchen, through the living room full of ladies enjoying one another, around the corner into the bedroom. She closed the door behind her.

Her bedroom is as bad as her desk at work. How in the heck can she find anything? Vanee thought, moving various articles of clothing to one side of the bed to make her a spot. The phone lay next to the bed on the connecting end table and headboard. Several pieces of paper were also scattered around.

"Yeah," Steffon answered.

"What's up, baby. You paged me?" she asked.

"Yeah. What time you swingin' home? I got some business to take care of. Where you at anyway?"

"Jersey at Talise's. I'm with the girls. I didn't plan on coming home until after midnight."

"That ain't working, Vanee. I got shit to do. You didn't tell me you was going to Jersey," Steffon said.

"What does it matter where I am? What's up with you and Talise? Y'all were good friends and now the mention of her name you get all bent out of shape. What did she do to you?" Vanee became increasingly inquisitive.

"Nothing. Look just bring it home a'ight. I told you I got shit to do," Steffon said.

Vanee looked puzzled. "If you'd like to make a call please..." The operator's voice startled Vanee's gaze back into focus. She maneuvered the paperwork back into place and noticed a final bill of sale delivered to one Talise Grimes. For a brief second she examined the paper when she noticed a piece of clothing that seemed familiar. She picked up what she thought to be a blouse, thinking Talise must have borrowed the item from her at one time or another. *This girl,* she thought. *She won't be borrowing another piece if she can't take care of my shit no better than this.* She picked up the light blue cloth and realized it was a pair of men's boxer shorts instead. "Ooh," she said aloud. "My bad. Not my blouse." She threw the underwear back into the ball of clothing, tried to place everything back the way it was and rejoined the ladies.

"Everything okay?" Talise asked, now passing out Key Lime Cheesecake for dessert.

"Yeah. Steffon wants me to come home because he has something to do," Vanee answered. She sat on the floor in front of the black couch and crossed her legs.

"You not going, are you?" one of the girls asked with her mouth full of the delectable dessert.

"She can't. I'm driving, and she ain't going nowhere until I'm ready, And I ain't ready," another said.

"I'm not trying to go anywhere. Hey, anymore lasagna left?" Vanee asked.

"Right in the kitchen. Help yourself," Talise answered. She was enjoying her evening.

"Wait just two minutes. I'm going to fix my plate and then we can get started." Vanee got up, stepped over a few ladies enjoying their delights and headed into the kitchen.

Talise who had finished serving followed her. "You okay? You seem disturbed."

"No, I'm fine. Steffon just flips the script so often, half the time I don't know what's going on. But I'm okay. I'll be back out there in a minute," Vanee lied. She watched Talise refresh her dessert tray as she walked out of the kitchen once again. She couldn't get the blue boxer shorts out of her mind.

"I told you dominoes is my game." Sack bragged about winning every round. The couples were having an excellent time. The restaurant fiasco had been successfully turned around. Calvin ordered a variety of local dishes and had invited Sack and Diamond back to his house with the two of them to enjoy the rest of the evening.

"So what would you like me to beat you at next?" Sack asked.

"If you're up to get whipped in a little game of acey deucey then, hey, I'm your man. Another brew?" Calvin asked.

"Yeah, I'll take another." Calvin and Sack headed off to the kitchen while the ladies remained cleaning up the dominoes.

"I like him, Tracee. What a small world though. We've been trying to hook up with Calvin for a little while but the wedding and everything afterward prevented the meeting. What better way for the two of them to get acquainted," Diamond said.

"I'm glad. I had no clue that Calvin was trying to hook up with you all. I just thought it would be nice for them to meet. Calvin's a brilliant guy. I thought Sack could use somebody like Calvin on his team," Tracee said.

"We'll be back. Cal and I are going into his office," they heard Sack yell.

"I hope you guys aren't going in there to smoke cigars," Tracee added.

"Oh, let us be, woman," Calvin answered. They disappeared.

"So…" Diamond asked.

"More wine?" Tracee offered.

"Don't play with me, heifer." Diamond followed Tracee into Calvin's kitchen.

"What?"

"You know what? I know this is not all business with the two of you. You really like him, don't you?"

"Di, nosiness isn't becoming," Tracee said, placing the wine back in the refrigerator.

"Oh, I see, you gon' make me hurt you. Answer my question," Diamond demanded.

"Well…" Tracee's thoughts were drawn out with her words.

"Well?" Diamond urged.

"Yes. I like him."

"A lot?" Diamond asked.

"Okay, yes, a lot."

"Why the reservations? He seems like a great guy."

"I don't know. He does seem like a great guy. He's everything I enjoy in a man but…"

"But what?" Diamond asked.

"I don't know, Di. I can't explain it, but my gut is telling me to go real slow. I'm not trying to get shot out overnight, you know. I have to gauge what I'm getting into," Tracee said. She continued cleaning up items left behind in the kitchen. "Oh, you know what, I have some pictures that I took at the wedding. They're in the car. Let me get 'em." Tracee dried her hands on the hanging towel.

"Tracee, I understand your reservations, I mean the relationship is new. But don't blow something good and solid on your sometimes overly zealous caution. Let yourself go and enjoy," Diamond reasoned.

"We'll see. Anyway, I'll be right back."

She clicked the automated release button on her key chain. She located the pictures almost immediately. She pulled them out and eyed them briefly. When she emerged from the car, she noticed a black stretch limousine sitting directly in front of Calvin's house.

Curiously Tracee walked to the end of the drive. As she stood, she noticed that the passenger or driver never rolled down a window so she sauntered back toward the side door to re-enter the house. The limo sat still.

Finally she entered the side door, dropped the pictures in front of Diamond who now sat at the island in the middle of the kitchen. Tracee went to the front picture window and made no bones about pulling the curtain back and gazing at the limo. Finally it pulled off slowly.

"Ooh, you scared me," Tracee said as Diamond seemed to sneak up behind her.

"What are you doing?" Diamond asked.

"There was a limo that sat in front of Calvin's house for a few minutes. I was looking to see who it might be."

"Why? You wouldn't know them. And besides there are other houses on this cul-de-sac. Stop being paranoid. Girl, these pictures are great. When did you have time to take them?" Diamond asked as she led Tracee back into the light.

CHAPTER 16

"You cock-sucking son of a bitch!" Vanee yelled. Their daughter wailed in the background. Vanee continued throwing everything her hands could grasp—his clothes, his shoes, his empty cologne bottles and toiletries all experienced her wrath.

Their little girl Trevorr's cry grew louder. Vanee got herself together for a moment. She called one of the girls from the sisterhood to come get Trevorr for the night. She planned to end this rampage. Moments later, one of the girls who resided in her same building came to the rescue. She grabbed the little girl and headed out the door. "Don't even worry about it, girl. Everything will be all right. Take all the time you need," she said, ushering their daughter out the door.

With Trevorr now gone, Vanee was able to cry her last cry. She screamed. She punched and flipped things over.

When Steffon finally came home she sat at the kitchen table as cool as a breeze. The tornado had passed and he couldn't have known what hit him.

"What the fuck?" he said, creating a mild wind compared to her earlier storm.

"Steffon, that's it. Get yo' shit and get the fuck out, now. Get yo' shit, whatever is left and get the fuck out now. I've had it."

"What the fuck you talkin' 'bout. I ain't goin' nowhere. Where's my fuckin' daughter?" he said as his storm increased.

"Don't worry about that shit. Get the fuck out. Get yo' shit, get yo' shit and get out!" she yelled. She ran toward him and pounded his chest. He saw a fire in her eyes, never apparent before. It stopped his retaliation cold.

"Vanee, what is wrong with you?" he asked, grabbing her arms and trying to calm her down.

"I'm tired, Steffon. I'm tired of yo' shit. Every time I turn around you fuckin' somebody new. You taking care of business outside the home and ain't never here to do what you supposed to do. Every once in a while when some street whore has dumped yo' ass and hurt yo' feelings you come crawling back here trying to make it right. No more. I'm tired of struggling the way I have to. We have a family." She smacked her chest. "We, Steffon. But with you it's always me, me and more me. Just get out. I have sniffed your last leg of dirty-ass drawers, motherfucka!"

"Vanee, Vanee!" he shouted.

She stomped to the bedroom. She emerged with the same blue underwear and a piece of paper. He looked puzzled.

She threw both articles in his face. The paper dropped at his feet and he caught the underwear. "Vanee, what is wrong with you? What is this?"

"You tell me, you son of a bitch! I bought you these three years ago. But I found them in Talise's goddamn bedroom. Oh, and this." She scrambled on the floor and picked up the paper that still remained at his feet.

"Vanee, you buggin'."

"I'm buggin'? I'm buggin'? I got furniture that's about to break down around my feet and you buying that bitch furniture. My so-called friend. Steffon, please get out of my face. Just get yo' shit, Steffon, and get out of my face. Please. I'm sick of the rumors of you fuckin' everything with a hole at that job," she mumbled on her way to answer the doorbell. Vanee opened it and directed the two guys toward Steffon. "I suggest you get him or there will be a murder," she said.

"Oh, it's like this. You must be kidding? Now Romy's actin' on your behalf?" Steffon said incredulously.

"Man, just get your shit and get out. I don't want to but at Romy's instructions I will hurt you. You have fifteen minutes," one of the henchmen said.

"No, he don't. His minutes have run out. Grab what you can and get the hell out. I will have the rest delivered to you later. Now get out." Vanee's voice trembled.

"You heard her, man. Let's go," the henchman said.

"I don't believe this shit," Steffon said as he stepped through the door. He heard the guys inform Vanee to please call Romy with anything else she needed. She agreed and thanked them for their help. Steffon continued to walk away, dumbfounded with no place to go.

Candace stormed out of the restaurant, causing a scene with her presence. Calvin placed several bills on the table and ran after her. He caught her before she reached her car. She struggled with her keys in the lock. He grabbed her from behind and held her tight. It was pouring and the rain didn't hide her tears. She doubled over in pain.

He helped her to the passenger side. He placed her trench coat on her knees and situated himself on the driver's side. They drove to his house, her instructions once her large gulps of air eased.

He led her to the couch where they talked some more. He tried his best to explain. But nothing seemed to ease her extreme pain.

Several hours later he walked her limp body to the bedroom where he tucked her in for what he considered to be their final evening. Their lack of passion could no longer be avoided, and it was time for them to move on with their lives.

"I don't want to hold you back either. I want you to be with someone who is right for you. That's not me," he admitted.

"How can you tell me who or what is right for me?" she whispered.

"I can't. But I know what is right for me, and Candace, this relationship isn't it." He could tell that his words stung. No matter how he sweetened them, the bottom line was that it was over, and he was no longer willing to sacrifice his happiness out of guilt.

He took off her shoes and placed them near his night table. She took her clothes off and he retrieved her flannels from the back of the closet.

She was shocked they were still there. "Would you like something to drink?" he asked as she snuggled into place. Her tears still flowed effortlessly.

He closed the door behind him and settled on the fact that he would occupy one of his guest bedrooms. The phone rang so loud that he was sure it disturbed Candace along with the dead.

"Hello," he said quietly.

"You sound sleep," Tracee said.

"On my way," he answered. He looked at the door praying all would remain calm. *I'm a one-woman man, Calvin. I don't tolerate infidelity on any level.* He recalled one of their passionate conversations. He knew he would never be able to explain this situation away.

"Well I just called to say good night."

"I appreciate that. Good night, baby," he said.

"Where were you tonight? I tried to call you on your cell phone but you didn't have it on," Tracee questioned innocently.

"Oh no, my battery ran down. I just needed to recharge it, but I left the charger at home."

"Everything okay? You sound nervous."

"Yeah, everything's fine."

"Okay, babe. Well I'll talk to you tomorrow. Oh, and I'll see you this weekend for the investment meeting. When are you meeting with Sack again?"

"I'm flying to Atlanta in two weeks. I'm viewing the plans and everything," Calvin said, elevating his voice slightly.

"Sack really likes you, Cal. You two seemed to hit it off really well. He said he was really impressed with the way you handled the situation at the restaurant that time. I wouldn't be surprised if a serious business venture is in the works, but you didn't hear it from me." She chuckled.

He responded with laughter as well. "Good. Well I'm going to go, but I'll talk to you first thing like always."

"Yeah, like always. I love you, babe."

"Right back at you." He laughed. "I'm only kidding, I love you too," he said as he hung up the phone.

An early-morning call jolted Candace out of a broken sleep. She reached to the other side of the bed and noticed it hadn't been touched. She remained in her spot.

Moments after the phone rang, Calvin poked his head in the doorway. He tiptoed to her side of the bed and noticed she was awake. He reached to wipe the tears from her eyes. She jerked away.

In silence she arose. She grabbed the clothes she had on the night before. Without a word she sauntered into the bathroom. Quickly she returned fully dressed. She searched the closets where she noticed he retrieved her things for any remaining items. She brushed passed Calvin, as he stood almost lifeless. Candace still hadn't said a word. She made her way to the kitchen and found a large garbage bag to throw the remainder of her things in.

She dragged the bag to the bathroom and placed a few decorative items she had recently purchased for Calvin's bathroom. She placed those on top. Confident that she had removed everything she ever had there, she made her way through, gave one last glance and proceeded to walk out.

"Candace, you want to talk?" Calvin asked.

She didn't say a word. She placed the bag at her feet and retrieved the carton of juice from the fridge. She pulled a glass from the cabinet and filled it halfway.

"Candace," Calvin called out.

She drank the last bit of juice in her glass, grabbed her bag and keys and dragged everything out of the side door and into her car without saying one word.

Talise went busting into Vanee's cubicle. "Girl, guess what?"

Vanee wasn't smiling. She sat at her desk with a cold stare that broke through Talise's soul. A friend from a different department stood guard.

"Girl, what's wrong? Are you okay?" Talise questioned with sincerity.

"I can't talk to you now. Meet me in the conference room in about twenty minutes." Vanee said. "You can go now," she said coldly and resumed her conversation.

Talise didn't argue. She had the familiar hollow feeling in her stomach that she always got when she just knew something was seriously wrong.

"She has a lot of nerve," she heard the girl say.

"Nope. Don't go there. I'm handling everything. Trust me I ain't 'bout to lose my job over this bitch. But she's gonna be sorry she ever fucked with me," Vanee said.

Talise had left earshot of the conversation. She made her way to the elevator. "Oh, I forgot which conference room," Talise said aloud, stepping into her office. Steffon was waiting. "What are you doing in here?" she questioned.

"What you think?" he answered.

"Steffon, I'm not up for you today. I have a lot to do and I have a meeting in fifteen minutes with…"

"Vanee?" he asked as he twirled the toothpick in his mouth.

"How do you know?"

"Put two and two together. You fucked up, you silly bitch. Vanee found my underwear at your house, and I wanna know how she got a hold of the delivery notice of your shit with my name on it."

"Vanee knows?" Talise said as her heart continued its fall to her knees.

"Yeah, she knows. Don't play stupid. Why you give her that stuff?"

"I didn't give her anything," Talise said.

"Well how she get it?"

"Steffon, don't start harassing me. I told you I don't know. Anyway, I have to go. And don't threaten me either about that furniture."

"I ain't sweatin' no fucking furniture. You fuckin' with my life, bitch, and I swear…"

"Get out of my office, now," Talise said, marching off. She left Steffon behind the glass.

Talise tried the conference room on the floor first. Talise checked the conference room on her floor. No one was in sight.

She went to the conference room on the floor below and that one was empty as well. Finally she tried the floor above. Vanee sat with her fingers tapping impatiently.

Talise slid into the chair just opposite her. "I'm sorry…" she started.

"Don't. I don't want to hear it. I have taken you in my home, allowed you to be around my child and introduced you to my family. I have been a good friend to you, always looking out for you at work, and this is how you repay me, by fucking my man? Well it's over. And I want you to know that you are responsible for me not trusting another woman in my home ever again. I would never…"

"Never say never, Vanee. I'm sorry but you don't know what you would do given the circumstances. I'm sorry, I was lonely and hurting. I didn't mean to hurt you. It wasn't about you. Steffon made his move on me all along and if it wasn't me it would have been someone else. I just—"

"Like I said," Vanee said, cutting her off, "I would never have played you like this. I will never, ever fuck my girl's man. If your ex-husband had come to me with this bullshit, he would have been off limits. And please don't think I didn't have the opportunity. On several occasions when I visited your home, Maurice hit on me. But like I said, I had too much love and respect for not only myself but also you. Now I'ma tell you like this…" Vanee leaned in closer. "Now for your own good, you see me coming, you better walk the other way. You hear my voice you better not say a word to me. Do you understand me? I'm telling you right now, I'm really angry, and I don't know what I'll do, so you better stay outta my way."

"Vanee, I'm sorry. I didn't mean to hurt you. I'm sorry…" Talise sobbed.

"Cut it. Your crocodile tears don't mean shit to me. Now step. Heed my words, Talise. Heed my words," Vanee said.

Talise retreated to her office. Steffon had left and the only thing left was a "see me" note from K.J.

"What now?" Talise questioned.

"So have you talked to Vaughan?"

"No."

"Why not, Gem?" Stephanie asked.

They walked along the corridors of the Princeton Halls. Their stride was steady and slow as they peered in each window like schoolgirls.

"Hold up, I need to rest, "Stephanie said as she sat on a wooden bench in direct view of a carousel. Stephanie pulled out her portable water bottle and a large packet of pills of various colors.

"It's that time," Stephanie said as she proceed to take them one by one.

"I'm proud of you," Gem said as she watched patiently.

"For what?" Stephanie asked.

"For fighting to live," Gem answered.

"Well it's not the dying I'm afraid of, but the living that scares me," Stephanie said, finishing her last dosage for the afternoon. "Ready to stroll?" she asked Gem.

"Yep," Gem answered as they continued their window shopping. They stopped in front of a jewelry store. Brilliant diamonds sparkled throughout the displays. One diamond in particular reminded Stephanie of her ring.

"Penny for your thought?," Gem asked.

"Just thinking about Alec. I'm sad that things turned out the way that they did. You know, I gave him the ring back," Stephanie said.

"Why?" Gem asked with exasperation.

"It wasn't right. I was never in love with Alec. And honestly I don't think he was in love with me. I'm sure I was a political pawn in his and his dad's game," Stephanie said, still marveling at the diamond. She set her sights on a pair of earrings that had to be a carat apiece.

"You obviously nailed that observation," Gem said, poking Stephanie and pointing out a laughing Alec emerging from the store. He wasn't alone. He was accompanied by a tall, slender, cocoa-colored woman. She sported a very neat short afro.

"Alec," Stephanie said in amazement. He looked stunned for a moment. Slowly he walked toward Stephanie and Gem, as his partner lagged.

"Fancy meetin' you here," Stephanie said.

"Uh, yeah. How have you been?" Alec asked as if their conversation of a few weeks, occurred months ago. "How are you feeling?"

"Great," Stephanie said with angst. She studied Miss Short Afro the entire time. "So, a new token in your life? And so soon, Alec. I bet you're trying to get married in the next few months just prior to the election—"

Alec cut her off "Stephanie, I loved you but you can't expect me to throw my life away," he said in a hushed tone. "Our entire situation, your situation would blow the entire election. I can't chance that," he continued.

"Blow the election! Blow the election! That's all I was to you? Another constituent to help you win your election?" Stephanie's voice raised dramatically. People began to stare while Alec tried to calm her to no avail. He smiled nervously as people stopped.

Gem tried to pull her away, but Stephanie's adrenaline kicked in. Stephanie would not sway as she stepped to Alec's friend. "So you're the new token in his life, huh? Well good luck, sweetie, because as soon as you don't fit into his well-orchestrated life, you, too, will be history."

"Stephanie, that's enough," she heard Gem say.

Stephanie felt a tug at her arm and backed off.

"I think she's right, Stephanie. You're causing a scene. Perhaps you should go home and rest," Alec said smugly.

"That is and was your problem. Trust me, sister, if he can control you and show you a thing or two, you're in, if not, he'll find another blackbird to latch on to. All in the name of looking good," Stephanie said as she allowed Gem to pull her away.

"Alec, what is that woman screaming about?" Stephanie heard the woman ask.

"Oh, nothing. She's just a scorned friend," Stephanie heard Alec reply.

Stephanie turned once again to tell the woman and Alec off, but Gem's tug was stronger.

"Let it go," Gem said.

"But I let him go," Stephanie whined.

"Come on, let's get some coffee and a scone," Gem said, leading her away as far as possible.

The elongated table resembled that of a Thanksgiving dinner in the middle of June. Calvin had assembled what he considered to be the finest of financial minds in the country. He rented the private dining room of the same rustic restaurant to which he once brought Talise. But this time he had the right set of people.

"Once you exit the highway you have to bear right. The restaurant is set off to the side. You won't miss it, and hurry because we've ordered appetizers and drinks. Everybody is here, we're just waiting on you, playa. Alright, see you soon. Call me back if you get lost," Calvin said, disconnecting the call.

Calvin was in his glory. His best friend, Grey, was present, along with twelve other highly financially astute friends and associates. Tracee also sat on the right of him.

She returned from the ladies' room and planted a kiss on his cheek. "Come on, babe. Let's get this party started. I'm starving," she said, picking from the onion loaf at the center of the table.

"We're waiting for one more person. But we can start ordering if you guys would like." They all agreed and Calvin called the waiter over. The waiter took orders and Calvin politely excused himself to take a call.

He flipped the phone. "Man, are you still lost? No, no, no, you're heading in the wrong direction. Turn around at the next exit and double back…I know the next exit is nine miles away but if you listened to me in the first place…" Calvin continued as he walked toward the front door.

He was stopped at the front server's podium.

"Hey, isn't that Calvin?" he heard a high voice ask.

It was Candace. He hadn't seen her or talked to her in months, and he had to admit *she looked rather, rather*...he thought.

He completed his conversation for what he hoped would be the final time and walked toward Candace.

"You see what I mean. I can't understand for the life of me what you ever saw in that idiot. He's so arrogant, Candace," one of the ladies said.

Candace hushed her. "Mr. Jones, so good to see you," Candace said with coolness. She allowed him to peck her on the cheek. They exchanged light pleasantries as her friends stepped aside to allow them space. Daggers shot from their eyes at a distance.

"Terrance, man, it's about time." Calvin's expected guest finally arrived. "We're in the private dining room in the back. Everyone's there, order something quickly so that you're not the only one sitting without food. Oh, I'm sorry, Terrance this is..."

"Candace Burton. It's wonderful to see you again. How have you been?" he asked, grabbing her hands and kissing her on the cheek.

"Great to see you too." She smiled.

"I take it you two know each other," Calvin questioned. He tugged on his ear.

"Oh yes. We go way back. All the way to ninth grade," Terrance answered.

"Yes, speaking of ninth grade, I didn't see you at the reunion we had a few months ago. It was really nice," Candace said, looking out of the corner of her eye at Calvin with disdain.

"Yeah, I was out of the country. I had business in Switzerland. I had been there for a year and a half, and I couldn't get back."

"Excuse me, Cal, the food is ready, babe, and we're all waiting for you." Tracee approached the group.

"Okay, I'm going to bleed the lizard, and I'll be right there. Terrance, continue with your reunion and you can meet us in the back. Oh, I'm sorry. Forgive my rudeness..." Calvin said. "This is Tracee. Tracee, this is Terrance, he's the man of the hour, and this is Candace."

"It's nice to meet you both." Tracee extended her hand. "Well I'm going back to the table. I'm a little hungry. I'll see you there." Tracee turned to Calvin and stroked his cheek.

Calvin noticed what he perceived as envy on Candace's face.

"Will you show Terrance the table? We've waited long enough," Calvin said, not looking back. He headed toward the men's room.

"See what I mean. He's so rude," one of the ladies in Candace's party said. She turned to hush her again.

"Um, Terrance, you're meeting with Calvin I see. Is Grey in your party as well?" Candace asked.

"As a matter of fact he is. What a small world," Terrance answered, following Tracee who sped far ahead of him.

"Oh, I want to say hello. I'll catch up with you girls in a minute," Candace said to her friends.

Candace approached the table.

"Grey, how are you? Good to see you." She kissed Grey on the cheek. She sat down in the only vacant seat available, which happened to be situated between Grey and Terrance.

"You too," Grey offered. "Take care of yourself, okay?" Grey dismissed her.

"So Terrance, I don't want to hold you up but…" she totally ignored Grey's previous comment. "here's my card, including my home phone and cell. Give me a call sometime," she said, leaving the chair.

"I would love that, Candace. I'll be out of town for the next few weeks securing my move back to the States, but I would love to get together with you after that," Terrance said.

"Well take care, everyone. Grey, it was great seeing you again."

"No trust me, Candace, the pleasure was all mine," Grey returned.

Candace turned on her heels and walked away.

Calvin returned, bumping Candace on the way. He sat down next to Tracee and kissed her lovingly. She responded with a smile. "Well let's get started," he said.

"Girl, what did you do?" one of Candace's friends asked as Candace took her seat.

"For once I showed Mr. Calvin Jones what he's missing." Candace held her hand up for a high five. They all gladly obliged with glee.

Gem left Stephanie fast asleep amid a sea of blankets with Blue curled up at her feet. She thought really hard about everything Stephanie had said to her during her hour-long drive home. She always listened, even though she didn't always take heed.

The night held an eerie stillness. She pulled into her driveway, now darkened from the burned-out bulb. *I forgot I have to get that replaced.*

That was one drawbacks of home ownership. She was responsible for everything. And when she was between gigs, house breakdowns as small as replacing a lightbulb could sometimes seem devastating.

She entered her cold, unfeeling home alone. Purposefully she headed straight toward the bath, drew the warm water and laced it with lavender-scented bubbles. She stepped out of her clothes and placed her toes under the tap. *Ahh perfect,* she thought as the phone rang. Immediately a strange feeling entered her stomach. Perhaps she had talked him up. *Would that be a bad thing? What should I say?* Gem thought as she approached her phone. Tiny beads of sweat appeared on forehead. She was sorely met with disappointment. It wasn't Vaughan, it was Talise.

She raised her shoulders tensely. She picked up the phone after she was sure her voice mail had already trapped Talise. She dialed three numbers and briskly hung up. *Just do what Stephanie would tell you to do. Pick up the phone. Pick up the phone. You have nothing to lose, but everything to gain. Life is too short....* Gem's brain and heart ticked feverishly.

So she followed the muscle that paced at more than 160 beats per minute and hit the speed dial.

"Hello?" a sleepy but sweet-sounding voice answered. "Hello?"

Silence.

Dial tone.

Sweat poured from her now wrinkled brow. "That must have been the wrong number," she reasoned aloud. She dialed again. This time she dialed from memory.

The same voice answered again. But at this point the woman's voice contained agitation.

"Um, hello. May I speak to Vaughan please," Gem asked cautiously. Maybe it was his sister, she prayed.

"He's sleep," the woman answered.

"Would you wake him up, please, it's an emergency," Gem said with slightly more confidence.

"No, I won't do that," the woman insisted.

"Then will you take a message?" Gem asked.

"Of course. And the message is?" the woman asked.

All of a sudden Gem heard the receiver being covered. It sounded as if a slight struggle ensued.

"Hello? Hello?" Vaughan's voice was music to her ears.

"Vaughan?"

"Yeah. Who is this?" he asked.

"Vaughan, this is Gem."

"And?"

Her heart pounded with more anxiety. He was playing her, and she suddenly felt sorry that she even bothered to pick up the phone.

"And, well I have a gig and was wondering if you would play the sax for me?" Gem lied.

"Gem, it's two in the morning? This couldn't wait?" He huffed. "When is it?"

"I guess you're right. Can I talk to you tomorrow then?"

"Yeah, sure, whatever," he said. The next tone she heard was the operator asking if she'd like to make a call...,

Gem seethed in anger. "Who the hell does he think he is?" she asked. She picked up the phone and dialed Talise. Even in her madness she thought enough not to wake up Stephanie.

"Hello?" another sleepy voice answered.

"Talise, are you sleep?" Gem questioned.

"That's what people usually do at 2:30 in the morning when they have jobs to go to that they can't be late for," Talise said now clearly awake. "I just called you a half an hour ago. Where were you?"

"In the land of embarrassment," Gem answered.

"What? What happened?"

Gem recounted everything, including her added verbal angst.

"Well, girl, you haven't spoken to him in weeks. You couldn't expect him to wait forever."

"Yeah, but I didn't expect him to fill his bed so quickly."

"Why not? You aren't willing to do it. I'm not saying you should, but Gem even I know that you can't have your cake and eat it too. You said yourself that with Vaughan, it's friendship and business. He's not your man and you're not his woman. You can't get mad if someone else declares that she is."

"All of this great wisdom is killing me. Too much. It's just too much," Gem said. She placed her head in her hands. She took the cordless phone into the bathroom with her and watched the bubbles dissipate.

"Gem, if you want the man and he's yours to have, go for it. If not then let it go and be done with it." Talise placed her head back onto the pillow.

"I guess you're right. I know you're right." Gem sighed.

"Yeah, well, I wish I could take my own advice," Talise said. She propped her head on her elbows.

"What do you mean?" Gem added more warm water and suds into her bath.

"Vanee found out."

"About you and Steffon?" Gem gasped.

"You got it."

"But you two are through, right? Or are you still dipping?"

"No, girl. We're done, and I wish before God we never started. This is was the worst nightmare of my life. I didn't mean to hurt her. It just happened. You had to see the hurt in her heart that penetrated her eyes."

"What did you say?" Gem asked solemnly.

"I tried to say sorry but she wasn't trying to hear it. It just happened, I mean…"

"What his dick fell into you?" Gem asked.

"No, but anyway…"

"I know, girl. It seems like we both have a lot going on. But hey…if that man is yours to have, get 'em. Don't break your code, but have him. You deserve happiness. Grab it while it's here, even when it doesn't look like it's present. Gem, I gotta go. I have to get some semblance of sleep before treading the jungle tomorrow."

"Oh, my goodness, Talise. You have to work with them?"

"Both of them. And you know she has a lot of pull around there. I don't know what I'm going to do."

"Pray, Talise. That's all I can tell you. Pray."

"That's all I can do. Good night."

"Good night."

The morning sun rose before five-thirty and Gem woke up right with it. In her green satin p.j.s she dropped to her knees. She asked God to guide her and be with each and everyone of her friends, guide them through their trials and tribulations no matter how strong her friends seemed.

"Th-Thanks for seeing me," Gem stuttered.

"I don't mean to be rude, but you have to make it short. I got a lot of stuff to do. We have a new singer coming in tonight and I have to set up,"

Vaughan said curtly. He sat with his arms straddled across the thin black iron back of the chair.

"I know. I first want to apologize for lying to you. I don't have a gig for you to play on…," Gem admitted.

"I figured as much."

"I just wanted to talk to you. And I was a little stunned when I realized you had someone staying with you…."

"Gem, that's none of your business, and if you're here to start grilling me 'bout stuff that ain't your concern, this conversation is over."

"No please, please, Vaughan. I'm not…" she paused. "Why are we over?" she asked with humility. "Vaughan, please. You don't owe me anything but we were a special team, and I miss that. I really miss you," Gem heard herself say. "Don't make this harder than it has to be." Her beautiful brown eyes widened.

"Gem, don't do this now." She still had her hook in his soft spot.

"I have to do this now." She clenched her fists until they hurt. She tried her hardest to fight back the tears but it didn't work. "Vaughan, I'm so, so sorry for pushing you away. You've become a bright star in my life that was—is—hard to ignore. I tried, believe me I tried." Her cheeks were soaked. "You've given me unconditional friendship and love, and I long to return that to you. I'm not begging you to get back together. But I'm begging to have your friendship."

"You don't have to beg, Gem. I'll always be your friend."

"But nothing more, huh?" she asked.

He shook his head. Physically he wanted to console her but mentally he knew it was not the right thing to do. He had committed his energy elsewhere. He took his time before he spoke. "Gem, there was a time when I did my best. I really don't how much clearer I coulda been about wanting to build with you. And you couldn't have been any clearer about not wanting to spend time with me. I asked you out. We kicked it with music and without. I offered coffee shops, museums and movies. When you felt charitable, you responded…thanks…thanks for an hour of your time, Queen Gem."

"It's my celibacy, isn't it? Well that's not going to change but…" Her tone changed from humility back to her comfortable state of defense.

He shook his head with a sarcastic chuckle. "That's what I mean. You have all the answers, don't you? Why did you come to me if you had all the answers? Your celibacy is not my bag." She tried to interrupt him but he wouldn't allow it. "You were something special."

"Were?"

"You are something special. But the fact of the matter is I can't be here for you when you want me to. I hear you but right now I have other things to focus on in my life. I'm real busy. The bottom line, Gem, is I'm a good person and I know it. I'm not the best-looking person in the world but I have a good heart. I don't deserve what you've been dishing out. We're just not flowing like that anymore. You gotta go." He rose from the chair. "If a gig comes up and you could use my services, give me a call. I'll do the same for you. I always keep my ear to the grindstone. Peace."

For the second time in less than twenty-four hours, he left her stunned.

Chapter 17

"Your limo is ready, Mr. Jones," a very sweet voice on the opposite end of the phone of the Peachtree Plaza said.

"Thank you, I'll be right down," Calvin said, gathering the gold that he was sure to get him the job.

"You don't need luck, babe. Your plan is flawless," he remembered Tracee saying.

She's right, he thought. He had done everything he knew to do by the book. Courtesy of Tracee, Calvin had an inside track to Sack's plans for Sack Enterprises for the next five years. He did the research, anticipated complications and devised solutions. Landing this account could mean serious financial independence.

He grabbed a white hanky, again courtesy of his beloved. Before shoving the material in his inside pocket he noticed his hands were clammy. He used his hanky reserved for the Atlanta sun, wiped his hands and sat down.

Why am I nervous? He couldn't recall ever feeling faint at the possibility of a prospect. He wasn't even this nervous right before what he considered to be the biggest game of his life.

It was senior year and his as well as a few other guys' last chance for a state championship. Coaches from Bucknell, Syracuse and Harvard looked on. He had rose in the ranks to be his school's first African-American quarterback. He had fought fast and furious to challenge the state's top contender.

"It's all on you, baby," Cal's star wide receiver yelled in the huddle. Cal had less than thirty seconds to decide on one of two plays. Everyone looked to him and even though he had to muster every bone in his body to show extreme confidence, his moment of truth felt like right now. Less than two minutes loomed on the clock and the score was 14 — 10, not in their favor.

Calvin called the play. Several of the other players looked at him in disbelief. He didn't repeat himself. He broke the huddle and took his stance. Needless to say when the clock ran down, the team held Cal in high esteem. The final score was 17 — 14 in their favor. Calvin never forgot that attitude of mental toughness. He had the game plan and the players in place. *Now I have to bring the mental fortitude that wins games every time.*

Calvin resumed his posture the same way he did once before. The sweat from his hands and brow disappeared.

He stepped through the glass doors sporting Armani's finest. And as always he turned heads. His Feragamo scent left a trail many wanted to follow but few could handle. He carried his plans in a brown leather attaché as if they were top-secret documents.

Calvin entered the room that held six of Sack's top executives. At a mahogany round table fit for a king sat Chancé Williams, Sack's Northeast district leader in sales and marketing. To his right was Shaun Fooshay, the all-American pretty boy import from Chicago, wheeling and dealing his way through the midwest. To his right was Celeste, the twin sister of Chancé and director of social affairs and The Sack Inc. nonprofit wing of the organization. Next to him sat Antonio Ladd, attorney extraordinaire. To close the deal and make it work, Cal had to go through him. Next to him was Brian Steele, college graduate, former intern turned limo driver turned head driver turned manager of transportation specialists in the Northeast region and finally, pulling up the rear with the sweetest honey smile and red-faced freckles was the beautiful lady responsible for it all, Diamond.

She was the lady of the hour, the lady of influence, Sack's love, his life and his partner in crime. Diamond's vote like Sack's, counted for two.

"Good morning, ladies and gentlemen." Calvin entered with pizzazz. He was eyed from head to toe.

"Good morning," they returned.

"I guess we should get started," Calvin said confidently. He didn't bother to sit. He pulled out his laptop and set it up for the show. He slipped the manila folders from the attaché and laid them on the table like a deck of cards.

"Sack, I don't have a lot of time. My flight leaves back to New York in three hours. I don't need the show, just the bottom line," Shaun snapped.

Sack tipped his head as if to serve Calvin to the lions.

"Mr. Jones, welcome," Chancé said. "Um, what are your goals for Sack Enterprises, and how would you go about achieving them?"

Calvin let out a breath. That was the easiest question of the day. He rubbed his hands together and proceeded as planned. He showed graphs of Sack's overall productivity in his existing regions as estimated in public records. He showed tidbits of his plan to increase Sack Enterprises' overall market plans by tapping into the fastest growing region in the country. "This would promote no less than a forty percent increase in sales because the Southeast region, particularly Atlanta, has so much growing industry to tap into. And who better than a person like me with the contacts and resources in all levels of commerce, industry and government than to do it," Calvin said.

The room remained silent. "Calvin, I currently run the Midwest region, which boasts more than fifty percent in Sack Enterprises current revenues. You think you can match that and in what time period are you speaking," Shaun challenged.

"I don't think, Shaun, I know I can increase sales overall in one year by forty percent because I have the jewel of the South in my grips. The Midwest, while a viable marketplace for entertainment and sports in Chicago will always be viable, is somewhat stagnate. Atlanta is the multicultural marketplace that prides itself as the gateway of the south..." Calvin continued explaining his reasoning and strategy. Eventually even Shaun seemed satisfied.

"Calvin, all of this sounds great. I like your presentation, your research, everything seems well planned. I'm really interested in your thoughts for sustaining Sack Enterprises for the future," Chance swiftly interjected.

"Quickly I'll say this. My focus is always beyond the superficial. Black businesses are sustained by doing what we do well. Expansion comes from necessity within the field. Sack Enterprises thrives as a limo company. Other forms of transportation can come from that in the future, alternative modes of transportation, but how do we expand S.E. as an automotive transportation giant? We manufacture our own product."

"Don't you think manufacturing limos is a little farfetched?" Shaun asked.

"Absolutely not. Sack is on his way to being the first black billionaire. Our thoughts and actions must encompass that. How do we manufacture limos? We invest in a major automotive company, let's say BMW. I would estimate that we would need to own twenty-three percent of its shares. Extend from them the right to own and operate a plant in the Southeast—" Calvin emphasized and glanced at Shaun—"where labor is reasonable, land is accessible and communities are amenable."

The meeting continued without a hitch. Even Shaun's bark seemed to subside as Calvin threw in a few perks to help boost his region as well.

Calvin was transported back to the hotel where he was asked to wait. His entrée into S.E. was to be decided by way of a quorum of the management team. Sack thought it best to put this proposal into action quickly. Calvin obliged them for another day. He thought of Tracee as he lifted his warmed snifter of brandy.

The gold rolled down his throat like velvet. He let out an *ahh* as the premium liquor gave him the stinging sensation he so loved. He picked up the remote and flipped on some music. He programmed several preselected jazz CDs to play until the phone rang causing his celebration or immediate vacation. Calvin had spent his almost last financially and definitely emotionally on this deal. Billie Holiday crooned, and he sang along. His head snapped to the catchy beat.

Finally, the phone rang. He had just kicked off his shoes and sat in the plush lounge area of the suite.

"Hello?" he said, balancing the phone, his drink and trying to tame the concert he had going on.

"Calvin, this is Sack."

Silence.

"Calvin, are you there?"

"I'm here, man. So what's the deal?" Calvin asked without reservation.

"Well providing you agree to the terms and conditions and salary…" he paused. "Welcome to Sack Enterprises, my man. You blew us all away!" Sack said with controlled excitement. "I knew you wouldn't, and you didn't let me down. I'm proud to have you on the team. Now all we have to do is get you signed up for the Omega men and you'll be almost perfect," Sack half joked.

"One accomplishment at a time please," Calvin said. He knew pledging at his age was the farthest thing from his mind.

"Of course. Listen I know Tracee is out of town and unfortunately the team and I are on our way back to New York, but I want you to have the suite for the rest of the weekend to celebrate. The limo is at your disposal for twenty-four hours as well. Antonio will fax all necessary documents to your office by morning. We'll need an answer fairly quickly, so be mindful."

For once things seemed to be turning around. And Calvin longed for the lady of his life to be there.

The detachable ring that held her car and house keys could not be detached. Ramon's step class would be starting in an hour and if she wasn't in line in the first fifteen minutes of the roster opening up she might not get a spot.

"Shoot," Talise yelled as she finally handed the valet the entire set of keys. *See that's why you always gettin' jacked for somethin'*, she recalled one of Steffon's lessons.

What? What are you talking about?

Your keys. Why would you leave all your keys and information about your address in your car? Steffon was always as cool as a cucumber.

We're only gonna be gone for a couple of hours. It's not like they have time to take my car and go to my house, Talise reasoned.

Hey, man, the keys will be ready in ten minutes. She lives in Jersey so you got plenty of time. Here's the address, Steffon mimicked as if he was talking on the phone making his point.

Get out of my head!!! Talise screamed internally as the young olive-skinned, dark-haired kid stood impatiently waiting to take her keys.

"I'm sorry," she said to him. "I'm having a mental-breakdown day." She stopped herself, noticing his disinterest. Finally against her better judgment and Steffon's penetrating advice she handed over the keys.

The muffled air full of sweat hit her nostrils as she walked briskly toward the door. "Doggone it." The line circled the front desk on its way toward the back locker room. "Shoot, I'll never get a spot," she said aloud again as she made her way toward the back of the line.

"Talise, Talise," she heard someone say.

Her friend and gym partner Chynna stood proudly as number three in line.

"Hey, woman." Talise kissed her on the cheek.

"Hey."

"How did you get here so early?" Talise questioned.

"Took off early. See you didn't make it," Chynna said.

"Yeah." Talise eased her way into the line, hoping no one would notice.

"Uh-uh, sister-girlfriend, don't even try it. Talk to your friend later. The back of the line is that way." The girl behind Chynna pointed.

Talise bid Chynna a "see you in a minute" and took her rightful place at the back of the line. It wasn't long before Talise was right back behind Chynna and the witch that banished her.

"How in the world did you get back here?" Chynna questioned.

"Nothing better than the power of a little rumor," Talise mumbled.

"What?" Chynna asked.

"I told everyone in the back that Ramon is absent today. I told them I heard it as I passed through. So the line disappeared."

Chynna cracked up laughing. "You are too much. I don't want to be anywhere near you when the herd finds out," Chynna said, signing in. Talise followed behind her and the girl in front of her who heard their every word and clearly showed her displeasure with Talise.

The girls laughed some more as they entered the locker room.

"So I haven't seen you in dog years. I think the last time we were here you were going to New Orleans for the…"

"Black MBAs conference," Chynna said.

"Yeah. How was it? You meet any hot honeys?" Talise asked, lacing her mid-ankle high-tops. She stood and stretched her slender legs.

"The conference was good. The honeys were good and I met a guy I liked but he was scooped right from under me by my so-called friend," Chynna said, placing her sneaker on the bench. Her head remained down.

"She knew you liked him?" Talise questioned.

"Of course," Chynna answered.

"That's foul." Talise crossed her arms.

"Yup. But what you gonna do? I started to talk to her about it but I have to hold my tongue for a minute. She's holding the key to this great job out of Atlanta, and I'm hoping she recommends me for it."

"If you ask me, she owes you one considering how she treated you. I tell you sisters..." Talise said, shaking her head.

"Yeah well, what you gonna do? He's as much to blame. I brought him around my friends and she swooped him up. He knew that I was interested in getting to know him better but C'est la vie. Hey, let's go grab our steps and get into our spots before the riot you caused ensues," Chynna said as she dragged Talise out of the room and to the exercise floor.

The music flowed louder than ever. A basket full of premium liquors courtesy of Sack and the team had been cracked open and lined up for consumption. Calvin was stripped down to a black silk calf-length robe courtesy of Tracee and Kenneth Cole.

Calvin Jones, entrepreneur, had done it. "I have weathered the storms of perserverance, low or no funds to not only sustaining and maintaining my own establishment but landing the fattest contract with the world's greatest financial conglomerate since Reginald Lewis." He hooped and hollered all over his club executive penthouse suite.

He continued his celebration of himself as the phone rang. He knew it could only be Tracee with whom he was anxious to share his grattitude and plans for the future, possibly their future.

"Hello." He caressed the phone joyfully.

"Hey, babe," Tracee said with glee.

"Hey. I got it. I got the account," he said before she could get out another word.

"I know. Congratulations! Did you get my present?" she asked joyfully.

"I did. It's really nice. I look great in it too." He laughed. "I wish you could see it."

"Maybe I will," Tracee said.

"Please tell me you're coming in early from your trip."

"How would you feel if I told you that I was in the air heading over Tennessee toward you right now? In fact the flight attendants are asking me to get off the phone now because we'll be landing soon."

"I would tell you that the champagne I've ordered will be on ice but the rest of me won't." Calvin's voice grew raspy.

"I like it, Tracee said. "Babe, I gotta go. I'll see you soon."

"Wait, you need me to pick you up?" Calvin asked.

"Why don't you send the limo that Sack gave to you for the rest of the weekend. Who's your driver?"

"Uh, Herman…"

"Oh yeah, Herman Gilmore. Cool. I'll see you soon."

He turned the music down and placed his snifter back in the warmer.

It was three glasses later when his pager suddenly went ballistic, allowing his groove to be disturbed.

He picked up the pager and was shocked to see Candace's number followed by 911.

Allowing his unspoken disappointment to dissipate a moment ago, he dialed Candace's number immediately.

"Hello," she answered.

"Candace. Hey, this is Cal. You paged me? Everything okay?" he asked anxiously.

"Oh, hey, Calvin," Candace remained calm.

"Oh, hey? Oh, hey?" His agitation rose slightly again. "You page me with 911 and all you can say is oh, hey?"

"Where are you? Atlanta?"

"Candace, what's up?" Calvin asked, dismissing her question.

"You're with your new friend, huh?"

"Candace, what in the hell are you talking about? And if this is why you called, to get into my business, I'm hanging up."

"Calvin, wait. Listen, I really need to talk to you, it's really important," Candace said solemnly.

"What's this about?" He retrieved another glass from the warmer in the oak-finished cordial bar almost burning the tips of his fingers.

"Us."

"Candace…"

"No please, Cal. I understand we're not seeing each other and I understand you are seeing someone else and…"

How does everyone know all my business, Tracee with the gig and now Candace about who I'm supposed to be seeing. "Candace, we tried too many years and…"

"So I guess this woman you're seeing has officially moved me out," Candace said.

"Candace, it's about us and what we tried to make happen. It can't happen. We tried and tried and like we agreed, we'll always be friends. Hold on, I have to get the door," he said, forgetting Tracee's arrival.

"Heyyy, baby!" He gave her a luscious kiss. She was dressed in a tan trench holding a bottle of what he suspected to be the bubbly he would savor off her body.

"So can I come in?" Tracee asked as she let the coat drop to her ankles. Her tanned skin glistened.

He grabbed her around the waist and kissed her some more. With the phone still in his hand he guided her inside and shut the door.

"You're on the phone?" she questioned seductively.

"Oh yeah."

"I'll put the bubbly on ice," Tracee said as she walked around him still nude.

"Um, hello?" Calvin returned to his phone call.

"So I guess she's there."

"Um can I talk to you another time?" Calvin mouthed toward Tracee that he would be a minute.

"So are you denying that you're seeing someone?" Candace pushed.

"I'm not saying anything but we'll have to talk about this another time." Calvin remained formal and coy.

"Will you call me when you return to town? Please? Oh, and good luck with your meeting with Sack."

"Huh?" Calvin was really confused.

"I read in the trade magazines that Sack is in Atlanta finalizing his land acquisition deals for S.E. and when your number came up on the Caller ID from Georgia, I just put two and two together. So good luck."

"Thanks." Calvin was speechless.

"Calvin, I'm ready," he heard Tracee yell from the other room. Somewhat disoriented he stumbled to meet her.

"So are you hungry?"

"Famished," Tracee answered as they lay in each other's arms. They never made it to bed; they remained in the middle of the floor.

"So what do you want to eat?" He asked as he kissed her shoulder and stroked the side of her face.

"Cheesecake Factory works for me," she said, snuggling closer to him. "So what are you going to do about your living arrangements?"

"What living arrangements are you talking about?"

"Well, I'm sure you'll be moving to Atlanta soon. I would offer you my digs until you get yourself set up but I'm not sure that's a good idea."

He rolled her from under him and got up, wrapping himself in the robe. He headed toward the oak cabinet. "Tracee, what is giving you the idea that I'm moving or that I want or need to move in with you? That's presumptuous of you, don't you think?"

"Well no, I mean you are moving, aren't you? It's part of your contract," Tracee said. She followed him toward the bar and discarded the now empty champagne bottle. She refused his offer of a warmed snifter of brandy.

"My contract. Tracee, I haven't received my contract yet. Furthermore I have no intention of moving to Atlanta. I like Charlotte and I will continue to run my business out of my hometown. I'm handling S.E. business like an outside contractor."

"Well how do you plan on doing that? Sack is going to have you pretty busy." She poured herself a glass of Dubonnet with a splash of Cointreau.

"Tracee…" He sighed.

"What? What?" she asked defensively.

"This isn't cool."

"What?" Tracee was obviously perplexed.

"Come on, you're a real smart girl. You are a businessperson, and you and what I suspect to be Diamond aren't handling your business. You know more shit about my offer, contract and life than I do right now, and I don't appreciate it. You know, I wondered how you knew to send this gift to me and how it conveniently reached my room shortly after I got the phone call from Sack. I mean I appreciate your concern and everything you've done, but y'all need to chill and handle your business."

"Who was that on the phone?" She changed her tone and totally stopped him cold in his tracks.

"Who, what?"

"When I arrived at your door, who were you talking to?"

"Candace, I mean Tracee…" *I fucked up,* he thought immediately. He shook his head hoping to rattle his thoughts back into place.

The room dropped in silence.

She chuckled sarcastically and began to mumble. "Candace…Candace. Who is Candace, Calvin? No, better question, who is Candace to you?"

"A friend," he answered coarsely and poured himself another drink.

"A friend. A friend. Could Candace be a friend whose presence seems to keep your thoughts occupied? Could Candace be a friend who I was introduced to at the restaurant for the investment club meeting that you and Grey found so important you all had to go into a corner and discuss? Could Candace be the picture of the woman found in your desk drawer face down? Could Candace be…I mean come on Cal, do I need to go on and on? And now the situation is so confusing that you call me by her name?" Tracee's anger rose with each question.

"Come on, Tracee, you're blowing this way out of proportion." Calvin had returned himself to the chaise with an empty glass.

"Am I? When we met, I specifically advised that I don't deal with men who are married, attached, committed or heavy with baggage. I also don't deal with men who aren't complete with themselves and who don't know what they want. I guess I've hit the jackpot," she said, gathering her trench.

"Tracee, Tracee, where are you going? I thought we were getting something to eat?" he said, following her.

She tightly wrapped the belt around her coat and headed toward the door. She turned to face Calvin and said, "I take my lumps for perhaps getting too involved. People I believe in, I stand behind them one hundred percent without apology. I'm honest and forthright about who I am and what I expect from the door. No surprises and I don't play games. For the last several months it's been all about you…"

"You too. I'm not playing any games…"

"Word to the wise, Calvin, nothing new or satisfying can ever be placed in a glass that's already full. Ciao," she said and walked out of the door. She left him standing there in the nude.

"It sounds like you both are overreacting to me. I'm sure he didn't mean any harm, but he's right. What you and Diamond discussed should have been left between the two of you. You've stripped his confidence. Even though he landed this on his own, your involvement or perceived involvement may always leave doubt. As for that other woman…that's your call, girl. You have to be safe, but I think you should at least talk about it…" a friend said to Tracee.

"Man, don't let her get away. She's pretty cool. Sometimes you have to fight. Everything ain't that easy. I know you a little pissed off right now, but playa, she's right. You coulda told her about Candace and all this coulda been nipped in the bud. You're giving her a reason to feel like you have something to hide. From what you tell me, Tracee seems like she's got it together. She's probably the best thing that's ever happened to you. Fight, playa. Fight."

Calvin heard every word Grey said. He cut his trip shorter than expected and told Sack he needed to take some time but he would get back to him in three days.

He walked around his office. He hadn't turned the lights on since he had arrived, and the room seemed darker than ever before. He noticed the picture of Candace still in the same spot he had placed it in months before when he thought Talise may have been the one. Now Tracee hung in the balance real close but almost unreachable. The funny part was that as he walked in the darkness of one room, he couldn't figure out why everything he just celebrated seemed to crumble.

What the fuck? When everything seems to be going prime, shit comes along like this, shit that always seems to be fucked up. Tracee, Candace, Talise and everybody else. Why don't they all just leave me the fuck alone? I'm just tired—tired of shit folks always dishing shit out but can't take it. Calvin, can we talk? Calvin, you can't put anything in something that's full. What the fuck!"

The phone rang several hours later. He remained in the dark. Vivaldi played on the CD over and over.

"Ma'am, there's no sign of forced entry. Are you sure you have no idea of who your burglar might have been?"

Talise sat on the cold, hard floor, her living room, void of the rugs and any semblance of crystal or jewelry she may have held in the apartment. She remained silent and shocked that the life she had built over the last six months had been stripped away like a thief in the night, literally.

"Where were you all evening, ma'am?"

"My girlfriend Chynna's. "We had drinks, I had a little too much and she snatched my keys. I came home a few minutes ago to no doorman, and my furniture, CD's—everything I own was just gone."

She cupped her face with her fingers and began to rock back and forth. Slowly but surely, the tears began to fall. *Why me? What else must I endure? Why?* She continued to rock.

The well-meaning officer grabbed the nearest towel and placed it under her kitchen faucet. He ran the cold water over it never taking his eyes off her. Finally he placed the cold cloth over her forehead, which made her shudder. Innocently he escorted her to her room and he laid her down to sleep. "We'll take care of this, Ms. Grimes. Don't worry. We'll take of it and you."

The two officers concluded their paperwork at her door. Officer Warren Raymond kept his eyes focused on Talise.

"Not bad, huh?" the second officer said.

Not only not bad, but real good." Officer Warren gave a goofy laugh. He closed his black book.

"Are you okay?" Stephanie managed to get out between coughs. She had just excused herself from the three-way conversation. Her throat had become so dry and hoarse from daily regurgitations that long-winded sessions such as this were a rarity. The sometimes thirty different daily medications usually taken to help combat situations such as these often caused more pain and complications then they were worth. She admitted to no one that she often skipped doses just because she would bring them back up before they hit the bottom of her stomach.

"Yeah, I'm okay. I'm just sitting on the floor again," Talise answered as she rolled herself to the other side of the bed. *Thank God they didn't take my bedroom set,* she thought. "Don't you have insurance?" Gem asked.

"No."

"Why not? That is really irresponsible of you, Talise, I mean geez…"

"Gem, it is not. I couldn't afford it and I don't need a friggin' lecture from you! I have enough stress on me without having to hear your smartass mouth about everything. You're forever putting me down, and I'm sick of it," Talise snapped.

Stephanie's coughing fit began again. "Okay you two, settle down," she said between deep breaths.

"No, she's always got something to say about everything I do or don't do. Right now I need your support. I'm at a job I hate with a boss who hates me and tortures me at every turn. I'm by myself doing the job of four people. I have to look a former friend in the face every day who won't look my way much less allow me to say I'm sorry for fucking her man, I have the friggin' Black Mafia after my ass for some furniture that I no longer have possession of, all to get you signed to their label, and I don't need to hear a lecture about me being irresponsible because I work for an insurance company and I have no insurance!"

"Talise, Gem, come on, y'all, calm down…"

"No, Stephanie, I'm sicka her shit. Look, I gotta go. I'll talk to y'all later," Talise said before she slammed the phone down. She clicked the lights off in her bedroom, rolled herself under the cover and begged her consciousness to let her sleep.

Chapter 18

Nervously Gem stepped into the dark smoky bar and searched around. Avoiding embarrassment she sat down at the once familiar black lacquer countertop with red specks. "I'm looking for Vaughan, Vaughan Winters. Is he here tonight?"

The somewhat protective bartender didn't bother to skip a beat as she continued washing glasses. "Who's calling?" the woman asked. Gem squinted at the familiar-sounding voice, trying to recall where she might know this woman.

"Gem. Gemmia Barnes is my name. Is he available?" Gem asked again in a syrupy voice, hoping not to cause any waves tonight.

"What can I get you to drink?"

"Excuse me?" Gem questioned, clutching her purse. *Stephanie, I'm gonna kill you,* Gem thought as she remembered Stephanie's insistence that she find this man and have a conversation with him.

"To sit at the bar during primetime you have to order a drink or I'm afraid you'll be giving up your seat," the woman said with a cool snip in her voice. She still hadn't looked up from washing her glasses.

"Give me a Shirley Temple." All of a sudden the place went black with the exception of the red lights that circled the inside of the bar. Vaughan appeared on stage as fine as he wanted to be, bouncing from side to side on his bowed legs. A chill ran up Gem's spine. *Stephanie's right. I do miss him.* Gem smiled to herself, recalling Stephanie's words and the sweet smell of Vaughan's cologne.

"Six-fifty." The woman placed the drink in front of Gem devoid of a cherry or any other garnishes.

"For a Shirley Temple? This doesn't have alcohol, does it? I wanted a non-alcoholic drink…" Gem ranted.

"I know what you ordered. Six-fifty."

Gem placed seven dollars on the bar. "Change please," she said to the woman who turned and sucked her teeth. Gem returned her attention to the dazzling superstar on stage.

"Before we get started with our main attraction for the evening, Miss Hope…" The crowd went wild.

W*ho is Hope?* Gem thought and looked around in envy.

"I would like to invite any wanna-be divas to the stage to try do your thang. Remember the rules, you have five minutes to showcase your best—acapella or with the band. Do I have any takers?" Vaughan asked.

One woman with a moderately talented voice and no riff did her best with a Celine Dion cover tune. Natalie Cole was the favorite medley of the next moderate performer. And Luther Vandross finally did his best background work underneath a wanna-be, and it still didn't help the third. *Why would you pick something so way out of your range anyway?* Gem thought. Finally without another thought she balanced herself behind the staircase and spoke quietly to the band. Vaughan began to announce the premier entertainer of the evening, but the drummer stopped him.

"Oops my bad, ladies and gentlemen, we have one more contender. What's she singing?" he whispered to the band.

"Don't worry we got it covered," the drummer answered.

"Okay, ladies and gentlemen, the band tells me this is a surprise. I don't know her name or her song but let's give it up anyway and see what she can do." Vaughan stepped aside in the silence and the lights dimmed.

In simple jeans with diamond studs at the cuff, perfectly manicured toes and sexy open-toe sandals she stepped across the stage. She nodded toward the band. Finally Gem's glittering smile stepped into the light. It was as if every person in the room held his breath.

Gem didn't let them down. She poured her heart out into Oleta Adams' "I Knew You When." The crowd rose to an incomparable several rounds of standing ovations. Vaughan stood in awe of familiar beauty, grace and the powerhouse voice of his angel. He couldn't hide his aura of longing. In her distinctive and poised stature she watched her bow, blew kisses, thanked them for their love and exited stage right. The crowd was still chanting and begging for an encore when she politely disavowed their request. *That was for you, baby.* She eyed Vaughan and took her seat back at the bar. *I hope you got it.*

"Okay so you did yo' thang. What can I get you, on the house of course?" the lady bartender asked.

"Mr. Vaughan Winters. I'll take two of those, nah, one is enough actually," she said as she watched him work himself from the stage.

"With a voice like that, you could probably have him and anything else in this place. But in the meantime how can I help you quench that throat?" the bartender insisted.

"Shirley Temple on the rocks, please with an extra cherry." Gem smiled. The bartender retreated and began to fill her request. She returned with the largest glass in the place. Gem counted at least five cherries.

Gem took her time, savoring her drink before she turned back to the stage. The band had taken a break and the deejay was trying his best to fill in. She sensed the air in the crowd as swarms of people crowded her to give her well wishes. Politely she listened but her attention was fixated on Vaughan's disappearing act. *Dag, he could have at least come over and said something,* she thought, looking around.

People hopped to the center of the floor when they heard the familiar horns playing everybody's get-up-and-dance tune "The Electric Slide." Gem, still sipping on her monstrous syrupy delight found her way to a secluded corner booth. Her eyes remained on the stage.

"Well, well, well, she's finally back." That deep voice resonated over her shoulder. The hairs on the back of her neck stood on end.

"Hey?" she said, trying to remain collected.

"Mind if I sit for a minute?" Vaughan asked.

Gem patted the cushion. *Don't blow it, don't play games, it's not worth it...*Stephanie's voice rang through to her brain.

"Thank you very much," Vaughan said, staring deeply into her eyes.

She blushed so hard she had to look away. "You're welcome. For what?" Gem's tone changed. *Be cool, just play it cool.*

"For scaring my premier singer back into her dressing room. She refuses to come out now. She's hysterical. So you're just going to have fill in for the night."

Gem chuckled. "No harm meant. I just thought what was rolling through needed a little help so I obliged. I would love to help you out tonight, but I really can't stay. I have an early call tomorrow and—"

"So what brings you here?" His abrupt tone cut her off.

She caught the hint quickly. She scratched the back of her neck, then she folded her arms in front of her. "That song was for you." She couldn't believe she threw her heart toward him like that.

Silence.

"Please catch it. Don't leave me out there like this," she thought aloud.

"What did you say?" Vaughan questioned.

"I said please catch it, don't leave me out there like this," Gem said as her candor startled even her.

"Catch what?" Vaughan asked.

"My heart," Gem answered and put her head down. Vaughan grabbed the back of her neck and pulled her closer to him. His shirt was now stained with her tears so he held her tighter.

"I'm sorry. I need…I want you in my life." Her voice was barely above a whisper.

"I want to be there for you but I'm not so positive you're ready for all that. I'm not going back and forth, Gem. I won't do it. So if you are stepping in my direction, you better be sure of what you're doing." His voice was loving but firm. "I need some time, not a lot, but I need some time. You cool with that?"

"I'm cool with that. Look I better go but I'll be talking to you soon." She stood trying to hide her disappointment and turned to walk out. *Don't be upset if he doesn't embrace you with horns and bells and runs lovingly into your arms. Just be patient.* She thought of Stephanie's words again. "Oh, hey, if you can, I do need help with one situation," she said, turning back around to him.

"What's that?" Vaughan was still calm and cool, as he remained seated.

"Blue Water asked me back. I put a band together and could use the best sax player ever in my corner to help me out. The pay is triple scale and the gig is during industry night, pre-Grammy nomination announcements," Gem said with her hands to her side. Her face was sullen.

"For real this time?" Vaughan tried to make light of the situation. He walked toward her and laughed.

"For real this time." She felt his sweet breath on her lips.

"No games?" he questioned as he grabbed her around the waist and rocked to Maxwell's Unplugged version of "This Woman's Work." He kissed her passionately and she returned his affection with relief.

"No games. Wait a minute, what are talking about, the gig or us?" She pulled slightly away.

"Both."

"No games. I promise. Know that I'm still celibate though, that's not changing..." He put his finger to her lips.

"I honor that."

"I thought you said that you needed some time."

"I did, I told you not a lot..." he said as they laughed and continued to sway to the music.

The playground was full of fun and sun as Trevorr reveled in it. Vanee sat at the bench taking in the fresh air and cautioning her overzealous little one to be careful. Steffon approached her from the shadow.

His handsome but somewhat disheveled mannerisms, led him to the small space beside her.

"Hey," he said. He noticed his daughter but didn't interrupt her playtime at first.

"You have it?" Vanee questioned coldly.

He handed her a bulging envelope. "There should be enough for her shoes, a couple of outfits and the down payment for school in the fall."

Silence.

"So how are you doing?" he dared to ask.

"We're fine, Steffon. Thanks for the money but we have to go. If you want to see Trevorr, you're welcome to come over tonight. I'm going out so you're welcome to hang out in the apartment while I'm gone," Vanee said. "Trev, it's time to go. Gather your things," she yelled to the little girl.

"Aw, Mommy...Daddy, Daddy, Daddy..." the little girl yelled. She jumped off the swing and ran toward her daddy's arms.

Steffon scooped her up and planted a huge kiss on her cheek. He held her tighter than he had ever held her before. Vanee continued to look away. But before he could relish in his daughter's glory, familiar sounds rang through his ears. In seconds, Steffon hit the ground with his daughter firmly underneath him. Shots rang out all around him as he dragged his daughter behind the bench where they sat.

Quickly he grabbed his piece and peered over the wood.

Silence.

The children, and their guardians, if they had any, scattered.

Finally the silence was broken with hysterical cries coming from all sides. Steffon checked on Trevorr who still lay flat beneath him. He placed his finger over his lips to bade her to remain quiet. Her tear-dampened eyes grew wider as he brought his piece to his chest and stepped beyond the bench. His eyes searched the perimeter for the person or persons that now declared war on his family.

No one was in sight.

He grabbed Trevorr once again and carried her behind the nearest tree, never straying too far away. His eyes darted everywhere, still unable to see the thieves who just stole innocence in the blink of an eye.

A very brave shadow had now emerged and headed straight for the bench he and Trevorr had just left.

Loud screams emerged from the shadow as a blood-stained figure's head was lifted. The lifeless body lay in front of the bench. As Steffon cautiously approached the bench with his piece still cocked a now loudly hysterical Trevorr shot past him, screaming "Mommy, Mommy, oh no, Mommy."

Steffon reached for them both. "Damn," he screamed.

"Hold on, baby, hold on!" he yelled as he heard sirens approaching.

Stephanie excused herself while she harshly coughed. Gem noticed her friend's now completely gray complexion and rail-thin frame. She complained of the sores that seemed to ravage her body and the extreme pain that she was often in. Gem didn't try and ignore her friend's condition but she tried her best to embrace the inevitable without tears.

"So I'm glad everything seems to be working out for you and Vaughan. You both deserve good people. Just continue to remain open and honest," Stephanie said.

"I will. So far, so good, though. I admit the exploration is nice." Gem smiled.

"I like that. The exploration of the relationship. Keep it going. That and open communication can help to sustain you. Now I have to ask, how is he handling the celibacy?" Stephanie asked.

"We both work hard to enjoy intimacy like cuddling and kissing but I admit that I pray every day. He's now praying with me. So when stuff gets hot we have to exit that space. It's not easy right now but I have to stay focused on God's path. I'm sure it'll get easier in time."

"I'm sure it will. Hey, hand me that tea over there on the counter," Stephanie said, noticing Gem's entry into the kitchen.

"Sure. So have you heard from Talise? I haven't talked to her in, what two weeks now." Gem raised her voice slightly now that she was fully in Stephanie's kitchen area.

"Her mom called and said that she's okay. She's taken some time from work and took a getaway. She promises she'll call us when she gets back," Stephanie said. The tea was lukewarm just like she enjoyed it. She allowed the vanilla-maple flavor to soothe her.

"You're worried, aren't you?" Gem asked.

"A little."

"Where did she go?" Gem asked. Stephanie shook her head and shrugged as if she didn't know. "When is she coming back?" Gem asked.

"Don't know that either. But her mom assured me that she's okay, she said she just needed some time away."

"Well when she gets back, she's gonna be the second person I apologize to. I can only imagine what that girl is going through, and my behavior toward her lately certainly hasn't helped."

"Don't beat yourself up. You all will get it together. You better. One never knows how much time one has," Stephanie said.

"Come on, Stephanie. Don't start talking like that. We're going to beat this," Gem said with sadness in her voice. She placed the cup beside her chair and sat at Stephanie's leg. She hugged the bottom of her friend's leg tightly to prevent herself from weeping. It only worked for a little while. "It's not fair. It's just not fair. Why you? Why not me, Talise or someone else who may have had a reason to get this horrible thing?"

"It doesn't work that way. Life is a funny thing, Gem. Lessons have to be learned, otherwise you just repeat them over and over. What my lesson is, I honestly haven't figured out. That's probably why I'm still here. But I do know that time isn't promised to anyone, and this disease doesn't discriminate. So be careful and take care of yourself and each other."

"Okay you been watching too much *Jerry Springer,*" Gem said as they laughed to keep from crying.

"You might be right about that."

"Where's Trevorr?" Vanee asked, finally awakening in the strange surroundings of recovery.

"Don't worry, baby. She's okay and you're gonna be okay too."

Vanee tried to sit up. Steffon gently bade her to remain. "What happened?" Vanee asked.

"It was a shooting. Right now it seems random, but I got my feelers out trying to find out if this was directed at me. The doctors say the bullet entered your shoulder. It grazed your collar bone and exited out your back. Your collar bone is bruised but not broken. Mainly it was a flesh wound," Steffon said as he stroked her hair. Vanee turned her head away. "I'm so sorry, baby, for everything," he said gently.

"You should be," she whispered as a tear rolled down her face. She lifted her arm to wipe it and felt a sudden surge of extreme pain. "Ouch," she cried.

"Try not to move. It's gonna hurt for a while," Steffon said gingerly. "They're going to keep you overnight, just to check on you. The doctor said I should be able to take you home tomorrow and—"

"No," Vanee interjected.

"No what?"

"You're not taking me home. This doesn't change anything, Steffon." Her whisper was firm.

"Van—"

"No. If anything, this situation shows me just how dangerous you are and how dangerous it is to be around you, for me and my daughter. You still sittin' on the fence, Steffon. Don't know who you are or who you want to be." Vanee coughed as her voice grew raspier.

"Vanee, you need help. You can't take care of yourself and my daughter alone," Steffon said.

"You need a place to stay, huh?" she asked.

"What?"

"You heard me."

"Vanee, I'm just trying to do right by you and my daughter."

"Shoulda thought of that a long time ago."

"You're awake." A nurse entered with mild enthusiasm. She held a cup of pills and proceeded to take Vanee's temperature. Steffon now stood on the side. The nurse poured water from a pitcher into a cup with a straw. "These are to minimize any infection and pain, so I need you to prop up and take them." The nurse placed the now-filled cup of water and pills on the table. She then lifted the headboard of Vanee's bed. "Great," the nurse remarked at how Vanee took the medicine without struggle. "You have quite a few visitors. There is a Jerome Graham downstairs to see you and several others. The doctor advises that you only see one person at a time."

"Send him up," Vanee said and turned her head away from the nurse and Steffon.

"Vanee, wait a minute—" Steffon interjected.

"Send Mr. Graham up, please," Vanee insisted.

"Sorry, sir, you're going to have to leave. You're welcome to wait downstairs until others have seen her then come back up."

"No, he can't," Vanee insisted. "Send Mr. Graham up please."

"Oh, surely. I'm sorry," the nurse apologized.

Steffon complied and walked out of the room and Vanee's sight. Lurking near the elevator but failing to get on he heard the nurse call to send Mr. Jerome Graham to Room 403. Moments later the elevator doors screeched open as several people emerged scattering in different directions. Last, but not least, with a dozen roses and balloons, Romy emerged with Trevorr holding a small stuffed animal by her side.

"What the fuck?" Steffon said aloud, approaching Romy and Trevorr. "Yo, Romy, what you doin' here, man. Better yet what you doin' wit' my daughter?"

"Daddy, Daddy," Trevorr said excitedly.

Steffon hugged her tightly. "I thought I told you to stay at Davina's across the hall."

"Yeah, Daddy but Auntie Davina called Uncle Romy and told him Mommy was at the hospital. He came and got me and said he would bring me to see Mommy. Auntie Davina said it was okay," Trevorr said as she looked down at her shoes.

"It's okay. Look Mommy's in there. She was worried about you so go in there and give her a big hug and kiss. But be careful, she's sore," Steffon said as he tapped her on the butt and sent her on her way. He stared Romy down. "I bet you're behind this shit, ain't you?"

Romy returned the stare.

"You not taking my family, man."

Romy laughed. "You right, partner. You giving it away."

"I swear to you—I will—"

Romy stepped in closer as he loomed over Steffon's frail five-foot-six frame. "Don't let your mouth write a check that yo ass ain't prepared to cash." Romy's breath touched the tip of Steffon's nose. He laughed again, turned and disappeared behind the door where Vanee lay.

Chapter 19

Gem raced out of the house, hopped in the car and sped toward the Kinko's on Route 22. As usual she was thirty minutes behind schedule to make her appointment with the band for rehearsal. Several songs and lyrics had to be photocopied and considering her schedule of late she hadn't had time to do it.

So with the finished documents in hand and finally gaining ground, she sped back down Route 22 to the Parkway North, dipping and dodging traffic to make her three o'clock rehearsal on time at the Peppermint.

She clicked the radio on for some soothing sounds. Most stations played commercials but one deejay promised a new song that everyone was requesting. The deejay ranted and raved so much about the song that Gem felt compelled to keep the radio tuned in.

Exiting the parkway onto the East Orange ramp she made her right turn into traffic up Central Avenue toward her destination. "And here it is folks, the most requested song of the day. Here's Chevron with 'I Brought It Back'...Kick it!"

The beats slipped in and Gem's head bounced along simultaneously. *Ooh, this is nice,* she thought as she waited at the light. Finally the lyrics began and after two words, Gem joined in almost word for word. She turned the music up trying to recognize the tune. "What remake is this?" she thought aloud. Her head continued to bob until the hook came. Once again she sang right along. *Who was the artist?* Chevron hit the bridge of the song with style just as Gem stopped short of hitting the pole that sat smack dab in the middle of traffic on a hugely busy Central Avenue.

"That's my song!" Her mouth flew open in astonishment. "That's my song!" she yelled again. Gem backed the car up and screeched toward the intersection defying the rest of the ten lights she had to go to get to her destination. She threw the car in park on the sidewalk in front of the door, neglected to grab her purse and ran inside.

"Gem, hold up baby, you can't park here." The bouncer's words couldn't be heard as she made a mad dash inside in search of Vaughan.

She found him in front of the stage, as he was about to pop a tape in for rehearsal. "Hey, babe, you are right on ti—" He couldn't get the rest of the words out of his mouth before she ripped the tape out of the box. She searched the top for the switch and turned it to FM radio. It was already on the right station. The end of the song trailed off, with Gem singing the hook.

"What's up with you?" He started to get indignant.

"That's our song! That is our song!" she yelled as hysteria started to set in. "Listen..." The tears went streaming down her face.

"Lady, that is some jam!" the deejay said over the airwaves.

"Thank you, thank you so much," the woman obliged.

"So do you write as well?" the deejay asked.

"I do. But actually my managers wrote this song and brought it to my attention while we were working on my demo. As a matter of fact I want to give a shout out to them, here with me in the studio, Will and Robb, heyyyyyy."

"Oh, shit," Vaughan said finally catching on to what was really going on. "How did they get the song, Gem, how?" he asked, grabbing her at the shoulders. She couldn't say a word; she couldn't do anything but cry. He pulled her into his chest. "Don't worry. Stop crying. We'll take care of this, I promise."

"So Miss Chevron, do you have a last name?" the deejay asked.

"No." She laughed.

"Chevron. Sounds like the gas station," Gem said.

"It is, baby. It is." Vaughan helped with the humor as the other band members now looked on to see what was happening.

"So I notice you are signed with one of the industry's newest and hippest labels, Honey Graham. How did you hook up with them?"

"Well, I was singing around Jersey, you know a couple of the usual spots and this kid walked up to me after a showcase I was in and offered me his card. He claimed he was with Honey Graham, a new label, and I checked it out. I won't mention his name 'cause he's not with the label anymore but…" Chevron explained.

"Yeah, that's how the business goes sometimes."

"I remember her. Hey y'all remember her? She was at the Peppermint and mediocre at best. The crowd booed her," Vaughan shouted to the rest of the members of the band.

"Yeah. You have to be careful, so anyway, I hooked up with Romy Graham, the president and told him I didn't have management, but instead of taking me for a loop he hooked me up with Will and Robb, and the rest is history. Romy liked the demo so much that it became my CD and the song you're hearing today—"

"You mean the song everybody's requesting," the deejay interjected.

"Yeah, that song became my single and I'm so grateful."

Gem finally got herself together and reached to turn the radio off.

Vaughan stopped her. "No, you can't do that. We have to get as much information as possible. We gon' take care of this."

"What are we going to do?" Gem questioned.

Vaughan pulled out his cell immediately. The radio played on.

Calvin retrieved the last box from the back of his car. He turned back and looked at the Gray Ghost with pride as it sat still in the space marked RESERVED. The large newly built glass building contained his destiny. Finally, he was moving into his own space—albeit three hundred square feet of it.

The square footage didn't matter. It was where The Jones Group was to make its mark. He rifled through several pieces of junk mail that had infiltrated the space before the ink dried on the lease.

He placed the small box of desktop trinkets in the corner and put the junk mail on top of that. *I'll let the girl deal with that when she gets here,* he thought as he picked up the ringing phone. "Yo speak," he said into the phone.

"How ya feeling, dawg? Moved in okay?" Grey asked, referring to Calvin's modest new office.

"Yeah, everything's cool. What's up with you, playa?" Calvin responded somberly.

"Cheer up, man, everything's gonna be alright," Grey said, remembering Calvin's last meeting with Sack Enterprises.

His relationship gone awry with Tracee not only left his heart empty, but also rendered his deal with S.E. dropped. Calvin suspected that Diamond reneged on her support of Calvin based on his disregard for her best friend. He spent an entire week between Sack's offices in New York and Atlanta trying to exert damage control.

Sack finally called Calvin and rescinded the contract offering. "You're good, Calvin, but not for Sack Enterprises at this time. We've decided to go with an in-house candidate," was the excuse Sack gave.

"So maybe it's better that you and Tracee are finished," Grey said. "I guess you all haven't talked?"

"No. She finally explained that there always seemed liked something or someone else was crowding my space. And to her it was the same as me cheating," Calvin said. He placed the mail back down and stretched the phone cord to the window. He gazed into his view of the parking lot, where an empty space sat next to his car.

"So have you learned anything?" Grey said.

"Yeah. That Diamond has a lot more influence over her husband than I originally calculated. And I don't need to piss anybody off right now. I lost the biggest account of my life," Calvin said with a hollowness in his voice.

"You did. Landing the Sack Enterprises account could have set you up for a long time," Grey agreed. "However, never say never. Keep trying, man, if you want it bad enough, don't quit."

"You mean Sack Enterprises or Tracee?" Calvin asked.

"Both."

A two-week absence felt like a much-needed lifetime as Talise wondered the corridors toward her corner office.

"They're not friends anymore, girl. She slept with her man," she heard one herd of hens say. "She's lucky that's not me 'cause I would have kicked her ass if that was my man," Talise heard another group say.

People smiled politely as she faced them but the minute she turned her back they whispered, they laughed or they scoffed. She finally made it to the safety of her office with the dusty files she had left some weeks ago to meet her and the red flashing light indicating messages to greet her. She was plowing through her final message when she heard "This is a general voice mail: There will be a meeting for all employees convening in the clerical section of the sixth floor at 9:05 sharp, this morning. Attendance for all is mandatory."

Talise checked her watch. It was now 8:38. She continued unpacking her soft green briefcase, emptying the contents on the desk. She continued to hold her breath for her clockwork visitor in ten, nine, eight, seven, six, five, four…

"Talise, I'm so glad you were able to come to work today. I hope you heard about the meeting at 9:05?" Dragon Breath made her entrance.

"I just heard the message. I'll be there with bells on," Talise said, ignoring Dragon Breath who looked on with a scowl.

"You know I was so sorry to hear about your friend Vanee getting shot. What a terrible tragedy. Thank God she's okay. The office sent her flowers. K.J. told her to take as much time as she needed. Were you able to see your friend during your hiatus?" Dragon Breath questioned with a hint of sarcasm.

"Uh no," was all Talise could answer.

"You didn't even know, did you?" Dragon Breath asked, noticing Talise's quizzical look. "Wow, you are really in knee-deep, aren't you?" Talise continued to ignore her.

"Well it's almost time. Should we venture upstairs together or do you plan to make a grand and late entrance as usual?" Dragon Breath questioned.

"You know what, I didn't ask for you to come in here. I just got back and you're on my case. I haven't had my morning coffee and you haven't had your Listerine!" Talise said angrily.

"Now you just hold on, missy…" Dragon Breath tried to interrupt.

"No, you hold on. Now, I'm going to this damned meeting but right after I'm calling human resources so we can have a discussion. I'm filing a formal complaint against you and your harassment and

K.J. and his sexual harassment. For almost a year now I've taken your guff, and I've had it. And I don't give a flying shit if you run to K.J. and tell him. So Sweet Breath get ready. I won't be the only one staying late tonight!" Talise said.

"Who do you think you are, you little twerp? You're nothing and you certainly don't make me shiver. I think your little sordid affair with Steffon Bryant has gone to your head. And guess what, you don't have to run to human resources, because your time is up. See this little meeting K.J.'s holding is to announce layoffs. Yours included, missy. So all that unpacking you were doing, you might as well reverse your action. Because in less than ten minutes, you along with several others including your little boyfriend are out of here. Sayonara!" Dragon Breath said and walked out.

"Bitch," Talise said aloud as she slammed her paperweight.

Dragon Breath didn't lie. K.J. announced that several departments in the New York branch of Great Raritan were defunct as of 9:00 A.M. Talise, Steffon and others were told they should gather their things immediately and exit the building.

Talise noticed that Dragon Breath looked smug from across the room. She also noticed that Steffon seemed extremely angry.

"Restructuring has also led to my transfer to the home office in Philly. I will be taking several managers and my administrative assistant," were the last words Talise heard K.J. utter.

I don't believe this. This mother—ooh, he's laying people off, messing with people's lives, and getting a promotion to boot. Where's the justice? Talise thought.

Talise made her way back to her office. Maintenance was scraping her name off the glass as she entered. She chuckled to herself. *And I thought them finally writing my name in gold on the glass meant I was here to stay,* she thought, recalling the first moment she stepped through the door and sat at the desk.

She sat down again and watched droves of people clean up and clear out. She checked her voice mail again for the last time.

"Talise, this is Gem. I'll be performing at Blue Waters tomorrow night. Your mom said you would be in town so I hope you can make it. Vaughan will be with me—yes, we're back and stronger than ever so please if you're around, I'd love to apologize in person, perhaps in song. Love you dearly."

Now packed and ready to go, a security guard appeared to make sure no one was left standing. He was also there to assure that Great Raritan's property was left intact.

"You don't have to worry about me taking anything that's not mine," Talise said to the guard. "Good night and good ridden to this dreadful place. It's funny, you know?"

The guard made no reply.

"Just as I was about to command my own justice, the rug was pulled from under me. K.J. abuses his power and gets rewarded for it. Dragon Breath completes her mission to make everyone miserable and is applauded for it, go figure," Talise said, grabbing her small box and shaking her head.

Lifeless she stood before the silver elevator doors one final time. When the doors opened a cool hollow breeze hit her face. She sucked in a big breath, stepped in and allowed the doors to close on that chapter of her life.

Extremely frail and worn, Stephanie took her place at the front table marked RESERVED. The place was packed and excitement was in the air.

Backstage, Vaughan was giving his final pep talk for the evening. Rehearsal had lacked focus since their song had been stolen from under them.

"Baby, this is your time, dance like nobody's watching. Remember they can't take this away from you," and he pointed to her heart. Those were Vaughan's last words before she heard, "Ladies and gentlemen, welcoming back to Blue Waters once again, simply stated Gem…" Cymbals rang, lights dimmed and a revolving crystal ball provided the perfect light for the sparkling baby-blue Swarovski gown in which Gem graced the stage.

Gem tiptoed through the first hour of melodic ballads, blues and jazz favorites. She looked back at Vaughan blowing on the sax. Finally during a spectacular musical interlude by their pianist, Gem made her way toward the sax. "Baby, the sound is bottoming out. I can't get any depth and I'm screaming. My voice isn't going to last throughout the show," she whispered. The pianist continued to dance across the keys. "Wow, he's really good," she acknowledged.

"Until intermission, eat the mike like I showed you," Vaughan whispered. "I promise, it'll be okay. I'll work the sound and lights for the entire second act if I have to."

"I love you" was uttered without thinking.

Vaughan flashed his killer smile that made her melt. "I know this. Now do your thing." He winked.

She walked back toward the center of the stage. She did exactly what Vaughan advised and placed the mike so close to her lips it looked as if the slender metal was about to go down her throat. She then tipped the mike down to catch the richness of her sound. "Everyone, please give him a hand. He is playing that piano, isn't he?" She allowed the spotlight to shine a little longer and noticed Vaughan's suggestion worked. "As a matter of fact, ladies and gentlemen, I'd like to take this opportunity to introduce my band to you…echoooo too much echo…" Gem sang trying to give hints for the sound man to get it right. She continued talking to test the sound during the adjustment. "Ladies and gentlemen, I have to give a special introduction to someone. Please put your hands together for my love and the brains behind all of this tonight, Mr. Vaughan Winters." The crowd applauded with fervor.

"I love you, too, and my sax is going to show you how much…" Vaughan sang as he blew the crowd away. Gem could do nothing more than blush.

It was time for intermission as Gem gracefully headed toward her dressing room to change. The door was slightly ajar and caused her some concern considering she knew she had closed it behind her. She walked gingerly toward the room and stuck her head through the door.

"May I help you change for your second act, madame?" Talise asked as she held up a fabulous black silk strapless jumpsuit with delicate rhinestones that shone like stars across the top.

"Talise, you made it," was all Gem could say before the tears flowed and they hugged.

Vaughan, pleased that his first surprise for the evening had worked so well, closed the door behind him to let the healing begin. He headed straight for the sound booth to make sure the second act of his baby's show was as flawless as her voice.

After intermission and many tears of joy had subsided. Gem changed her lineup as a tribute to her best girls who embraced as they sat in the front row. Vaughan had taken a place behind the booth for sound.

Gem moaned before starting her first line and realized the sound was perfect. Gem then poured her heart into "You Are My Friend." She concluded to a standing ovation. She also noticed a stranger was right next to Talise and Stephanie. Stephanie remained seated but her support was loud and clear.

Gem smiled. *Who is that? I can't tell...Oh shoot, that's Wincey! What is she doing here again?* Gem thought. *It's okay, it's okay, she's here for whatever reason, Dance like nobody's watching, just keep singing.* She pumped out a load of dance tunes that had everyone bouncing in the aisle.

"First of all this was a dream come true. I've had a wonderful evening of song with each and every one of you. I hope I was able to lift you as you've done for me."

"Thank you everyone, and good night!" And as usual she exited with grace—and tears.

"It's nice to meet you," Gem said cordially.

"I am so impressed with your performance. Your showmanship is excellent, and the way you worked the crowd was just wonderful. Vaughan told me you were a gem, pardon the pun, but I must agree."

"Thank you. Thank you very much, Wincey." Gem remained cordial as she watched Vaughan and Wincey chat as if they were old friends.

"Well the night is still young. I was hoping perhaps we could continue our discussion over a bite to eat," Vaughan said to Wincey and Gem.

Why is he wiggling like he has ants in his pants? Gem thought.

Vaughan's phone rang and he excused himself to the far corner of Gem's dressing room.

"So please, have a seat." Gem offered, not really knowing what else to say. *Stay cool, don't get starstruck.*

"Thanks but I can't. I'm actually on my way to the airport to catch the redeye to L.A. I promised Vaughan that I would come by the show before I left. It was well worth it."

"Thanks." Gem's silence was overwhelming.

Vaughan remained on the phone.

"Well, here's my card. Vaughan has my numbers but like I said I'll be in L.A. for the next three months. Tell him we'll talk when I get back." She turned to walk away.

"Um, working on a project?" Gem managed to get out.

"Actually putting the finishing touches on my next album. I'll see you around again, I'm positive of it." Wincey exited the dressing room, leaving Gem in awe.

Gem turned back to her dressing room mirror and began removing her makeup.

"Hey, diva!" Talise ran in with Stephanie not far behind.

"Excellent show! Your best yet!" Stephanie said.

"Girl, what was Wincey doing in your dressing room? I was excited when she sat down right beside us but we didn't want to disturb you. We saw when she was escorted back here," Stephanie said.

"I don't know what she was doing here. She seemed to have more business with Vaughan than actual interest in my show," Gem said, smearing Noxzema cream all over her face.

"You still use that stuff?" Talise said, picking up the jar and examining it.

"It's the best thing for removing makeup and preventing zits, like the one forming on your forehead." Gem playfully placed a dollop of cream on her friend.

"Don't change the subject, Gem. What was Wincey here for?" Stephanie insisted.

"I told you I don't know," Gem said. Vaughan was wrapping up his conversation on the phone.

"Don't get upset, Gem. Vaughan is probably working something out for you, like he was the last time when…" Talise stopped.

"I see your relaxing hiatus didn't bring anymore wisdom," Gem snipped.

"Okay, ladies, you're welcome to join us. Gemmie, we have an appointment. I promised we'd be at the Shark Bar uptown in the next thirty minutes, so pop like popcorn, baby."

"Hold up, Vaughan, what meeting? I'm tired and what was Wincey doing here? And…" Gem whined. She took a deep breath and rubbed her temples.

Her girlfriends looked on with pleading eyes for her to calm down and not blow this thing.

"Look, baby, I appreciate everything you're doing but you have to keep me in the loop of what's going on. You can't just go making decisions without informing me."

"Baby, you're right. You're absolutely right. I was hoping to strike a deal with Wincey about becoming her musical director for her band and then perhaps hooking you up with a part of her organization so we can hook up with some folks. But Wincey said that she couldn't stay—"

"I know she's completing her album in L.A," Gem interjected.

"Oh, is that what it was? Anyway, my sister, the attorney, just called, and she can meet with us for a late dinner. Straighten out the situation concerning your demo and the stealing of our song. Now I'm not trying to be pushy, baby, I'm just trying to take care of business. So can you help a brother out?" Vaughan asked playfully.

"Attorney, stealing of song? Hellooo? What's going on?" Talise asked.

"We'll have to bring you up to speed later," Gem said, waving Talise off.

"So you ready?" Vaughan asked anxiously. "My sister is a stickler for lateness so we have to get rollin'. I called for a car. Talise, Stephanie, you're welcome to join us for dinner but the first half will be all business," Vaughan said with increased anxiety.

"Thanks, Vaughan, but I'm going to have Talise take me home," Stephanie said.

"Since tomorrow's Saturday, you can stay at my place if you're too tired to go home. Thanks, Vaughan, Gem. Your show was wonderful, girl. We love you," Stephanie said, turning.

"Yes. We love you. We'll talk to you tomorrow," Talise said, allowing Stephanie to bulldoze her into leaving.

They all exchanged hugs and kisses and left Gem to do her thing.

Chapter 20

Gem's pedal was to the metal as she raced behind the ambulance that screamed with blaring red and blue lights. The ambulance held her and Talise's best friend who fought for breath.

Stephanie's mom called them in the middle of the night to let them know things did not look well for Stephanie and they should rush over.

By the time they reached Stephanie's doorstep, the ambulance doors were closing. Stephanie's mom jumped out and told them to follow the truck to the hospital.

Tears silently tumbled down Talise's face as she tried desperately to contain herself. "Gem, you okay? Do you need me to drive?" Talise asked.

"I'm okay," Gem said as she raced through the traffic. "You okay?"

"No," Talise answered.

"I'm not either," Gem confessed.

"I'm scared. I don't want to lose her," Talise said.

Finally they reached the front doors of the hospital, where in dramatic fashion a team of white coats rushed Stephanie in the stretcher. Stephanie's parents emerged from the ambulance and followed closely behind.

"Go to the waiting room," Stephanie's mother shouted as she allowed her husband to lead her in.

"Talise, go inside, I'll park the car," Gem said.

Talise folded her arms as if to keep herself warm and disappeared beyond the glass doors.

Talise handed Gem a cup of freshly brewed coffee. They sat extremely close, side-by-side.

"So, I take it, you haven't heard anything?"

Talise shook her head and continued to sip.

Patiently they sat and waited.

Dawn broke when Stephanie's parents emerged through the doors of the waiting room. They both looked worn and disheveled.

"She's in ICU," Dr. Alphonso finally said.

"She's breathing with the aid of a machine. Her lungs collapsed," Mrs. Alphonso said softly.

"Is she conscious?" Gem asked.

"She opened her eyes when we yelled her name, but she didn't speak," Mrs. Alphonso answered. She put her arms around Gem and Talise and led them back to the hard light-blue leather couch they had fallen asleep on earlier.

Gem stared directly into Mrs. Alphonso's eyes. Gem noticed the deep-seated sadness and pain masked by a brave front.

"Ladies, it's time you said good-bye," Mrs. Alphonso said.

Talise's eyes welled.

"But you said she acknowledged you when you yelled her name," Gem spoke.

"She did, but she's not going to last on that machine much longer. She's not conscious any longer, girls," Dr. Alphonso answered as his wife looked to him for support.

With Stephanie's parents' permission, the nurse led the ladies into the room where their best friend lay. Machines dominated the pathway to her bed. Stephanie's chest heaved like a balloon from the steady, rhythmic piece of metal that forced air into her tiny body.

"Steph, we're here," Gem said, approaching her lifeless friend. Her grayish hue was now charcoal. Talise held one hand while Gem clutched the other. They noticed how cold and thin they were. Talise proceeded to rub some warmth into them.

"Steph, we love you. I'm not ready for you to leave me, but I know it's time for a better space and place for you. I don't want you to suffer anymore. We will be okay," Gem said, sobbing uncontrollably. "You have a permanent spot in my heart that no one can penetrate. Oh, by the way, thanks. Vaughan and I are doing well. We're in love all because of you! You're always there lifting me up and helping me through. Now it's your turn. Take care of yourself, my friend, my sister, I love you."

"Stephanie, it's me, Talise. From the moment I met you, you were always my confidante. Gettin' me out of jams and loving me unconditionally. Because of how you loved me I've learned to love me and others unconditionally. You never judge me. But I'm now judging you. I'm sentencing you to peace, love and happiness. But most importantly, I wish you rest. But after you've rested just a little bit, come down and visit us. I know you can't resist that. I know you'll keep me on the right track. I will keep you in my heart like a steel trap. And every time I trip up— which will be often— I'll hear your voice and see you angelic face. I love you." Talise then kissed Stephanie.

Gem followed. At that moment they felt a slight squeeze of Stephanie's hand. Just then the nurse stepped in to escort them back to the waiting room. Stephanie's hand fell limp.

With swollen eyes, Gem and Talise finally fell back asleep on the hard couch. As long as Steph's chest pulsated from the air, they weren't going anywhere. Steph's parents remained in her room.

It was only twenty minutes after Talise and Gem closed their eyes, when the nurse returned. She woke Talise first and rubbed her back. "I'm sorry," the nurse said.

Chapter 21

"Talise, come on. It'll be fun. Besides, it's the end of the summer and we need a lift. We deserve it. Come on, let's go," Gem pleaded.

"But I don't want to be a third wheel. I don't have a date," Talise said.

"Is it money? Because Vaughan and I will pay…"

"No, it's not money. My unemployment checks have come in regularly. I just don't want to be a third wheel. I'm not in the mood."

Gem remained focused on persuading Talise to go to one of the biggest amusement parks on the East Coast. Six Flags Great Adventures was perfect to ease their minds and hearts of the most horrific year in their lives. Besides it was Vaughan's suggestion, and Gem was willing to try almost anything to snap Talise out of her depression. Gem was determined to bring Talise along for the ride.

"I really miss her, Gemmie. Every time the phone rings, I pray that

I'll wake up from this nightmare."

"I know, I miss her, too, but just like Vaughan says, Steph wants us to have life to the fullest. Let her life be a lesson to us," Gem said.

"Oh, by the way, I got a call from the police station yesterday. Remember, I told you about the investigating officer, Warren Raymond?"

"Yeah," Gem answered.

"Well, they made an arrest."

"What? Will you get your furniture back?"

"No. That stuff is long gone. It turns out that a ring of theft originated from the valet guys at my gym. They would park your car, find your home address off something you may have left and have your keys duplicated in minutes. Then when they were sure you were at the gym, they'd strike. Since I'm a regular it was easy to determine when I wasn't home," Talise said. "You know, Steffon was right?"

"Steffon? I thought you forgot about that loser," Gem said.

"Well, yeah, but he used to always tell me stuff like never leave your full set of keys on one ring. Don't leave things that have your full address in your car…"

"You mean, common sense?"

"Anyway, Warren and his partner broke the case. And the gym is offering free lifetime premier memberships. If we take the membership, we can't sue. Warren advised me to take the offer because he said settling a suit would be years and I won't ever see that furniture again."

"Warren? You two are speaking on a first-name basis?" Gem asked.

"Oh, we talk from time to time…"

"That's perfect!"

"What?" Talise asked. "You know I often wonder how Vanee and Steffon are doing. What, Steffon…?"

"Oh, forget about Steffon. And I hate to sound cold but you and Vanee aren't friends anymore—never really were. Why don't you ask Warren?" Gem said.

"Ask Warren to accompany you to Great Adventures, and you won't be a third wheel, as you say."

"Gemmie, I don't know. He's cute and all, but he's a little loud. I'm not sure if I like him yet. He's a know-it-all."

"I'm not taking no for an answer either. It's with Warren or without, but you are going," Gem said.

Vaughan pulled his Eddie Bauer Limited Edition SUV into Talise's circular driveway. Gem called from the cell phone, urging Talise to put a move on it.

Hey, girl," Gem yelled as Talise opened the front door. They hugged and planted a kiss on each other's cheek.

"Talise, over here, please." The man ordered her over to his car.

What is she, a lapdog? Gem thought disappointed with this new man's tone.

Vaughan was busy making sure the backseat was clear.

Talise finished her business and proceeded back to the car.

"A little pushy, don't you think?"

He's a cop. He's trying," Talise answered, planting herself firmly in the backseat.

Vaughan exited the driver's seat to properly greet Talise with a kiss and a hug. He attempted to give Warren a pound but Warren opted for a handshake instead.

"How ya doing, dude?" Warren said in a nasally tone.

Vaughan stopped cold and bugged his eyes. He looked at Gem who attempted to hide a chuckle.

"So you guys have the directions?" Warren asked loudly.

"Haven't you been to Great Adventures before? We don't need directions. Talise, what's in that bag you're guarding so carefully?" Gem asked.

"Oh, Vaughan, would you mind putting this in the back, please, it's—"

"They're sandwiches Taleesy made." Warren cut her off. "PB&J's, tuna, ham. We brought enough for everyone."

"What's PB&J?" Vaughan asked, getting back into the car and proceeding to pull off.

"Peanut butter and jelly, baby." Gem chuckled. "And how do you and Taleesy propose to keep these sandwiches fresh? They're going to spoil," Gem said.

"I don't know, it was Warren's idea." Talise added, feeling slightly silly.

"Aw, they'll be alright. It's a cool day…"

Record highs today, Gem thought.

"…Besides food in the park is way too expensive, so you're better off bringing a few snacks. We'll just get them to stamp our hands and come back out to the car when we're hungry. If we get thirsty we'll just have some of the water in the back." Warren smiled.

And he's cheap, hmm, Gem thought, giving Vaughan an incredulous look. *Hey wait a minute, water in the back? That's our water, what were they going to do if we didn't bring that water. I hope Taleesy brought her own money.* Gem's thoughts trailed off as Vaughan continued to drive with a smirk on his face.

"…Yeah. You know dogs are about four bucks apiece. I'd rather spend my money on the rides like the roller coasters." Warren hadn't stopped talking.

"But once you pay for admission, the rides are included. Besides having to come back to the car is a hassle. Y'all will be doin' that by yourself," Gem offered.

"You know you're right. Besides I don't eat hog, man," Vaughan said.

"Suit yourself. Hey, can we listen to something other than this rap stuff. I have a couple of great tapes here, Ozbourne—"

"Oh, Warren's going old school on us. You got Jeffrey Osbourne?" Vaughan interjected.

"No. I have Ozzy Ozbourne, Van Halen, Aerosmith, ooh this is probably your bag, Hootie and the Blowfish," Warren exclaimed with glee.

Oh, brother. Talise hid her face.

Hmm, are you an alien? Because you spend so little time on the planet, with the rest of us, Gem thought.

"Ooh, Talise where is a gas station around here? We need to stop," Vaughan asked.

"Oh, wow, you guys should have stopped earlier. What were you doing? I mean you were late…" Warren chimed in.

"Right before we hit the parkway entrance there is a Merit Station," Talise instructed, ignoring Warren and hoping that everyone else was following suit.

"Merit is so ghetto. You have to pay before you pump. They wouldn't allow that in White neighborhoods," Warren interjected once again.

"We are in a White neighborhood, Warren," Talise corrected.

"We're in agreement about that," Gem said. *What a miracle.*

Vaughan found a gas station. He asked if anyone wanted anything. They all declined.

"My little cousins are coming to visit for a week," Gem struck up a conversation with Talise.

"Who? Danasia and Shanique?"

"Danasia, like the Dijonnaise mustard? Shanique?" Warren began to think out loud again. "I tell you Black folks and these names. They're awful and we're doing our kids a disservice with these made-up names, I tell ya. My kids are going to have normal unassuming American names like…"

"Bart, Beth or Sue?" Gem cut him off sarcastically.

"Personally I like the name Abigail for a girl…" Warren droned on completely unfazed by Gem's comment.

"Warren. Warren!" Talise stopped him. "That was so inconsiderate. Even if you feel that way, your comments are so uncouth and inappropriate."

"What, what? Oh, come on your friend knows I meant no harm, I was just saying—"

"Let it go, Warren. Just let it go," Talise said, cutting him off.

They drove for almost two hours with Warren talking about everything and anything in a fake West Indian accent.

Finally at the park with their space secure they all hopped out of the vehicle and stretched.

"Okay, everybody, last one to the monster coaster is a dirty rotten criminal," Warren yelled. Vaughan and Gem both turned and eyed Talise as she sighed. *This is going to be a long day. A very, very long day.*

It was their seventh time on this particular ten-story ride. *Why didn't I sit this one out?* Talise thought just before the drop plunged her stomach out through her toes.

"Wasn't that fun?" Warren exclaimed some forty-five seconds later. "I could do that all day, couldn't you?"

What, stand in line for forty-five minutes for a silly ride that lasts forty-five seconds? Not! Talise didn't say a word. It didn't matter though because he continued talking for the both of them, nonstop.

"Hey, look, the Batman coaster line is short, let's do that one again, please," Warren pleaded.

"Warren, you go, I'm going to sit this one out. We've been riding nonstop all day, I'm tired and I'm hungry," Talise said with Warren trailing behind her. "Ooh good there's a concession stand. I think I'll get a hot dog," she said, looking toward the booth.

"Oh, I'll get it for you," Warren said, catching up with her.

"Thanks, I appreciate that," Talise replied. *Okay, he's trying*, she thought.

"...But if I were you, I would get a yogurt cup or something. You're thin but you have little fat handles on the sides here. You need to change your workout," he said loudly as he pinched the skin that protruded outside of her cute shorts.

And he's obnoxious, she thought. Of course the line that had formed behind them seemed to go for a mile and Talise was sure everyone heard him. But the look she gave him didn't stop him from droning on. *And he says this in my face with this White woman smirking behind us.* "Warren, shut up! Just shut up for ten minutes, please! Do you try really hard to be this much of a jerk or does it come naturally?" Talise yelled back at him and walked off with her hot dog.

"What? What did I say?" Warren asked, trailing behind her. "What did I say?" he repeated.

Talise remained quiet as if the only existence at that moment was her and the hot dog. Just then two giant pink teddy bears strapped to the shoulders of a robust man and several little ones in the arms of an equally stunning woman approached them on the bench.

"Oh, my God! What happened to your hair! And what is that black stuff on your face and look at your clothes all disheveled, Talise," Gem said, sitting down and placing several cute little stuffed animals in her lap.

"Hey, you guys having a good time?" Vaughan asked, standing near Gem.

Talise just looked at him.

"Warren, you look like you're having a good time," Vaughan teased.

"I'm having a great time. I thought Taleesy here was having a good time but she's not talking to me right now."

Gem cleared her throat. "Honey, hold these please." She handed Vaughan the stuffed animals.

"Where are you going?" Vaughan asked.

"Taleesy and I are going to freshen up. You know girl talk." Gem smiled and lifted Talise to her feet.

When they approached the bathroom mirrors, Talise screamed.

"What is wrong with you?" Gem asked.

"My hair, my face. I can't believe Warren was allowing me to walk around like this. That man…" Talise looked as if she had been through the mill. Her hair sat atop her head like a porcupine on alert. Mud or some very dark substance made her look like she was either in a parade for raccoons or she was suited up as a linebacker for the Minnesota Vikings. Her cute outfit was twisted and frayed at the ends and her skin was protruding from the halter-like top as if she had love handles.

"So I take it you're not having a good time?"

"No," Talise answered, desperately searching her bag for a comb.

Gem handed Talise her own comb. "Why?"

"Why what?" Talise asked combing some order back into an Afro that sat on top.

"Why aren't you having a good time?"

"Because Warren wanted to ride every roller-coaster ride in the park twice, and I hate roller coasters! I've been throwing up every thirty minutes since we've been here. Do you know he insulted me in front of a bunch of people?"

"You don't say…" Gem said wringing a paper cloth she had run under warm water. She began to pat Talise's face. "What did he say?"

"He criticized my physique in front of a bunch of people. He's been criticizing me all day actually."

"This guy is a jerk! Why are you putting up with him, Taleesy?" Gem laughed sarcastically.

"I know, I cringe every time he calls me that."

"Answer my question. What about him is making you give him chances? Didn't you pick up on his personality when you all talked on the phone?" Gem asked as she threw the towel in the trash receptacle. "When are you going to value yourself, honey?" she finally asked with compassion.

"Is there a Stephanie echo in the room?" Talise looked around.

"No, I'm serious. Stephanie was right, you know. When are you going to value yourself and begin hanging out with men, people who are uplifting rather than a putdown? This man takes liberties he shouldn't. He opens his mouth and inserts his foot on a whim, and worse than that he's disrespectful and appears to have no clue. You're better than this, Taleesy. Let's drop this zero and get us a hero." Gem laughed.

"A hero like Vaughan?" Talise questioned, putting her face to the bowl to splash water in her eyes.

"He is pretty amazing, isn't he?" Gem said.

Talise nodded.

"But you know when I got him—or got him back, I should say—is when I believed with all of my heart that I deserved him. As Stephanie would say, via *Oprah,* it's what you believe about yourself that determines your success, not what you desire or what you hope for but what you believe about yourself. When you begin to believe, have and practice faith in what is true and right, your life as you know it will transform. Transformation happens by choice, not by chance," Gem said, hugging her friend with all of her might.

"Stephanie via *Oprah,* huh?" Talise looked up.

"Yup."

"I wish she was here with us."

"I do too," Gem said, hugging Talise.

"You know, you have a lot of nerve. You're the one who convinced me to come with this jerk," Talise said.

"Yeah, but since when did you start listening to me?"

They laughed and walked out of the lavatory together.

"I was about to send the calvary in there after you guys. Everything okay?" Vaughan asked.

"Everything is going to be just fine." Gem smiled.

"Well we still have a little time. Y'all want to go home or catch a few more rides before the park closes?"

"I'm ready to go, I've ridden everything I wanted to ride and—" Warren interjected.

"No, I'm not. I'd like to ride some rides I haven't ridden since we've been here," Talise cut him off. "First I want to hit the bumper cars, and I can't leave the park without doing the Ferris wheel and the merry-go-round.

"Aw, those are kiddie rides. We should do the monster coaster again and then…"

"Warren, you can do what you like. I just told you what I'm doing, if that's okay with you all." Talise looked to Gem and Vaughan.

"That's fine with us," Vaughan answered.

"But Taleesy…"

"Warren, my name is Talise, *Tah-lease,* not Taleesy. Please call me by my correct name. You can even call me Tal, but only because I say you can," she exclaimed and walked off.

Gem winked at her friend and Vaughan gave a look of approval.

"I don't know what you fed her in the bathroom, but I like it. Oh, and thanks, her hair looks much better. I wanted to tell her but I didn't want to hurt her feelings." Warren turned and said to Gem. "Hey, Taleesy, I mean, Talise, wait up, I bet I'll beat you on the bumper cars…" he yelled.

Vaughan and Gem walked off not far behind them.

He pulled the Gray Ghost into the spot marked RESERVED. "This all you, playa?" Grey remarked, impressed.

"Yeah. The spot next to it is for my new assistant," Calvin said proudly as he used his special-entry laser key for the back door.

Grey immediately admired the lush green-and-white decor along the black glass exterior.

"Man, this is your fifth assistant. What's going on? Don't tell me you keep getting involved with these girls. Don't answer that," Grey said. Calvin didn't plan on it.

"Speaking of involvement, have you spoken to Talise since her girlfriend passed away?" Gray asked.

"Not really. I tried calling a couple of times, but no answer. I left a message once, but she didn't call me back. We'll never be the friends we once were," Calvin said as he led Grey to the modest office space. There was enough room for two desks and a partition that sat between them.

The front entrance barely opened without bumping the first desk already occupied by a middle-aged woman typing away.

"Hello," Calvin said with a quizzical look.

"Mr. Jones?" The woman rose and extended her hand.

"Yes," Calvin said and shook it. "And you are?"

"I'm your new temp. My name is Ethel Konce."

"You're prompt, but I see you're working on something already. And what might that be?"

"Oh, that's my time sheet that you'll be signing. I'm very organized and didn't feel a need to waste time," she said.

"Great," Calvin said. "But how did you get in?"

"The janitor," she answered.

"Wow, efficient, prompt and organized," Grey said.

"Oh, Ethel, right? This is my friend Grey, he's visiting this week and will be hangin' out with us for a few hours this morning."

"Good morning, Ethel," Grey extended his hand.

"It's a pleasure to meet you, Grey, and I'm Mrs. Koonce not Ethel," she directed her comment to both of them.

"Small but nice," Grey commented. "How many of us would love to come to our own space like this. So business has been just flowing steady for the last couple of months, huh?"

"Yeah.

"Hold up, partner, so you and Candance swinging again?" Grey asked, noticing Calvin placing Candance's picture on the shelf across from the desk.

"Somewhat," Calvin continued to place things on his desk.

The intercom buzzer rang. "Mr. Jones?" Mrs. Koonce said.

"Yes, Ethel?" Calvin answered. "I'm sorry, I mean Mrs. Koonce.

"A Miss Candace Burton is on the line. Shall I take a message?"

"Uh, no, Ethel I'll take it. Thanks," Calvin said as Mrs. Koonce put the call through.

Grey picked up before Calvin could grab it. "Hey, Candy, what's swinging, sweetie?" Grey placed his feet on the desk and reared back in the plush black leather chair.

"Yeah, it's Grey. I'm just in town for a bit, thought I'd check out Cal's new digs…Oh so you helped decorate, huh? Well you did a wonderful job, I knew this knucklehead couldn't have done it by himself…Yeah, I know, I met Mrs. Koonce and she don't play that… Yeah well Cal is holding his hand out so I take it that's my cue to get off the phone. Hey, I'm in town for a few more days, so hopefully we can all get together for dinner or something…Great, well I'll talk to you later." Grey handed Calvin the phone.

Calvin conducted a brief conversation.

"So…"

"G-man, just drop it." Calvin kicked Grey out from behind his desk and sat down.

"So I guess you're back to the old standby. Man, you and Candace been trying for years, and it's obvious that she is always waiting for you but you're not happy with that situation, so why you keep trying?"

"I'm not trying, we're just friends who…"

"Who you manage to make your way back to every time something else doesn't work out 'cause you give up so easily. Just friends whose picture now sits up on a shelf of your new office."

"Grey, drop it man. Just kill the noise, okay. I'm handling my business. I know what you're trying to say and what you're trying to do. I'm okay. You know Tracee…Tracee, man…" He clenched his fists. "It was cool. She was everything I wanted, I thought, but you know I can't…"

"I know. Look, we don't have to discuss it anymore. I just want you to be cool. Hey, I'm here," Grey said, giving his friend a pound and a hug. "I'ma head out for a while, I'll check you at the crib tonight," Grey said, walking out of the door.

"So what are you ladies doing for Thanksgiving?" Mrs. Alphonso asked, savoring her final bite of chicken parmesan.

"Vaughan and I are going to my sister's house with my parents and everyone," Gem said.

"Well, I'm supposed to be going to Warren's aunt's house with his family. I haven't told my mom yet though," Talise said, stabbing at the veal parmesan.

"Ooh, your mother is going to have a fit, Talise. Will this be your first Thanksgiving away from your family?" Mrs. Alphonso asked.

"Yes, ma'am," Talise answered with her head still down.

"Well, I certainly don't want to be around the area when you break the news to your mom and dad. We'll probably hear her some sixty miles away," Mrs. Alphonso said as they all enjoyed the laugh.

Each of them seemed to chew their food in slow motion. The meal was being consumed as if it was the Last Supper.

"So what are you and Mr. A going to do?" Talise asked.

"We're going to St. Thomas for a few months. We both need some time to recuperate from all of the stress. We've reserved the house for three months but if we need to stay longer, that's an option."

"Oh," Talise said.

Mrs. Alphonso dabbed her eyes and swallowed. "You know, I found this in the back of Stephanie's closet. I suppose she received it from some thrift shop or some little kid." Mrs. Alphonso held up a pink-and-white striped jump rope with wide plastic pink handles. It was somewhat worn and old as if it had been used. "You know when Steph was a little girl, she had a rope just like this. We went to the park one day and she ran back to our picnic site just in tears. Some other little girl had walked off with her rope. She tried to stop her, to tell her to put her rope down but the little girl didn't listen. Finally, Stephanie claimed the little girl disappeared. I tell you Mr. A was furious that someone had skipped off with his baby's favorite toy. It was dark when they finished scouring the entire park for that little girl. The funny thing was that the little girl, according to Stephanie looked just like her. Needless to say we never found the rope or the little girl, and for weeks Stephanie cried and cried and cried. Her father tried his best to replace that rope with other things—a new bike, hoola hoops and balls, even an identically colored jump rope but nothing could replace it. Just like this one, it had a dent in the handle. Anyway when she found this, wherever she found it, I bet it was like Stephanie found a piece of herself. I tell you." Mrs. Alphonso rose from her chair and walked toward the sink where she fixed herself a glass of water. "I really miss her."

"We do too," Talise said. She walked and placed her hand on Mrs. Alphonso's shoulder. Gem followed.

"Well," Mrs. A. said, composing herself, "this has been a strong day. We've accomplished everything we set out to. I want you two to never be strangers, okay?"

"We won't," Gem said, looking at Talise for agreement.

"No, we won't. And Mrs. A?"

"Yes."

"Thank you again for trusting me and being so generous with Steph's things. I promise I'll take good care of them. In fact when I go back to work again, I'm going to write myself a renter's insurance policy to protect everything. Thank you," Talise said.

"You're welcome, dear. I'm going now," Mrs. Alphonso said as they all began to exit from the place Stephanie called home.

"I better call Vaughan. He made me promise to let him pick me up," Gem said.

Talise was already at the front window peering out. "Wait a minute, Gem. I think Vaughan is already here. There's a blue SUV out front."

Gem ran to the front. "You need us to drop you off?" Gem asked, putting on her coat.

"Warren is picking me up."

They all hugged and followed one another out of the door. Blue lagged behind confused. Mrs. Alphonso lured him into her Mercedes Benz and shut the door. She mouthed something and waved her finger at his blank stare. Talise laughed because she imagined Mrs. A reading Blue the riot act about not destroying her leather upholstery.

Gem and Talise watched as she seemed to turn in slow motion toward the front door. The lights were all out and Mrs. Alphonso for what they imagined to be the last time turned the key to Steph's door. She turned it left then right and finally removed the key from the lock. She shook the knob to assure its security and let out a deep sigh.

"Mr. Jones, I'm out for the day. Do you need anything else?"

"No. Uh no, Ethel, thanks for everything, I'll see you in the morning," Calvin said over the intercom.

"Mr. Jones, I'm coming in there before I leave. Do you have a minute?"

"Of course. Always for you," he said curiously.

"Mr. Jones, are you pleased with my work here?" She wasted no time.

"Of course I am. You really are the pulse of this madness." Calvin laughed.

"Well good. I enjoy working with you too."

Oh, please no. You're old enough to be my mama. Not you too? I can't swing with you, no offense but you're not my... Calvin's thoughts rambled.

"However, don't take this the wrong way. I'm not one of your little girlfriends coming in and out or calling every other day. I'm old enough to be your...well sister." She coughed. "But as a matter of respect and professionalism as I address you as Mr. Jones, I need you to offer me the same courtesy. I am Mrs. Koonce, not Ethel."

"Yes, ma'am," Calvin said. He jumped from his seat and sat casually on the corner of the desk. Mrs. Koonce continued grilling him on the do's and don'ts of their successful merger. Jovially and relieved, he gave her this time to air anything she wanted and conceded to all of it.

"Are we clear?" Mrs. Koonce concluded.

"As a bell." Calvin stood.

"Good, now I'm leaving. I want you to have a great holiday, and I will see you on Monday. By the way, I'm cooking a small dinner for my husband and myself—you know the usual turkey, stuffing, gravy, sweet potato pies, candied yams, collard greens, string beans, corn, cranberry sauce, potato salad, chicken, chocolate cake, lemon cake, lemon pies—you know nothing special. You and a lady friend are welcome to join us."

"Thanks, Mrs. Koonce, but I have the holiday covered." Calvin smiled.

"Speaking of lady friend, your friend Grey called and asked that I remind you to call your friend Talise. He said you knew what it would be about. Good night and happy holidays to you."

"Thanks, Eth—Mrs. Koonce, I'll get on it right away."

"You're welcome," she said and scurried out the door.

Not knowing what to say or how to say it, he picked up the phone and dialed some once familiar digits. *Thank God...her answering machine,* he thought.

Talise scampered around the house, zipping her pants, fluffing her hair. Warren arrived and now the phone was ringing off the hook.

"Hello? Ouch," Talise said, bumping into the newly delivered sofa. She still couldn't believe how acquiring her best friend's furniture turned her desert of an apartment into an oasis.

"I still can't believe you're spending Thanksgiving at Warren's family's house. I made all of your favorites, including barbecue. I mean, Talise, you don't really want to spend Thanksgiving of all holidays with people you don't know. Besides, Talise, Daddy and I don't really like him. He's a loudmouth." Her mom spoke candidly.

"Ma, that's not nice. I promised the man that I would go. Maybe we can stop by your house afterward. Please, Ma, be patient." Talise knew getting her mother off the phone would be an impossible task, and once again Warren would show up with an attitude because she wasn't ready.

"So what are you taking?"

"Nothing."

"You're not taking a pie or cake or something?" Talise's mother asked indignantly.

"Nope. I asked Warren if I should bring anything and he said just myself. So I'm taking him up on his offer," Talise said.

"That's tacky, Tal. I taught you better than that. Come by before you go. I'll give you one of my homemade sweet potato pies from the freezer. It'll thaw by the time you get to their house. Where do they live anyway?" her mom insisted.

"I don't know, besides we don't have time. Anyway, if we come to your house first, you'll guilt us into staying there. Look, Ma, I gotta go and finish getting dressed. He'll be here any minute now. I love you, and I'll see you and Daddy later," Talise said, abruptly hanging up the phone. But no sooner than she hung up the double ring on the phone indicated someone was at her door.

Talise clicked the special button.

"You ready?" Warren questioned.

"No, but give me five minutes and I'll be down."

He sucked his teeth. "No, I'll be up," Warren said. Quickly he arrived at her front door. She scampered away and retreated to her bedroom to finish dressing.

"Look at you, you're nowhere near ready," he said while she remained in the room. "Talise, I said four o'clock. What's the problem?"

"I told you I'm coming," she yelled defensively. With that she took an extra twenty minutes hoping he would get so pissed off that he would leave. Then she would be at peace to partake in some of her mom's famed barbecue. Unfortunately he remained unfazed.

Finally with the finishing touches placed on her hair and makeup she waltzed out of the room and gathered her things. "I'm ready. Are you sure you don't want me to bring anything? We could stop by my parents' house and…"

"Nonsense. We're almost an hour late as it is. Thank goodness they don't live too far from here. Besides you look fantastic," he said. "I'm sorry I snapped earlier but I wanted to be on time because I wanted an excuse for leaving early. Anyway, my family did a lot of cooking so there is no need to bring anything except your pretty self."

She batted her eyes and accepted the compliment as he helped her into a fox wrap her parents had given her for her birthday.

Warren turned onto a street that Talise silently prayed was not their destination. The houses were dark and old. Some houses contained windows that seemed to hang off the hinges. Paint was peeled away, and the roofs of some homes appeared as if they were about to fall at any minute.

Talise pushed the locks down when she noticed Warren's car slowing.

"See that's why I hate being late, there's nowhere to park." He sighed.

Nervously she walked up steps that screamed in need of repair. Warren practically left her behind he was so excited.

She took a deep breath and stepped into a dark foyer. The wooden door had a large hole on the lower left-hand corner. She walked through the doorway and almost tripped on a purple-and-turquoise shag rug over blood-red-colored carpet. Coats, hats, toys, blankets and other unidentifiable objects were strewn about. The television was blaring and all kinds of people were scampering throughout. Talise clutched her pearls. *The house is as loud and messy as Warren,* she thought when Uncle Cephas and Aunt Reesee and their matching gold teeth greeted her at the door.

"Come in, chile. Make yo'self at home. What did you say ya name was ugin?"

I didn't. I want to run, she thought. "Talise. My name is Talise." She extended her hand while she hung on to the coat Uncle Cephas was bent on relieving her of.

"And who's you kin to, chile?" Aunt Reesee asked.

"Uh, no-no one," Talise stuttered. "I'm a friend of uh, uh Warren's." Her heart sank in despair.

"Oh. And who is Warren?"

"That's Betsy's child. Girl, come on in here and sit down." Warren's uncle said.

Talise followed Uncle Cephas through the maze of people and things and tried to secure herself a spot on the couch. "Ooh," she said jumping up. Just then a kid came and snatched a toy from the middle of the seat.

"Lady, you squished my action figure. Maaaaaaa," the little boy yelled out, "that stupid lady sat on Mr. Flash Avenger." The kid ran off.

"Well if you took it off the seat like I told you fifty times, maybe she wouldna a ruined the thing." A woman walked toward Talise. Talise prayed she was coming to her rescue.

"So you Taleesy, Warren's girlfriend?" A short, fat woman, wide as she was tall asked.

"Yes, ma'am. I'm Talise. Are you his mom?"

"No, I'm his aunt. His mama's in the kitchen. Now here take your coat off, girl. Ain't nobody gonna steal it."

Where would you like me to put it, on the wad of bubblegum stuck on the arm of your chair perhaps? Talise thought as she complied with the woman's wishes.

"Now here's the tradition. This here is Warren's other auntie's house. She's in the kitchen; you'll meet her later. Now the tradition is that the wimmens do all the cooking and cleaning and the mens be loud to watch the game. Now you come with me." The woman led Talise to the dining area where a vacuum cleaner sat in the middle of the floor. "Now what I want you to do is run this vacuum cleaner over the floor for me. If these chilren get in yo' way, just kick 'em out."

No, I'd like to kick you, all of you, Talise thought as she smiled.

"When you finished that, come in the kitchen and you can help clean the greens."

Clean the greens? It's 5:30, when is everything going to be ready. I'm starving. Greens take at least three hours to cook properly. Lord, what did I get myself into? Talise thought.

"You know how to make greens?" the woman asked Talise.

"Uh, not really. My mom does all the cooking for holiday dinners."

"Well, honey, you ain't gonna get Warren to marry you if you can't cook no greens," the woman said and walked off.

The next thing Talise knew she was running the vacuum cleaner over the floor.

Some three hours passed. She had spent all of three minutes with Warren when he and the others emerged from the basement laughing and joking about the game. "Hey, babe? Having a good time?" Warren pecked her on the cheek before taking her seat.

"Of course she is. We're taking good care of her," Warren's mother said.

"My family is great, aren't they?" Warren said, sitting next to his uncle, leaving no space for her to accompany him.

Just wonderful if you like waiting until nine o'clock to eat Thanksgiving dinner and having to work for your dinner before you can eat. I've never heard of such nonsense, Talise thought. Finally she noticed a seat next to Warren's cousin's girlfriend whom she deemed sane. She, too, seemed to be out of sorts but obviously learned her lesson from years of practice. They had just joined the family some minutes ago. "Dawn, right?"

"Yes," the young lady pleasantly answered.

"Anyone sitting here?"

"You are now, please," Dawn said.

Warren, his cousin, aunts and uncles continued with their loud conversations and stories as if the two ladies didn't exist. Talise suddenly clutched her nose. She looked at Dawn who had done the same thing. Everyone looked around at everyone. Finally one of Warren's aunts exclaimed, "No, you didn't, that's so rude. You farted!" she yelled at Uncle Cephas. Everyone's laughter filled the room. All except for Dawn and Talise who looked appalled. And it was at that moment that Talise's appetite had said a long good-bye.

Losing her appetite was probably the best thing, too, because as soon as the grace was said, the cousins, aunts and uncles and Warren dived into the dry-looking food like the end of the world was coming tomorrow. People were grabbing turkey with their hands. One of the kids wiped his nose and then searched the bird for the perfect piece. Several adults saw him and no one chastised him before he settled on a drumstick.

I'm gonna be sick, Talise thought as she excused herself to the ladies' room. Her plate hadn't been touched. On her way to the bathroom she noticed that Dawn had a similar look of horror.

"I see Miss Priss didn't put anything on her plate and left to go to the bathroom. She ain't slick, Warren. I don't like her. She too uppity. She ain't as nice as that other girl you used to bring by," his mom said across the table.

She continued her babbling, not noticing that Talise had re-entered the room. Uncle Cephas cleared his throat as a hint. Finally realizing what was going on, his mother placed her head down and devoured her greens and sweet potatoes.

Talise sat down politely and poured herself a plastic tumbler of red Kool-Aid. She eyed Warren's mom and thought, *Old fat cow...* Talise sipped on the drink for the rest of the dinner.

After dinner proved worse. Talise could tell that like herself Dawn was fed up with the evening. As the couples exited to their cars Warren announced loudly. "We don't have to leave, guys. Let's go to the movies!"

Talise watched Dawn pulling Warren's cousin aside. She seemed to be trying to convince him of something. Talise hoped that it was for them to go home but he didn't budge as he walked toward Warren, with Dawn in tow.

"But honey, we promised my parents that we were going to stop by their place for dessert. You promised."

"Yeah, but Warren and Talise really want to go out. We can't disappoint them."

"Actually, Warren, I wanted to stop by my parents' too. They were really disappointed that—" Talise said.

"Oh, Talise, I'm sure they don't mind. So what movie?" Warren interjected. "I know the new James Bond flick is out." Warren grabbed his cousin around the shoulders and walked toward his car.

They don't mind! They don't mind! Negro, you have some classic nerve. You don't even know my parents that well. And James Bond, James Bond? That's it. After tonight I'm kicking this no-class, loud-mouth overbearing boar to the curb, Talise thought, stomping off behind them. She rewrapped her shawl around her neck and felt something hard and cold against the grain of the fur. “What is this? What?” Talise realized that the same wad of gum on the sofa was now on her coat.

Chapter 22

Mr. Jones, Candace is on the line. She's confirming your dinner plans for six this evening at Chez's under your name."

"Thank you, Mrs. Koonce. Please tell her I can't talk to her now but to meet me here at five-thirty."

"No problem. Also your three o'clock is running late but will be here shortly."

Calvin gazed out of his picturesque corner window at the light dusting of snow Charlotte was receiving. He enjoyed the sight as he picked up the paperwork for his latest marketing acquisition. He was meeting with the client of a steel company.

The intercom buzzed. "Your appointment is here," Mrs. Koonce announced.

Calvin eyed his watch and became incensed. *It's 3:40. This guy is definitely going to have to do better than this. My time is way too valuable.* Having told Mrs. Koonce he'd be with him momentarily, Calvin decided to allow the guy to wait longer as a lesson to his valuable time.

Finally, Mrs. Koonce ushered in The Jones Group's latest client. "Mr. Jones, this is Ms. Natalie Washington. Ms. Washington, this is Mr. Jones of The Jones Group.

Calvin noticed right away that he was going to enjoy working with this chocolate Vanessa L. Williams type. "It's a pleasure to meet you," Calvin said as they exchanged equally strong grips.

"Would either of you care for herbal tea or coffee?" Mrs. Koonce offered as she led Ms. Washington to the seat before Calvin's desk.

"I'd love some herbal tea without sugar. I'm not used to this brisk air. I thought Charlotte was a bit warmer," Natalie flirted.

Without sugar. Calvin thought noticing her svelte figure. "It usually is but we're having a cold snap."

"I see. Better yet I can feel." She chuckled. "I'm really sorry I'm late. As you know I'm not used to the area and I got turned around. My assistant was incorrect in her directions. She's new to using the directions online and well you know the rest…"

"It's quite alright. I understand. I'm just a bit surprised. The specs sent over indicated a man in your position though. Turnover is that quick in your company?" Calvin asked.

"Actually my assistant mixed up the papers again. The name you received is handling the Southwest. I'm the Southeast director. I'm happy about the assignment. My roots are here. I attended University of North Carolina at Chapel Hill for undergrad. But Charlotte is so different since then."

They continued talking about their backgrounds and laughed about their similarities. It was apparent to Calvin that she was not only attractive but bright as well. He didn't take his eyes off her. They explored The Jones Group's style, publicity routes and other functions of the contract.

"This sounds great. My company is sponsoring a formal opening celebration in two weeks. I'd love to have you there. You'll be able to meet some of the other top managers in the company and make a few contacts," Natalie said.

"That would be great. I'll just have to clear my calendar with the boss out there," Calvin said, reaching for the buzzer. "Mrs. Koonce, would you please check my evening calendar for…" He looked to Natalie to provide the date.

She did, and Mrs. Koonce filled it with their new plans. "If there is nothing else, I'll be going, Mr. Jones. It's after five." Mrs. Koonce said.

"It's five already? Wow. Time flies. I'm hungry. How about you?" he said to Natalie.

"Famished. I was planning on eating alone tonight, but company would be great."

"Good. Mrs. Koonce, do me a favor before you go, please."

"Yes," Mrs. Koonce answered.

"Call and cancel my five-thirty but keep the dinner plans, Ms. Washington and I will be dining there instead."

"Sure, Mr. Jones," Mrs. Koonce said.

"We'd better get going," Calvin said, placing Natalie's coat on her shoulders. He then placed his suit jacket on and they headed out the door. "Mrs. Koonce, I'll see you in the morning," he said, bidding her a good night.

Mrs. Koonce held the phone to her ear. "Oh, Mr. Jones?" Mrs. Koonce called out now with her hand covering the receiver.

"Yes." Calvin turned back around. He told Natalie he'd meet her downstairs.

"Be careful," Mrs. Koonce said to him. "Just be careful."

"Trust me, I always am." Calvin laughed and rejoined his guest.

"Uh yes, Candace, this is Mrs. Koonce. I'm sorry but Mr. Jones had to cancel his date this evening. He said he'll be sure to call you later but his afternoon's appointment ran late and…"

Gem and Talise convened at their once favorite spot, Je's. Even though the food held the same flavor, it wasn't the same. A major piece of the meal was missing.

"So when are you and Vaughan leaving?" Talise asked, biting into the stewed chicken.

"Well, it hasn't been deemed a tour yet, but Wincey is performing at the Superdome in New Orleans and then on to Las Vegas. I'm lead backup singer and Vaughan is the musical director. Who knows what happens next," Gem said, demolishing her fried chicken wings and greens with hot sauce.

"What about the lawsuit against Will and Robb?" Talise asked.

"We're settling out of court. Everyone and their grandma was subpoenaed. Did I tell you that your boy Steffon is nowhere to be found? He was depositioned and didn't show up. He got into a shootout with Romy Graham at Romy's nightclub in Queens. And guess what?"

"What? Steffon, I mean is he okay?" Talise asked frantically.

"Girl, please. Why are you worried about that thug? Nobody knows if he's okay or not. He couldn't be found. Anyway, even more shocking news..." Gem tried to get back on track to her original conversation. She seethed that Talise could still be concerned over a man who would have stopped at nothing to ruin her life. But in the spirit of peace she held her tongue. "Anyway, Romy and Vanee are married, girl. They appeared together for the deposition. She showed up on his arm. None of his assets are in his name, but hers so we couldn't go after everything we felt we deserved. But we were able to get a settlement out of court. So with a little money socked away, Vaughan and I are on our way."

Talise's face remained sour.

Gem couldn't tell if the sadness she noticed was due to her and Vaughan going away or if Talise was really still pined away about her ordeal with Steffon.

"What?" Talise asked.

"Romy is now married to Vanee. All his assets are in her name. He couldn't be held fiscally responsible but like I said we've settled out of court. So with a little bit of money socked away and an opportunity to make more, we're on our way."

Gem paused for a moment and took notice of Talise's sad demeanor.

She put her fork down and touched Talise's arm. "Don't be sad. This is a wonderful opportunity for Vaughan and me. We are going on the road with one of the biggest names in R&B, pop and jazz. This is far greater than the gig I pined over a few years ago. I'm making a lot more money and a lot more contacts. For the first time I see my way through to getting my own deal. Besides, I need—we need—to get away from all this. With everything that's happened, I have to make a choice about what's possible, not what's probable."

"But you're leaving me too," Talise said, all choked up. "I don't have anything now. No friends, no job and no clear-cut direction."

"I'm not leaving you, girl. Our hearts can't be disconnected no matter how far apart we may seem physically. And as for that job, take this time to rejoice. God has lifted you out of doom and despair that if not for His glory you would have stayed there and your soul would have withered away. Thank Him for His blessing and ask for His guidance.

You have a new opportunity to make better choices in your life. You have opportunities of belief and completion. Go for it. When I get back, I don't want to see you in the same space and time in your life. If nothing else I should see growth. And you're going away for some seminar with your friend Chynna, right?"

"Yeah. I don't know if it's going to do me any good but…"

"But nothing. Make the best of it. It must be something else if she's even paying for the weekend. I think I read something about it in *Essence* magazine. These women were talking about how it literally changed their lives and gave them new direction."

"I'm not sure of anything," Talise said quietly.

"No one ever is." Gem shook her head. "No one ever is. That's the beauty of this thing. Just remember what Steph used to always say: It's not what you hope for or aspire to that determines your success but what you believe about yourself that gets manifested."

"Did she say it like that?" Talise asked.

"Well no. But you get the picture." They laughed.

"So are you ready?" Chynna's voice asked from the intercom.

"In a minute. Come on up." Talise screamed over the box. She was placing her last few toiletry items into her duffle bag. *I don't know how I let this girl talk me into doing this.* Talise thought about the self-enhancement seminar Chynna had roped her into. Chynna was so sure that this weekend would give Talise the tools she needed to put her life back on track.

Chynna walked through the door. "Girl, if it were left up to you, you'd be late to your own funeral. But since it's not left up to you, we're going to be on time, so let's go," Chynna said, cramming what she thought Talise needed into the bag for her.

The phone rang and Talise ran to get it.

"No, let your machine pick it up. We have to go," Chynna said, tapping her watch.

"Hello?" Talise said into the receiver. Talise was stunned when she finally recognized the voice on the phone. "Yes, I'm surprised you called. I thought I'd never hear your voice again." Talise sat quietly and listened.

Chynna became intrigued.

"No, actually I want to tell you how sorry I am," Talise said. "No, no trust me, it's not your fault and by no means do I blame you. Well thanks but I'm not interested in anyone else's misery. Besides that chapter of my life is behind me, and I honestly I don't want to revisit it ever again. Thanks, please take care," Talise said as she hung up the phone.

"Who was that?" Chynna asked. "That wasn't who I think it was, was it?"

"I don't know who you thought it was but do you remember my ex-boss, the maniac as you used to call him?"

Before Chynna could answer the phone rang again. As Talise reached to grab it, Chynna pursed her lips displaying her disdain with Talise retrieving the phone rather than them leaving.

"Hello," Talise said somewhat cheerfully. She immediately heard a recording that made time stand still.

"This is a collect call from the Rahway State Prison from…Steffon Bryant." Talise heard his name in his own voice. "If you accept please say yes after the tone or hang up to deny." The operator's voice chimed in. Talise stood there lifeless. It was Chynna's voice rushing her to come on that brought Talise back into reality.

"Yes," Talise said. "I accept."

"Yo, baby girl. What are you up to? It's good to hear your voice."

"Steffon?"

"Oh, I know you are not keeping me waiting for no Steffon. Talise hang up the phone," she heard Chynna say.

Talise turned her back and continued her conversation.

"Yeah, it's me. Missing the hell out of you," Steffon said.

"Are you okay? I mean what, why, what happened?"

Vaguely Steffon tried to explain how Romy Graham had set him up and how he had ended up in a situation he couldn't work his way out of. He further explained how his public attorney wasn't worth a grain of salt and he believed that his attorney might have worked on Romy's behalf as well. "But you know I'm hangin' in there. I was wonderin' though if you could hit me up with a couple of dollars, seein' as I'm not far from you anyway. I tried callin' Vanee but she changed the number on me. I don't know where she or my daughter is."

"Steffon, I'm not sure where Vanee is but she and Romy are married. They showed up at Gem's deposition."

"Hellooo. Talise, hang up the phone from that thug. Let's go," Talise heard Chynna impatiently say.

"I'm coming," Talise answered. "Anyway Steffon, I have to go. I really don't have any money to send you. Sorry."

"That's cool. Hey maybe you could come see me once in a while. You are on my visitors' list you know," he said with a sad tone.

"Um, Steff, I don't think that's a good idea. Listen take care of yourself, okay. I don't think it's a good idea that you call here anymore either," Talise said, sounding tentative.

"Wait, wait, babygirl, before you go. I'm real sorry about everything that happened between us. I really care for you and well, seeing as though I don't' really have anything else…well I'm getting out of here in about six months, I was hoping I could come and stay with you until I get myself together, you know get back on my feet…"

Before Talise could muster the strength to respond Chynna snatched the phone. "Listen, you son of a bitch, you make sure you don't ever mess with my girl again. Lose her number, and don't you call here. In fact, you forget she even exists…" Chynna went on while Talise remained lifeless.

The next sound Talise heard was the slamming of the phone.

"Well, with that out of the way, can we please be on our way?" Chynna said. "Talise, make sure you change your number as soon as we get back. Don't go chasing any more waterfalls, got me?"

"Yeah but…"

"But nothing. That man was bad news. It's time you move on. And I'm not taking no for an answer. Now please, can we go?" Chynna said, grabbing one bag and opening the door.

"Yes, we can go. Hey, thanks. I do feel sorry for him though."

"I know. But he made choices and brought this on himself. No sense in you carrying that burden anymore," Chynna said, letting Talise into her car.

"Oh yeah, I did finish telling you. The first call was a follow-up call from my former head of human resources."

"Don't tell me they're offering your job back?" Chynna said, starting the engine.

"No. She called to see if I changed my mind about testifying. K.J. was escorted out of the building by security. He came back from lunch one day and his office was cleared and locked up. He went to the main office of the company and within three months he had at least five charges of sexual harassment lodged against him. The company is thinking about pressing charges and decided to do an investigation going back to when he managed the New York office. So they called me and asked if I would go to Philly to give a statement."

"And you said?"

"I said no thank you," Talise answered, noticing the vast plush greenery in her own neighborhood as if she viewed it for her first time.

"You're not scared, are you? I mean if that…"

"No, I'm not scared. I just want to move on from that chapter in my life. You know, when I got laid off, I thought, where is the justice in this world. Moments before I got laid off, I was going to report him myself but once they let me go, I thought there was no reason."

"So do you forgive him?"

"I'm learning to. I believe like Gem always says, vengeance is mine saith the Lord. Gem says for me to give it over to God and let him handle it. I've tried everything else, so why not. Gemmie said God will handle it better than I can."

"I like it. You know the first step of forgiveness is forgiving yourself," Chynna said, heading down the highway.

"This seminar you're taking me to taught you that?" Talise asked.

"It gave me the tools to open up to the concept. After I finished the seminar, you know I called my girlfriend Tracee and apologized for the role I played in that situation I told you about in New Orleans. We're rebuilding our friendship again. Besides she's not even seeing Calvin anymore and regretted that she allowed him to come between us in the first place."

"Was that the situation where you said your girlfriend knew you liked this guy and she pulled him from you?"

"That was the situation, but that's not really how it happened. Calvin wasn't really at fault either, it was my expectations of the situation that got me."

"Calvin is his name?"

"Yeah. He's a self-made brother from Charlotte. I have to admit he did have it going on…"

"His name wouldn't happen to be Calvin Jones, would it?"

"Yeah. You know him?"

"Oh, girl, do I. Ain't this a blip? Six degrees of separation at it's best. The story goes like this…"

The Garden was packed. Lights and smoke filled the vast arena and the electricity was in the air. Talise had a front-row center seat and a bona fide backstage pass to what was deemed the kickoff show for the world tour of the decade. Talise screamed with the rest of the crowd when lights sparkled all over the place and each backup singer was showcased in her own right. First the spotlight hit a Brian McKnight sound-alike. He riffed a scale that sent every woman in the audience soaring. Then a Lalah Hathaway sound-alike nearly blew the mike off the stage with her part. Finally the light sparkled one last time and her best friend, Gemmia Barnes, let out a riff that had the entire concert arena on its feet.

Finally the strings appeared. Then the horn section blew. Two sets of drums ascended to the stage. And finally the bass, several guitar players and two sets of keyboards appeared. And right before Wincey made her grand entrance, there was Vaughan with his conductor's baton in hand. He took his bow and the music filled the air. Wincey entered, and the crowd went wild but Talise was still yelling about Gem. Talise was so proud. She yelled, "That's my friend…that's my friend!"

Finally the two gentlemen sitting next to Talise looked over and said, "I take it that's your friend." And laughed. Talise screamed and didn't bother to notice the faces behind the black coats, brim hats and sunglasses. "She's pretty good. I like her," one said to the other.

The show was fantastic. Wincey and her background singers changed five times, each outfit more fabulous than the last. Talise was so overwhelmed she had to take deep breaths to keep from fainting.

The limo pulled up in front of the Peppermint as crowds of people gawked to see who was getting out. They didn't recognize either of them but the electricity in the air made them scream anyway. Gem and Talise were protected and ushered through the doors with the rest of the band members and backup singers. It was rumored that Wincey was stopping by these old stomping grounds for a befitting farewell to Vaughan and Gem as they embarked on their world tour with Wincey.

"Girl, I feel like a star." Talise beamed.

"Me too," Gem said.

"I can't believe Wincey let you showcase like that at her concert. You blew it up."

"She's generous like that. She likes my talent. She's trying to help me get a deal. I might even be able to get signed to her label as her protégé. Of course Vaughan will be named as my executive producer." Gem sparkled like the diamond on the third finger of her left hand.

You would have thought that Talise lost her voice by the way she screamed at the concert. But she had plenty left to spare. "Oh, my goodness, I'm so happy for you. Look at that rock! When is the big day?"

"No time soon. We're going to wait until the tour is done. Things are going so well that we may go international. And Vaughan has accepted the Lord as his personal savior, so we're really handling our business."

Gem spotted the front table marked RESERVED and led Talise to it. Talise asked, "So what about your song? Did you get it back?"

They reached the already occupied table. Gem introduced the two ladies. "Talise, this is Vaughan's sister. This is my best friend, Talise."

They exchanged handshakes.

"Speaking of court cases, Lyn here is the reason everything was resolved. We settled out of court. I can't sing the song but Vaughan and I will reap writing credit and royalties. But it's okay because I have a new song to sing." Gem flashed her ring.

The crowd inside the place and outside went wild.

"What the heck is going on?" Gem asked, trying to see above the sea of faces.

All of a sudden, Vaughan appeared fighting through the crowd with Wincey on his heels. He spotted Gem and they all ended up at the table. Wincey greeted all of them warmly.

"Whew, that's some crowd out there," she said, sitting at the table.

"Hey, baby," Vaughan greeted Gem. He then kissed and greeted his sister and Talise as well. "Alright I'd love to hang and talk but Gem and I have a show to put on. Thanks for coming, Wincey."

"No problem. This will be a great night out for me too," Wincey said.

Vaughan and Gem disappeared behind stage. Talise sat speechless. She couldn't believe she was sitting eye to eye with some of the world's biggest stars. Finally Wincey waved to a couple of people who made their way to the table.

They all greeted with Wincey with a kiss. "Talise, right?" Talise nodded. "This is my best friend, her husband and my husband. This is Gem's best friend," Wincey said as she coaxed them to sit.

"Girl, that crowd is something else. I had to ask who's coming that they have to have all these barricades and police presence," the woman said adjusting her seat.

"I'm coming," Wincey said and the two women laughed. "It's a private joke," Wincey offered to Talise.

Talise still sat starstruck.

"So where is Toni?" the woman asked Wincey.

"In L.A. She's shooting another film and meeting me when we do the L.A. Forum. But her hubby is coming tonight. He's in town."

Wow I wonder if they're talking about the actress Toni Kennedy? They have to be... Wow this is exciting. Gem's hangin' out with everybody, Talise thought.

The moment finally arrived. Vaughan took on a slightly different role for the much smaller band that accompanied his wife-to-be. First Vaughan blew a solo on the sax that brought Wincey, Talise and everyone crammed in the joint to their feet.

Finally Gem appeared. And just before she sang, she spoke softly. She thanked everyone for their presence. She thanked her best friend, Talise, and said how without God, Vaughan and Talise, her whole existence wouldn't be possible. Talise broke down in tears before Gem could finish.

Gem then gave a tribute. "This woman is in heaven right now, smiling down on all of us, but she always said I could do it. And I want each and every one of you to know that I don't know what chances you've taken in your life or what choices you've made. Some may be good, tough or not so good, but I want you to know that whatever you're going through, joy always comes in the morning. Now your morning may be tonight, tomorrow, next week or next year, but remember to always endure because joy always comes in the morning. Stephanie, this is for you. The cymbals rang...her voice boomed...

It was Stephanie's favorite and had become Talise's anthem. It was Donny Hathaway's great song of encouragement "Someday We'll All Be Free." And at that moment that's exactly how Talise felt...free.

EPILOGUE

Hey, Girl,

It's me. Normally I would open up with I hope all is well but I saw you during your Grammy presentation, and you looked absolutely fabulous so I pray and know that you and Vaughan are doing very well. Tell Vaughan I said congratulations on his Grammy-winning work with Wincey's album, that diva is still going strong. I'm looking forward to you not only presenting a Grammy but receiving one next year too. So when is the debut album dropping? Everybody's talking about you—BET, MTV and VH1 have all been pumping your single. And you know I'm proud to tell everyone that's my friend, that's my friend! The fellas always say oh yeah, so when you gonna hook me up but I quickly let them know you're married!

I'm doing well too. My surprise birthday party from me to me was wonderful. So many blasts from the past showed up, even Warren! Do you remember him? Picture that! But no I'm not hanging out with any of them. No more rafts to the beach. I'm enjoying my freedom to be me. I'm a paid counselor with the self-enhancement seminars with other high achievers, and I'm enjoying it. I'm still learning a lot about me and how I can get the best out of life. The pay is not a lot yet but I'm so much happier. I'm doing what I love and it's helping me to explore and reach for other loves as well.

The group leaders of the self-enhancement seminars have asked us all to start memoirs or written reflections of the last three years of our lives. Now that some of us have hit the big three-O, we need to reflect on what the twenties meant to us and what we can expect out of the thirties. Girl, that's the easiest thing in the world. My memoirs are entitled The Terrible Twos of Talise! *Yes, I'm giving it a title and writing it in the form of a story, you know like a novel. Who knows, maybe one day it'll be published or something and you'll see me on* Oprah *as her book of the month (I'm laughing as I'm writing right now!). But I'm free now. These enhancement seminars of course along with a job have really helped me to see how I am responsible for my own self and actions and character. A long time ago Stephanie said that we are what we believe, not what we hope for or aspire to but what we believe about ourselves. I've learned to capture a new belief about myself. I'm worthy! And my worthiness is not determined by some man, money, job or social status. But my voice is worthy and I am who I choose to be.*

Choice. *What a powerful word. If I got nothing else out of this part of my life—the terrific threes I call them—it's that I have choice. And when you don't choose, chance chooses for you but that's still a choice. We are not where we are by chance. We don't end up in situations, good or bad, by chance. It's all by choice! Something or someone we've chosen in our past, present or future has brought us to where we are. And if we are traveling on the same roads, with the same people, doing the same things, and (this is a big and) we don't want to be, then we have to look at our choices! Isn't that deep? Nothing happens by chance, but everything happens by choice! Well I'm gonna go now. I'll e-mail you as soon as my new computer comes, but I wanted to get into a writing mode tonight. I'm starting my reflections later.*

Oh, and before I forget, I answered an ad today and made an appointment. My friend Chynna was reading the newspaper and there was an ad asking in bold letters: **DO YOU WANT TO BE AN ACTOR...IF YOUR ANSWER IS YES, PLEASE CALL...** *anyway, I called the number and it was* *to* The World Famous Harlem Theatre Company. *It's an acting school but to enter you have to audition. I have an appointment next Tuesday. Isn't that exciting? So, all we can do is see what happens next. Maybe I'll meet you in the spotlight someday! Besides you and Stephanie always said I had a flare for dramatics. Anyway that's it with what's going on with me.*

Oh, and to answer the questions from your last letter, yes I've heard from Calvin on and off. He's still doing the same old thing, not married, barely committed and still seeing Candace off and on. He's struggling with his business. He never landed Sack Enterprises. We maintain a cordial friendship, we can't go back to being the close friends we once were. And you know what? I'm okay with it. Our friendship has passed on. But Grey and I are still cool. Anyway enough of that stuff. I'll talk to you real soon. Like I said, I'm getting a real computer soon so I'll e-mail you next time. Yeah, yeah, yeah, I said next time the last time but I mean it. I miss you and I love you dearly.

From the Bottom Up,

Talise

P.S. I've talked to Stephanie's parents and they are doing okay. They are really proud of you and said they keep you in their prayers always. In fact my memoirs are going to be dedicated to Stephanie.

Talise sealed her latest letter with a kiss and wrote the latest address given to her for Gem in Minnesota.

She placed a stamp on the letter and set it in front of her purse to mail the very next day. Talise took a deep breath. She was about to embark on fulfilling one promise to herself for the evening.

So with her glass in hand, Talise sauntered over to her multi-CD stereo that held twenty-four CDs at a time. She checked the digital display that advised which disks were already loaded. Her favorites: Diana Ross and The Supremes' anthology, Earth Wind & Fire, The Emotions and Joe Sample featuring Lalah Hathaway were among them. She also loaded Rachelle Ferelle, Anita Baker, Ray Charles and Betty Carter, Billie Holiday and Etta James.

She promised herself that since her memoirs would be a story, the story would have characters and names to protect the innocent. The outcome would be, as she wanted her life to be, another suggestion of the self-enhancement seminars she had attended. And whatever the outcome, it would be all hers.

Talise sat down in front of the dinosaur of her computer and began to relive the last three years of her life. The words flowed effortlessly as her story took form…

Talise did everything in her power to disrupt. . .

Ooh, I can't use my name, she thought as she interrupted her first sentence. *Okay, I need a character name …The Waiting to Exhale* CD and Toni Braxton kicked into her head. She also thought about the time she met that famed actress Toni Kennedy and the impact it had on her, so she erased the line and began again.

Toni did everything in her power …

She thought of a few more names to protect the innocent and wrote them on a note pad she had next to her computer. Her writing resumed.

It was four hours later and 5:30 A.M. when she finally stopped. She picked up her head and checked the page and word count displayed in the far right hand corner of the screen. Fifty-six pages later and almost three chapters, Talise had a book! She re-read each line. Her mouth salivated with the content. "Watch out, world, this is going to be one heck of a book!" she said aloud.

About the Author

Toni Staton Harris resides in Newark, New Jersey, with her husband, Injeel. She is originally from East Orange and Hillside, New Jersey, respectively but boasts proudly of her old-fashioned North Carolina and Virginia roots. She is an actress, author and flight attendant. Her hobbies include reading, writing, movies, traveling and collecting porcelain dolls.